Zero In, Zero Out

Evan Willnow

LEGENDARY PLANET

SAINT LOUIS

TRADE PAPERBACK – ISBN 978-1-939437-14-3

TYPESET IN ALEGREYA AND SOURCE CODE PRO.

HENRY BRIDE, A HENRY BRIDE THRILLER, AND THE HENRY BRIDE THRILLERS ARE TRADEMARKS OF EVAN WILLNOW AND LEGENDARY PLANET LLC.

MANUFACTURED IN THE UNITED STATES OF AMERICA

LEGENDARY PLANET, LLC
PO BOX 440081
SAINT LOUIS, MISSOURI 63144-0081

legendaryplanet.com

Contents

For Dad - my editor in books and in life

one: input

1> Time Off

THE BLOOD RED CROSSHAIRS zeroed in on the steel and glass doors of the towering courthouse. The focal point remained steady on the southernmost set of five entrances, each between six-story-tall pillars, each providing access to and from the semicircular enclosed portico of the structure's east face. These particular doors, like their twins on the portico's far side, were the standard, double, pull-to-open affairs. A second set of inner doors formed an airlock to maintain the government's precious air conditioning. The three middle entrances were revolving doors. But there was nothing extraordinary about the southern doors except each had, below a universal handicap symbol, a notice on the glass reading "Handicap Entrance Around The Corner" followed by an arrow pointing right. That and a piece of white gum some savage stuck to the left door's handle. For the past hour this embodied Henry Bride's entire world.

That was just fine for Bride. Between work issues, girlfriend issues, and the doldrums of ordinary life, lately the outside world had kind of sucked, leaving him wondering how he fit in. But on this rooftop, gazing through a Swarovski z6 3-18x50 BT scope, Bride's mind pulsated its own inner soundtrack, drowning his daily preoccupations. He had developed this technique of using inner music as a means to concentration years earlier. His Navy shooting instructor had taught him to clear the mind while waiting for the shot. Bride never mastered that trick but discovered, for him, music, generic music, served the same purpose while conjuring no thoughts, no emotions, only stopping the mind from wandering and yielding the needed even trickle of adrenaline.

"Crosswind is up to seven west-southwest. And are you singing?"

"Why? Do you have a request?" Bride re-set his sights while answering his spotter *du jour*'s readings. Bride had met Harrison "Spiro" Agnew, a fellow DHS agent, just two days prior at a debrief on this situation. Spiro immediately struck Bride as one of the good ones. Lanky with a fuzz of dark stubble around all but the top of his head.

"You know any Zeppelin?"

Bride tried to ignore Spiro's jest.

"Or how about something from *Hamilton*?"

His eye never leaving the scope, Bride gave a short silent chuckle then said, "Spiro, what part of 'piss off' don't you understand?"

"You didn't say, 'piss off,' partner."

"It was implied," Bride said as his sole focus returned to the door, but the interruption had halted the music in his head. Then, after a few minutes of silence, Bride's outside world crept in when the image of a photo stuck in his mind like a knife. It was that simple 8x10 of the seventeen-year-old face of Garrett Jackson donned in cap and gown.

Garrett Jackson AKA Abu Bakr Hamed, was both the reason Henry Bride was on this rooftop and why he shouldn't be here at all. This day was supposed to be another day of Bride's mandated desk duty. He unquestionably shouldn't be staring through the scope of a LaRue Tactical 14.5 Inch PredatOBR 7.62 tactical suitcase rifle toward the Thomas Eagleton Courthouse in downtown St. Louis. But here he knelt on the flat rooftop of a restored historic multi-story brick warehouse across Clark Avenue, rifle in hand and attired in full tactical uniform; "Police – Homeland Security" emblazoned in yellow across chest and back.

Nine days prior, Agent Henry Bride of the Department of Homeland Security shot and killed a terror suspect in DC. By all accounts, it was a clean, by-the-book shooting. The terror suspect, Abu Bakr Hamed, had already fired on agents and was swinging a Glock G40 toward Bride and his fellow agents when Bride put two chunks of lead in Hamed's chest. The concern was not that the suspect had converted to radical Islam. The concern became that the suspect was black, and in the ongoing *Black Lives Matter* climate, it seemed no one had Bride's back as the inquiry progressed. And the face the world saw of the suspect was that three-year-old photograph of an innocent Garrett Jackson, with all his potential, graduating high school early, ready to face the world. It was that face, not the rage-filled face shouting, "All police must die!" that haunted Bride.

Bride's old supervisor, recently retired Deputy Director of Operations Coordination Robert Blackwell, would have gone to bat for him, but to the new boss, Bride was an unknown quantity. After three eight-hour days at the desk and nights alone suffering through the first episodes of season two of *True Detective*, Bride persuaded the new supervisor to allow him to travel to St. Louis while the investigation continued in DC.

This St. Louis trip had not been solely to escape his work problems. It was also intended to resolve his love problems. The trip offered one last attempt to rekindle his long-distance relationship with Leta Sinn, the young woman whom he had dated after they survived a traumatic event together. He hoped to procure a transfer to the DHS's area office and strip "long-distance" from the relationship's descriptor. The rekindling quickly failed, and the transfer inquiry turned into being drafted as a stand-by sharpshooter and "floater" in an ongoing terror investigation.

The local office, situated across the river in East St. Louis, was short on men, particularly sharpshooters, and required help with this terrorism alert. After reading Bride's Navy records and his firing range scores, the agency honchos enlisted Bride into duty. He didn't bother to point out his desk duty assignment or the pitfalls of giving a "killer cop" a high-powered rifle in one of the primary ignition points of the *Black Lives Matter* movement. That information about his status should have arrived with his file. If they didn't read it or they chose to ignore it, that was their damn problem. Bride was happy to return to active duty even if simply in a support role.

Bride closed his eye in his scope for a short second, refocused, and restarted the music in his head. The photo faded from mind and returned to today's terrorists, the handful of men holding hostages inside the courthouse. These jihadists weren't the homegrown variety like Garrett Jackson. No one in this country would protest their loss. These were Syrian-born terrorists, and the DHS trailed them for months. But the day hadn't gone off without glitches on both sides.

In the pre-dawn hours, the team from Homeland Security, in addition to local officials, took positions surrounding the Wainwright building, the target intel had deduced. Command had stationed Henry Bride inside the parking garage across Seventh Street above the Hooters. The complications compounded when the agents assigned to following the lead terrorist lost him en route. When the silent alarms sounded blocks away at the Thomas Eagleton courthouse, they finally understood where the real target was.

The scramble was on.

The Department of Homeland Security knew the actual target intimately. Besides the Federal courtrooms, the building also quietly housed a DHS substation and was under the constant eye of the department. This day, possibly by plan, the tower had a smaller DHS presence than typical because of the higher alert at the Wainwright.

Bride was aware of the courthouse, observing it in the skyline while cruising through the city with Leta. He pointed out that the towering take on a traditional courthouse looked like R2-D2; Leta had thought it looked like a penis.

At present, Bride's exclusive focus through the Swarovski Z6 3-18x50 BT scope was the southern-most of the courthouse's five entrances on Tenth Street. He awaited anyone—terrorist, hostage, or the bastard who stuck their gum on the door—to appear behind the glass.

Eyewitnesses who had escaped the ordeal in the courthouse atrium in the early minutes gave the DHS the little intelligence they had. It ran down like this:

At roughly 7:40 am four, possibly five, Middle-Eastern men entered the federal building. They split into the two security lines. Each carried various benign metal objects in their pockets and various other hidden locations on their persons. When they attempted to pass through the metal detectors, they repeatedly set off the alarms. The prolonged delay clogged the security lines. All people entering the courthouse's primary entrance behind them were forced to wait for the metal detectors. The lines grew long. Eventually each man was detained. It was then that another man in the midst of the crowded security line shouted. He declared he had a bomb strapped to his chest. Witnesses identified this man as Jabr Muhannad, the man the DHS had lost earlier. The accounts say Muhannad held a handheld detonator above his head, yelled something threatening in Arabic, and depressed his thumb on the trigger switch.

It seemed, according to the terrorists' plan, the security policy intended to protect the building's occupants would doom them instead.

But Muhannad's trigger had no effect, save a slight sizzle inside his overcoat. This was because Muhannad had obtained the "explosives" from an undercover Homeland agent, but the failure of the explosives only began the chaotic scene.

A second after the apparatus should have exploded, Muhannad again screamed in Arabic and withdrew a handgun from his belt. He shouted once more, this time in English, "Everybody to the floor!"

From there, with the ensuing bedlam, the eyewitness stories get confused. But the factors that are certain follow: The crowd panicked. People screamed. Many ran. Many did as ordered. Some knocked over other people to escape. In the confusion, the guerrillas stripped the pistols from the guards at the security gate. Shots were fired, and many hostages were taken.

Privately, Bride was glad to be on duty and not wallowing in self-pity about the events in DC. Seven times since leaving the Navy, Bride had had his sharpshooter skill utilized and so far he'd yet to fire a shot. Despite the weight of the trouble inside the courthouse, he found this part of his job calming, meditative. The calculations were instant and intuitive. He was no longer sure if his mind performed the math or recalled the charts; the processes had merged into instinct. For Bride, time at the rifle range brought him what he imagined others sought from a round of golf. At least with range shooting, unlike golf, there seemed a point to the impossible chase of perfection.

Even the voices of his various colleagues chirping in his in-ear radio were each processed and dismissed with the back his mind but not allowed to break his melodic concentration. Instead each voice melded into the beat of the meditative atmosphere. "North side clear." "Team three in position." "Sighting, possible subject."

A new voice on the radio broke a protracted silence and passed through his conscious thoughts. "We have a rooftop watcher. West—"

The incoming message was unceremoniously interrupted by a heavy pop in Bride's earpiece. So much for concentration. A sequence of screeching electric tones and scrambled voices followed. "Ardfkrek durkn grkun torkr khankch." Another pop promptly stifled the voices. A sharp volley of static burst out and then music—loud, angry music. A live recording of "Blind" by the band Korn raged through the supposedly secure two-way radio. At first Bride kept his sight on his target door, but the meditative state ceased. His colleagues on the surrounding rooftop clambered for clarification over their radios, but nothing came through over singer Jonathan Davis' creepy, repetitive proclamation that he couldn't see and was going blind.

In frustration, Bride broke orders by yanking out his earpiece and swinging his scope westward, scanning the rooflines of the surrounding buildings. He saw nothing except other friendly sharpshooters and forces, all sharing the same confusion and chaos that existed on his rooftop. The eerie echo of a hundred radios all playing "Blind" sounded through the nine-block range of the operation. Bride lowered the rifle to take in a broader view of the full scene. All eyes searched westward.

Through complaints about the radios Bride heard Spiro's deep voice calmly say one word, "Drone."

Bride traced the gaze of Spiro's steel, melancholy eyes to a hundred-or-so feet over the Filippine Garden, the two-acre public park opposite the courthouse on Tenth. There, hovering as if suspended in space floated an unmanned octocopter. It was hard to determine the size with no nearby reference, but it was large. It was no hobby drone, spanning five- perhaps six-feet wide. Large for a modern camera drone. Bride raised his rifle and focused the drone in his scope for a better look. It was a homemade drone built from mixed parts. Beneath the central body hung a camera and possibly homemade armaments. It presented a potential threat to the mission, his fellow officers, and the public. With no orders, Bride made a unilateral decision it must be downed.

"Wind?" Bride barked to Spiro.

No response came from the spotter. The drone's camera, and what Bride took as weapons, swiveled toward them.

"Wind?" Bride repeated.

"Hang on, I've nothing to read from."

The drone appeared to be looking directly at them. It remained centered in the crosshairs despite buffeting of the wind. Bride grew impatient to pull the trigger, but a miss would send an HSM 308-12 AMAX Match bullet at 2875 feet per second through the heart of metropolitan St. Louis. The camera lens spun, seemingly to zoom or focus. It was studying him.

"Spiro?" Bride shouted.

"Six point—"

Before Spiro completed the reading, the drone zipped up and eastward over the nearby Stadium West parking garage.

"What the hell was that?" Spiro asked.

"News maybe, but I think it was armed." Bride said, examining the skyline for the drone to return.

"CNN has been getting very aggressive."

"By the design, I'd say MSNBC."

As he spoke, Bride had an epiphany. He lifted the riflescope eastward and scoured the rooftop of the Westin Hotel, a block away on the far side of a parking lot. "Westin," he said to himself, "not west."

His hunch proved right. Atop the hotel he spotted a masked man. "There he is. I have a subject on the top of the Westin Hotel," Bride said, focusing his lens. "Black ski mask, black coat, black trousers, holding what looks to be a controller." For a full second Bride centered his scope on the stranger before the masked man turned away. He caught small details through the hundred times magnification of his scope; electric blue eyes, a loose button on the coat, a grease stain on his left knee. One further detail after the man turned, a sizable lump protruded on the back of the knit stocking mask and a sprig of bleached hair peeked out below.

"We got him!" Bride yelled to Spiro as the masked man on the rooftop bolted for an open window in the hotel. "Follow me."

Bride laid his rifle against the roof ledge. Instinctively he checked his belt holster and found his SIG Sauer P229R DAK in its place along with a complete collection of DHS tactical gear; stun gun, baton, handcuffs, knife, flashlight, and the now useless radio. He snatched up one of the rope coils the SWAT boys had tied off and tossed it over the old six-story warehouse's east side. After latching his safety harness, Bride followed the rope over the wall and, a bit too swiftly, rappelled the six tall floors down to street level. Startled but ready, Spiro descended right behind him on a second line. A third man wearing a DHS flak jacket, who Bride had never been introduced to, trailed down behind on Bride's line. With the radios still refusing anything but Korn—now *Freak on a Leash*—Bride waited on the street to provide verbal orders to the two men.

"Spiro, the man on the Westin roof; blond hair, ponytail, blue eyes, wearing all black. Take the north side of the hotel. I'll get the south. And you..."

"Jennings," the other agent said.

"Jennings, search that rooftop on the Westin, the nearest one with the air conditioners."

Spiro and Jennings nodded their understanding, and the three men split as each ran toward different zones around the Westin. Bride sprinted east on Spruce Street through the police barricades and a small, curious crowd. He arrived at the hotel and identified a man in all black with the bleach-blond ponytail exiting one of the rear doors of the hotel. The man turned east through a cluster of onlookers who were disappointed the city police force was rousing them to a position where they could see nothing of the incident inside the courthouse. One city police officer took hold of the ponytail man and escorted him to the rest of the crowd. Bride's yells to detain the man went unheard.

By the time Bride reached the crowd, excited about the DHS agent running toward them, he had closed to about half a block from the ponytail man. But his target must have detected the commotion of the crowd. He peeked over his shoulder at Bride and burst wide around the east end of the hotel. The chase was on.

In a heavy sprint, Bride reached the hotel's east corner, but his target was nowhere to be seen. The sidewalk hugging the Westin's east wall was empty. He scoured the space and found no hint of the man with a ponytail. Bride looked across the street to the baseball stadium. The super-heroic sculpture of Stan Musial towered at the tip of the "T" of the intersection, waiting for the next pitch to come right down Spruce Street. But neither Bride nor "The Man" could locate the man with the ponytail.

Bride spun and discovered he had passed a stairway headed downward below street level. It was the entrance of the MetroLink, St. Louis' light rail transit system. Looking down into the lower level, he caught sight of his target again on the train platform seeking to blend by standing near a trio of businessmen. When he caught sight of Bride bounding his way toward the stairs, the ponytail man spun and darted toward the tunnels that conveyed the commuter trains below downtown St. Louis. Bride pursued, taking the concrete stairs downward two at a time. His target, eager to lose the DHS agent pursuing him, vaulted from the platform down on to the tracks and his black attire dissolved into the dark tunnels under the city.

2> Last Day

DIA REYNOLDS STOPPED TYPING and adjusted her seldom-worn black skirt, just one of the things bothering her today. She tried to rush her report on what she had dubbed Nuqu, a successor to Duqu, an advanced piece of spyware believed to be created by the Israelis. She wanted to leave work at the National Security Agency by noon at the latest, only she couldn't concentrate. What would it matter if she didn't finish her report when she had already committed treason?

For months she planned a just-in-case escape when her current role at the agency changed to run contrary to the reasons she had joined. Then after the apparent suicide of fellow programmer and friend, Alec Holloway, two weeks ago she knew it was time to get out. She had spent her free time getting everything in place for her exit. If she didn't leave now, her next opportunity might not be available for weeks, possibly months. She had asked her boss for personal time for today and the following Monday. Her boss had granted her the days off so long as he had her report before the weekend. This left Dia having to come in for a short while this morning as a crucial detail was due from another department by 8:00 am and, unfortunately, that information didn't arrive until 7:58.

She had wanted to ask for the whole following week off, but that would throw up the red flags with Staff Security Officers in the Office of Security. They would take account if she used a third week-long vacation in this short calendar year. The SSOs have been touchy since the contractor, Edward

Snowden, famously left the agency's employ. Today, Dia needed no such red flags since they were intended to detect the exact thing she was planning.

Like Alec, Dia was one of the wunderkind at the NSA, a group of young-genius, white-hat hackers. The agency recruited sixteen such young geniuses to stay on par with the skills of the black- and gray-hats of the world. The collective—discovered and dubbed "The Equation Group" by the outside world in 2015—took the NSA's capabilities far beyond the capabilities of independent hackers. Only Israel's similar team competed with their coding skills—though judging by the code of Nuqu, the NSA's hackers might have slipped a few steps behind.

Today, other things occupied her mind. She needed to finish her report and write a dozen-or-so lines of mundane coding, a proof of concept on exploiting Nuqu. Instead her mind jumped from one thing to the next. She thought about Alec and her escape and... No, she needed to work. To retreat from her racing thoughts, she re-checked her desk for anything she wanted to keep. Her desktop held the maximum three sentimental knickknacks. The NSA frowned on such trinkets as each needed to be scrutinized, searched, and x-rayed by the Security Protective Officers to be sure they contained no clandestine devices. Of course, objects removed also needed to pass through the layers of security.

Dia satisfied herself that she could live without all of her things until she noticed the frame containing a selfie taken with her sister, Ruby. Crap, that must go. She couldn't leave a picture with her sister. She cursed herself for not having thought of that. The picture would have to be replaced with something that wouldn't hint at her escape route.

"Dia did you hear what's happening in St. Louis?" the voice of Denis Ayers interrupted her thoughts. Ayers also worked as a programmer in the area they called "The Lab" and, thanks to a caret on the makeshift sign, re-christened "The Equation Lab."

"What's happening?" Dia asked.

"There's an attack on the Federal Courthouse. They've got the news on the big screen in five-D." He started to leave before he added. "Oh, and some new SSO is here doing interviews."

Dia spun around. "What?" She realized straight off she overreacted. Visits from Office of Security's investigators were not a rare thing. Informal interviews conducted every six weeks was standard, with the more formal polygraph interviews coming every quarter. The occasional spot interview sometimes came at three to five weeks after the regular ones to keep everyone's toe muscles well exercised. More visits happened after something occurred, twice a week for a while after the Snowden defection. And now with Alec's suicide, interviews were inevitable. Dia played off her response. "Don't those guys always travel in pairs? Who'll play 'good cop'?"

Ayers laughed. "You mean 'less-bad cop'?"

Dia feigned a laugh.

Most of NSA employees not assigned to the case spent the morning watching the events in St. Louis on CNN in break rooms in the building's less-secure Administration area. The NSA higher-ups huddled in the Situation Room. When Dia showed up to the room something had happened to the feed from St. Louis and all of the news stations were scrambling to re-establish the connection to their crews on the scene. Two of the news stations even aired ten to twelve seconds of an icon image of a skull with blackout sunglasses over a hard rock song. Dia realized that with everyone distracted by the events in Missouri this was her chance. She was left in peace to take care of what she needed to and get out. A few harmless security bypasses and Dia printed a picture of a dog from the internet, trimmed it, and substituted it for the selfie with her sister in the frame. The selfie and the scraps from trimming the dog's picture went into a protective sleeve, through the shredder, and into the burn bag. She finished her coding and her report. They weren't her best work, but they would be expected to be done and she had put more effort in to each than she had planned. By quarter till ten she was ready to go.

Everything was set. She passed out through the inner layer of security, grabbed her jacket and bag from her locker, threw them both over her shoulder, and headed for the exit. Before passing through the outer security perimeter she saw Anthony Thorenus. The NSA's Deputy Director of S32 – Tailored Access Operations, Thorenus was her boss and the last person she wanted to see. He stood near the front doors on the far side of the lobby. He was talking to a short, stocky, and bald gentleman wearing wire-rimmed glasses. Dia tried to recall if she had ever seen this second man. Perhaps it was her paranoia speaking, but she worried this new man would be able to see straight through her thoughts with the all-knowing eyes of his. She paused before entering the lobby and searched for a path to avoid the two men, but she found none. Not one that wouldn't arouse suspicion anyway. Instead she decided to power right past them with a laconic nod goodbye. She had no luck.

"Just a moment, Miss Reynolds. I need a word. Can you meet with me inside in five minutes?" Thorenus stopped her to say. The second man thankfully ignored her, checking his phone or something.

Dia smiled; said, "Sure"; nodded; and circled back toward the core of the building, leaving Thorenus and the unfamiliar man alone.

"Inside" meant back in the secure area. No talk of classified material was allowed in the common areas and administration areas of the building. It was a frustrating system, but Dia, and everyone else at the NSA, understood why it was needed. So Dia put her jacket and bag back in the locker. While waiting to pass once more through security, Dia caught a glimpse over her shoulder of Thorenus exchanging words and shaking hands with the other man. Something felt wrong, but she sucked it up and passed back through inner-security. Once again she waved her badge over the keypad at the secure area's entrance and punched in her PIN. Inside she asked the desk for a small meeting room and informed them to tell Deputy Director

Thorenus that she would wait inside. She repeated the badge swipe and PIN on the meeting room door.

She sat down and tried to keep her cool, but found herself fidgeting. How long would this take? In reality she waited ten minutes though time seems to stretch in empty meeting rooms under the best of circumstances. This was far from the best circumstances.

At last, the door beeped, and Thorenus entered and sat across the table's corner from her.

"I'm so glad I caught you before you left. How's that report?"

"On your desk." Dia almost added "sir" but stopped herself. Showing the man that kind of respect now would stir suspicion.

"Good," he said. "Could you give me the quick layman's breakdown?"

"It's almost surely Israel again," she said, "but they've added a new coder. One who's taken their game up another notch. This stuff is genius."

"Why target anti-virus companies?" he asked.

"Again, hard to say, but it seems it's to find out if they're creating anything that will detect their spyware. I'm not sure why they install the whole package. I would've gone smaller and targeted. Like something that wouldn't respond unless detected. They may have needed the whole package to infiltrate, but once you're in why leave something for them—and us—to analyze?"

"Perhaps they're just not as clever as you, Reynolds."

She blushed, "I don't know about that."

"I do," Thorenus said. "You've really upped your game. You're even dressing the part lately." Thorenus swept his hand up and down to highlight her attempt to finally fit the NSA dress code with her black skirt, wide black belt, and a gray tweed jacket with black lapels. He was probably most happy her tattoo was covered. Thorenus continued, "But I'm afraid I need that genius this weekend. I know you're supposed to have a long weekend off, but I'm sorry I'm going to have to ask you to cancel your plans. I need you tonight and at least tomorrow. You can take off next weekend and have an extra day or two."

"Sure, I understand. It'll be no problem." She said, contradicting her thoughts. The bastard was just buttering her up to once again disappoint her. She added, "Is this for the St. Louis situation?"

"No," he said, "it's for project Wonderbread. Can you gather up your data on Wonderbread and meet in the Fishbowl?"

"Yes, sir," she said.

Thorenus dismissed her with a wave of his hand and a curled lip of a smile that Dia was sure was because he finally coaxed a "sir" out of her.

Crap, she thought as she exited the meeting room and headed back into the building toward the Equation Lab and the glass walled conference room nicknamed the "Fishbowl." Her escape window was closing, and Wonderbread was the reason she wanted out. She wondered if Wonderbread was why Alec... She hadn't worked with Alec on Wonderbread. She only worked alone on Wonderbread, but she recognized Alec's work.

It seemed there was no getting out.

/ / / /

Robert Liptmann adjusted his wire-rimmed glasses as his eyes followed on the girl exiting the meeting room. The Senior Special Investigator for the Office of Security kept his short, stocky frame out of her view when she headed back into the core of the building. He didn't trust this new breed in the NSA. The agency had a need for "fresh blood"—he understood this—but let these newcomers conform to the agency's ways, not the other way about. According to her file her work was impressive, and she had the skills the NSA needed. She had found and created more active backdoors in target software than anyone else at the agency. She had also created many of the systems to use those backdoors undetected. He ran his hand over his smooth, hairless scalp as he yearned for another way for the agency to get her skills. He didn't trust her kind. She was pretty though, but too young.

"That was Diamond Reynolds?" Liptmann asked Deputy Director Thorenus after the director had exited the meeting room though he was sure of the answer.

"Yes, that was Miss Reynolds." Thorenus answered. "She goes by Dia. Is she on your list?"

"No." Liptmann took a hard breath through his nostrils to delay as he thought about his assignment for a second. "But I'll want to talk to her as well. Can you arrange that for this afternoon?"

"This afternoon? Sure. I'll arrange it. Is 4:30 fine? I have her on a time sensitive project with St. Louis and all."

"4:30 will be fine," Liptmann said, though he nearly said, "no," and demanded the interview be earlier. But he didn't want to demand because he wasn't sure why he wanted to talk to the young programmer, as he watched her step on to the elevator.

/ / / /

It took Thorenus twenty-five minutes to make his way to the Fishbowl. Dia sat resting her head in her hands and her elbows on the table and the folder containing her data on Wonderbread. She straightened herself when Thorenus stepped in.

"Dia," he said, "I won't need you this weekend after all. I hope I haven't made you miss your plane."

"No." She tempered her excitement. "I'm still good."

"Great. I hope you have a good time off and we'll see you Tuesday."

Dia thought the situation was weird, but wasn't going to question it. This time she passed through the layers of security in record time. She would give Thorenus no chance to change his mind. Her window hadn't closed after all. It was time to put her escape plan in motion.

/ / / /

A few minutes earlier, Steven Burgess had been watching the action of the St. Louis courthouse standoff on the main one-hundred-and-five-inch screen in the dark underground control room. The drone's camera streamed overhead video of the whole affair.

"Look at them scramble. They have no idea what just hit them." Warren, one of the two technicians in the room laughed as they watched the video feed of the feds and the police reacting to their radios being hijacked. The smaller, flanking monitors were showing the coverage of the event from various news outlets—CNN, CBS, Fox News—all of which were scrambling to reestablish connections with their crews on the scene in St. Louis. All except NBC, which had restored contact to its cameras through the wired connection of its local affiliate, which was conveniently located directly across the street from the courthouse.

The Blind Worm—Steven's Blind Worm—the worm he had captured some five-years ago and modified in his spare time—worked. It worked better than everyone had expected. Not only did they take down the police's and the fed's radios, it took down the network's TV cameras. They apparently worked on a similar system to one of the select systems Steven had the worm target. He secretly wished the Korn song would have broadcast over the network coverage. That would have been funny.

But unlike the technicians, Burgess wasn't laughing. He had a job to do. His boss had concocted this "field test" of the Blind Worm. Steven didn't even know how the boss was aware the attack on the courthouse would happen. He just knew the boss wanted to test Steven's cross-platform worm against the modern radio systems that the government was using. It was another success. The question was now, would the government be able to figure out how to stop it. He spoke into his headset microphone, "Pan around. I want to make sure we got everybody."

"They're on to me," the voice said over the speakers. "I'm pulling out."

"Can you get a wide shot before—" Burgess started to ask.

"It's the snipers," the voice cut in. "I'm moving out Oscar." Oscar was the codename they gave the drone. "And then I need to go."

"Understood. Transfer control of Oscar to me and get out."

3> **In the Tunnels**

BY THE TIME BRIDE reached the platform the mouth of the century-old twin train tunnels had swallowed his black-suited quarry into its darkness. The near-dozen commuters standing on the platform clamored about the crazed individual who leapt to the tracks below and entered the tunnels. Not far behind, Bride dropped from the platform to the tracks in stride and followed Ponytail. Ignoring the yells from the platform, Bride attempted to scan the tunnel interior. Unfortunately, his eyes had yet to adjust to the dark. The light near the entrance had allowed him to at least assess the tunnels' geography and speculate how it progressed into the black.

The old stone walls with a barrel arched ceiling. Wide arched passages joining the dual tunnels repeated every thirty or so feet. Luckily for Bride—and for the man he chased— St. Louis used light rail commuter lines. This meant no live, high-voltage third rail on the tracks as there are in cities such as New York. Instead, a bare cable that hung just below the center of the ceiling delivered the trains' high-voltage power. Bride slowed his pace as his eyes reached the wall of dark. He found, for some reason, the line of caged light bulbs that hung every few strides on the outer wall was shut off. *Great.* He advanced down the tracks, knowing with the trains' wide turn radius the worst pre-existing obstacle would be something he would glance off. Bride assumed tunnels' design repeated for a good distance under the city. He not-so-safely assumed the man with the ponytail would continue deeper into the tunnels. As Bride's eyes grew accustomed to the darkness, he found the man had vanished.

"Shit," he whispered to himself while slowing to a walk. He unholstered the SIG Sauer and his flashlight and gripped the two together in both hands so where one aimed so did the other. Cautiously he passed each connecting arch hoping he somehow hadn't overtaken the ponytail man. He wondered about the train schedule. In the eastbound tunnel, where he was, trains would approach from behind, assuming the rail line was running at all. With the terrorist activity at the courthouse a few blocks away, would they keep the commuter trains running? The police had not closed the station, but as he passed, the police seemed to have been widening their perimeter. Does the lights in the tunnel being out mean the trains weren't running? If they kept a normal schedule, trains would stop at the stadium station, where he had entered the tunnels, and would noticeably block the light.

These assumptions made it more surprising when a loud whir rose behind him. He immediately stepped into the nearest connecting arch to avoid what he took as an approaching train. He peaked around the stone corner to discover an empty tunnel stretching back to the station. *What the hell?* he thought. The whir sound rose, and—though the echoes made pinpointing its location impossible—it definitely approached from behind. Bride slid along the stone surface to the edge of the westbound tunnel and glanced again toward the station. No train but something was coming. A silhouette floated in mid-tunnel and was expanding. *The drone!* he nearly said aloud.

/ / / /

Steven had guided the drone to the opening of the MetroLink tunnels and would have preferred to return command to Chip, his man on the scene. Vast clear spaces were fine for controlling the drone's flight with the roughly quarter-second lag he was getting from the approximately fifteen-hundred mile distance between his location and St. Louis, but underground where space was cramped and signals were sporadic, that kind of remote control wasn't practical. The tiny radio relay the drone had dropped near the tunnel's mouth helped its signals enter the underground passage, allowing Steven to communicate with both Chip and the drone inside.

But Chip declined to take back command, reasoning that his scant seven-inch monitor's glow would give his position away. Fair enough.

But now Steven felt claustrophobic. Though the drone's video played on the one-hundred-and-five inch screen, thanks to the camera's fish-eye lens, the shadowed walls seemed mere inches from the octocopter's propellers. Screw it, he'd flown his drone through tougher obstacle courses.

"Help is here, Chip." Steven said into the mic then mumbled, "Let's take this bastard, Oscar."

Steven twisted the dial on his controller to switch off the safety on the drone's weapons and then flipped on its underbelly lights.

/ / / /

Bride ducked back into the connecting archway as the drone lit the tunnels with a rack of LED lights. Gun in hand, Bride hugged his back to the stone wall, standing out of the drone's light. When the light dimmed, Bride snuck a peek around the corner. As his eyes cleared the corner, he spied a glint of flame followed by a furious hiss. *Rocket.* He leapt back, flattening himself to his wall. The rocket whizzed past and erupted in flames on the far side of the archway. Fire charred the stone wall for a full ten seconds as Bride scrambled into the far tunnel. The rockets must contain an accelerant, Bride assumed. If it can burn stone for that long then it would burn something even the slightest bit flammable for perhaps minutes. Someone has been playing with their chemistry set.

Bride worked his way to the previous archway, hoping to get in behind the drone. As he stole a look around the arch, another rocket fired, this one striking the corner and spraying pellets of flame across the tunnel. One flame pellet hit Bride on the sleeve, igniting the jacket's fabric. The half-inch circle of flame slowly widened. The tactical uniform's material was supposed to be flame resistant, but the unknown chemical in these rockets didn't care. With the vest and all the straps he was wearing over the jacket, pulling off the garment wasn't a viable option. In the time he weighed options, the blaze had spread to two inches, and he was feeling the warmth through the heavy material. With his off hand, Bride reached across his torso to holster his handgun and unsheathed his Smith & Wesson Border Guard 2 Rescue Knife. Carefully, yet urgently, he slipped the knife blade under the burning sleeve, twisted the blade up and sliced upward at the cloth. Before he made a second cut though, the drone rounded the corner into his archway.

"Bastard," Bride swore at the electronic beast.

Sleeve still aflame—the fire at least no longer contacting skin—Bride sprinted back to the far tunnel. He was greeted with an automated announcement that reverberated through the train shafts, but he only caught some of the message over the drone's whir. "Attention passengers, the next … bound train will arrive … seconds."

Ducking into another arch, Bride cut away the rest of the burning sleeve with his blade, but as he worked a fresh sound swirled in the air. Deeper than the last rumble produced by the drone, this charge of air and noise was omnipresent and growing. This time it must be the train, but Bride couldn't identify which line, eastbound or westbound, without emerging from his hiding place in the center arch. He would know soon enough, but more importantly what would the drone do? Would it also seek cover in one of the connecting arches? Either way Bride could make a no-risk bet that it would emerge or already be in the tunnel opposite the train. If he were wrong, at least he knew the drone couldn't sneak from behind him. What to do with this knowledge was the challenge.

He conjured a plan. He closed and sheathed the knife and unholstered his Taser X26P. When the train arrived—it was westbound—Bride rolled out into the eastbound tunnel and sighted the drone hovering near the intersection of the next pass-through. The drone apparently had spotted Bride as well because as he rolled back to his knees another rocket screamed over his head. But Bride had already taken aim, rolled forward under the drone and discharged the Taser. Its twin bolts launched upward toward the drone through a shower of swirling anti-felon identification confetti that every Taser load contains. The bolts flew narrowly over the drone as Bride released the Taser's body from his palms and tumbled back along the rails away from the drone. The Taser's line tangled with the electrified catenary wire hanging inches below the tunnels ceiling that carried the electricity for the commuter trains. The weight and momentum of the Taser's body pulled the line down into the drone's high-speed blades. Between the jolt of 50,000 volts DC of the Taser, the constant 750 volts AC of the ceiling's power line, eight high-speed rotors, Taser confetti, and the incendiary chemicals of the remaining rockets, the mechanical beast burst into a hell storm of electrical, chemical, and mechanical explosions.

4> Lost Contact

"OH, JESUS!" Warren yelled.

"What the hell happened?" Chris, the second technician, blurted.

"We've lost the feed," Steven said calmly. "Rewind. Let me see that frame-by-frame, but put Oscar's live feed on to monitor five in case it comes back"

The three men re-watched slowly as the DHS agent shot from a Taser and missed high.

"But he missed," Warren said. "What the hell went wrong?"

The next few frames told the story as the Taser's wire dropped through the Taser's swirling confetti and into Oscar's rotors.

Warren was the first to react. "Fuuuu—"

"We need to tell Axeworthy," Chris said. "We have the streamed footage, but Oscar had other cameras recording and it recorded all the data transmitted from the worm. We've lost all that. Are you going to call him, Steven?"

"I think I better brief him in person. Ask if Chip can double back and check if Oscar's flash drive is intact."

"Oscar's dead, man," Warren said. "And Chip's still gotta lose the fed who toasted Oscar."

"Ask him anyway. The flash drive might still be working. We can't let the feds have it."

"There's nothing left, and the feds will never break that encryption. No use in Chip risking getting—"

Steven stopped Warren's argument with a stare.

"All right, man, I'll ask, but Chip's not going to like it."

"I'm driving up to visit Axeworthy in person. Keep me informed."

/ / / /

The tremendous eruption of chaos had subsided, but flickers of the chemical flames still seemed to stain the old stone walls. Henry Bride quickly checked himself. It seemed no more of the rockets' chemicals had landed on him. It took a moment, but Bride regained his feet. He staggered to the wreckage. He felt no physical injury from the explosion, but he found it difficult to balance. Staring down at the burning carcass of the octocopter, he absentmindedly put his hand on the back of his neck. Something stuck out of his skin. With a sharp tug he wrenched it from his neck. The pain rushed through his upper body and he sank back to his weakened knees. He examined the blood-covered pointed fragment of carbon fiber and supposed it must be a sliver of one of the drone's rotors. He checked his neck wound again, not too much blood, but an inch to the left and it would have struck his spine.

A loud clanging emanated from elsewhere in the tunnels. He realized he had dazed out, but he now recognized what he needed to do. It was time to locate the ponytail man. With his weapon and flashlight back to ready, Bride left the fire and proceeded deeper into the tunnels. Ahead, he noted that the eastbound train had gone dark and had halted shy of the station. *I suppose I did this*, he thought. Across the MetroLink car he saw passengers struggling to open the doors. He removed his badge from his vest, thumped it against the door's glass, and commanded, "Stay on the train and keep down." He repeated his command to the passengers in the front car of the train. So far no trace of the ponytail man, but he observed people in the Eighth Street station ahead—also dark—peeking down the tunnel trying to determine what happened on the tracks. Ponytail mustn't have passed the station yet.

Bride moved arch to arch through the foul-tasting, smoky haze given off from the drone's wreckage. Ahead, the mid-nineteenth-century stone tunnels widened into the late twentieth-century concrete of the Eighth Street station. With two arches remaining to investigate before the station, Bride caught sight of movement in the last archway. It was him, the ponytail man. Bride sprung forward to the last arch just in time to catch a glimpse of the ponytail man sprinting for the Eighth Street station in the opposite shaft. He sprinted and raised his weapon. But when he sighted his quarry rounding the next pillar, he hesitated to squeeze the trigger, the photo of Garrett Jackson flashing into a frame of his thoughts.

Damn it, Bride! That was your chance.

He gave chase again, but the effort brought a bout of lightheadedness, and Bride needed to support himself on the old stone surface to maintain his footing. *Come on, he's getting away.* With determination winning out over fatigue, Bride pressed on.

Inside the station, dim ambient sunlight that snaked its way down the access stairways eerily lit the lingering haze. A couple of disoriented riders made their way along the wall toward the stairs up. *Why are there no lights? When did they go off?*

Bride found himself on the opposite tracks from Ponytail separated by a four-foot concrete barrier oddly topped with dark louvered florescent tube lights. Ponytail was attempting to climb the far platform. Bride steadied himself, took aim, encompassing the man inside the flashlight's beam, and hollered, "Stop! Hands up."

The man did not comply. Instead he dropped to the track and rolled across the rails toward the barrier that separated him from Bride, utilizing the concrete wall as cover. The man scurried along the wall deeper into the darkness of the tunnels.

"Bastard," Bride swore below his breath. There was no simple or safe way for Bride to top the barrier, not in his condition. He had to count on his instincts and follow where he thought the ponytail man was heading. If the echoes weren't deceiving him, the noises coming from the other side of the obstacle seemed to validate Bride's choice of direction. Bride hoped to make it to the next segment of the old tunnels first, but tried not to pass the man. Agent Bride, being the cat in the game, understood in a maze the mouse had the home field. And this maze contained no dead ends to corner the mouse. He'd need luck to help him catch his quarry.

At the first archway Bride caught another glimpse of the figure running past in the far tunnel. Bride kept on straight. He struggled to pick up his pace, but his head wouldn't have it. He wondered what was slowing him? Concussion? Blood loss? Whatever it was, after seeing less of the dark figure at the next arch, Bride knew a short, hard sprint would be all it would take for Ponytail to escape. Bride prayed the man didn't realize that.

He slipped in his earpiece and clicked on his radio. The blasted thing still looped Korn. A hasty check of his phone confirmed no cell signal penetrated this deep underground. He continued moving but had lost his target. The outlaw may have doubled back, took off running, or simply stopped. Any could let him disappear. The hunt had become desperate. There was no backup. Spiro and Jennings had no idea Bride had trailed the man from the Westin's rooftop. The rest of the team had the hostages in the courthouse to worry about, and with no radios they probably were scrambling to reorganize their tactics. No evidence said this man was associated with the extremists in the courthouse, and Bride suspected he wasn't. Why? For one, he told himself, Ponytail was purebred Caucasian, most likely American, and the terrorists in the courthouse were all Middle Eastern. It's conceivable, but to Bride's knowledge it was rare. It was an odd bit of racial profiling that led Bride to question who precisely he was chasing. The rockets on the drone proved this guy wasn't a journalist.

The thoughts surged through Bride's mind as he pressed on deeper into the dark with no sign of ponytail, until he spotted a sliver of light ahead. It was a door. In the middle of the tunnel, along the outer wall on his side, light snuck in from a cracked doorway. Without a plan hatched, Bride shut off his flashlight and backed himself against the stone support column in the tunnels' center. His hope was Ponytail would consider the door as a chance to exit.

Until he had leaned against the wall, he didn't realize how exhausted he was. He wanted to sink into the old stone pillar. Was this a plan, or had his mind surrendered and tricked him into resting? Bride convinced himself this was his best course. He wasn't going anywhere.

He waited against pillar for minutes and questioned how long to wait before giving up. During the stillness, he felt an intermittent drip down his back. Was it sweat or blood? Bride held little hope. Ponytail could be out of the tunnels, leaving town, or getting a haircut by now.

While Bride wasn't looking, the florescent lights of the Eighth Street station relit. It was farther away than he remembered walking. The stranded passengers were filing from the train, someone taking charge and leading them to the platform.

As he watched the activity back at the station, a figure passed just to his right from the archway. Bride calmly steadied his stance and brought his eyes around to the figure, careful not to turn his head and show motion. The figure seemed not to spot him as it slunk forward toward the dim crack of light framing the doorway. It was the ponytail man.

Bride leveled his pistol as Ponytail approached the door. Ponytail gave the handle a simple tug and to both men's surprise the door swung open. Sunlight poured in the doorway silhouetting Bride's target. It made little sense. They were two or three levels below the city, but outside the door stood the red granite outer wall of a building lit by natural, albeit indirect, light.

"Stop. Hands up." Bride repeated, trying to replace the gusto he lacked with intensity.

Again, the individual refused to comply, bolting forward out the doorway. Bride fired toward the man, intentionally a bit high and wide. The warning shot proved as effective as the verbal warnings; the man in black spun from the doorway to the right. Bride lunged forward after the man, rounded the doorway, and found himself in a twenty-five foot deep, stone-walled dry moat around the Second Empire-style building known to locals as the Old Post Office. The moat was apparently used for getting sunlight into the tall windows of the basement floors. The door led to under a walkway below the building's entrances. Bride was surprised that the non-direct sunlight was so blinding. He'd stayed in the dark too long. At this point he was only worried about Ponytail, who, after Bride's eyes adjusted to the flood of light, he saw sprinting for the corner of the moat. Bride plodded after, losing distance with each step.

Bride rounded the building just as Ponytail, still in a sprint, neared a stairway of open steel grating that led up two levels to the street. With no hope of catching the fleeing man if he chased up the stairs, Bride tried for what he considered as the shortest of long shots. With his last effort, he ran under the stairs, reached between two risers, and grappled at Ponytail's leg as the man climbed upward. He got it. Ponytail tumbled forward, crashing his shins and forearms into the unforgiving steel, then letting out a sort of grunting scream.

He tried to kick himself free, but Bride held tight, wrapping his hand in the fabric of his quarry's pant leg. Bride held his gun over his head, pointing its barrel through the grating at the man's chest.

"Don't move," Bride said calmly.

It was the first real view Bride had of Ponytail's face, though through the stair tread's grillwork. The face disproved the theory that symmetry equated beauty, the eyes equally too inset and too close to the nose. The skin was too smooth, almost as if freshly shed or at least over-exfoliated. The expression on his face suggested Ponytail had given up. For a moment he lay still except panting until the same thought apparently went through his head that had already gone through Bride's. A wide smile curled up too much equally on both sides of the too-thin mouth.

"Or what? You going to shoot an unarmed man?" the man asked in a distinct California accent.

His bluff called, Bride doubled down. "Unarmed? When I find your remote controller and mention you threatened to blow up the something-or-another building—maybe this one, it looks important—the shooting will be fully justified."

Through the grate, Ponytail eyes looked startled, but the startled face quickly returned to the curled grin.

"Sorry fed, I don't believe you." Ponytail shook his leg free of Bride's grip and scrambled up the stairway. At the top, he leapt over the ornamental metal gate and disappeared.

Gaunt and exhausted, Bride's body slumped into the wall, his pistol dropping from his hand to the concrete. There was no chase left in him. It was even an effort to slide his hand into his pocket and pull out his phone. Great, he thought noticing the bars at the screen's top, it had a signal. He held down the button until he heard the familiar, friendly tone.

"Dial 9-1-1."

5> On the Case

"WHERE'S DIA REYNOLDS?"

Robert Liptmann wanted to gauge the reaction of Anthony Thorenus. The Deputy Director of S32's eyes shot up from the sink where he was washing his hands. Liptmann's ambush in the third floor men's room had worked; Thorenus acted flustered and desperate as he tried to compose himself.

"What?" Thorenus uttered.

Liptmann could tell he was stalling, but why? "Where is Dia Reynolds?" Liptmann repeated.

"She's not at her desk in the Equation Lab?"

Thorenus stalled again by grabbing a paper towel from the dispenser and drying his hands, all while avoiding eye-contact. Liptmann wondered how a man so easy to read reached such a high position in the NSA. Perhaps he was having a bad day. "No." Liptmann said, keeping it short to keep his original unanswered question hanging.

"Did you check..." Thorenus paused and stared too long into a blank section of the wall. Finally, "Oh, she left early. I had forgotten she had filed for a half-day."

That was the truth, but Liptmann sensed Thorenus still hid something. "I asked you to set up an interview with her at four-thirty. It's..." he looked at his watch, "...five-o-nine now. When I ask for an interview, I expect the person to be there."

Another pause. "It's totally my fault, Robert," Thorenus said. "Don't blame Miss Reynolds for my mistake. She's not at fault here."

38

"I understand where the blame lies." If Thorenus wished to fall on the sword, Liptmann would inform him the sword already pointed his way. "I expect to see Dia Reynolds Monday morning at nine sharp."

Thorenus struggled to say, "M-miss Reynolds is off Monday as well."

Liptmann couldn't believe this man's gall. He was hiding something. He was hiding Dia Reynolds. Why? Liptmann shook his head to demonstrate his disgust at Thorenus; he turned and walked away.

"I can have her to you on Tuesday," Thorenus pleaded. "Or I could tell her to cancel her plans and come back Monday."

Liptmann kept walking. Let the man squirm. It will be interesting—and telling—to watch what he does. Thorenus tried to say something else as Liptmann passed through the bathroom door and let it automatically shut behind him.

Something was going on and it involved Alec Holloway, Dia Reynolds, and Anthony Thorenus.

Liptmann headed back to The Lab. Upon arriving, he found it empty save for one man working away at a desktop computer. Liptmann recognized the man as Denis Ayers from his files.

"Pardon me, Mr. Ayers," He interrupted Ayers's concentration.

Ayers jumped, momentarily startled by the disruption. Liptmann wondered if he just had that effect on people.

"Yes?" Ayers said.

"Can you show me Dia Reynolds desk?" Liptmann flashed his credentials.

"Sure." Ayers stood. "It's right over here." He led Liptmann to a desk in the corner, the only desk in the Lab not on a right angle to the wall. Ayers started to go back to his own desk when Liptmann stopped him.

"Hold on, Mr. Ayers. Can you tell me if anything looks out of place?"

Ayers took a moment and scanned the desk. "No... No, it looks fine to me."

Liptmann eyed the desk himself. It looked normal. He dismissed Ayers who went back to his desk. He went through Dia Reynolds's drawers. Nothing stood out. Liptmann raised his voice to speak across the room. "Hey Ayers, I've been in interviews all day; what finally happened at the St. Louis courthouse?"

"Oh, then you didn't hear?" Ayers said animatedly. "The terrorists surrendered. The scuttlebutt says the police radios at the scene went into Helen Keller mode and when the police and Homeland scrambled to communicate with each other, the terrorist with the bomb thought they were preparing to breach. He freaked out and surrendered. The rest surrendered about fifteen minutes later."

"Was anybody hurt?" Liptmann asked while looking under the desk. He noted that Ayers was the type to spread unsubstantiated rumors. Liptmann didn't know what to look for, but his concerns with Ayers would wait for another day. Ayers wouldn't be so cavalier if whatever nagged Liptmann about Alec Holloway and Dia Reynolds also involved Ayers.

"Four victims died in the initial firefight. A judge got beat up bad and taken to the hospital, and a Homeland agent also ended up in the hospital. I don't get how though. The terrorists never made contact until they surrendered."

"Shame." Liptmann said picking up a sliver of freshly trimmed paper from the floor. "Any one claiming responsibility?"

"Not yet," Ayers said. "But I bet ISIS does. They claim everything. I got rickrolled the other day and ISIS claimed responsibility."

Liptmann rose from the floor and examined the desktop again. He changed the subject. "Can you tell me where Miss Reynolds is going this weekend?"

"Up north. Cape Cod, I think." Ayers said.

"Is she going by herself?" Liptmann picked up and inspected a stapler.

"Hmm, I'm not positive." Ayers stopped typing for a moment. "She usually vacations with her sister."

"Her sister?"

"Yeah, that's a picture of Dia with her sister on her desk. That one was taken at the beach in South Carolina."

Liptmann looked around the desk again. He found no picture of Dia Reynolds with her sister. He picked up the only picture on the desk, a framed picture of the dog, and stared into eyes of the basset hound in the photograph. "Does Dia Reynolds have a dog?"

"Not that I know of."

CLARENCE AXEWORTHY FASTENED the top mother-of-pearl button of his white Paul Smith shirt while looking into his full length dressing mirror. He tucked the tails of his shirt into the Hugo Boss trousers. He would again forego the silver cufflinks he had made with his company's logo, the padlock above crossed axes of Axeworthy Internet Security. Too garish, he thought. Why did he have those made? Well, they seemed to please the senior employees. The plain round ebony cufflinks would serve him today.

Axeworthy was a towering individual, six foot six, whose neat ash blonde hair had half melded to gray in his approach to fifty. He selected one of the black silk bands that his tailor had created for him. With both hands he strapped the band around his neck, twisted until the fastener was at the back, then drew the shirt collar down over the strap. This left a clean black square visible atop the white field of his shirt. All that was lacking to complete his signature look was the matching Hugo Boss suit jacket.

The lights automatically switched off behind him as he strode from the dressing alcove and then faded on ahead in the master bedroom where the jacket was staged on a valet chair.

The expansive bedroom was impeccable. Decorated in white, with the floor and accents in a natural Brazilian hardwood, the only blight on the room was the nude, gaunt woman poised on the rumpled sheets of the bed. Axeworthy looked at the woman disappointed. The raven-haired woman lay sallow, unmoved since he left her for his shower. To him, sex—like all matters concerning a woman—was best with a submissive, but this one had lost all vitality. He will have to call Lloyd to exchange her for a fresh woman. Axeworthy slipped on the suit jacket and was dressed for his meeting, but now he had to deal with this. He kicked the king-sized bed with enough force to move the mattress. "Out, you damned cow!" He screamed at the slave. "Get to your room, woman!"

The scrawny woman rolled off the mattress and scurried to the simple door in the south wall of the opulent bedroom as rapidly as the weak, bony limbs could carry her.

"What the hell?" Axeworthy's question echoed in the empty room. "If being a millionaire can't buy you a decent sex slave then what the hell good is it?"

He straightened the suit jacket, calmed himself with a stiff breath, and headed out the double doors. "Irma," he called out to his assistant as he descended the stairs that opened on the great room. With a point of his hand, the vertical shades slid away on the massive floor-to-ceiling wall-to-wall window revealing morning on the desolate expanse of Salton Sea, the largest body of water inside California. Another point and the room's lights adjusted to daytime. He no longer marveled at the tricks his experimental chip implants could accomplish. It had become his way of life.

"Irma," he called again, "when is my conference call?"

"It began fifteen minutes ago. They are waiting for you, sir. The video call is already live in your office." Irma, a squat grey-haired woman who did little to highlight what natural beauty remained from her youth, came scurrying into the expansive room with her tablet in hand.

"Good, then I'm not late. What are my messages?"

Irma checked her tablet. "Your mother wants to know when you will visit. And sir, Steven Burgess is here."

"Hmmpf. Where is he? What does he want? I don't care for guests showing up here uninvited."

"He's in the front room. Also, Attila wants a report on St. Louis."

"I guess I have to talk to Steven then. Do you know what he has?"

"He said he has most of the footage, but is missing the data collection. Apparently the drone was destroyed."

Axeworthy looked displeased. "Tell Steven to wait. I'll talk with him after the call and let him know I'll need a written report by tonight so he might want to work on that while he waits."

"Yes, sir. Next, Allen asked if you had seen the posting by the new NSA defector?"

"What?" Axeworthy spun and grabbed the tablet from Irma's hands and furiously read the email from his chief software programmer. His face shook in simultaneous glee and anger. "Irma, I need to see this sort of thing first."

"Yes, sir."

"Call Allen." He handed the tablet back to Irma and headed toward his home office. "Tell him we need this. I'll call him after the shareholders, but tell him don't wait for me. This acquisition is exactly what we need. Move on it."

"Yes, sir."

When Axeworthy walked toward his office, he found Steven Burgess sitting in a chair by the door. He hadn't noticed the gangly man there. Neither apparently had Irma. As Axeworthy approached, Steven stood to a slight inch taller than Axeworthy, but with his lankier frame and plainer dress sense he cut a much less imposing figure.

"Steven, I thought Irma asked you to wait in the foyer." Axeworthy strode past, continuing into his office.

"Hello, Clarence," Steven said, nervously trailing his boss into the wide modern office. "Yes, sorry, I didn't think this could wait. I wanted to tell you personally about St. Louis. It worked. The damned old thing worked. All reports say we infected all the Police and Homeland Security's radios over the air by my ... er ... our modification of a twenty-year-old worm. It's just so wicked cool."

Seeming to ignore Steven, Axeworthy stood at his desk, a glass-topped table held up by three stainless steel columns with no wires going to its monitor, keyboard, or lamp. It was the perfect height for working while standing. The office was spacious, yet spartan, the west wall of glass overlooking the desolate sea. Sizable video screens filled the opposite wall. Each contained the face of a shareholder closed captioned with their name and a running transcription of what they were saying. The center screen was black with light, white, sans-serif font reading, "Clarence Axeworthy – not connected."

Finally Axeworthy gave Steven's enthusiasm a judging sideways glance. "You must learn to calm yourself, boy. What happened? What warranted the drive from Yuma?"

Steven took a deep breath. "The Blind worm we captured, we were able to modify it to infect the operating system in the police and feds' radios using the zero day hole we found. We've achieved our proof of concept. In theory, this worm should be able to get root—technically above root access—on about seventy percent of Unix-based systems. So long as we can manage all types of user access, even guest access, on most systems."

"I understand you collected usage stats on the drone, but someone destroyed the drone."

Steven tried to stammer an excuse, but Axeworthy pressed on with his lecture. "We needed that data, Steven. We must be careful with this worm. Without feedback from the drone we can't know if the worm self-destructed. We can't have this worm in places it could be discovered. If Blind does as you promise, Steven, it puts us on top. I've examined your modifications. They are the type of hacks we need, but we'll also need the NSA's router hack. The Hacking Group's leak has closed up too many of our backdoors. If we're to infect the routers, we need new vulnerabilities. The NSA router program allows us to complete at least two of our A-list projects."

"StasisZero, you mean?" Steven asked. "We've tried reverse engineering the NSA's StasisZero. That thing is a master class in obfuscated coding. We're going nowhere with that without source code."

Axeworthy pulled up a wheeled office chair and sat down, the streamlined desk automatically lowering as he did. He typed something into the keyboard and worked his finger along the glass desk as a trackpad. "That may just be coming available soon," he said. He spun the monitor toward Steven, showing him Allen's email about the NSA defector.

When Steven finished reading the email he said, "Whoa. Is this real? Someone's threatening to release NSA source code. *Balls.*"

Axeworthy ignored the freshman language. Smart boy, but not very mature. "We need this," Axeworthy demanded. "Find this post's author and get this source code. I expect to have the code within the week."

"Yes, sir."

"And Steven, when you get back to Yuma tell marketing to make Axeworthy Internet Security free starting this Thursday."

"Really? The whole suite? Don't you need board approval first?" Steven asked.

"The board is my problem. Just do as I ask." On an invisible cue, Irma entered the room. "Irma," Axeworthy said, "show Steven out." He added, "And call Lloyd and tell him I need to make an exchange." He stood, pressed a key on the keyboard, and joined the conference call.

7> Sault Ste. Marie

"CALM DOWN, D. We're almost to the border," Ruby Jarrett told her sister as she checked the amount of gas in her 2004 Jeep Liberty. Ruby confessed to her sister, Dia Reynolds, for the last six months the old Jeep had been sputtering and dying when low on gas. With three different mechanics giving her three different expensive remedies, she had opted not to worry about it. Dia bet she worried about it now.

"We've been stuck on this bridge for forty-five minutes," Dia said, close to panic. She crooked herself to try to see through the rear view mirrors from the passenger's seat. She finally spun her torso around in the seat for a good view behind the Jeep, then ducked half down to avoid being seen. "I think that's the car, four cars back, the one that's been following us."

With no concerns about being seen, Ruby twisted her body to look. "You're paranoid, D," the older sister chided. "The border crossing is slow because of that thing in St. Louis. We'll be across in no time."

"I'm in the NSA, Ruby. I'm paid to be paranoid." Dia slumped in her seat.

"*Were* in the NSA, Ducky. Or did you forget what this trip was about? And don't forget until two days ago I thought you were working for the Department of Defense."

Dia hated her childhood nickname. Ruby pulled it from her quiver whenever she desired to remind her seven-year-junior sister who was the older and wiser of the two of them. The nickname worked; Dia stopped arguing. Instead, she surveyed

47

the situation. The half-century old, two-lane, steel truss, dual arch Sault Ste. Marie International Bridge spanned the locks of the St. Mary's River that bordered the United States and Canada at the twin cities of Sault Ste. Marie, Michigan and Sault Ste. Marie, Ontario. Today, traffic clogged the two-and-a-half mile bridge deck in both directions. This made sense to Dia. What wasn't understandable was why the traffic heading into the US advanced a half car length every minute while the traffic into Canada had not budged in five minutes. The truth may have been that on this day, the Americans had better prepared for the sudden high security alert than the Canadians. In Dia's conceit it was on her account.

"This isn't going to work." Dia was in a full panic. "We're not going to make it. I need to go back."

"Dia, calm down. You can't go back. Even if there was room to turn around, we'd still have to pass through the US checkpoint. If you remember, they're the ones you think want you back. We're in no man's land."

"That *is* the car I saw before. They're waiting to trap us at the Canadian checkpoint. I have to turn back."

"You're being crazy, D. We have no choice but to go into Canada."

But Dia might have spotted a means of escape. A family in front of them heading south took advantage of the stopped traffic. They left their van, and were at the edge of the bridge taking photographs of the St. Mary's River and the locks and canals. Near them was a gate in the fencing put up to keep people from climbing on the bridge's support arches.

Dia pulled her olive drab laptop bag from the backseat, checked her supplies in the tool kit within, and slipped the bag over her shoulder.

"Give me your phone."

"What?" Ruby protested. "What's wrong with your phone?"

"I told you; they'll be tracking my phone. Please, give me your phone."

"Damn it, D. What am I supposed to use?"

Dia released a condescending sigh. "Stop at a Best Buy or Walmart and get a pay-as-you-go phone. Send a text to your number when you get it. We'll meet back up. Maybe we double back and catch a boat from Mackinaw City or Mackinac Island."

"And where are you going now?" The elder sister said in a maternal way.

"I see a way out." Dia cracked her car door open, peeked over her shoulder to confirm whoever was inside *that* car couldn't see her.

"Well, be careful, and don't forget..." before Ruby completed her sentence Dia slipped out the door and pressed the Jeep's door closed quietly behind her. Though her sister could no longer hear her, Ruby completed the sentiment. "...I love you, Ducky."

Dia took care to stay out of the line of sight of the car that had spurred her paranoia, but also took pains to walk naturally as to not arouse suspicion from other drivers. She walked forward on the bridge until she could cross in front of a northward van and behind a southbound truck. She stood on the steel rail, took out her sister's phone, and took a picture of the majestic scenery. In truth, Dia was killing time until the truck progressed enough to obscure the view of the gate. As was her luck with lines, the northbound traffic into Canada commenced moving and the vehicles heading into America froze. Dia moved along the truck until she could just glance between the cab and the trailer. There went Ruby's Jeep; there was little time to change her mind and get back in with Ruby. Before she thought it through, the Jeep moved out of view.

Only moments later, the car Dia thought was following her, a brown early 'eighties sedan, probably a Buick or an Oldsmobile, came into the narrow view. Dia backed away. She longed to get a view of the driver but that meant the chance the driver might also see her. Instead she stayed hidden behind the truck. After a half minute she checked again. The car had passed. It was time to try her hand at the gate.

"Warning: Injury May Result From Unauthorized Access." Another sign warning of security cameras sought to intimidate people from doing what she was on the verge of doing. Dia scoffed.

The chances of someone currently watching a camera showing the same image it had for decades was minuscule. All bark.

Dia dug what she needed from her tool kit and returned to the gate. After confirming the truck obscured any views of her, she examined the padlock, a Master keyed lock. She frowned, she'd only done this hack on a combination lock. She figured she had under a fifty-fifty chance of her crack working. Dia took out a tiny aluminum shim, cut from a beer can following instructions on YouTube. She had tested the hack on padlocks at home, but when she attempted to slip the thin shim into the body of the lock in the gap around where the shackle entered, it wouldn't go. The shackle was too tight in the hole and the effects of the lock's years of exposure to elements thwarted Dia's hack.

She whispered a curse. She hatched a riskier plan, but it would have to wait for the next truck to obscure her again. Until then she shot more photos of the waterway. Then she realized the grandeur of the scenery laid out in front of her. The tumbling white clouds mottled the azure afternoon sky. The St. Mary's River below matched the sky's azure as it expanded west into Lake Superior. Industrial buildings and newer housing dithered into the spring green foliage on both the US and Canadian river banks. Canada's chilled winds swirled her freshly colored hair. With the temperature just above forty Fahrenheit, Dia should have felt cold. Instead she felt invigorated. In a better time, Dia would have had the urge to spread arms and declare, "*I'm the king of the world!*" Her DiCaprio hatred be damned.

After temporarily surrendering to the majesty of the vista, Dia snapped back to focus and waited for the opportunity to put her plan in action. After too long, the next truck pulled aside her and the gate. She searched her bag and fished out her cordless Dremel 8220 rotary tool. She selected a cutting disc, tightened it on, and attacked the lock's shackle at full speed. Her prayer was that the sound of the car engines would drown the high-pitch squeal of the Dremel. It wasn't the perfect plan. It would be obvious someone cut the lock, and she wouldn't be able to lock the gate behind her, but in forty-five seconds the Dremel sliced clean through the shackle.

Dia pushed the gate open and stepped out on to the tiny concrete ledge. What she saw over the ledge awed her. She assumed there would be a ladder down and she had misjudged the height of the bridge. It appeared to be more than 200 feet off the ground. "Christ," she said—half in vain, half in prayer.

Noticing that any movement of the truck would leave her exposed, she squeezed the gate closed behind her, took a deep breath, and went over the edge. Clinging to the electric cables strung down the side of the bridge, she scurried down until she was out of sight of all traffic. She paused. Her arms were strained, and she'd barely gone down five feet.

"Don't look down. Don't look down," she adopted as her mantra as she methodically descended hand over hand, four inches at a time. The climb progressed, four inches, then four inches, then four inches, over and over until with four more inches her leading foot found nothingness. No foothold, no surface, nothing. She had reached the bottom of the bridge deck.

She froze. There was no going up, and there was no going down. The cables continued under the deck, but they were taut to the bridge's underside. There was no wrapping her legs around them. Dia steeled her thoughts. There had to be a way. She eased herself lower another foot-and-a-half by squatting her legs beneath her at the deck's bottom edge. With a tight grasp of the cables with her hands, she thrust her legs down below the deck and searched wildly with them for some purchase, but again found nothing. It had been an all-or-nothing move and nothing won. She hung still for a moment and realized that this might be the end of her. Ruby would return to the US to identify the body. How much damage would this fall cause? Would she be able to identify her?

No, she thought, *this is defeatist thinking. Just go.* With a bit of reasoning she theorized if there was something to grab, it would be to her right, toward the piling, out of view under the deck. Her hands loosened on the cable for enough time to slide down another half foot. With her legs under the bridge deck, she swept her legs forward to the right and back to the left. On the third pivot forward, when she sensed she had swung her legs as high as possible, she let go the cables with her hands.

For a moment, Dia hung suspended in the air by momentum, but gravity grabbed hold and she was falling. But in less than a second of tumbling her left leg hooked over something at the knee. On only instinct, the right leg wrapped itself around the other way. Her arms clutched for their own hold, the left hand landing one.

Her legs and one arm wrapped her cylindrical savior, but she still wasn't sure what she caught. When her right hand, swung back and landed atop the left, Dia peeked around to determine she hung from a ten-inch round downspout pipe. *Thank the gods.* But before she even tried to grab the downspout tighter, Dia began to slide.

"No, no, no!" Dia's slide picked up speed, her right hand slipping loose. Suddenly her legs hit a pipe clamp, knocking their grip loose. Her left hand held the pipe only long enough to make her fall not head first.

Dia screamed. She was falling again.

Much faster than she expected, her back slammed into something solid whipping her head back, clanging the back of her skull to the surface. She closed her eyes for a moment to access the pain. Not too bad, but her head throbbed both inside and out. Opening her eyes, she found herself only a short distance below the bridge deck. Carefully she turned and felt what had caught her fall. She was saved by a floor of corrugated metal, presumably put there for bridge inspection. She lifted herself to one knee and examined her environment. She was still in the bridge's web of steel structure propped atop the hundred-plus foot concrete support. Her corrugated floor butted to the nearest support.

Dia took one second and cleared the fog from her head. She heard voices calling from atop the bridge. "Who's there? We need you to come out where we can see you," a male voice called. She needed to move fast. If they were at the gate, they were on their way toward the ground below, but at this stage they probably didn't know what they were dealing with. They'd be assuming a jumper or someone sneaking across the border. A look down and Dia saw she still had a tremendous way to go.

The downspout and the cables both continued down the pier. Dia removed the strap from her toolkit and gave it a good examination. It was a strong, woven strap. The whole tool kit was a military-quality build, but right now Dia would've been more comfortable had it been actual military surplus. Dia stood over the opening, extended the strap to its full length, clipped it around her waist, and wrapped it around the downspout. With more voices clamoring above her, she steeled her nerves and descended the pier.

8> Sunshine Asks for Help

THE BLADE PASSED just under Henry Bride's left arm. He had missed the parry but still dodged to avoid taking the hit. While the foil's tip extended beyond him Bride stepped into the attack and swung his own foil around for a close-up attack of his own. His opponent turned sideways and slipped beyond Bride along the painted line that acted as the edge of the strip. Technically, the move should cause a stoppage and reset in fencing. However, an unspoken gentlemen's agreement in the club stated when fencing "dry," without being attached to electronic scorekeepers, the fencers would simply switch sides, come to *en garde* position, and continue. Bride cursed the gentlemen as he went *en garde*. He could have used the breather; his opponent had him on the run, and this was his first real physical activity since the doctors patched up his wounds from the incident in the tunnels. He had thought a little fencing would show he was ready to resume duties, but when he struggled to fend off the next barrage attacks, he knew the answer. Parry four, parry eight, parry seven; Bride's foil swept back and across as he scrambled to defend attack after attack without a chance for a decent riposte. Finally, Bride held a parry, disengaged the riposte, and landed the tip of his blade on the shoulder of his opposite.

Bride started to remove his mask and congratulate his friend, Gordon Greene, on a good match, but Greene interrupted. "Sleeve," he said, pressing his finger to the spot just outside the seam where Bride's blade had landed.

Greene was right; Bride hit off target. Bride had never had this much difficulty fencing Greene before. Whenever Bride came to town over the past couple of years, the two men had made it a point to get together at the St. Louis Fencers Club. They would follow up fencing with a small, late meal at Elicia's Pizzeria. They'd only missed one time when Bride's visit coincided with Greene's Army Reserve duties. Bride had always gotten the best of Greene, but tonight his friend made Bride work harder for a win.

Bride came *en garde* again. Greene mirrored his position. The two men struck forward near simultaneously. Bride lunged into Greene's own lunge. Bride believed he had right-of-way—attacking forward first—so the point would be his. Before his attack landed, however, Greene's blade made nominal contact with his blade and moved Bride's point off target. Greene's tip caught the slight amount of Bride rib.

"Touch," Bride called, pressing his finger against the spot where he felt Greene's rubber tipped blade through the heavy white canvas jacket.

It took a second for Greene to realize what had happened, but when he did, he pulled of his mask and hoisted it into the air. "Ha!" he cried in amazed victory.

"Good match, Gordon," Bride said as he removed his mask, then held out his left, bare hand for the customary shake.

Greene was ecstatic when they shook. "I thought I'd never beat you, Henry, and you couldn't have made it easy, could you? Thanks for the match."

After a few minutes more of Greene's gloating, Bride sat down on the gymnasium's bleachers, toweled the sweat from his face and three-day off-duty whiskers. He ran his fingers along the stitches at the back of his neck, everything seemed intact, but his energy hadn't returned to one-hundred percent. There would be no more fencing for him tonight.

He packed his fencing gear and changed to his street clothes, then sat in the bleachers and watched the other fencers. Greene's technique had improved; it wasn't just Bride's skill slipping that allowed Greene to beat him this time. Gordon

55

Greene was a gifted athlete, but fencing wasn't a sport he took completely seriously. Aikido was Greene's sport. He held a black belt and taught that art. He even had plans to open his own dojo someday. This evening, Bride observed that Greene's aikido skills had bled over into his fencing.

As he rested, Bride ran his fingers over the healing scar on the back of his neck. The ER doctor had glued the wound shut, so far it was holding. It was probably a bad idea to test the repair so early. Had the doctor warned Bride not to exert himself? He couldn't remember. He'd never been good at listening to doctors, being only interested in when he'd be cleared for duty. He told himself at least he was smart enough to know he was being an idiot.

After Greene finished two more matches with two of the better fencers in the club—winning one and losing one—he asked Bride if he was ready to go.

Bride was. The two men headed toward the parking lot, discussing where they would meet for a late snack that would serve as an excuse for continued conversation.

"How's Leta? Gina asked me to invite you two to dinner on Friday if you're going to be in town," Greene asked.

"We broke up." Bride answered, treading into a subject he had hoped to avoid.

"Ah hell, Henry. Where are you staying?"

"The company has me in a hotel until ... well, until my current project is done."

"Nonsense. You're going to stay in our guest room. Gina would insist. I insist."

But when they emerged on to the parking lot Bride spotted a familiar figure standing near his car, the white 1973 Apollo GT he had recently acquired.

He turned to Greene, "Listen Gordon, I'm afraid I'll have to cancel this evening."

Greene glanced over toward Bride's car and saw a charming black woman who, with pride, wore a five-inch tall Afro. "I understand, Henry," Greene replied.

"I wish I did," Bride murmured to himself before giving his goodbyes and promising to stay in touch. He took a deep breath and strode to the car.

Waiting by the car, Bride recognized someone he had never seen outside the DC area and had rarely seen outside the headquarters of Homeland Security: Krystal Carrie, the head of the DHS's Digital Technologies section.

"Sunshine," Bride called to her using her nickname, "what are you doing here?"

"Henry!" She said, startled, uncharacteristically using his given name. Apparently she hadn't seen his approach. "I need your help." A look of worry had replaced her usual glowing smile.

"How did you find me?" He knew it was silly question the moment he asked. He carried with him five gadgets he could think of that came from her division.

"How I got here doesn't matter, but how I figured out this was your snazzy new European sports car, that's a different story." For a brief second Bride saw that smile return.

"Yes, well, a man must have his hobbies, but for the record, it's an American sports car. However, you didn't come all this way to give me trouble about my automotive choices. What do you need?"

"I need a favor. A big one. A friend of mine is in trouble. My friend Dia was with the NSA, now she's gone on the run. The NSA thinks she's taken some of their software and toys. They want her back. And as jumpy as Fort Meade is post-Snowden, I'm afraid it's not likely she'll come in unharmed.

"When I saw her last Thursday night, she was on edge and nervous, but wouldn't tell me why."

"What makes you think she's on the run?" he asked. "There's a lot of possibilities. Granted, few are good."

"When I last saw her she gave me this." She handed Bride a photo—showing him the note written on the back. It read:

Sunshine, You were always there for me.
Thank you.

Bride noted the tense of the word "were." He flipped the photo over to the front and examined the picture. It was Sunshine with a vibrant young woman with bright bleach blonde hair tipped in vivid blue and an eyebrow ring. The girl looked familiar, but he couldn't place where he had seen her before. The pair of women were mugging for the camera inside a sports bar or restaurant.

"How did a girl that looks like her get hired by the NSA?" He asked.

"She's a programming genius. This girl hacked an al Qaeda forum's server when she was sixteen, and she found a plot to attack the American embassy in Egypt. *When she was sixteen.* She emailed this information to the head of the NSA on his private internal address."

"They recruited a sixteen-year-old?"

"No, no, no. They recruited her three years later after she filed similar reports to the NSA five more times. You have to understand, despite her rebellious looks, Dia is a solid patriot and has been fiercely loyal to the NSA. Something has to have made her go on the run. But that's not all. I'm afraid Dia has taken out escape insurance. Take at look at this."

Sunshine handed Bride an iPad Air open to a posting on a website addressed as codeofresistance.onion. It read:

```
To all it may concern,
Recently, I have left my position with an
American government agency. Though I intend
no harm to this agency, I am concerned with my
ability to leave its employ. As such, I have
posted on https://whitehouse.gov/encrypt7777
encrypted copies of certain files and software
that the agency would not want made public. I
have created four fail safes around the world,
some human, some computer. The fail safes will
release the password to unlock these files to
the public should certain events happen that
```

either prove my death or show my inability to
prove I am alive.

As evidence that I possess the software I am
listing each application's name, version number,
build number, and a string of twelve bytes at
position 1000 in application file.

GRAYVACUUM v.7.30.761 b.d0881263
B6223FDE100AC1F2994C0008
BRIGHTUTAH v.1.10.201 b. f71002231
CITYGRATER v.0.10.106B b. s36700311
HEADWATER
SCHOOLMONTANA
SIERAMONTANA
SUFFIXMONTANA
STUCCOMONTANA
STASISZERO
STEADYZERO
RINGANDRUN

These listing should be sufficient proof to the
agency that I have access to these applications.
However, as further proof I have placed a copy
of the SLANTZERO app v.5.55.002 on a server open
to the public. SLANTZERO is only one component
of a bigger system and harmless by itself. It
can now be found at https://whitehouse.gov/
slantzero555
/<X>

Bride recognized a few of the application names from
both internal memos at the DHS and from the leaked NSA
ANT catalog. He scanned through the replies to the post.
Most of the first dozen were essentially saying, "Got them"
followed by a few declaring "It's down now." Then various
users posted links to sites where they were hosting copies
of the file, and a discussion began about the validity of the
original post of the thread.

"This is your friend?" he asked.

"Yes, it has to be. Did you see the sign-off?"

"Sure." Bride looked at the X surrounded by the greater-than and less-than symbols.

"Dia is short for Diamond. Her name is Diamond Reynolds. That symbol, it makes a little diamond. I'm betting that's her new hacker name. It all makes sense."

"Why would she do this? She's certainly burning the bridges."

"I have no idea. She's always seemed rational."

"If you don't know the 'why', what about the 'how' and 'where'?" Bride asked.

"There I might be able to help you. Don't forget, Mr. Bride, the border boys and the TSA are on our team." The trademark Sunshine smile returned.

9> **Road Trip**

THE WHOLE WEEK had gone to hell. Bride originally flew to St. Louis on Monday with the sole purpose of mending his relationship with Leta Sinn. The long-distance relationship was always a long-shot relationship. Bride tried to spend any free time he mustered either in St. Louis with Leta or by flying Leta to DC. This led to large gaps in the relationship, some as long as three months. He planned this week to visit the head of the DHS regional office and request an assignment closer to St. Louis, preferably in the metropolitan area proper.

Leta and the fates had other designs for the week. Leta took the visit as a chance to break off their affair in person rather than electronically. What was to be a week, or possibly more, with Leta turned into six nights alone at the Quality Inn Airport. The meeting to explore positions at the local DHS branch, located across the river in East St. Louis ended with Bride volunteering on what turned into the Eagleton Courthouse situation. He also scheduled to pick up his recently purchased Apollo GT from the garage who turned it from another man's failed restoration to his simple, yet fun modernized "driver." He would either ship it to DC at the end of the week, or, if things with Leta had gone better, have it as a daily driver in St. Louis.

With plenty of free time, thanks to the mandatory paid-leave following the DC suspect shooting and the tunnel incident, he contrived this trip as a test of the untried Apollo. The long-distance journey to Michigan's Upper Peninsula was an effort to track down Sunshine's friend fleeing her presumably former employers at the NSA.

So far, the Apollo performed admirably as it sped along I-196 on Lake Michigan's eastern shore. It still slowed his journey having to check for leaks every few hundred miles in the new 3.4L V6 crate engine that replaced the blown Buick V8 that came with the vehicle. There was also an issue where the oil temperature gauge wasn't functioning, and, because the water temperature gauge was just plain missing, he prayed the engine didn't overheat. Bride caught a streak of luck finding the Apollo. He spotted the heading "Italian designed Sports Car – needs work" in a local CraigsList ad on one of his trips to St. Louis. A call to the seller in Quincy, Illinois reported it as an American-built Apollo GT. A visit showed good bodywork but a need for considerable mechanical work to make it drivable. He recently parted with his old Triumph so he had the money to pay the seller's $12,000 bargain of an asking price before any serious collector found the ad. Fully restored an Apollo GT started around $75,000. This car was far from fully restored, but, with the body work nearly complete, this car made a perfect candidate for Bride's plans. He wanted modern workings under the classic shell. He found a St. Louis garage to do the work. It gave him both another excuse to visit Leta and a diversion on the days she went into work. So far the car had proven competent, save the temperature gauges, so Bride decided this journey should be made by car. Airplane would have been faster, but offered little flexibility. Sunshine had used some of her computer magic and phone records to locate Dia Reynolds's sister fourteen hours ago in northern Michigan, far from her southern Indiana home. It was a good bet Dia was with her and the two women could be in Canada already or hidden in a cabin somewhere in the Northern Peninsula. Of course, there was a high probability that Dia wasn't with her sister at all. Bride might need to reverse course and head for Miami, San Antonio, or Paducah. In those cases air travel would be required. Bride had to admit the choice of traveling by car stemmed as much from a gut feeling as it did from logic. But his gut wanted to play with his new toy.

He wasn't sure why he was even doing this. Yes, he owed Sunshine several dozen favors, but this situation lay beyond the scope of any of those. He may run afoul of his own government. Something about the girl in the photo made him feel she needed his help. Was he being sexist? Would he make this journey if the person were male? If it were Edward Snowden? That wasn't it, he told himself. Maybe he was just bored. He didn't relish the idea of spending the rest of his forced leave in either DC or St. Louis. This gave him a perfect excuse to get away from his troubles. He'd rather not reflect on Leta or his job because he couldn't do a thing about either. Instead, he occupied his thoughts with the Apollo, Dia Reynolds, and the Springfield XD Mod.2 9mm that Gordon Greene loaned him before he left St. Louis. It was a solid gun, though more of a civilian weapon than the SIG he was used to. Bride wanted more range time with it. So far he only had the ten minutes on the range when Greene had let him try it out.

The highway turned inland toward Grand Rapids. Bride decided it was time for some music, so he fired up an upbeat playlist on the music app on the phone mounted on his dash. The stereo made it four bars into Imelda May's Tainted Love before his ringtone replaced the music. The screen displayed the temporary number Krystal Carrie had given to him. He pressed "speaker."

"What do you have for me, Sunshine?" He answered.

"Bad news." The tone of Krystal Carrie's voice echoed her words. "Ruby Greer's car was in an accident on I-75 near Kincheloe, Michigan. An ambulance brought the two women to War Memorial Hospital in Sault Ste. Marie. The driver is in serious condition and not expected to make it. The passenger was injured but left the ER before seeing the doctor."

"That sounds like our girl. Kincheloe, where's that?"

"Near the tip of the northern peninsula—about twenty minutes from the border crossing into Canada."

"Sounds like she's making a run for the border."

"Except the car was heading south on I-75."

"Odd." Bride couldn't make any sense of that. "Any luck with contacting her?"

"No, I'm not sure where I'd try if she's taken herself off the net. She's just... Hang on..."

"What have you got?"

"Give me a minute."

The minute dragged on to two then three, with Krystal Carrie still silent. Bride sped northward wondering if he should pull off the road and wait for her response.

Finally, her voice blared over the speakers. "Got it! The sister's phone hit on a tower in Mackinaw City, Michigan. That's—"

"Yeah, I've been there. If she's trying to get off grid, she's headed for the right place."

"Wait." Silence again then finally, excitedly, "I have another hit! This time it's Dia's phone on a tower in Duckwater, Nevada."

"What?" This perplexed Bride. Was the whole Northern Michigan situation a diversion? He considered whether he needed to get Nevada but then thought about his original theory, "Oh, she is a clever one." Bride expressed. "I'm pretty sure I know where she is."

/ / / /

The wall of video screens was black except the center screen which contained a silhouette of a man.

"How are your plans for our new sub-net?" the silhouette asked.

"Everything is on track," Clarence Axeworthy said, standing facing the screen with the glass wall looking out to the Salton Sea behind him. He instinctively checked his black Roman collar, an indication he was concerned. Without his natural intensity, he continued, "We have one technical issue with the routers." Before the figure on the screen responded, Axeworthy added, "But another avenue has come to light that we are exploring."

"What is this issue?" the dark shadow asked. "We turned to you because you convinced us your people could solve these sorts of difficulties."

Axeworthy cupped his palms together and inhaled deeply. "We will, I assure you. Our people are the best. If our programmers can't solve the issue, we have other..." he hesitated for dramatic effect. "...specialists who can resolve these matters in their own creative methods."

"Yes, I understand, Axeworthy, but what is the issue?"

"We're working to solve the problem of overwriting router firmware externally. Our current network isn't wide enough to scatter the packets efficiently to guarantee an anonymous transfer. If your people want true online anonymity, we will require more ghost routers online. That calls for more than just routers controlled by the Axeworthy Internet Security suite."

"I understand that as well." Frustration was clear in the silhouette's words. "What are you doing about it?"

"You can assure your people matters are in hand. We are implementing three steps. First, starting Friday, we will offer the entire AXIS suite available for a free download. We expect this will at least triple our user base. Second, our people are preparing to deliver a unique virus that will silently install our firmware on to the computer's routers. If successful, it will self-destruct. If not, the virus will transform and stop being silent. This will encourage users to install anti-virus software. At first, the Axeworthy suite will include the only anti-virus program effective against the new form of virus, and this virus will be nimble, staying ahead of our competitors' anti-virus definitions. Third, we are attempting to acquire a set of zero-day router exploits to install our router firmware remotely."

For a time the silhouette was silent—perhaps processing what Axeworthy had spelled out, perhaps in anger. Finally the figure spoke again. "Are you talking about the leaked NSA software?"

Axeworthy didn't want to admit it, but humbly said, "Yes."

10> Dia Slips Away

DIA REYNOLDS DOUBLE-CHECKED her work and grinned. The small metal electronics box on the wall fit in with the wires, boxes, and additional electronics that occupied the cramped, single-windowed room. The trouble was her project box appeared brand new when the rest of the equipment appeared untouched for at least a year. To disguise her work, she withdrew a three-ounce can of WD-40 from her toolkit and shot a light spritz of the all-purpose lubricant over the metal box. She scooped up a handful of dust on a sheet of cardboard and puffed the dust over the box. *Perfect,* she thought. Her controller box blended with its surroundings. The box contained one of the few items whose design she appropriated from the NSA to aid her escape. She intended to use the device to mask her whereabouts in Canada, but, with her personal upgrades, her handiwork should fool the Americans—including those "in the know." She packed her tools into her kit, whose case appeared to the world like a hipster's, medium- to large-sized purse.

Again she checked her phone's screen. The map showed her current position as rural Nevada, travelling west at 65 mph. She grinned again. With Dia's upgrade to the design, combined with exploits in her phone, even her phone believed it was road tripping the back roads to Reno. Not only was it safe to use her phone, but it would throw pursuers off her trail.

Dia took a deep breath—perhaps her first in ages. After running for days, this was her first opportunity to relax. With eyes closed, she exhaled slowly and allowed her heart rate to calm. She was absent without leave now at the NSA. If any doubts existed at the NSA to who posted SLANTZERO and the note of codeofresistance.onion, they would be erased now. She needed to plot her next move, but her cell-phone signal cloaking box should buy two days, perhaps three, to develop a plan. She schemed better when calm.

After a few stolen quiet moments, she exited the room full of pure, raw technology and stepped out into a prim world virtually void of tech. It was a world where horse-drawn carriages and bicycles owned the streets and not a single gas-combustion vehicle was in sight. Quaint houses and stores of nineteenth century, or older, design lined the streets. She peered back at the simple white homestead she had left and directed her gaze up to the brick chimney that rose above the house a tad too high. The chimney disguised a cell phone tower that served the populated portion of Mackinac Island. Situated in the straits connecting Lakes Huron and Michigan, Mackinac Island lay between the two major peninsulas that make up the state of Michigan. So long as Dia's phone stayed within range of the antennae hidden inside that painted brick chimney, her control box transplanted its signal to a set of preprogrammed towers. Dia used towers recorded from the route of an unsuspecting traveler the prior week.

Dia dodged a pair of jovial horseback riders and crossed the street to The Gate House, a restaurant and pub that's decor combined old world and Detroit Tigers memorabilia. It was mid-afternoon, so most of the lunch crowd had deserted the dining room. She scanned the black-and-white striped arched ceiling and wood walls eclectically decorated with Tigers memorabilia and various maritime imagery. After being greeted by a cordial hostess, she requested a table at the far end of the main dining room. The hostess seated her past the stone fireplace and under a hanging ship's wheel. After a hasty glance at the menu Dia ordered a brim-full glass of Stag's Leap Wine Cellars Chardonnay and an order of fish and chips. That would feel nice on the stomach and take the edge off her nerves.

The wine came promptly. After a healthy swig she checked her phone while waiting for the food. The screen showed one-hundred–plus missed calls, forty-something voice messages, and the badge on the text messaging app read, "7,493". Had everyone she ever met called to find her whereabouts? The "do not disturb" setting would help keep them all oblivious while she used her phone to dig up information to create a new plan.

Dia remembered the phone borrowed from her sister and wondered why Ruby had not called. Had her sister had enough of her drama? She couldn't blame Ruby. Dia had put her through a lot, abandoning her on the bridge in Sault Ste. Marie, springing it on her about being in the NSA. Of course Ruby wanted nothing else to do with her. Dia had to move on without her sister, and this was the perfect place to regroup and devise a new escape plan.

She flipped open the old phone to see if perhaps she missed her sister's call. A notification announcing one text message from "unknown." She opened messages:

```
1 message:
>3ma - ☼
```

Dia audibly gasped. She understood the exact meaning of the cryptic message. She powered down her sister's phone and returned to her own. Her finger flipped through her app pages until it found the folder titled "crypt." Inside the folder she found an app labeled "Threema" with its signature three green dot icon below a padlock in a speech balloon. She launched the ultra-secure messaging app, typed in her PIN, and it opened straight into the "Messages" panel. Dia put faith in Threema as a messaging app because she knew the NSA had not cracked it. Atop the list was the name "Sunshine" with a picture of Krystal Carrie in a tiny, round icon followed by the words "contact me." She touched the icon and opened messages page. A saw tooth line separated the new message from a prior conversation about meeting for cocktails. This was all below the reassuring three green dots indicating Dia personally scanned the 2D code from the screen of Krystal's phone to verify her ID and public encryption key. Assuming it was Krystal using her own phone, Dia could be definite that Krystal had written these messages.

Dia stared at the glowing screen. She believed she could trust Krystal, one of her few friends in this dirty business not in the NSA. But at this point Dia was hesitant to divulge anything to anyone. By now Krystal's app would have flagged the message as read on her end. Dia pressed and held on the message until a pop-up appeared. She chose "Acknowledge."

Within twenty seconds, another message appeared.

Help is on the way to you.

Did Krystal figure out where she was, or was she sending help toward her decoy signal in Nevada? As long as Krystal was alone, Dia could trust her. The message wasn't the sort she'd send if the DHS or NSA bosses were watching over her shoulder. Dia acknowledged the latest message.

Another message appeared.

Stay where you are. My friend should be on the 4:00.

Dia quickly acknowledged. The four o'clock ferry? Krystal had determined where she was. She wished she had set up code word with her friend. But Krystal was just that, a friend. Someone fun to hang out with and with the benefit of a high enough security clearance to talk agency gossip and brag about work accomplishments. Never did she expect to rely on Krystal for something like whatever this was.

Dia considered what a code word with Krystal would be. Some test to ask if her friend was alone or with higher-ups dictating what she said. It hit her, the perfect code word test. She typed the single word message into Threema:

Vodka?

After two seconds Krystal's reply popped onto the screen.

Pearl.

Dia stifled a cheer. In her mind if "They" were watching Krystal, she'd have replied "Absolut" or "Grey Goose." Only Krystal could comprehend the reference to their evening with a bottle of Pearl Vodka.

At that moment the waitress arrived with her fish & chips startling Dia. *Crap*, she thought. *Be cognizant of her surroundings.* She typed one last message to Krystal before closing Threema.

Gate House.

////

Robert Liptmann stood near the information desk in the waiting room of the Emergency Room of War Memorial Hospital in Sault Ste. Marie, Michigan. Twenty-three minutes had passed since he flashed his Department of Defense credentials and asked to speak to someone who treated Ruby Greer and the other woman. The twenty-three minutes piled on to the hours spent in traffic, on the Boeing MD-88 and then a cramped Canadair RJ, at the airports in Baltimore and Detroit, waiting for service at the car rental booth in middle-of-wherever Michigan, plus the drive to Sault Ste. Marie. Exhausted and wearing a layer of dried sweat, he remained standing by the information area so he could not be ignored. The wait gave him time to think about everything that led him here. Starting Friday evening, after checking at her apartment and finding no one home, he issued a POI bulletin on Dia Reynolds and her sister, Ruby Greer. Afterward he researched young Diamond Reynolds; her history with the agency, her assignments, her co-workers, her childhood friends, her personal life, her five ex-boyfriends, her classes and teachers during her two-and-a-half years at the

Rochester Institute of Technology, every vacation taken since the age of ten, and the restaurants and shops she frequented.

Saturday morning came news that the agency had another defector. Liptmann told his bosses he might have an angle on it, but it was just a gut feeling. Liptmann had already decided to go back to Dia Reynolds's apartment sooner rather than later. If Dia Reynolds couldn't be found, whole teams would descend on her home and Liptmann wanted the first look. To do things by the book, he took Tatham, a junior member of his team. As expected, Dia Reynolds wasn't there. This time he planned to enter. No need for a warrant, her employment agreement with the NSA gave him permission to search her properties. The locks on the front door succumbed to his lock picks and he entered the loft-style apartment. He slipped on a pair of latex gloves before turning on the lights, telling Tatham to stand by the door, observe but keep his mouth shut. The book said not to conduct this type of search alone, but it didn't say the other party needed to participate.

Despite it being a one-hundred percent legal search, Liptmann felt ashamed as he studied the small apartment. He was intruding in the girl's private world. Ironic as at any given second his agency was peeking into the lives to millions of people, but here it felt like he was rummaging through her underwear drawer. Which, he thought, he would have to do.

The walls of the open-concept apartment were a vivid light blue except the black far wall. The decor struck Liptmann as a post-Ikea motif. A bed cantilevered in a loft over a work area. Half computer desk and half electronics lab with circuit boards, soldering guns, wires, and other electronic chips and gizmos, it was her own little Radio Shack. Liptmann disturbed nothing; he could order the teams to dig harder, but to search for what? He used his phone to take pictures of the whole apartment and close-ups of anything he didn't understand.

There wasn't a lot to learn from Dia Reynolds's apartment except to learn more about her personality. She was either tidy, or had cleaned recently. Everything was in its proper place.

Nothing screamed, "This girl is a plant, a spy, or a traitor." There was even a framed and spot-lit American flag on one of the blue walls. Liptmann took down the flag and examined its frame. Some, he thought, might use the flag ironically to hide evidence. He hoped this wasn't the case with Dia Reynolds. Despite his suspicions he found himself liking this young woman and her youthful rebellious streak. Her type will mellow with age and inch toward conformity, though she never would one-hundred percent fit. She would hold on to a bit of youth, but with fifteen to twenty more years at the agency she would blend well with the ex-military like himself.

Liptmann found nothing in the frame. Carefully he remounted and rehung the flag. The apartment revealed no clues to where Dia Reynolds had gone on her weekend. Other than a missing slot in a closet where a suitcase or a backpack would fit, there was no sign Dia Reynolds had left town. There was also no sign of the dog from the photograph on her desk; no food bowls, no dog food, and no tiny short hairs that a basset hound would have shed everywhere.

The following day, Sunday, the agency conducted its own extensive search on Dia Reynolds's apartment. A handful of NSA employees who had access to the programs the online message cited were unaccounted for. Each's home received the same treatment. Meanwhile Liptmann, with Tatham again as his silent partner, interviewed most of Dia Reynolds co-workers from The Lab. Only a few of the so-called Equation Group worked in the office that Sunday, but he started there. Next they visited the homes of the group members off for the weekend. With each, Liptmann started with an apology for interrupting their Sunday, then preceded to ask them questions about four of their coworkers, Dia Reynolds always being second or third. The questions were simple, "Have you noticed this person acting oddly or differently lately?" "Do you know where this person is this weekend?" "Have you made contact with this person outside the office?" He got next to nothing from the interviews except another "up north" when asking about

Dia Reynolds's weekend plans and one person remembering something about Florida. Liptmann thought it told him Dia Reynolds had hidden her weekend plans. He found nothing concrete, just growing suspicions.

It was 2:41 Monday morning when the phone next to his bed rang and woke him from a good sleep. He looked at the caller ID box; it read "UNLISTED." He noted the period at the end of the word. It was the office. He picked up the black bakelite receiver and answered, "Liptmann."

"We've received a hit on a subject from your bulletin," the voice on the line said.

"Subject one or subject two?" Liptmann asked.

"Subject two."

"I'm coming in," Liptmann replied. "Give me ten minutes." He hung up the receiver.

He dressed with the suit he had laid out the previous night, wet and combed his hair, and left his one-bedroom house in Jessup. Subject two was Ruby Greer nee Reynolds, Dia Reynolds's older sister. Ruby Greer was five-years the senior, married once, divorced once, resided in suburban Philadelphia, and worked as a technical writer for a company that built ATMs. The two sisters appeared to be close, vacationing together and making regular trips between Philadelphia and DC for weekends of what Liptmann imagined as shopping and bar hopping.

Eleven minutes later, he arrived at the office, passed through security, and checked in with William Franco, his junior counterpart covering the night watch.

"What have you got, Bill?" Liptmann asked, skipping the pleasantries.

"Your subject two was involved in a one-car accident on I-75 on the Northern Peninsula of Michigan." Franco—a tall ex-Marine, half-Italian, half-something-Scandinavian—gave Liptmann a hand-written report. "She is in intensive care. A second female in the car was also taken to the hospital but took off without receiving treatment. The Michigan Highway Patrol is looking for the second woman, but the EMT who brought her in gave a vague description. They are trying to get the EMT back in for more details, but he hasn't been seen since he went off-duty."

Liptmann scanned the report. It was thorough and detailed, as he came to expect from Franco. "Thanks, Bill," he said. "I'll call you if I need anything else."

It took several hours for resources to arrange his travel. Liptmann snuck in a few more hours of sleep in his office. There would be no sleep on the airplane. There never was. On the first leg between Baltimore and Detroit, Liptmann went over everything again; the photos of the Dia Reynolds's apartment, the tapes of the interviews, all of Dia Reynolds's files, and the note that the defector put online. He had yet to take the time to mull over the note of the so-called defector and the sample programs posted on whitehouse.gov. Obviously the defector wanted the world to know they had access to top level government sites, but why the White House site? Perhaps it was fake. Someone acquires an otherwise useless NSA program and software list, and they hacked the White House site because they found a vulnerability. He thought that was a definite possibility, but what if he assumed Dia Reynolds had posted the note and the supposed bundle of software? Why would Dia Reynolds post on whitehouse.gov? She could post this anywhere, nsa.gov might make the note more convincing. Perhaps she thought it would be taken down faster on nsa.gov. There must be more to it. If Dia Reynolds put this app on whitehouse.gov, she did it for a reason. It was a message, a purposeful clue.

During the layover, he called Franco and asked if he was on the defector case.

"Everyone's on the defector case," Franco said. "You missed the meeting. Its code is Slipfish."

"Who comes up with these codenames?"

"I'm convinced they have a monkey with ping pong balls."

Liptmann laughed. "Bill, do me a favor. Find out if subject one worked with anything involving the White House."

"We've checked that for all suspects. There's no connection. But I'll dig some more for you."

Liptmann caught another forty-five minutes of sleep on the flight to the Northern Peninsula.

Between the red tape and the convoluted path to northern Michigan, more than a day had passed before he landed at Chippewa County International Airport. Since he was closer to the site of the crash than the hospital, he chose to visit the crash site first. Crews had cleared the accident, but Liptmann still easily found its location. He stopped in the median of I-75. From there, he still could see the swirling tire mark where the Jeep Liberty spun out, the divots in the asphalt where it began to tumble, and the missing median divider posts where it came to its final rest. He pictured the whole accident in his head from its aftermath. But why? Why had the Jeep suddenly spun out? Why were they heading south? Did the Jeep have a mechanical failure? Or did a hit-and-run driver strike it? The highway didn't answer his questions, so he took his rented Chevrolet Malibu and drove to War Memorial Hospital in Michigan's half of Sault Ste. Marie. It was the closest trauma center and where an ambulance had taken the two women and where he now had waited thirty-four minutes.

At last, a young, flaxen-haired woman in nurse's scrubs approached him. "Mr. Lipman?"

"Liptmann." He corrected her pronunciation without over-emphasizing the "t" she had omitted as he showed his credentials again. "And it is Colonel." The corrections weren't the friendliest way to start, so he flashed his best paternal smile and offered his hand. "And you are?"

"I'm Monica Crawford. I was on duty when Ms. Greer was brought in." Miss Crawford did her best to not seem unfriendly when she didn't take Liptmann's hand.

Liptmann pulled his hand back and tried to pretend it was never there. Of course, she wouldn't take his hand; that would be unsanitary. He smiled again. "I'm concerned with the woman brought in with Ms. Greer. Did you see her?"

"Yes," the nurse said. "She was dazed and probably suffered from a concussion when they brought her in, but no visible injuries. After her mind cleared, she refused to answer any questions. She just got up and left."

Liptmann pulled a photograph of Dia Reynolds from his inside jacket pocket and showed it to Miss Crawford. He asked, "Is this her?"

"No."

"Are you sure?" Liptmann asked. "She may have different hair and makeup."

"I'm sure. That doesn't look a thing like her. Wrong eyes, wrong age, totally wrong look. This woman looked more like..." The nurse paused, seeming to build a picture in her mind. "...like Mark Wahlberg dolled up in a really good Connie Stevens drag."

"That's not my girl."

"Not even close."

/ / / /

After searching through the horse- and cycle-filled street, Bride thought he spotted the mark. If he had found Dia Reynolds, she knew how to play it safe. He speculated she would be outside the Gate House Restaurant—rather than inside—and there she seemed to be across the street. She tried to stay inconspicuous by petting a white-spotted saddle horse, likely a rental from Jack's Livery Stable around the corner. He had passed the stable on the way from where the carriage driver had dropped him a block away. With caution he approached as if passing on the sidewalk. It was definitely her. The hair was shorter and a different color from Sunshine's photograph—now an almost-natural bottle red—but this was Sunshine's friend.

Suddenly he understood why she, Dia, looked familiar. He had seen her before in one of the many generic halls of government. Every time they passed each other she had smiled at him. They had crossed paths at least a dozen times, and she always shined a pleasant, genuine smile for him. What the smile implied he never had a clue. Did it mean "good morning"? Or "that man is dead sexy"? Or "that's the guy I saw with a piece of spaghetti on his chin while he was talking to General Such-and-such"? The worst possibility in Bride's mind, they had previously met, and she remembered, and he didn't. Unfortunately enquiring about a stranger in the black halls of government isn't something one does.

The current question was would she recognize him? Would it be a good thing if she did? She would realize he was a government man. Would she know more than that? If she pegs him as Homeland Security then she might put together that he is the help Sunshine promised. If not she most likely would presume the US government had sent him to bring her in. Or take her out.

Bride halted his approach. Another woman moved in next to Dia. He eased close enough to overhear some of their conversation.

"Dia?" The tall, solid woman said.

"Yes?" Dia seemed surprised and pivoted toward the stranger. This woman loomed a head over Dia. The straw hair flowed retro and short—like Grace Kelly's in *Rear Window*—but it didn't altogether suit the round, wide face. Her form, while not masculine, appeared strong and square. Handsome was not a word Bride used often to describe a woman—most would incorrectly assume it meant as an insult—but for this woman the word was apt. She wore a soft leather jacket over a pale green tee unwisely tucked into loose khaki slacks. Put the pieces together right and she might look stunning without ever being accused of being pretty, but as-is, she was an odd mess.

"I'been sent to help. You're bein' watched. Hop on the back of the horse." The woman's voice clipped in a way sometimes heard in educated children of uneducated parents.

With one movement the woman lifted Dia, only half-voluntarily, on to the horse, seating her behind the saddle. The unknown newcomer stepped up on the stirrup and mounted the steed in front of Dia. With a small heel kick, the horse reared slightly. This caused Dia to clutch to the woman in front as they trotted off as fast as a rented horse would take them.

Already moving toward them, Bride took off in a full run. After a few paces he slowed as the chase became obviously futile. He cursed himself for running. *Way to blend in Agent Bride*, he thought. *I'm sure no one thought that scene looked strange.* He moved off the street to behind the little stone church. Who was that woman? Was she NSA? Did someone else send help? Bride could identify the woman, but not well enough to pick her from a mug book or describe her to a sketch artist. He took out his phone and dialed Krystal Carrie.

"Sunshine, I've lost her. She left with some woman."

11> Biscuit & Grits

FROM DIA'S PERSPECTIVE from the rear of Biscuit the horse, the pursuing man disappeared from view. She kept peaking over her shoulder to try to catch another glimpse of him as she clung to the woman in the saddle. The pair of women galloped away northwest on Cadotte Avenue between the Grand Hotel Jewel Golf Course and the tennis courts. Biscuit cut violently left to avoid a pair of cyclists and a carriage, prompting Dia to turn her sights frontward. She was awestruck by the enormous Grand Hotel, the 1887-built Queen Anne-style goliath that still claims to have the largest porch in the world.

Worried and frightened, Dia's cheek pressed into the soft leather jacket, her arms clutching her apparent rescuer's waist. Her legs had already been doing the same to Biscuit. The bulge of a small pistol under the woman's left arm inside her jacket simultaneously terrified and reassured Dia. She realized she was trusting her existence to a person who entered her life in the last minute. But the woman was correct, there was a man following her. Dia first caught sight of him running after them—after her—while the woman mounted the horse in front of the Gate House.

This woman had to be the help sent by Krystal. It felt right. For some reason, Dia assumed Krystal would send a woman. She really didn't want help; she wished she hadn't gotten Ruby involved. After backing out of the border crossing at Sault Ste. Marie, Dia had begun to gain confidence on her backtrack to Mackinac. But she had to admit this was beyond her depth. She'd been with the NSA for close to eight years, and like most of the agency's employees, she had never been in the field. It was one thing to create hacks and gadgets and surveil from the office. It was another to be in the real world where every person was an unknown.

Dia wasn't sure how long they had been riding when they slowed. She saw they had ridden out of the developed area of the island and were following a line of telephone poles along a clearing through the woods.

Dia didn't know what to say to the woman because she wasn't sure what had happened. She chose the least important thing on her mind.

"I only rented the horse for an hour."

The woman looked over her shoulder back at Dia with a look that said, "That's what's got you troubled?" After returning to facing forward, the woman tried to placate Dia. "We'll see you get the horse back. Might need to pay for some extra hours, though."

"Where are we going?"

The woman seemed to ignore the question. With her right hand, she reached into her jacket's inside breast pocket, pulled out her phone, scanned her thumbprint, then opened an app. She typed a quick message with her thumb. After a dozen seconds, the stock message bing rang back. She read the message, typed a quick reply, and returned the phone to her pocket. "There's a private stable. I don't think's being used right now. Not far, but we'll need to double back a bit."

"Who are you?" Dia finally asked.

"Name's Margaret," the woman flashed a smile, "but people call me 'Grits'."

"I'm Dia."

"Yeah, got that."

"Of course." Dia paused. "Of course you did. What happens next?"

"We get to a safe place, maybe that stable. Then I check in with your friends, and find a way back to the mainland."

Yes, Dia thought, this Grits girl will check in with Krystal and then... But she said, "friends", plural. Who is working with Krystal? Perhaps she shouldn't have trusted Krystal after all. She should have talked to Krystal longer and found out more about her plan. But Dia was still reluctant to give anyone more information. She still wasn't sure. Krystal may have recruited more help. That had to be it. Krystal must have recruited this Grits and a select few others.

Grits turned the horse on to a seldom used path deeper into the woods. They ducked under some low branches and Biscuit stepped carefully over various natural debris lying on the trail.

"'Tisn't far." Grits reassured.

Dia was growing comfortable with Grits. Perhaps there will be a way out of this mess.

The trail opened to a small field with an old wooden stable. At the far end of the field Dia saw the back of a large three-story Victorian villa. Grits turned the horse toward the stable.

"This's the place. Hop off."

Dia dismounted as told, and Grits came down off the horse as well. She handed Dia the reins.

"Take the horse in. I'll suss out our next move and make sure the area is clear."

Dia petted Biscuit's head and led the beast through the wooden doors into the barn. Biscuit had been a good horse. She wished she paid attention to the stable hand when she had rented her. He said Biscuit liked something. Petting her mane? Rubbing her ear? She couldn't remember, and settled for petting her neck and saying, "Good girl. Good girl."

In the meantime, Grits stayed outside and Dia observed her walking the area while talking on the phone. Dia guided the animal into a stall and closed it from the inside. She sat on a bench, put her head into her hands and tried to fight off thoughts of panic. This whole escape—if that's what you call it—took months to plan, and it had drifted out of her control. She couldn't fathom how everything had slipped so far off plan. She didn't like relying on Krystal and this stranger for the next move, but so far she has none of her own.

Dia looked up to see Grits standing in the doorway with her reassuring smile. "Good news," Grits said. "I've a way off the island. Your friends arranged a plane. We just have to—"

Grits stopped speaking and her eyes locked on to something behind Dia. The tingle in Dia's shoulders and neck told her the something was a someone. The man's voice confirmed that intuition.

"Don't move."

Dia froze. Her gaze fixed on Grits whose body almost imperceptibly constricted as her muscles coiled. There was an instant of silence followed by cautious footfalls from the back of the barn.

Grits sprung. Her body twisted and somersaulted back toward the door as twin gunshots rang out. Dia flinched but remained frozen on her feet. The horse whinnied and bucked in its stall. When Grits regained her feet, a small, chrome revolver was in hand and aiming in Dia's direction. Dia squeezed her eyes shut as another gunshot cracked. Two more. Then another.

She heard a voiced muted in her fatigued ears. "Get down!" She dropped flat to the ground and covered her head with her arms.

Two more shots.

She no longer could tell where the shots were coming from, but thankfully the shooting seemed to stop. Through thirty-seconds of no sounds but that of the horse fighting its stall, Dia prayed the man was dead. She opened her eyes when two more shots sounded from just above where she lay. Another three shots came in precession. The third kicked up the dirt near her head. Before she had a chance to react, a hand grabbed the back of her jacket and drug her from the middle of the room into an empty stall.

Swinging her head around, Dia glimpsed the man as he lugged her behind the stall's door. It was the man who ran after them back at the Gate House.

"Get back into the corner and stay down." He barked.

Dia scrambled to the corner and curled into a ball as commanded just as two more shots splintered the wooden door of the stall inches from her head.

The man returned fire around the door. After a second Dia heard the sound of a body thump to the ground.

He checked the clip in his pistol, then rose to his feet and, gun first, walked out into the stable. Dia cautiously stood after him. She moved to the door. Grits was laying on the ground, eyes open, and shaking. The man approached her. He kicked the tiny revolver out of her open hand back into the room, holstered his gun at his belt, and knelt to Grits's bleeding side.

Dia looked at Grits's gun in the dirt. The man was paying no attention to her. She watched him carefully as she skulked toward the gun. When she was close enough she sprung forward, grabbed the pistol from the ground, and poised it in her hands. The gun warmed her hands as she aimed it at the man. She yelled, "Stay back! I want to be left alone. Please."

He turned to her and stood. For the first time he became familiar. She recognized those fierce smoky eyes from the NSA offices or... He was a government man—an agent. Her brain raced. Nothing made sense, and before she could digest any future possibilities, he spoke one of the last words she expected from him.

"Pearl."

12> Voted Off the Island

"WHAT?"

"Pearl," Henry Bride stepped assuredly toward Dia and spoke in a calm tone. "Sunshine said to tell you, 'Pearl'."

Dia shook her head in dubiety. "Krystal sent you? What the hells? I thought Krystal sent Grits."

"She sent you what?"

"Grits. That woman, she said her name was Grits, or Margaret. Is she alive? And who in the hells is she? How do we get out of here? How did you find me? And who are you?" Dia's anger grew as she spouted her rapid-fire inquisition.

"Hang on. Slow down." Bride said. "She is alive, and I have no idea who she is, so we need to tie her up. Can you find a rope?" Bride went to the unconscious woman, rolled her onto her stomach, and yanked her arms behind her, preparing for Dia to come back with rope.

When Dia returned, she held the leather straps from a set of reins. "Will this do?"

"That'll be perfect." Bride took the straps and tied Grits's wrists while he continued answering Dia's questions. "I found you by disabling your box at the cell antenna so your phone would show your true location again, which means you need to shut it off and we need to leave the island soon. Sorry."

Dia shouted. "You did what? That's my only—"

Bride cut her complaint short. "Had I not found you Grits here had planned to kill you. I don't know who she is, but I overheard enough of her phone call to hear her accept orders to 'take you out'." Bride flipped his captive back over, pulled out his phone, and snapped a picture of the woman's face, and sent the picture off to Sunshine with a message:

Need ID. Goes by Margaret or Grits

Bride stood and turned his attention to Dia.

"Did I answer all your questions?"

"You missed the big one, Sparky. Who are you?"

"I'm Henry Bride. I'm from Homeland Security."

"Are you here to take me in?" Dia asked.

"No, I don't have those orders. To be honest, I'm not sure what I'm here to do, but I came to help. It works like this: my friend Krystal said she had a friend who needed the kind of help I could provide. I'll assess the situation, and if taking you back is for the best, that's what we'll do. But right now you're in danger, so first we get you away from here. We do, however, need to figure out who this is." Bride gestured to Grits and went back to searching her pockets. He pulled out a set of keys to an old GM car, a parking lot ticket, and a phone. No wallet or ID, just a money clip with a couple hundred dollars in twenties. He examined the phone. It was one with fingerprint lock. He clutched the index finger from the bound hands of his unconscious captive and started to place it on the sensor.

"Wait." Dia stopped him. "It was her thumb. She might have a phone that hard locks if you use the wrong finger. We do."

"Thanks." Bride placed the thumb on sensor, and the screen unlocked. He tossed the phone to Dia. "See what you can do with that."

Dia dug through the contents of the phone as Bride searched Grits for hidden pockets or any other secret hiding places. Bride was searching the cargo pants when Dia dropped the phone. Bride spun to see her face had blanched.

"She ... she was going to kill me. Someone was paying her to kill me."

Bride stood and grabbed the girl by the shoulders to stabilize her weak knees. "Yes. I told you that."

Her frightened eyes stared into Bride's. "I thought she was NSA, but she's not. She is being paid 25 Bitcoin to kill me and make sure my body is found and identified quickly."

Bride helped her to the bench and sat her down.

Dia continued, "Crap. It's because of me. They wanted to verify my software from the NSA was out there before she killed me. I put that software on the net to be released if I die, as a safeguard. It was supposed to protect me from the NSA. It never occurred to me that someone else would want it enough to kill me for it."

Bride picked up the phone and read the conversation between Grits and someone listed as "Unknown". The exchange was brief, and Dia's summary had been perfect save the one detail she had seemed to have missed.

```
G: 130 as promised
Unknown: We have all exchange numbers for
         transfer to the one who provides proof
         of completion.
```

To Bride "numbers" and "to the one" indicated that this Grits had competition. There was an open contract on the life of Dia Reynolds. Bride felt it may not be the best time to bring that fact to the forefront.

"We need to leave," Bride said.

/ / / /

Honey Chase had not been the one to communicate with the employer. That had been all Grits. But with Grits gone, Honey had no funds coming in, but she wasn't qualified to do the job herself. Honey usually just gathered the intelligence and carried out some of the legwork. And this time they... she had intelligence. She wondered if it would be worth anything.

For fifteen minutes, Honey sat in the corner at Starbucks staring at her iPad and the empty field on Grits' message app. She felt useless. Her irrational fear of interacting with strangers kept her from typing what she needed to write. *Damn it, just type. You don't have to hit send.*

That solved it, she persuaded herself to type the message.

```
G: could not carry out the nsa job. but have
   information about the subject. is that worth
   something to you?
```

The cursor blinked as the unsent message sat on the input box. Honey stared at the letters. The message was good, but could she send it? Her nerves shot tiny spasms to her upper arms and shoulders. She hated this. She tapped her index finger next to the enter key while she tried to summon courage. *Tap. Tap.* Why was this so hard? She looked up from the screen and inhaled. When she did, her finger unconsciously moved and tapped enter.

Christ. The message was gone. She had tricked herself into sending the message. Her chest tightened around her heart and her breathing shallowed as she anticipated the response. After thirteen seconds of distress it came.

```
Unknown: What kind of information?
```

She was still nervous, but she breathed much better. The proverbial bandage was off. It was like this every time; Honey would sweat making first contact for minutes, hours, or days. Sometimes she couldn't do it at all. But once the conversation started, she could act fairly normal.

```
G: acquired information about dia reynolds's
   recent travels. what's that worth?
```

She waited again, nearly a minute this time.

Unknown: 4B

Now came the negotiating. She hated negotiating.

G: 10

Was that too much? Should she have asked for six?

Unknown: Done.
Unknown: Send the information and your Bitcoin
          address. We'll send the Bitcoin.

two: throughput

13> South

ALL THE GIRL HAD SAID was head south on I-75. That was eleven hours ago. The whole of the lower peninsula, Ohio, and Kentucky was behind them. She questioned Bride early in the trip, seemingly trying to get a sense of if she could trust him—and how far. Bride believed he had succeeded in gaining as much of the girl's trust as possible. At least, she trusted him enough to fall asleep in the car. Or as likely, she had just been exhausted.

The most difficult part had been talking her into not leaving the States. After returning the horse to its stable back on Mackinac Island, Bride asked the stablemate where one might hire a private boat. The stablehand told them only fishing charters might hire out this early in the season. Those, he said, usually required a reservation. The harbor didn't sound promising, but might be worth a shot. They might get lucky and find a charter boat dropping off its day's passengers. Looking at a map, though, the harbor appeared too public to try to "procure" a boat in a non-legal way. Bride wasn't sure he wanted to cross that line. He'd already be in trouble over not reporting the incident with Grits. It would be the ferry, whose last boat left at 6:30, or gamble at finding a charter boat.

"Try one of the vultures," The stablehand added.

"Vultures?" Bride asked.

"That's what I call them. A few unscrupulous boat owners hang out by the docks. For a mighty pretty penny they'll take suckers who missed the last ferry to the mainland. They're usually only on the weekends this time of year, but I've seen them lately by the ferry docks in the last couple of weeks. Probably because the last ferry leaves so early until they expand the schedule next week."

Bride tipped the stable hand and he and Dia headed off through the Victorian streets toward the main strip and the harbor. They walked through the light clusters of tourists of the historic island and passed clapboard-sided homes in Victorian and Federalist style. The island appeared peaceful in spite of the gunfight that happened earlier. The girl was not peaceful.

"Are we going to wait and get a boat directly to Canada?" Dia asked as they trekked the old-fashioned streets. "I bet we can find one who'll take us up to Lake Superior."

"We can't go to Canada, Dia. We're going to Mackinaw City, where my car is."

"What the—?" she protested. "You realize I can be hung if I don't get out of the country, right?"

"Hanged. The word is hanged. Curtains are hung. People are hanged." Bride chose the cleaner version of the mnemonic.

"Wonderful. I feel much better with my life being protected by the best man from the Department of Homeland Linguistics."

"Sorry about that. Understand though, I can't protect you in Canada. You leave the country, and you're on your own. Not only will you have to deal with any yahoo wanting to collect the bounty on your head, but I'll also have to report what I know. That will bring the full force of the US Government down on you."

"You wouldn't." She was near tears at the prospect. "I just want out."

"Listen Dia, if you help me stop the NSA software from being released, then I'll do everything possible to see you get the best possible deal." He turned down the rhetoric. He had scared her enough.

"So I won't be hanged."

"...or hung," he added.

His quip brought a hint of a smile to her lips. Perhaps her attitude was improving.

"Okay, you're right. That does sound dirty."

Bride brought the conversation back to the serious matter at hand. "Tell me how to stop the software from being released."

"It's not that simple. The software is out. But it's encrypted so tight that not even a quantum computer could brute force it. And no one has the password. You see, I have several nodes— little computers—that are looking for evidence of my death or incarceration. If these nodes see either, they will release the password. And after that anyone can decrypt the package. If we want to stop the password, we have to turn off the nodes."

Bride guessed that her explanation implied a passive agreement to his offer. *I'll take it.*

"Okay, what do you need?" he asked. "Can you deactivate your nodes from an internet café? I bet there's one on the island." He watched a horse and buggy pass. "Or maybe not."

"That won't work. I made these things digitally bulletproof. We need to go to the nodes and disconnect them and make sure they stay offline. And you'll need me there to do it. 'Cuff me now. I'll show you where the nodes are."

"Handcuffs won't be necessary," he said. This was becoming a bigger mess than Bride thought. Today's lesson: Don't do favors for friends. "But tell me, where are the nodes?"

"Hang on, agent. I'll show you where the nodes are, but one at a time. And it's got to be just you and me. I wouldn't put it past you boys in Homeland to devise a scheme to send Mr. Handsome to come, quote, save my life, unquote, to get me to give up the node locations."

"And I'm the 'Mr. Handsome' in that scenario?"

"Yup." She walked ahead.

"All right. Where's the first node?"

"South," she said.

At least he pried from her that they need to take I-75 out before they got to the car. After that he got dirty looks and the silent treatment. He countered with his own silence, unsuccessfully. Seven-hundred plus miles on I-75, he hoped his assumption that she wanted The South, and not to turn right in Toledo, was correct. Of course it was south, silly girl, there was little north of where they were if you planned to stay in the United States. He wished he had opted for the handcuffs when she offered, but he also didn't want to wake the girl. The silent treatment was easier to take when not accompanied by angry stares.

Bride utilized the quiet time by calling Sunshine and apprising her of the happenings. Sunshine, in turn, told him what she had learned about Margret "Grits" Owenn. "She was a suspect in two murders-for-hire involving a .22 caliber pistol. But without the gun the connection didn't stick." Sunshine said.

".22 caliber, you say. Well, if you're talking .22 magnum, we might have something for the prosecutor when this issue is finished."

"Cool. If this Grits survives, they might be interested."

"Yes, that might make a difference." Bride said and then paused. "Listen, I understand this isn't your area, but I need false identification for Dia. It'll have to pass muster with the TSA and not come from any official channels."

"I'll see what I can do, but I can't promise anything. None of my connections fit into the unofficial category."

"I've got a private cobbler. I'll send you his info."

"You're not sending me down a dark alley for you, are you?" she asked.

"This guy lives in Georgetown."

"Is he married?"

The conversation with Sunshine continued for a while with Bride using it as a way to keep alert through the long drive.

The Apollo GT motored through the morning twilight of Tennessee. This was The South. Were they driving all the way to Atlanta? Or perhaps Key Largo? Somewhere this, first tiny computer waited for the girl asleep beside him to die.

Bride peered at her slumbering in his passenger seat. He sighed away his anger for her. He didn't know exactly what she had done, but the girl looked innocent now.

The girl. Why had he thought of her as "the girl"? Maybe it was because she needed protecting. Maybe it was to protect himself from falling for her when he clearly had found her attractive while exchanging smiles in the halls of government. His recent breakup was too fresh and unwanted. It would be too easy for him to use *the girl* to bury his sorrows and...

"We'll turn at Knoxville."

She surprised Bride, not as much by her voice as by her morning beauty. Her sparkling eyes seeming to forgive him. She radiated the kind of beauty Bride previously attributed to morning afterglow. Unless there is an afterglow to violence and car rides, he had to assume the girl ... the woman... Dia was a natural. Damn, he needed to keep focused.

"I-40?" he asked, mind back on business.

"Yeah, east on I-40 into North Carolina. Can we stop in Asheville?"

"Sure. Are we close?"

"Fairly close. We need to go to the mountains, but first I need supplies and breakfast."

"Breakfast sounds good," he said. "Better than more rest-stop coffee, anyway. And I need a couple of hours sleep and a shower. Are you all right with spending a few hours in a hotel before you get your supplies."

"That'd be perfect." She smiled. "I'll need to build a few things so don't go cheap on me. Get a room with a desk or a table."

"No problem," Bride said.

14> **New Freak Capital**

IT WAS HENRY BRIDE'S first visit to Asheville, North Carolina, the retro-urban city cradled by the Blue Ridge Mountains. Dia directed him through the winding avenues leading to downtown. Asheville churned with a remarkable volume of early morning foot and bike traffic flowing in harmony with the automotive movement. Bride guided the Apollo through the Bohemian city's ravel of streets faced by preserved art déco storefronts and neoclassical office buildings. With the Apollo parked in a municipal garage, they set out on foot and their first order was breakfast. The nearby patio of the Early Girl Eatery on Wall Street supplied the meal.

"What's our plan?" she asked. Thankfully she no longer appeared angry at him. A prolonged night of the silent treatment must have burnt away her frustrations.

"Long term or today?" he volleyed.

"Let's start with long term."

"To start, how many nodes are we talking about?"

She thought a moment, likely deciding what to reveal. "Three."

"Are they nearby?"

"The first two are, somewhat. They're both in the Carolinas."

"And the third?"

Before Dia answered the server arrived and took their orders. Dia confidently ordered a dish called the Benny, grit cakes with poached eggs, tomato, spinach, and—to make it what Dia called perfect—avocado. Bride tried the black bean and cheddar omelet, later confessing to its delectableness.

Short-term plans were discussed over drinks; hot herbal tea for Dia, water for Bride. He hoped to find a hotel for a brief sleep. Dia said she wished to visit a boutique electronics store downtown while Bride slept.

"That's not a good idea, Dia," he told her. "Give me two hours' sleep and I'll go with you."

Dia reluctantly agreed. "I figure it might save us time, but if that's how you want to play it."

On the long-winded recommendation of the perky young waitress, Bride and Dia headed for the Downtown Inn and Suites on Patton. He checked in under the name Harold Brennon, an off-the-books alias he activated for this trip. His preference was to use a different false name than the one used in Michigan, but with only two available to him, Bride gambled this identity had yet to be burned. He might require his spare.

Appreciatively she put up no fight about the quick hotel stay. Bride wasn't comfortable letting Dia wander Asheville on her own. He had considered letting her go. If he proved he trusted her, she might start trusting him, but hopefully further opportunities to build trust would arise.

As they settled into the hotel room, Bride headed straight for the luxurious bed. Perhaps he was being overcautious about Dia. Nobody could know they were in Asheville. A few side jaunts off of I-75 had ensured they weren't followed. Nobody but Dia, including Bride himself, knew where they were headed. Bride wasn't altogether convinced Dia knew. They should be safe in Asheville, but he didn't understand how Grits found Dia on Mackinac. So that was a worry.

/ / / /

Robert Liptmann flashed his credentials to a stoic Michigan Highway Patrol officer standing guard at the edge of the police tape surrounding the weathered horse stable.

"What's the Department of Defense's interest in this?" the junior officer asked.

"This shooting may be tied to an ongoing investigation of one of our employees," Liptmann answered. "Why, if I might ask, is the Highway Patrol interested in this case?"

"Gangland shootings go beyond the capabilities of the island Police Department. So they called the big boys."

Liptmann faked a smile and held it a few seconds until the officer realized the brief conversation was over and lifted the tape to let Liptmann pass.

Gangland? Did the Highway Patrol already have this case pegged, or was the rookie officer jumping to a conclusion?

Liptmann entered the undersized barn to find an older plain-clothes detective leaning against the stable's gate. Liptmann sized up the investigator. He stood five-ten with a prominent slouch, over six-foot without it. His slicked-back black hair showed he mastered personal grooming pre-summer of love, but the pork-chop sideburns were all 1970s. His dark skin was presumably more from Mediterranean heritage and smoking than sun. The eyes were slate gray and sharp as a tack. His polished badge hung in an open, weathered leather case on the breast pocket of a brown pinstriped suit.

The detective spotted Liptmann, stepped around the primary crime scene, and casually began introductions. "You the man from the DOD? Liptmann?"

"Yes, and you are?" Liptmann knew the answer, having been briefed on who he was meeting, but asked anyway.

"Detective Tom Rodgers, MIOC. This scene was wrapped, photographed, and ready to release until our office got your call. What's DOD's interest here?" Rodgers crooked his head and placed his fists on hips signing to Liptmann that this better not waste his precious time.

"It may be tied to one of our ongoing investigations." Liptmann re-used his stock answer. "Your patrolman at the tape claimed this was gangland."

"He did? Well, then he's an idiot."

Rodgers candid response proved to Liptmann that the veteran detective himself was anything but.

"What is it you do have?" Liptmann asked.

Rodgers walked Liptmann through the items that the paramedics and forensics team found. He explained how paramedics found the female gunshot victim—whose fingerprints had identified her as Margret Owenn—alone, bleeding, and unconscious in the stables. Rodgers indicated the asymmetric blood stain in the dirt floor. The victim was alive and flown to a nearby hospital where she was listed as critical. Rodgers spelled out the preliminary forensics. Their team collected bullets and shells of two guns, a .22 magnum and a 9mm. Excluding the paramedics, they identified footprints of four people; they suspected three females and one male, and one horse.

"A horse?" Liptmann was confused. "Are you sure the horse wasn't the stable's permanent resident?"

"That's the thing, Col. Liptmann, the stable has no permanent resident. The stable only houses horses three months a year. The property is owned by an old money Michigan family. They stay south during wintertime."

"Winter ended in March," Liptmann pointed out.

"This is Northern Michigan, Colonel," Rodgers said. "Our seasons are June, July, August, and winter."

/ / / /

Despite her promise, Bride hadn't been asleep five minutes when Dia removed Bride's security bar and silently slipped from their hotel room. She had told Bride she intended to visit an electronics store. While not strictly a lie, it was a healthy strain to the truth. She set out toward the loft of a fellow hacker she had met when last in North Carolina. The morning's light but steady rain dampened her hair as she traversed the twisted streets of Asheville, but the drizzle could not dampen her newly found sense of freedom. For the first time since implementing her escape plan Dia Reynolds felt free. Asheville was her kind of town. These free-spirited people, many who also ventured out in the cool rain, were her people. In spite of her upstate New York upbringing Dia sensed a belonging with this Southern recusant community. She strode past the bohemian downtown markets, diverse local eateries, and eclectic galleries like this was her home. By the time she reached her destination, a studio apartment situated over an art gallery a short ten blocks from the hotel, she was damp with tiny water drops gathering on her arm hairs. Despite that she bore a cheerful smile. She didn't bother standing under the shelter of the porch when she rang 3N on the panel of buttons alongside the main entrance. After twenty-odd seconds the intercom chirped.

Dia affected a fan-girl voice to the intercom. "Oh. My. God. Ohmygodohmygod. Is this where the handsome, super sexy, and brilliant Kosmic Krunk Seven Eight One lives? I soooo need his autograph. I'd do anything to meet the world's greatest hacker slash builder."

After ten awkward seconds of stunned silence a puzzled voice sounded from the intercom. *"Dia?"*

"Koz, let me up, you sexy devil," she said back to the speaker.

Five more seconds, then the latch clicked and buzzed. Dia entered and climbed the narrow marble stairway to the third floor. The building interior was art déco, not entirely restored but in nice shape with a good spit shine. This was Asheville's unique hipster-retro ambiance Dia loved. 3N was the apartment with a Dropcam mounted over its peephole. The camera tilted up and down Dia, stopping centered on her wet shirt. Frustrated Dia covered the camera with her palm and said, "Let me in, Koz, before I rip this camera off the door."

The deadbolt clicked and a ring around the keyhole glowed neon blue. Dia pushed the door open and entered the studio-style apartment packed with tight rows of metal shelving. Each shelf was crammed with cardboard bins, each with its own Avery label identifying its contents in Sharpie.

A young, heavyset man—bald, bearded, and bespectacled— came into the room. She recognized him as Emerson Kosma. The hacker/builder community knew him as [KosmicKrunk781;](#). His friends knew him as Koz. Dia had graduated from former to latter when the two hackers met during Dia's vacation two years ago. While in the region, Dia had attended a meetup with a group of Blue Mountains region hackers. At the meeting, Dia realized Koz was the genius she had chatted with online about his CAPTCHA defeating scripts on hackaday.com.

"Hey, Koz." Dia smiled. "Give a girl a hug."

Returning a wide grin, Koz said, "D, what lands you in my burg?"

Dia came in for the hug, wrapping her arms around her builder friend's neck. Koz snuggled his arms around her middle and appeared to relish the wet female contact.

She broke their hug and turned to the nearest shelf, sliding out random bins and peeking inside. "I need parts. I figured you might hook me up." She pulled a loose motherboard from a bin, sniffed it, made a hard blink, put it back, and turned toward Koz. "You're my new Radio Shack, if you don't mind."

"Sure," Koz said. "What'd you need?"

"I have a list." Dia pulled a sheet of notebook paper with a handwritten list from her back pocket, unfolded it, shook some water off, and handed it to Koz.

She believed they both understood the score with their relationship. Dia flirted, but no more. Koz gave Dia whatever she wanted and enjoyed the fantasy. Dia was cautious not to abuse the relationship, seeking only hospitality and a few hard-to-obtain parts. She would follow by sending Koz rare *Firefly* or *Buffy* collectibles as thank-you gifts. For all she needed today she'd need to send something big—perhaps a screen-used prop.

After Koz scanned Dia's list, he said, "I have most of these parts. What kind of signal booster do you need?"

"Something universal," she said. "I'm not sure what I'm going to use it for, but I'd like one in my bag of tricks."

"I've just the thing." Koz smiled. "But I notice a few items on your list I don't stock, like the RTL-SDR. I can procure one tomorrow."

Dia scowled, "I'm leaving town later today. Got anything I can sub out?"

"Can you work with Airspy?"

"Out of my budget," she said.

"I've got a used one you can have."

"No, Koz," she protested. "That's too much. I can't have you doing that for me."

"Don't worry. I got it thrown in on a trade. It's no big deal."

"Have any burner hotspots?"

"Plenty. How many do you need?"

"Two and a handful of SIMs. What about a Ublox GPS Module?"

"Yeah, I got that," he said. "What are you trying to build? I can help you figure it out."

Dia considered how to reply. She couldn't tell him she intended to build her own version of an NSA passive wifi GPS mapper, codenamed Sparrow II, without violating the Official Secrets Act. Did that matter at this point? *Yes,* she thought, *yes, it does.* If for no other reason than having one less justification for lining her in front of a wall. "I'm building a kind of specialized wifi extender."

"Oh. For a minute there I thought you might be building a Sparrow II."

Dia gave her best "genuine" laugh. "What the hells is that?"

"Haven't you read the Snowden slides? The NSA have these spying devices equipped with what they call Sparrow II. It's a GPS enabled wifi mapper built to use on drones."

"Do you think you could build one?" She asked.

"I started one, but never got it working yet. I got sidetracked."

With flirty bats of her eyelashes she asked, "Can I see?"

"Sure," said the putty in Dia's hands. "It's back on my bench."

She trailed him past the complex rows of crowded shelves, through plastic sheets hung as dust barriers, and into the workshop in the studio's rear area. Koz's current project, an elaborate Roomba modification, sat neatly with an organized tool set on a stout wooden workbench centered in his shop. Koz stepped to the back wall and pulled one of dozens of plastic bins off the shelf marked "projects". He placed the suitcase-sized translucent bin on the bench, popped open its lid, and removed the incomplete gadget. The bare circuit board had an attached keypad, hand wiring, and a small, home-built dish antenna. "Here it is. I hit a dead end building it, but I'll get back to it, eventually. Fresh eyes, you know." Koz handed the raw gizmo to Dia.

Dia examined the customized board, top and bottom. At first she didn't understand what he had attempted. Maybe the great and wonderful Koz wasn't as brilliant as she gave him credit. But then she grasped his innovative approach. The design was nothing like the NSA built Sparrow II, but Koz's novel idea was splendidly brilliant.

"It's completely off-the-shelf, just like the Snowden documents disclose. Nothing custom." Koz said.

"This is sweet, Koz," Dia said. "Wicked tight design. Did you plot these board mods yourself?"

"Yeah. The Snowden papers offered no schematics just a detailed description of Sparrow II's function. So I winged it."

Dia flipped the board again. "Doesn't work though, huh?"

"No."

Dia picked up a precision screwdriver and poked at the components. She frowned. "You're using an Arduino as the brains, huh?"

"Yeah, it should do the trick." Koz moved closer to observe Dia's examination.

"What frequencies are you scanning?" she asked.

Koz said, "The microwave band, two-point-four, three-point-six, and five megahertz, but it's adjustable with a swap out."

"That should work." She placed the nonfunctional device upon the table, sighed, gazed into Koz's eyes, and said, "If I show you the fix, can I have this one?"

Koz's eyes lit up. "Yeah. That's fair. What do you need?"

"Have you got any of those old USB wifi cards? You know the ones with the external antennae?"

Koz nodded and considered a beat before replying, "I think so. I'll go check."

"And grab a mix of potentiometers. I'm not sure what pots I'll need. Trimmer pots possibly."

He spun back, grinned, and said, "Sure."

Dia smiled back until he passed outside the dust curtain, then she got to work. With a pair of snips and a soldering iron, she flipped the board and started modifying the device's under side. Just when her circuit modifications were completed, Koz re-entered the workshop.

She flipped the device back over and acted like nothing had happened.

Koz piled the stuff gathered on the bench corner, then he noticed his soldering iron. A wisp of white smoke rose from the iron's tip.

"Were you using my soldering iron?" Koz asked.

"Yeah," Dia confessed but then lied. "A connection was loose."

"Oh. Thanks."

"Let me show my fix," she said demonstrating her repair to the board. During her instructional to Koz, she over complicated the build's explanation, but was careful not to expose the circuit board's underside. As long as she hid her patch he wouldn't understand how to build the Sparrow II clone and she wouldn't break the Official Secrets Act. The whole ruse took about twenty minutes, and, when tested, it worked like a charm.

"Did you get all that?" Dia asked.

"Yeah. I— I believe so," he stammered.

"Great." She wrapped one arm around his waist and pulled him close to her side. "Can you grab the rest of my list?"

"No problem," he said. He then returned to his stores and gathered the dozen additional items written on Dia's list. When finished collecting everything, he handed her a reusable shopping bag full of her new parts.

"What do I owe you, Koz?" she asked.

"Don't sweat it. Get me next time."

She guessed that would be his answer. This one time, she wished simply to pay her friend too much money and be done with it. Would there be a "next time"? If she survived... And that "if" weighed heavy. If she survived she expected never to revisit any aspect of her previous life. These thoughts nearly brought her to tears. To hide her approaching emotional outburst and merely to appreciate her friend, she wrapped her arms around Koz and hugged him tightly. After several seconds of the hug being one sided Koz brought his arms around her waist and fondly reciprocated. To Dia, just the embrace of someone's arms felt wondrous. Despite this fellow Bride that Krystal sent, Dia had felt alone since she abandoned her sister on that Sault Ste. Marie bridge. Why hadn't Ruby called? Dia was convinced Ruby simply had enough of her little sister's recent drama. Dia dreaded leaving the warmth of Koz's arms, but needed to return to the hotel. She raised her head from Koz's shoulder, gazed into his eyes betraying her emotions, and she kissed him. Though intended as a simple thank-you peck, she held the kiss, and it became something else.

Why had she done that? It was as if she kissed her former life goodbye, Koz being the final vestige of her past life. She mumbled, "Thank you," gathered her bag of goodies, and exited the apartment. She stopped in the doorway, glanced behind her to the friend she'd just kissed too passionately, and said, "Goodbye, Koz. And sorry."

When the door closed behind her, she cursed herself. Koz didn't deserve that. "That" meaning not the kiss, but rather the lead-on. She had no romantic intentions for Emerson Kosma though she was aware it was his dream. Koz would, at best, be confused; at worst, be in love.

Dia realized she was still standing in the hall in front of his apartment. She shook her head to clear her mind then left the building. She had kissed her old life goodbye. It was time to head into the new one.

She started back toward the hotel. The rain had stopped and once again the jaunt through Asheville aided in lifting her spirits. After walking a block-and-a-half, though, she got that odd sense, the sense of being watched. Dia cursed herself for taking no precautions; she had headed straight for the hotel. Dia glanced over her shoulder. A running woman was pushing a large-wheeled baby carriage in the opposite direction. A pair of hipsters walked together a block over. But no one appeared suspicious. Still she couldn't shake her belief she was in trouble. At a break in the traffic, she picked up her pace and crossed to the west side of Biltmore Avenue, also known as US-25. While using the street crossing as her excuse to look about, she spotted a businessman in a gray suit carrying a black umbrella under his arm. The gray-suited man also attempted to cross the road about a half block behind her. She wanted to run, but decided a brisk walk would draw less attention. Trying not to peek obviously behind her, she headed up the sidewalk. The shop windows of street-side stores became her next excuse to surveil the neighborhood, but the technique wasn't helping track the businessman. *Don't panic, don't panic,* Dia thought, *just get away calmly.* With her new plan developing, Dia cut down a narrow one-way street between a salon and another art gallery. Once out of the main street's view, Dia sprinted, her bag flapping in the wind behind her until she reached the salon's back corner. She ducked around the brick wall and caught her breath before peering back from where she had come. After an instant, the gray suit walked by, never glancing down the side alley. Was he not her pursuer? She gave the businessman thirty seconds and then jogged back to the main street. It would be less likely for someone take her on the busy thoroughfare than the empty roads behind the shops. Of course, the government wouldn't care if they made a scene, but she'd rather be arrested than killed.

Back on the corner of Biltmore, Dia assessed her surroundings. She feigned appearing lost and struggling to regain her bearings. She could have pulled this ruse before now. *Wise up, Dia.* The gray suit was already three blocks away. If he wasn't following her, who was? A moderate number of people rushed all around on the busy street, but none she recognized from earlier. Dia constructed quick mental sketches of each face along the street. With smaller crowds on the far side, she decided to cross again. At the next break in traffic, she jogged across and wandered further up Biltmore.

She planned to continue until she came to a coffee shop with a red double-decker bus permanently parked in its outdoor patio where a short line of people waited to order their morning cups. Dia queued up at the back of the line, and when it was finally her turn, she ordered a tall, black coffee to go.

After her coffee has ready, she took the sleeved paper cup, exited the café's patio, and headed west on Aston Street. Dia had no intention of drinking the coffee, this steaming hot cup of liquid was her first-use weapon. If anyone gets too close, they earn hot coffee to their face. She diverted to the aptly named Church Street with its brick Gothic Revival Presbyterian church on the right and the limestone Romanesque/Gothic Revival hybrid Methodist church on the left. But Dia was nervous again, this route was empty. There was no winning. Too many people on Biltmore, not enough on Church. But she approached the heart of downtown Asheville, she decided not to hit the big streets again just yet. Instead, her path led her down the alley behind the Romanesque Revival style Drhumor Building where two delivery trucks unloaded their goods along the narrow alleyway curb. The truck drivers should be safe, she assured herself, though one gave her a wolf whistle as she passed. *Watch it, buddy,* she thought. *I'm armed with coffee.*

Dia turned the corner and emerged on Patton Ave, one of Asheville's main drags. Bride and the inn were a block west, but, still believing she was being pursued, Dia decided against walking straight back. At the least, she wanted substantiation all had been done to lose her pursuers. After the traffic light changed, she crossed Patton's four lanes, headed east, and branched off on College across from the aluminum "Deco Gecko" sculpture in Pritchard Park. Turning again on Haywood, Dia entered her favorite Asheville street. On a previous visit, she had devoted an entire afternoon on Haywood, exploring its unique shops, galleries, restaurants, museums, and flea markets. This visit, however, only the crowds held her attention, as she tried to suss out her pursuer. At first she dismissed all the hipsters and obvious tourists, which were approximately fifty percent of the crowd, but as she continued up Haywood, she rethought that. Why couldn't an assassin dress like a hipster or a tourist? Grits wasn't a typical killer. So Dia again watched everyone. Had she seen that slacker in the maroon hoodie before? Her mind was overloading with the faces of every pedestrian she passed. What about that jogger pushing the stroller? She seemed familiar. And then there were the cars. What behavior would give away an assassin in an automobile? Every vehicle on Haywood cruised the lane in a suspicious manner. She had to leave this street. She crossed again. Passed several more storefronts, then cut through another alley. This one between a café and a construction site. When she emerged from the alley, she found herself across from the Grove Arcade. *Perfect.* Dia jogged across the street, dropping her coffee when a blue sedan nearly hit her. The car slammed its brakes, and it blared its horn at her in protest. She waved "sorry" to the agitated driver and continued her short run until she was off the street and into the majestic hall of the Grove Arcade. Completed in 1929, the Grove Arcade Public Market was conceived to be "the most elegant building in America." Inside it, was hard to argue against its success in achieving this claim. The regal center hall was lit by its wall-to-wall skylight. The hall's exquisite arched terraces lined the upper floors, and its ornate spiral stairways playfully infringed the hall from the terraces.

Dia spent a half-minute in awe of the great hall's grandeur. She reminded herself of the purpose of her visit and stepped into the nearest store. The display in the Goddess Shop's window became her watch point to discover who followed. When she exited the hotel, she felt free for the first time since... Well, she didn't remember how long. Despite the astonishing wonders of her favorite American city she had become trapped by her own paranoia.

"Oh, I tried that soap my last visit here. It's wonderful. It made my skin so smooth."

Dia registered the voice was talking to her. To her right she found a smartly dressed lady in her early-to-mid-thirties smiling at her. Dia looked down at her hand and found she held a bar of handmade soap. She didn't know what to say. Her mind wasn't processing for this random encounter. Dia returned the lady's smile, set the soap down, and exited the store.

Dia followed the hall south and exited through the west entrance, near the barber shop. From there she decided she had done enough to lose any follower and made a near bee-line the two blocks back to the Downtown Inn & Suites.

Inside the inn, Dia unlocked the door with her keycard and slipped into the hotel room's functional blackness. She struggled to replace the security bar in the dark. After her eyes adjusted, she found Henry Bride lying unmoved on the nearest queen-sized bed. She began to appreciate this champion sent as her protector. Could she trust him? She needed to, and she had no reason to not. Despite the second empty bed, Dia kicked off her shoes and laid down back to back with Bride.

"Did you get what you needed?"

"I did," she said, surprised.

"Good." Bride said. "Don't go anywhere without me again."

"Don't worry. I won't."

"PULL OVER THERE." Dia said, pointing to a thin gravel parking area for a trailhead on the opposite side of the road. They had been winding their way along North Carolina Highway 107, a two-lane highway that twisted through the mountains south of the small town of Cashiers.

"Are you sure these falls are the right ones?" Bride asked, passing the trail with a sign reading "Silver Run Falls" that Dia had pointed out at the last second. They had just driven through Cashiers and the South Carolina border was the next feature listed on the map. Bride suppressed his urge to spin the Apollo about with a power slide. Several bends downhill he found a gravel shoulder wide enough for a proper U-turn without drifting off the road either toward the cliff face upward or off the cliff downward.

Since leaving Asheville, this had been the third waterfall they had stopped at based on Dia's description of "just off the road". She thought for sure it was Dry Falls, so-called because it was possible to go beneath without getting wet. At first glance she ruled out Bridal Falls. Those falls you could drive under with a car. Dia studied the scene as they again approached the trailhead. Tentatively she answered. "This must be it. I'll be sure when we see the falls."

Bride pulled the Apollo into a tight spot behind a minivan parked with no regard for what space it left for other cars. The pair stepped from the car and examined the path to the falls. "This has to be it." Dia said. "There are no more waterfalls before the state line, right?"

"According to your map." Bride said with a touch more anger in his voice than he had intended. Dia had insisted on using paper maps, claiming GPS allowed them to be tracked. Bride had to concede that she'd be the one to know.

Dia hopped out, dressed in faded denim cutoffs, a sleeveless white top, and white Doc Martens. Bride took a moment to admire her spirit and other things before joining her on the trek along the path leading into the woods. Looking around on a wooden walking bridge spanning a narrow creek, Dia declared ninety percent certainty that this was the right spot.

"Explain again how you don't remember." Bride showed more frustration.

"I never planned on coming back here," she said. "It was never supposed to come to this."

"What exactly are we looking for?" Bride asked. "How does a network node even operate in the woods?"

"You'll see." Her expression instantly changed from worried to an ain't-I-clever grin, and her pace intensified. She was in a hurry to show what she had concocted.

Bride could smell the fresh water before they glimpsed the falls. As they approached, the mist gathered on his arm hair and the roar of the tumbling water amplified.

Finally the trail opened to unveil the twenty-odd foot water falls spilling into a wide swimming hole. A young woman swam in the water below the falls while a man, presumably her husband, stood on the rocks at the water's edge with a toddler on a leash. The man warned the young boy, in German, to be careful before exchanging pleasant, yet meaningless greetings in English with Bride and Dia.

They stepped past the man and boy and Dia started to head away from the falls up a path. Bride silently signaled for her to stop and spend time enjoying the falls and the luxurious natural setting that surrounded them. He would explain to her later that it would be suspicious to not spend any time at the falls.

After a few minutes they wandered onward, adhering to the trail Dia had been in a hurry to forge earlier. It led them to a near-vertical, twelve-foot incline of mud and roots.

"This is definitely the spot. We go up there," Dia said.

Bride took a second to examine the climb before he scrambled up the roots to the top. Dia followed right behind him, but with her muscles still strained from her climb in Sault Ste. Marie, she struggled to crest the ledge.

"Where now?" Bride asked as Dia pulled herself to her feet.

"We follow the creek." She walked back toward the creek above the falls. "We'll need to cross, then find a black hose leading up from the creek into the hills."

After finding a place to cross, Dia came close to dropping her bag into the creek. She looked lost, scanning back and forth the water's edge. She became worried and slightly panicky.

"What's wrong?" Bride asked her.

"It's all different. The water was lower when I was here in October. The hose will probably be below water now."

A hose, or any sign of mankind, would have been incongruous to the saturated scene of nature surrounding the Silver Run Creek they followed up into the mountains, Bride thought. The insects, birds—even a pair of chipmunks—continued their routines as if oblivious to the two human intruders among them.

Dia led the foray through the thickening undergrowth along the waterline. She examined every inch of water's edge. The whole endeavor frustrated Bride. If she trusted him enough to say how this needle of rubber hose in the haystack of nature related to an internet relay set to release her password posthumously, then perhaps he'd have more enthusiasm. He flicked off a tick searching his arm for a good place for bloodsucking.

"Here it is!" Dia declared.

Bride stepped up beside her. Sure enough, she had found a black hose entangled with ivy. A slight tug on the hose moved plants up the steep incline heading straight up into the mountain.

"We follow that hose," Dia said, "but it'll be easier if we go upstream and cut back along the top of the ridge."

Even Dia's "easier" ridge was a difficult climb, but with Bride helping her along they made it to the top. They spent five minutes trying to find the hose again.

After locating the hidden pipeline, Dia said, "Now it gets dangerous. The hose meanders into the woods, but watch carefully for booby traps."

"Traps?" Bride said. "Why the hell did you put traps?"

"They're not mine," she said and set off into the woods before turning her head to him. "Oh and try to avoid the cameras."

After a thousand feet of tracing the hose, Dia was forging on, scanning through the woods when Bride saw something moving strangely near Dia's boots.

"Stop!" he yelled.

Dia did as commanded, freezing in her somewhat unbalanced position.

He slowed as he caught up to her. He knelt just behind her, and it was as he thought; a trip line was resting on top of the laces of her boot.

"What is it?" She asked trying not to move her head or face.

"Trip line," Bride said as he tried to trace the line to its trap. "It's taut. A slight move will set off whatever it—" Bride stopped when spotted the device.

"What?" Dia was obviously nervous.

"The line is attached to a spiked pendulum hanging from that tree," Bride said, "so keep still."

Dia went from frozen to rock still. Bride was devising a plan to get Dia out of the danger when he noticed she wasn't breathing.

"You need to breathe," Bride said in calm tone. "Do it slowly. I can't have you passing out on me. Got it?"

"Got it." She nodded her head a millimeter, and something ticked up in the tree.

With no time for anything else, Bride grabbed Dia's belt and collar and yanked her backward with all of his might. A square yard of wooden spikes split through the tree's leaves and swung to Earth faster than Newton's law allowed. Dia was horizontal, four feet off the ground, a foot above the dropping Henry Bride, and nearly clear when the wooden spike plate struck. Three of the spikes clipped the side of Dia's boot and sent the girl—who was already in the air—spinning. From Bride's vantage point looking up from the undergrowth, it was like a slow-motion scene of a helicopter flying overhead with a woman for blades. The spikes, vibrating from striking Dia's boot, slammed into the soft dirt marked by the trip line. Dia pulled her arms, legs, and head in to prepare to roll, but the action only increased her revolutions per minute. She careened off two small trees nearly eight feet from Bride before landing on her side and tumbling another ten. She screamed out in pain a word too filthy for such a pretty girl but apropos for the beating she had just taken from the forest.

"Are you okay?" Bride shouted.

She repeated her swear with a tad less ferocity.

Bride stood and moved to her, but she stood on her own, albeit shakily.

"We have to move fast," she struggled to say.

"Take a break," Bride commanded. "I'll scout for more traps."

"No," she said with determined defiance. "That trap triggered the alarms. We don't have much time." She trekked up past Bride and the now harmless square of sharpened two-inch thick wooden spikes, a fresh hitch clear in her step. Cautiously she stepped over the pendulum's arm, pushed the branches of some low bushes aside, and disappeared into the brush. Bride tailed with more caution. When Bride moved aside the bushes, he found himself in a rough acre of marijuana plants growing on the slope of the mountainside. The pot plants' musky sweet stench lolled heavy in the air. The forbidden horticulture was situated randomly and grew in broad variants of green, presumably to help camouflage the field in satellite images.

Dia limped a direct line to a grove of trees at the field's edge. Bride followed.

"Do you see that hornets' nest up in that tree?" She said when Bride pulled even to where she had stopped.

"Yeah, I see it," he replied.

"That's a wifi camera the pot growers use to monitor the fields. Inside it I piggybacked a tiny computer to leach off their solar power and wifi. That is the first node. We need to get it down and disconnect it. There is little time. We're on camera right now."

"How did you place it up there without—"

She cut him off. "Not much time. Give me a boost."

He knelt and intertwined his fingers to give her a place to step. When she did, however, she cringed in pain.

She stepped off and rubbed her ankle. "Give me a minute," she said.

"You said we don't have time," he said. "I'll get it."

"All right," she capitulated. "You get it. Take this."

Bride took the multi-tool she offered from her bag, then grasped the trunk and scaled the fifteen feet up to the hornets' nest.

He squeezed his legs around the trunk, resting one foot on a small branch, but using the vice of his legs to carry his weight.

"What next?" he shouted down to her.

"Bust off the nest until you get inside to the electronics."

With his right hand he flipped the multi-tool until it had transformed into a knife. The piece of hornets' nest fell off easily until he exposed two small, black plastic boxes, one obviously a camera.

"Done," he said.

"The lower box, you need to disconnect the power line coming out the back."

"And then I'm done?"

"Yes."

"Does it matter what happens to the camera?"

She thought for a second. "I suppose not."

Bride folded away the multi-tool, took one black box in each hand, and leapt off the tree. The thin power wires gave no resistance to Bride's full weight and snapped with little effort. Bride rolled when he hit the ground, stood, and handed Dia her box.

"We done here?" he asked. "Because we should go before someone comes for this camera."

//// /

"Irma?" Clarence Axeworthy called out from his office. Where was that woman? Usually she knew when she was needed, and now she hadn't responded to his signal that buzzed her watch when he pressed the glass on the edge of his desk. Axeworthy stood from his chair, flicked his wrist, and called out to the house's intelligent control system, "Where is Irma?"

"Unknown," the house responded in a voice like, but unsatisfactorily different than that of Majel Barrett, the original computer voice on *Star Trek*. The difference bothered him more today than usual.

"Has Irma left the compound?"

"Unknown."

That wasn't the response he wanted on multiple levels. First, was it "unknown" whether Irma was on the compound, or was it "unknown" if that was even a function the system could perform? Artificial Intelligence had a long way to go before it lived up to the dream.

"Is Irma wearing her watch?" he quizzed the system.

There was a long, frustrating pause before, "The watch has detected no heartbeat." Again, a discouraging response.

"Where is Irma's watch?"

"Irma's watch is in the vicinity of her desk."

Now he was getting somewhere, but it still required him to get up and find out what was happening himself. He exited his office into the grand room of the seaside house. Irma's desk was vacant and curiously out from the wall, the position it should only be in when Irma was working. *Damn, that woman.*

"Have any of the compound's doors been opened in the last half hour?"

No response. Axeworthy realized his mistake, flicked his wrist again, and repeated his question.

"The rear, lower-floor door is currently open."

"What!?"

The house speakers, not realizing Axeworthy's confusion, repeated its last phrase. "The rear, lower-floor door is currently open."

Axeworthy stormed across the wide room and out the door above the stairs. Outside he heard Irma's voice, "Hurry, girl. Hurry." Dressed in one of Axeworthy's old shirts and what he guessed was one of Irma's oversized skirts, hair unkempt as always, the young trollop rightfully was frightened to exit her room. "Please girl, we don't have much time," Irma urged.

Boisterously, Axeworthy descended the wooden stairs. "Where do you think you two are going?"

Irma stopped in her tracks and turned to face her boss, moving herself between Axeworthy and his sex slave who had reluctantly begun following.

"You can't give her back, Clarence," Irma pleaded. "You know they will kill her. She promises she won't say anything, don't you darling?"

But the gaunt woman, fear hanging on her face, simply slinked back into the darkness of her room.

"Please, Clarence," Irma cried, "you can't..."

But Axeworthy ignored Irma's pleas for the girl as his blood boiled. Besides, at this point she pled for the wrong life. Axeworthy stepped toward the bleating aide, and grabbed her fat woman throat.

His eyes moved to those of the slave as he choked the final life out of his assistant of five years. The terror in his slave's expression excited him as much as the feeling of power he felt taking Irma's life. As the final, desperate gasp creaked from Irma's throat, Axeworthy shouted orders to the terror-filled slave who had just witnessed the murder.

"Remove those God-awful rags and wait for me in my room."

16> **A Round of Golf**

DIA AND BRIDE SCRAMBLED through the deep shadows of the mountain pines. They ignored the trail and cut a direct route through the brush back to the car which was still parked on the gravel patch along Highway 107. Upon arriving at the Apollo, they found the white sports car obstructed by a silver 1998 Volkswagen Golf GTI. The Volkswagen was empty.

"Those bastards," Dia said. "They've blocked us in. It's probably the pot farmers."

"Possibly," Bride said. "But a Volkswagen is a strange vehicle for marijuana growers." After slipping in to the driver's seat, he reached over to unlatch her door. *Mental note: Install remote locks.*

"It'd be less suspicious," she argued as she climbed in.

"I suppose." He started the Apollo, looked behind him, then gently backed the centimeters until his right rear bumper contacted the VW's front bumper. After gently touching bumpers, Bride floored his accelerator pedal. The fresh radials spun spitting forward rocks, dust, and smoke as the Apollo pushed backward against the VW. The stones surely wreaked havoc on his fresh paint job, but that was a later worry. At first the Golf didn't budge, but Bride kept the Apollo's tires spinning and thanks to the newly installed limited slip differential the newer car succumbed and inched backward.

At that moment, two men clad in denim and flannel ran out of the trailhead and stopped when they saw what was happening with their car. The plucky Apollo pushed and pushed until it forced the VW back a foot and a half.

That gave Bride enough leeway in front to drive the Apollo out. He trampled down the clutch and the Apollo's wheels immediately stopped spinning. He jammed the stick shift into first gear, rotated the front wheels outward, then drew his foot from the clutch pedal. The rocks now spat rearward, showering the Volkswagen and the two newcomers with gravel as the Apollo bulleted forward onto the pavement. The Apollo's Firestones chirped then squealed indignantly as they climbed onto the blacktop. Pivoted one-hundred-and-eighty degrees, the spirited white car lunged south down the mountainside roadway. The onlookers sprinted for the Volkswagen as the Apollo sped past.

Dia laughed as they rode off. "That'll teach those trolls to crowd you." She appeared oblivious to the fact the Volkswagen would soon be pursuing them, so Bride let her remain in the dark as he focused on putting distance between them.

The mountain highway relentlessly threw bends at the antique sports car. The Apollo sped downhill through the zigzags of Highway 107. Bride worked the transmission methodically up and down through the gears. Proper straightaways were the anomalies on State Highway 107. With dense forest and cliff faces on the right and the deep crevice cut by Whitewater River on the left, the road seemed to cling to the mountainside.

The VW incident apparently reminded Dia of something from her past. She began regaling Bride with a story of a girls' night out with Krystal Carrie. She described when they escaped a bar after Dia punched a womanizer making improper advances. Apparently this was an infamous night where "Pearl" became a thing with them and somehow the story segued into vodka recipes. The tales were entertaining and endeared Dia more to him. His druthers, nevertheless, was the silent treatment here and the girls-being-girls tales back on the long dull I-75. That preference aside, he'd drink one of those coffee and caramel vodkas right now.

"Want to know how to mix one?" Dia excitedly continued. "Take an ounce and a half of caramel vodka, some good but simple coffee—we went with a Columbian dry roast—mix 'em together and add—"

"Hang on," Bride interrupted, checking the rearview mirror on the dash. "Our VW friends are back."

Dia spun and observed their pursuers out the rear window. "That silver Volkswagen? Are they serious? That's some big fahrvergnügens."

"It's a Golf GTI. They're serious." Bride increased the pace, but the snaking mountain road only allowed the Apollo to gain the tiniest amount of momentum. As soon as they rounded one cruel turn, the road threw another, and the Apollo was revealing a weakness for oversteer. In the rearview the Volkswagen shared no such weaknesses. It hugged the turns like a sidewinder through the rocks, keeping pace with Bride's Apollo with little effort. Who were these guys? Were they the pot farmers as Dia suspected? More assassins? Doubtful they were government. It seemed unlikely an agent of the US Government would drive a '98 VW Golf GTI, but then here was a Homeland Security agent operating a white '73 Apollo.

Dia followed the Golf's movement intently out the rear window.

"What do you see back there?" Bride asked.

"There's two dudes in the vee-dub. The old geezer is driving and a younger hilljack is in the passenger seat," she said, clinging to the seat tops to prevent being tossed about as the car slid through curve after curve. "The passenger is on the phone. Both are still rockin' those black baseball caps. If I'd guess, I'd say father and son. Pops is saying something to Junior."

Bride picked up speed beyond the Apollo's ability to execute the turns in only one lane. "Straightnin' the curves," Waylon Jennings called it. Meanwhile the Golf GTI kept pace while remaining in its proper lane.

"They're keeping up." Dia continued the running commentary. "Junior set his iPhone on the dashboard. He's using speaker phone."

Bride slid the old aluminum-bodied car through another hairpin to find an oncoming minivan in the far lane, which was also occupied by the Apollo's tail end. Dia turned forward in time to hurl a reactionary expletive toward the innocent family in the minivan. Bride popped the clutch, removing power from the rear wheels during Dia's missed heartbeat. The tires' rubber regained traction and propelled the Apollo's back end into the correct lane.

"Dude!" Dia said. "You can't cash the bounty on my head if we're both dead."

Bride ignored the comment and cut the Apollo fully over to the far lane to widen the highway's next twist. The Apollo was managing over sixty miles-per-hour on curves marked twenty-five. The back of Bride's mind compiled a list of refinements for Gonzo Rodgers, his mechanic back in St. Louis. He recalled the last words Gonzo said when he picked up the Apollo. "Put 'er through 'er paces."

Check.

Dia, back to watching the VW, said, "Shit! Junior's got a shotgun."

Bride confirmed Dia's warning in the tiny rearview. He was left no option but to outrun them. The only exits off the two-lane highway were the occasional driveway or roads that most likely dead-ended up in the mountains. Those would do no good unless he preferred gunfight to car chase. He didn't.

"Why aren't they trying to pass?" She wondered aloud. "They could have us dead to rights."

Bride realized the game the VW was playing. "They're pushing us toward something. If they try to pass, I'd spin us around and head the other direction. We need to get off this road before we arrive where ever they're driving us toward." He decided to test this hypothesis. On the next bend, he attacked the arc a bit too fast, ducking the Apollo into the far lane and letting the rear skid out into a power slide. After the corner's apex, he cut the front wheels in further and let the rear slide past, spinning the car backward on the road.

The VW flew around the turn just behind and slammed its brakes to avoid striking the Apollo. The Golf came to rest nose-to-nose with the sports car. For an instant the two cars sat stationary in the center of the blind mountain curve. Finally the VW's passenger door swung open and Junior cautiously climbed out with his 12-gauge double-barrel shotgun. Without moving anything but his foot Bride depressed the clutch and gravity rolled the old car quietly backward down the mountain road. Junior hesitated until Pops yelled for him to get back in the car. Still rolling backward Bride released the clutch into first gear and floored the accelerator pedal, propelling the Apollo forward at the Golf. He veered toward Junior nearly clipping the VW's bumper and crashing into the still open passenger door. The entire weight of the Apollo mangled the VW's door and slammed it into Junior's trailing leg. They could hear Junior's scream over the roar of the Apollo's Crate engine.

Dia responded with a victory cheer. "That'll take care of them," she said, peering back at the wrecked side of the GTI.

"It'll slow them down," a more sober Bride said, back to driving his lane. He wondered how much damage he had inflicted on the poor Apollo that was out one headlight and slightly pulling to the right. Less than he dealt to Junior he hoped.

"Pickup truck coming!" Dia yelled just as Bride caught sight of the blazing headlights cutting through the dusk. A Ford F-250 Super Duty with wood-railed bed and chrome exhaust stacks rumbled down the center of the roadway around the inside hairpin turn ahead. In the falling sun's light, Bride caught the driver eyeing them across the chasm. The truck was after them as well.

The Apollo stood no chance against this newcomer. Bride dropped two gears and moved far to the outside as they entered the hairpin. He turned the car overly sharp into the curve and jerked up on the emergency brake. The old Apollo spun around its center. When the Apollo continued its spin after a complete about face, Bride realized he had lost control of his maneuver.

"*Hang on!*" he yelled, though Dia already hung on to everything she could hang on to. Now drifting on the thin gravel shoulder, the Apollo headed nose first toward the cliff face at the turn's apex while the F-250 continued barreling toward them.

The Apollo's front end crunched into the rock face as the old sports car came to a rest. His gearbox already in reverse, Bride peered over his shoulder, and floored the accelerator. The Apollo smoked its rear tires once again, and they retreated backward down the mountain road.

The Ford Super Duty cut around the hairpin and loomed close enough to the Apollo for its overpowering headlights to flood the car's interior.

Dia yelled, "Go! Go! Go!"

No time to explain that cars only have one reverse gear.

"He's trying to push us off the side of the mountain!" she exclaimed.

With the truck's massive after-market steel bumper inches from the Apollo's grill, Bride noticed a strange detail. The center of the grille, spray painted in red, proudly displayed the word "Rooster".

They lurched hard when the two vehicles' front ends collided, but Bride fought the nudge to the left and continued steering the Apollo down the asphalt track. The Apollo's low split bumper design was at a decided disadvantage versus the F-250's high chrome monstrosity. The beast's bumper overtopped the old sports car's hood, crunching it down and losing part of the Apollo's front grill. Bride was horrified by the damage to his freshly restored car, but the matter at hand was staying on the road and not dying. His best hope was not to fight the momentum of the Ford half-ton, but to keep his wheels rolling to at least direct the Apollo along the mountain road. With that in mind, he slipped his gearbox in neutral to stop the Ford from overrunning the Apollo's reverse gear and having his tires lose traction.

"Are we seriously being stalked by a guy named Rooster?" Dia asked out of the blue.

"I'm a bit busy right now," Bride said, focusing on steering the Apollo GT backward down the mountain highway. Meanwhile the oversized pickup truck endeavored to force the old car any direction except on the road. So far Bride kept the wheels on the asphalt but only by employing the entire width of the road. They weren't traveling as fast as they had before. But with essentially rear wheels steering, anything more than slight braking meant relinquishing the tires' spinning grip on the road and thus ceding control to the presumptive Rooster. Control was precarious. Rooster allowed the Apollo to roll ahead on the short straightaways only to bang his bumper again into the Apollo's hood at the next turn.

Dia swore as Rooster's truck pounded the Apollo's nose once more, jolting everything inside the car and almost causing the Apollo to spin out of control.

While Bride managed to limit the Apollo's path to the asphalt, with each subsequent turn he wondered where the Volkswagen was. He expected to see the hatchback again. Even if the Golf GTI lollygagged turning around, they should have come upon it by now. The next turn met those expectations. After another vicious hit from the chrome monstrosity, steam sputtered from beneath the Apollo's hood. Bride spied the VW standing watch on the roadside gravel pad where the VW and Apollo met. Junior and Pops waited, rifles in hand, behind the Golf's open doors.

Balanced on one leg and leaning against the Golf, Junior leveled his hunting rifle and fired—the bullet striking the rear of the Apollo. Bride took stock of the situation and decided to hell with it. The F-250 had allowed the Apollo to slip ahead again for the straightaway but followed mere feet from the car's crumpled front end. Still driving over his shoulder, Bride aimed the Apollo's rear toward the stationary Volkswagen. Junior recognized the danger immediately, pushed away, and dove from behind the door into the plant life along the gravel pad. Pops, however, froze in terror, seeing the 2,500-pound sports car and the 6,600-pound pickup heading directly for him. Just before the Apollo hit, Bride veered the vehicle partially back on to the road, but not enough to entirely miss the Volkswagen.

The rear passenger side of the Apollo's steel bumper clipped the Volkswagen's reinforced vinyl bumper on the front driver's side. The metal of the two cars crunched, pushing the Volkswagen back and trapping Pops behind its door. Pop's scream penetrated through the Apollo's glass as both his legs snapped with the impact and he was hurled from the VW's side. While the Apollo's rear quarter panel accordioned with the impact with the VW, the front end spun around, turning it perpendicular with the road. Rooster, witnessing the bedlam in front of him, slammed the truck's brakes and dodged back onto the highway's asphalt. The pickup's front end now aimed square with the Apollo's front passenger side fender and it impacted with another jolt. After the Apollo spun another quarter turn, it came to a rest. For a second there was a stillness on the mountain side, save the steam rising from all three vehicles.

Then Pops resumed his screams of agony.

"Are you all right?" Bride asked Dia, who was stunned, shaking, and staring out into the aftermath. She spun her head to glare at him. He took her expression as a "yes", slammed the gearshift into first, pressed the accelerator pedal, and let up the clutch. The Apollo's rear wheels screeched as the car took off down the mountain again.

They were moving, but the crippled Apollo now had a significant pull to the right and a shimmy whenever it tried to go straight. To make matters worse, Bride caught sight of Rooster's pickup starting after them as they rounded the first bend.

When the shock wore off, Dia yelled at Bride. "What the hells were you trying to accomplish? You nearly squashed us."

"Just trying to point the car the right direction," Bride said. "And I'm chalking it a plus. I knocked two of them out of play."

Dia thought about matters and calmed. "Aw, but your car. You've really trashed your poor car."

Bride frowned, "Well, it wouldn't have done me much good if we hadn't lived to enjoy it. But I'll let you tell Krystal that I expect her to help me fix it again."

"Yeah, I will," Dia said. "And you're right. At least we're safe."

Bride checked the rearview mirror and saw Rooster's truck rumbling around the previous bend.

"Don't jump the gun," Bride said.

Dia looked over her shoulder and spotted the pickup. "Son of a..."

This trip down the mountain was a bit slower with Bride's control of the Apollo limited by its front end damage. But the big pickup didn't handle the curves as effectively as Pops' little hatchback. So after determining the limits of the Apollo's current steering situation and pushing those limits Bride put some distance between them and Rooster. But he knew it wouldn't last. With steam spraying from its cooling system, it couldn't be long before this new engine overheats. Without temperature gauges he had no way of guessing when. Except maybe when the steam stopped misting from beneath the hood. At least they were still driving downhill, so as much as he could Bride let gravity power the car, gathering as much momentum as he could around the turns. He guessed that as long as they didn't push it, and continued traveling downhill, he could keep the old car rolling ahead of Rooster. He knew, however, that wouldn't be forever, and he remembered that Pops was trying to herd them into something.

"Can you fire a gun?" Bride asked.

The question's implication clearly scared Dia. "Why? You don't think we can out run him?"

"Not likely," he said. "The engine's on borrowed time. We may need to make a stand. And I think we'll have more company soon."

"I've fired guns before. Mostly rifles, but have had pistol training. My uncle—"

He interrupted her. "Skip the details. How good are you?"

"I wouldn't say great, but I can hit the target."

"I'll find a spot to make a stand. You grab the guns."

"Okay," she said.

"In the back get in my duffle bag and unzip the end pocket." She did as told. "Inside there is a small hand towel. Carefully take it out. I wrapped Grits' .22 Magnum inside the towel."

"Got it," she said.

"Now take my pistol from the glove compartment."

Dia collected that weapon as well.

"Hand me that one." He held his right hand open, and a second of hesitation she handed him the XD Mod.2. He tucked it in next to his seat.

The next turn unveiled what Bride had been dreading.

17> **Showtime at the Apollo**

HENRY BRIDE BELIEVED he may have driven the Blue Ridge Mountains as much in reverse as in any forward gear. The instant he spotted the blockade across the shadowed mountain road, he recalled the small gravel drive back around the last curve. He locked the Apollo's new disk brakes and slapped the stick shift into reverse. The question was how far behind was Rooster's thundering Super Duty pickup truck?

The blockade consisted of four armed men, a Jeep Wrangler with a box trailer, and a Toyota RAV4. The pair of vehicles did a sufficient job of blocking the full width of state highway 107 and its median. That explained the lack of traffic on the journey down. The Apollo GT crashing through the blockade seemed highly unlikely, perhaps a bigger vehicle could smash through the box trailer, but the crumpled sports car stood no chance. So they reentered the dangerous game of chicken with the Rooster. Their new odds didn't seem much better.

The air wasn't hot, but sweat dripped off Bride's brow as he rounded the last turn and simultaneously spotted both the gravel drive and Rooster's oncoming headlights. The Apollo was less than half the distance to the drive than Rooster was. He could make it. Or so he thought until the Apollo's new replacement engine sputtered and the old sports car shimmied.

"*Come on,*" Bride urged the beaten Apollo, "Just a little farther."

He momentarily eased the throttle. The engine smoothed, and the Apollo stormed up the mountain road powered by unleaded gasoline and determination. It would be close. Rooster's F-250 rounded his turn and gained speed into the Apollo's straightaway. The gravel drive was now barely a couple of car lengths away.

"Get ready to run," Bride shouted to Dia.

She grabbed her bag from the floorboard and shoved the .22 magnum inside the side pocket.

Bride ceaselessly drove backward through the mountain highway dusk. A second more, then he could turn off the highway. Then what?

The question became moot as the Apollo sputtered a last gasp and died. Bride had prepared. The instant the Apollo engine stuttered again, he depressed the clutch to prevent the dying engine from sapping all the car's momentum. With Rooster approaching rapidly, Bride spun the steering wheel and backed the coasting sports car at a forty-five degree angle into the gravel drive's mouth. The F-250's tires locked as the driver slammed down his brake pedal, but the beast stopped well past the side road's entrance.

Before the Apollo rolled to a stop Bride shouted, "Go!"

Dia popped open her car door and, bag in tow, sprinted into the mountain forest. Bride yanked the emergency break, grabbed his gun from the gap by the break lever, opened his door, and followed Dia. As he reached the tree line, he fired a shot at the F-250, shattering the spray-painted rear window. He didn't wait for the aftermath of his shot; it should, at least, slow down any pursuit, as was its intention.

Even with her newly acquired limp, Dia plowed her way through the tall pines and thick underbrush at a surprising speed. Fast enough that Bride worried he would lose her. He followed her rough path, dodging the trees and pushing through the undergrowth as they climbed the sloping mountainside.

Sufficiently beyond sight of the road, Bride spoke to her in a loud whisper. "Wait, we need to double back to the car."

She paused, allowing him to catch her. "Are you insane? They've got shotguns."

Still for the first time since entering the forest, Bride heard their pursuers' distant rustle.

"We need a place to hide before they spot us," Bride said.

"Why?" she asked. "Let's keep going."

"No time to explain." Bride was already scanning the mountain wilderness. "Over there." He pointed to a rock outcropping just visible in the deepening dusk.

They altered course and dashed to the rocks finding the far side had a ten foot drop to a dry creek bed.

"Here." Bride pointed to a narrow crevice that supplied handholds for a quick climb down.

At the ledge's base, Bride realized its shadowed underside formed an imperfect hiding spot. Though spacious enough to fit Dia, the undercutting never would fit them both. It would have to suffice.

"Squeeze under that ledge," he ordered.

"Where will you hide?" she asked while lying on her side below the outcropped edge. She tucked her bag behind her, and wedged into the tight, rocky space.

Bride examined the area for another locale to hide. A tree or shrub seemed his only options, but a terrible one if the searchers fanned out through the forest. Bride spotted a sizable felled limb still replete with its leaves. He tucked his gun away so he could work and crossed the rocky creek bed. After lifting the branch from the ground, he discovered it already hid something, a pile of trash—aerosol cans, boxes of decongestant, and empty cans of paint thinner. Bride cursed his luck. After dealing with spiked traps in a marijuana patch, he now stumbled upon a meth lab dump. With no other choices, he proceeded with his idea, hoping the trash didn't call attention to the location. As quietly as possible he hauled the branch which was larger and heavier than first estimated, to the ledge bottom. He dropped the branch in front of Dia, leaving a gap to allow a way to climb in. He wedged himself between the limb and Dia's position against the ledge, scooting back until his backside pressed against her. In as tight as he could muster, he pulled the branch over top of himself, hoping no one else heard the noise. Dia wrapped her top arm over him, and, for a second, the touch of her soft breast against his shoulder blades distracted him from his purpose. The second over, he reached back between them and unholstered the Springfield XD again, held the gun out, and waited.

"I hope they don't have an Indian tracker guide with them," she whispered. "If they do, we're dead meat."

Bewildered, he grumbled. "They don't have an Indian tracker."

"How do you know? Did you get a decent look at them? The one guy's name is apparently Rooster. That sounds Native American."

"Odds. That's how I know. The odds say they don't have an Indian tracker."

"But they could. Or they might have a dog."

"Hush. If they hear us, they won't need a tracker or a dog."

Bride shimmied tighter into Dia and pulled the branch closer. They lay silently waiting. The odd silence of the forest's breaking night was excruciating. To make matters worse, he sensed bugs crawling along his legs, and judging by Dia's squirming, she felt them too. He slowly reached his left hand back and laid it on her leg to calm her. It seemed to work. Her squirming quieted to an occasional twitch, but as the bugs bit his legs under his trousers, Dia's bare legs had likely become the insects' smörgåsbord.

As the westward sky bled from red to indigo, Bride perceived the footsteps of the first pursuer climbing up through the underbrush. He tapped his hand on her leg to signal the searchers were coming and hoped she understood the touch code he just made up.

Through the thick leaves Bride spotted a flashlight's beam. Silhouetted against the trees and swinging a shotgun and the flashlight back and forth around the woods, a stocky pursuer scanned across the forest as he trekked up the elevation. Bride gripped Dia's thigh. She, in return, squeezed his chest with her arm.

Time dilated as they waited for their stalker to pass. Bride aimed his pistol through the leaves, centered on the approaching man's torso. One long glance in their direction and Bride would put two 9mm slugs into the bastard's heart. Bride steadied his gun arm against his hip and timed his breathing. Their hunter stepped closer and closer, approaching to five yards of the dry creek. The light beam swept their direction but diverted to the trash pile. After hiking to the pile, the silhouette's hefty hiking boot kicked at the rubbish then diverted his light to the crest of the craggy ledge and waved someone over. Another pursuer would soon be ten feet above them. If Bride fired at the original target, he and Dia would become fish in a barrel for the person atop the ledge. After ten seconds of suspense, Bride heard footsteps above. The shadowy figure on their level pointed at the trash pile with his shotgun and flashlight. A whisper from above said, "It's nothing. It's been here too long." After stirring the trash with his gun barrel, the silhouette seemed satisfied and pivoted to continue his search up the mountain. Finally he was leaving. It seemed they ultimately wouldn't be found. But suddenly Dia produced a muffled squeak and kneed Bride's leg which in turn rustled the leaves of their hiding place. What the hell was she thinking? They were Scot free. Now the silhouette with the shotgun aimed his flashlight directly at them and was edging closer.

A second later, Bride understood the cause of Dia's reaction when the scales of a snakehead slithered over his ear and cheek.

Bride froze, resisting even breathing. The snake's belly traveled across his face using his nose as support to cross to the branch. Bride was too close to identify the snake breed, but it was long and as thick as his big toe. Eventually the entire six-foot serpent slowly slid off Bride's head into the bough's foliage.

"I see you," the approaching man whispered behind the blinding spot. The beam penetrated through Bride's pupils straight into his retinas. But Bride dare not close his eyes. Whoever's on the ledge and this serpent be damned; Bride needed to shoot this guy.

"Aren't you cute," the silhouette said kneeling a scant four feet from Bride's horizontal position.

It was the snake this guy spotted, Bride realized and removed pressure from the trigger.

"Go on, buddy. I'd take you home, but I'm busy, today."

The flashlight beam followed the snake slithering off down the creek bed, before the silhouette stood and continued his trek up the mountainside. But the two hiding under the branch remained unseen. Thank God that guy wasn't a snake hater.

Now came the tricky part. Bride's plan was to double back to the road. What would happen after? He didn't know. The Apollo was out of service, but he would save the bridge crossings for the bridges. The dilemma became when to go. Too soon and risk being seen by the goons climbing the hill; too late and risk them returning.

He decided to wait two minutes after the last sign of the searchers, for no rhyme or reason other than gut. Dia, however, was getting anxious.

"When are we going?" she whispered.

He quietly shushed her.

"I'm being eaten alive, and I'm worried that snake might have friends."

"I know," Bride whispered back. "Wait."

She had broken his concentrating on counting out the seconds in his head. He remembered passing sixty, so he decided thirty more would do.

"Get ready," he whispered.

As gently as he could, he lifted the limb from on top of them. It created more noise than he hoped, but he heard no response so he stood, holstered his gun, then helped Dia to her feet.

She checked her bag for critters, and he pointed down the slope from where they came. She nodded and the pair quietly scrambled back toward the road where the vacated Apollo rested.

About halfway back, a voice echoed through the forest, "They're behind us!"

That was their signal to run. Both Bride and Dia shifted from a scramble to something near a controlled fall, both bouncing off trees and leaping down ledges, anything to keep upright and moving fast.

"Stop!" the voice yelled punctuated by the deep bang of a shotgun firing.

Bride glanced behind them as he caromed off another tree. He caught no sign of the pursuers in the forest twilight. Ahead through the gaps between the trees, however, stationary headlights had become visible. And unfortunately, someone was moving about down there amongst them. Dia, who had built a sizable lead on Bride, seemed oblivious to the waiting thug near the cars.

He was near certain the straggler assumed their approach, but yelling would betray their exact location. And Dia wasn't looking back. So at the next tree he broke off a small limb and threw it toward Dia to get her attention. The stick whirled right past her left ear. That got her attention. She slowed, spun, and stared at him with an expression that said, "What?"

Bride pointed toward the man down by the cars as he caught up to Dia. From where they stood Bride could count four vehicles lined up on the road, the Apollo, the F-250, the RAV4, and the Jeep with its trailer. The latter three blared their headlights into the trees. Looking behind them, multiple flashlight beams had appeared rapidly careening down the hillside.

"Follow me," Bride said, "but don't leave the woods until I get this guy under control."

She complied, and they descended the slope at a diagonal hoping to exit behind the lingering man. Upon reaching the forest's edge, Dia ducked down beneath a low, wide tree. With weapon drawn, Bride emerged from the woods in the shadow past the Toyota RAV4. He leveled the pistol at the figure standing guard over the cars. The man held a hunting rifle and was still scanning the woods.

"Put the gun down," Bride ordered.

Without lowering his rifle, the lanky, bearded stranger turned to Bride. He stood about a dozen feet away wearing jeans, flannel, and a trucker's cap that read "Rooster". He grinned.

"You're not going to shoot me," Rooster said. The rifle barrel was not aimed at Bride, but it would only take milliseconds to raise and fire.

"What makes you say that?" Bride asked.

"You could have shot me when you shot out my window."

"Your logic is flawed there, Mister Rooster," Bride said. "Just because I'd rather not shoot you, doesn't mean I won't."

"I don't think..." Rooster stopped speaking when Dia casually ambled from the woods holding a small black device in her hands. She smiled and nodded at Rooster and walked behind Bride to the RAV4. She double-pressed a small button on the SUV's door handle, and the doors clicked unlocked. Dia opened the door and climbed into the driver's seat.

"Come on," she said. "Let's go."

Bride didn't understand what happened. How had she unlocked the car's doors? He'd raise that question with Dia later.

With the gun kept aimed at Rooster, he eased around the front of the SUV. Rooster, still grinning, backed up as Bride stepped forward.

When he reached the far front side of the vehicle, Bride turned the gun and fired two shots putting holes into the tires of the Jeep and F-250. With his pistol again aimed at Rooster, Bride eased back and opened the passenger door. He stepped up on the door frame and held the gun over the SUV's open door.

"Let's go," he repeated to Dia.

For a second, things were silent.

"It won't start." Dia whispered to Bride, loud enough for Rooster to get a chuckle out of their situation.

"What?" Bride said still eyeing down Rooster.

"I have this range extender," she explained in a low voice. "It extended the range of someone's key fob, but the metal car body blocks the frequency and it's not receiving the fob's signal inside the car."

Rooster used the opportunity of Dia's slight distraction of Bride to duck and roll away and behind the Jeep. Bride fired as soon as Rooster moved, but the bullet only damaged the Jeep's hood.

"Can you hot wire it?" Bride asked.

"No," she said, "just give it a second."

Staying low, Dia held the black device outside the open door. A second later, her window shattered accompanied by the crack of Rooster's rifle. Bride again fired in Rooster's direction for no other reason than to give the hillbilly pause.

"We don't have a second." Bride said.

"Keep calm. We won't die in North Carolina."

"Great, except I'm fairly certain we're in South Carolina now."

"It'll work," she promised holding the box a little lower, below the broken window.

A second, then third, thug emerged from the trees, guns aimed at the RAV4. Bride ducked below the dash before they could fire.

"It better, or we are dead."

Simultaneously with the word "dead", two more individuals appeared from the woods and a tiny light lit on the black box's side. Dia pressed the brake pedal and start button, and the Toyota roared to life. Still ducking, she yanked her door shut, threw the RAV4 in reverse, and sped backward onto state highway 107's dark asphalt, guiding the SUV through the tiny reverse-camera screen.

Once on the road, she sat up, shifted to drive, and they sped south. Bride's door slammed shut when its momentum didn't match the SUV's.

/ / / /

All the math was correct, but the woman's body still refused to sink into the boiling mud. Clarence Axeworthy simply stared frustrated at the corpse's lethargic dance about the mud pit. The macabre choreography was accompanied by the two long shadows begot by his car's twin headlights being cut by the twisting corpse jutting up from the bubbling earth. Under his breath, he swore, "Sink, you crusty old cunt. Sink." But Axeworthy knew, once again, his ego had been his undoing.

Since first setting eyes upon the famous mud volcanoes near the south end of the Salton Sea, Axeworthy's curiosity drove him to discover what would happen should a person find themselves stuck in the field of the continuously rolling land. He had doodled possible scenarios, and drew the conclusion that a weighted body would totally submerge in roughly thirty minutes to an hour. After nearly two hours he realized his conclusion was only wishful thinking for the body of his assistant—ex-assistant, he corrected his thought—hadn't seemed to sink any farther in past half of that time. Early on, after dumping Irma's body into the natural mud caldron, Axeworthy sat, popped open a bottle of Bollinger, and savored the end of Irma's judging stares and ceaseless questions. Soon he tired of just how slowly the body sank, Axeworthy pulled out his phone and checked his emails and texts. Not much important there, mostly things that Irma would have handled. He sighed, for the first time regretting her loss, and began slogging through the mundane communications.

He did have one message of interest. The "package" he had been searching for was seen in the Carolinas. *The Carolinas?* he thought, *wasn't there something in the files about a vacation in North Carolina? Or was it South?* He realized he now had to check files that he purposefully made inaccessible from the cloud. He would have to deal with that when he was back home. Whenever the hell that would be.

Now, at nearly two hours, he was back on his feet, trying to solve where this plan had gone wrong, and, more importantly, how to fix it.

He should have added weights to both the arms and legs. The leg weights must be on a ledge below the surface. That had to be the problem, but too late for that now. He had used all of the weights he had brought with him. Had he not been uncomfortable leaving the body sticking from the ground with its arm waving about like a slow-motion video of Horshack vying for Mr. Kotter's attention, he could go retrieve some weights.

Axeworthy walked to the rear of his car and opened the trunk. He took off his jacket and folded it over the trunk's lip, then rolled up his sleeves, and pulled a spade from the back. He cursed that modern cars didn't have spare tires. The wheel of one of those doughnut spares would make a fine extra weight.

Spade in hand he returned to the edge of the pit and started shoveling the bubbling mud from beside Irma's torso and dumped it over her head and on the side of the body.

He continued digging to one side of the corpse and dropping the liquid earth on the other side. By the time it was obvious that progress was made, Axeworthy dripped sweat. "This is exactly the work I try to avoid," he said to his dead assistant.

He should have just thrown her into the damned sea. After all, the over-salinated waters held a reputation for mob body dumps. This time he cursed Steve Jobs for putting it in his mind that he had to be different.

He took a moment's rest, standing up straight, stretching, wiping his brow with one arm while leaning on the shovel with the other. As the thought that he should have brought water instead of Champagne, he caught sight of a set of headlights bouncing over the flat desert toward him.

"Shit," he said. "Now what?"

It was probably because of his headlights. Could be the police, but, more likely, some stoners who spotted his lights and assumed there was a party over by the mud pits.

Forgetting the fatigue he had felt shoveling the mud, he shot over to his car window and reached in to shut off the lights. He returned to the spade and redoubled his efforts of encasing the body under the pit's surface.

He allowed the occasional glance over to check the progress of the intruders. They slowed after his headlights went dark, but they still kept moving closer. But finally his efforts were paying dividends; the old hag's body slipped further into the pit's surface. Another peek over and he could now see the differences of the headlights and the running lights. They were almost here.

As he watched the approaching vehicle, Axeworthy abruptly lost footing, and his left leg slipped under the ground. He shouted in surprise as he saw he had stepped into the bubbling earth. He cursed Irma again and leaned away from the pit's edge, pulling up against the gulping mud.

With a great splooshing sound, his foot pulled free. But his shoe did not surface with it. He hiked his left sleeve higher on his arm and plunged his hand below the mud before the hole that had swallowed the Salvatore Ferragamo loafer completely disappeared. His hand immediately grasped the back of the shoe, but the terrible mud refused to release his footwear without a fight. He pulled and pulled slowly against the suction behind the shoe, adding his right hand to the fight under mud when progress was too slow. Finally the shoe popped free, spraying mud over Axeworthy's face and torso, just as the car with the headlights pulled to a stop behind him.

"Hey, dude. Whatcha doing out here?" said a voice from the van that had just pulled up and opened its doors.

Axeworthy looked back at the boiling ground to see half of Irma's head and one forearm still protruded above the surface, though both encrusted with the mud he had shoveled over them.

He looked back to the would-be party crashers, and, judging by what he saw of their shadowed expressions, they had not noticed Irma's remains.

"I was out here looking at the stars," he said, "Then my foot got stuck in the mud. I nearly lost my shoe." He held out the muddy evidence to the pair of skinny twenty-something men in what Axeworthy thought of as "Skater Gear". The taller one, the driver, was looking at the mud-covered shoe. The short one was looking down at where Axeworthy had just pulled the shoe from the ground, a mere yard from the corpse.

He needed to think fast.

"There's one," Axeworthy said, pointing up into the southwestern sky.

"What?" the tall one asked, gazing up toward where Axeworthy pointed.

More importantly the short one looked up too.

"Shooting star," Axeworthy lied.

"Cool," said the tall one.

"Shut off your lights, Paul," the short one said unprompted. "We'll be able to see them better."

Paul, the tall one, stepped to his van, reached in and doused the remaining unnatural lights before returning to his friend's side.

As their eyes adjusted to the dark, the clear sky over the Salton Sea presented the magnificence of the Universe to the three men. Billions of stars filled the once black sky.

For the next twenty minutes, the three men stood staring at the sky, the two newcomers in awe, each occasionally claiming to see their own shooting star.

Axeworthy, while impressed with night sky, tried to sneak peeks at the slowly sinking woman and wondered what he could do to rid himself of his two new "friends."

Finally the short one gave him the opportunity. "Hey man, you wanna do some 'shrooms?"

Without moving his eyes from the sky, a sly grin formed at the corner of Axeworthy's mouth. "I'm a cop," he lied again.

/ / / /

Bride pumped gas into the stolen Toyota, leaving the engine running since it could not start with the vehicle's key fob miles away. Based on road signs they were near the confusingly named Six Mile, South Carolina. Even with no sign of being followed, Bride wanted to dump the RAV4 soon in case it had GPS tracking or if someone reported it stolen.

While Dia drove, Bride asked her to explain how the signal range extender allowed them to steal the SUV.

"Key fobs for cars of this era have a limited transmitting range—roughly three feet," she said. "The doors only unlock when whoever possesses the fob is in proximity of the car. The trouble is the design is vulnerable. With a high-powered range extender set to the fob's frequency it extends the distance, the door locks open. It amplifies the signal from under a yard to over a hundred feet. The same goes for the push button ignition. Except inside the car its steel body blocks the signal.

Then the fob needs to be within ten to twenty feet. That's why this baby," she patted the RAV4's dashboard, "didn't start until those goons came out from the woods."

"I understand," Bride said, not certain if he did.

"Newer lock designs count the milliseconds the signal takes to travel from car to fob and back. If it takes too long, they won't work. The update stops range extenders like mine from doing their thing."

That he definitely didn't understand, but they had escaped, and that was most important. But where now? Dia still didn't trust Bride enough to divulge the whereabouts of the remaining nodes.

When Dia strolled out of the gas station's mini-mart toting a plastic bag of travel supplies, Bride was examining a prominent bullet hole on the stolen RAV4's hood. It might draw unwanted attention.

"Don't worry," she said. "I got something that'll fix that."

"Oh," he said.

From the bag, she pulled out a paper-thin object, squatted, and pressed it over the bullet hole. Bride examined the sticker. It read, "South Carolina Sasquatch Hunting Permit."

"You're welcome." Dia grinned and then surprised him when she stood tiptoe and kissed his cheek. Equally surprising was Bride starting an exchange of flirtatious smiles.

Dia circled to the SUV's passenger side and said, "We're going to North Myrtle Beach next. You drive."

18> Tea and Tee

THE NEAR-PICTURESQUE INFINITY POOL of the Wyndham Ocean Boulevard Resort seemed to extend out into the Atlantic. The concrete pool deck lay between towers one and two and also featured two hot tubs and some fifty-odd deck chairs. A rough dozen beautiful vacationers frolicked in the resort's amenities. A husband and wife leaned tranquilly on the rail absorbing the view of North Myrtle Beach's seemingly endless stretch of the Grand Strand, the 60 miles of continuous beach on the shores of South Carolina. Henry Bride and Dia Reynolds gazed the opposite direction, over Ocean Boulevard toward the smattering of holiday condos and hotels of the vacation destination city.

While they drove overnight, they had contacted Krystal—on Dia's insistence, via Threema—who during the course of the conversation had managed to book them into the resort by un-canceling someone's last minute change of plans. A cancelation within two weeks of a booking, she had explained, meant a forfeit of timeshare points, why not put those points to good use. Bride didn't bother asking how she had come across or accessed any of this; he knew Krystal's response. "Magicians, and nerd chicks, never reveal their secrets."

Krystal also had arranged for a tow truck to retrieve the Apollo. Bride had worried it would be gone or torched, but this morning she sent a message that, in addition to the damage he knew of, the old car had also had the rear window and one tire shot out. Fair play, Rooster. Fair play.

"That's the condo, the light blue three-story on stilts?" Bride asked the girl.

"Yup. That's the one. Top floor, there's a utility closet in the back bedroom with attic access."

Bride raised his binoculars and panned across the variety of vacation housing, from gleaning hotel towers to stilted multi-story condos to ranch bungalows built before the requirements that living space be above base flood elevation that put the newer buildings on stilts. He slowed when his sights passed over the top-floor balcony of Dia's three-story to observe a pair of heavily tattooed bikers in Harley-Davidson tee-shirts and jeans teasing a blonde girl in similar ink and similar but tighter attire. Inside the windows he could see at least four more bikers.

"This is your definition of 'cake'? Could you've picked a busier condo?" He asked. "I don't know if there'll be a time when it's empty."

"Sorry, but they didn't have a schedule available when I was last here." Her comment was wet with sarcasm.

He pulled his eyes from the binoculars and smiled at the girl. "That's fine. We'll just have to choose infiltration over cat burglary. Where can we get a motorcycle?"

"Try motorcycles. Unless you want to be the one riding bitch."

"Two motorcycles it is then."

She made a gesture for him to hand over the binoculars for which he complied. As she raised the glasses to her eyes, Bride couldn't help but to take her in while her eyes were elsewhere. Seeing as she had planned to go to Canada, she hadn't packed a swimsuit. Instead she wore a red sports bra on top and a paisley scarf tucked in to ... um ... something worn as a skirt. It wasn't a common look around here, but she didn't look out of place.

And for the first time Bride got a good look at her tattoo. It was of the style called trash polka—sharp, realistic black and white imagery with kinetic splashes of red. It was a chaotic design like most trash polka, but not as violent as some Bride had seen. It featured a depiction of a stone angel standing in front of a maze of circuitry that connected to a triangular computer chip. On the chip was the all-seeing Eye of Providence, except this version seemed to be blind as it had no iris or pupil. The red in the background was harder to decipher but it contained dripping geometric circles, the words "Black Algebra" and the moon apparently exploding. Bride tried to make sense of it all and how it related to the NSA, but then it could just be a reference to *Doctor Who*.

"Well, if we're going to pass as bikers, we'll need to do some shopping for you." She said then lowered the glasses and looked him over.

"Me?" He raised a brow.

"Yeah, you. I can pass with what I have in my bag. But if you plan on wearing those loafers on a Hog..."

"Point taken."

A cab ride and a morning of clothes shopping at Barefoot Landing and Dia proclaimed Bride's new look to be like "a right handsome member of the Sons of Democracy, but it'll do." His six-day-old whiskers helped the cause.

Barefoot Landing was also hosting many Bike Week activities including Harley-Davidson who were offering test rides and rentals. At first the man working the Harley seemed to treat Bride with disdain. Bride figured he had him pegged as a cop, most likely a narc. After they had picked their motorcycles, a Fat Bob in Vivid Black with the Twin Cam 103 engine for Bride and an Iron 883 in Olive Gold for Dia, it came time to pay for the rentals and the rep asked for I.D. Bride showed him his Homeland Security identification. From that point on the rep treated them with much more respect. Apparently Bride was his kind of cop.

Bride and Dia mounted their new rides and headed back toward their condo, Bride leading the way. He had had enough motorcycle experience from his days in the service where he and a bunkmate had a mid-'70s Hodaka 250SL that they shared as transport. This Harley's 1690cc engine was a harder beast to tame, but it wasn't long until Bride was feeling natural riding through the streets. Dia seemed to be able to hold her own as a rider as well.

Cruising down Highway 17, Dia pulled even with Bride and hand signaled for him to pull into a parking lot of a gas station whose lot was hosting one of the numerous tents selling tee shirts. This one had a banner boasting "3 for $10".

After they stopped and parked the Harleys, Bride asked, "We don't have enough new clothes?"

"We do," Dia said. "The trouble is it all looks too new. With souvenir tees at least we've an excuse for wearing new. I'll pick us out a few tee shirts. You go into the shop and get us a couple of boxes of tea bags. Lipton, preferably."

Bride thought he knew what she had in mind so obeyed without question. He gathered up the tea bags and some drinks for them now. As he was checking out he noticed Dia was talking to someone. The man was around five-foot-nine and three-hundred pounds. He wore his espresso-colored hair in what Bride thought of as a dead mohawk—a long mohawk laying down to one side rather than spiked up. He had a dark tan making him look Latino, but his features were more Caucasian. He finished paying, checked that the XD was in place on his rear hip, and rushed out the door to the racks of tee shirts under the open-sided tent. Who was this guy? Bride moved up to the other side of the rack Dia was browsing. The man, all dressed in denim and leather, was speaking to her.

"We came down from Indianapolis. This is our fifth time. Have you been to bike week before?"

"No. First time." Dia answered.

"Oh! You're going to love it," he said with a bit of arm animation.

Bride loosened his guard a bit. As he rounded the clothes rack and approached Dia. She spotted him and said, "Henry," she feigning a smile, "come and meet Boo. He was just telling me about a party tonight over on Hillside."

"Hey Henry," Boo said with a Winnie-the-Pooh-esque charm under the dead mohawk. "Dena here—"

"Dia," she corrected. Bride thought that he must have a talk with her about using real names.

"Yeah, Dena here was saying you guys had other plans, but she'd ask you if you'd rather hit this party. It's going to be stoked."

Dia was making strange excited signals with her eyes. She probably thought Bride should be able to decipher them.

"Yeah, it sounds like fun," Bride said.

Dia rolled her eyes in frustration.

Bride continued, "We'll try to make it."

"Beast," Boo said. "Hope to spot you there." Boo headed back to his waiting girlfriend, who Dia later told Bride was named Karma.

Dia threw the tee-shirts she had picked out at Bride and in a huff said, "Go pay for those."

"What?" Bride inquired.

"What the hells, man. 'Sure, it sounds like fun.'" Dia's imitation of Bride sounded like Eddie Murphy from his *White Like Me* sketch.

"That's not what I said," he protested.

"You'd blend right in if this party was at the Cleavers."

Bride wasn't going to argue any more so he went to the register to pay for the shirts.

She mumbled as he walked away still in the Murphy's white voice, "Sure, it sounds like a gee-willy fun-tastic of a swell time. Count me and the little missus in."

/ / / /

Oscar Kerns nervously sat at the antiquated Dell computer on his desk at the taxi company where he worked as a dispatcher. He opened Internet Explorer, the only browser on the old Windows XP system. He typed in four three-digit numbers separated by periods followed by a slash and the term "exit372". The browser window re-drew a simple white rectangle on a black background. Kerns pecked in the password provided to him, mopped the sweat from his brow, and pressed "return."

The window again refreshed, now showed white with a single flashing cursor. He sat for a minute waiting for anything else to happen. Finally, he typed:

```
I believe I spotted the girl you are
searching for.
```

He waited. After a half-minute the cursor dropped down a row and typed:

```
                        What makes you think it was her?
```

The new type was flush right, opposite his. Kerns stared at it, hit "return," and punched in:

```
She has the tattoo.
```

```
                                    Where was she?
```

```
A cab picked her up at the Westin
on S Ocean Blvd and took her
to the mall.
```

```
                                    When was this?
```

```
Four hours ago. I just got
thru reviewing the morning in
car cameras.
```

```
                                    Did she take a taxi back?
```

```
Not one from my company. She was
not alone.
```

```
                                    Who was with her?
```

```
A man. I have the video feed I
can send you.
```

The cursor flashed for a short time before jumping down again.

Send it to
bhgg23874dnql2@hmamail.com

Kerns took the MP4 file, opened another window, and did as instructed.

Sent. When you get the file, will
you delete the pictures? I want
this over.

Kern waited for a response, but instead the window flashed black then loaded Google's main search window.

19> "That's a Compliment"

THE HEADLIGHTS of the rented Harley-Davidsons lit up Hillside Drive as Dia and Bride, both in full biker regalia, rolled down the resort town street. Since the time they had spied the three-story building through the binoculars, the area below the building's stilts and the lot next door turned into a rolling display of two-wheeled American chrome and steel. They eased their bikes into the lot, found a couple of free spaces near to the street between a batch of Harley street cruisers and a beautiful restored late-'40s Indian Chief Roadmaster. They dismounted and each walked their bikes into the tight open spaces. The Allman Brothers' "Trouble No More" was blaring from speakers on the top-floor balcony of the condominium building. Dia peered up to the scantily leather-clad dancers on the balcony. The party was apparently in full swing. The building itself was tall for Hillside Drive, but the towers of Ocean Boulevard, one block east, dwarfed the pale blue building and consumed most of its occupants' ocean view. The main offender was the Wyndham, where earlier Dia had faux-aged their outfits with the tea, a pair of scissors, a serrated knife, and a cheese grater. After removing the sleeves of the denim jacket with the proud Harley-Davidson eagle across the back she frayed around the arms and turned it into a well worn denim vest. She then took the cheese grater to the knees and rear pocket of his new jeans. His new boots were scraped on the concrete patio to get that road worn feel. Tonight he was looking good to her. A few tats and maybe something to keep his mouth shut, and he'd be perfect.

She gazed up at the three condo units in the building she had stayed at with Ruby in what seemed a lifetime ago. If the balconies were an indication, every condo was part of one large party for the bikers visiting Myrtle Beach for the week's festivities.

"Top floor?" he asked her.

"That's the one with an attic." She replied.

"Brilliant."

They walked under the structure between the stilts to the wooden stairway where two large bikers were flanking the steps. It wasn't apparent if they were the party's bouncers or just hanging out. Dia split the difference.

"We're looking for Boo."

"Boo?" one said.

"I think he's on the second floor," the other stated.

"Cheers," Bride said as he and Dia entered the stairway.

Leading the climb up the stairs Dia asked, "Is the second floor the first condo up or the second?"

"What?"

"I mean the stilted space below the building might be considered the first floor then one level up from that would be the second. Or the space below might be the ground level and one level up is the first. Do you get what I'm saying?"

They arrived at the first condo. The open doorway revealed two guys carrying in a keg to the delight of the other partygoers. Right next to it was a sign that read, "Condo 1".

"I think we take condo one as being on the first floor." Bride said and continued up the stairs.

"That's fine as long as that's what the lug-headed gate keeper downstairs was thinking," she went on.

"If Boo's not here, then we'll go back to condo one."

"All right, but then you must admit you were wrong."

"And...?"

"And I was right." She smiled.

"How were you right?" Bride asked. "You didn't express an opinion."

"That's how clever I am. By not expressing an opinion I can be right, but I can't be wrong."

They reached the next level and entered the wide-open door of condo number two. As soon as they walked in they heard the jovial voice of Boo.

"Hey! Henry! Dena! You guys made it."

Bride motioned to Boo and whispered to Dia, "You were wrong."

Boo approached and gave Bride something that was three-quarter handshake, one-quarter hug. "Brother, it's ultra-beast that you're here." He turned to Dia. "Dena! Bring it in." For Dia, it was all hug. With the lovable bear of a man, she was content to be called "Dena", particularly after Bride's lecture about using real names.

They stayed on the second floor for a half hour while Boo told them—and whoever else would listen—stories of Bike Weeks past and offered various alcohol. Both Bride and Dia turned down the harder liquors, Bride pretending to nurse a beer for the entire time. Dia went drink-less.

When Boo excused himself to use the restroom, Bride informed him they were going to check out the other floors of the party. Done performing their party guest duties, they headed straight for the top floor. No one questioned their right to be there. Dia directed Bride to a bedroom door in the back hallway. "It's in here," She said.

Bride peeked in the door. "It's clear."

She debriefed him again. "The attic's trapdoor is in the closet ceiling. It has a cheap padlock on it that's an easy pick. The junction box you want is in the southwest corner under the insulation. Why am I not doing this again?"

"Wait here by the door." He ignored her question. "Signal me if anyone tries to get in the room."

"Signal you?" Dia said. "You want a secret knock? Three slow, two fast, two slow? Or will 'shave and a haircut' do?"

"I'll be in the attic so perhaps a text."

"Why didn't you say that then?" she said as he slipped into the bedroom.

She began by waiting by the door, but realized she had no pretext if anyone asked what she was doing. And if she was texting him—or more accurately using Threema to signal him—she didn't need to be at the door, just in eyesight. So she blended back into the party and kept her phone out to appear occupied so no one bothered her. It didn't work.

"You are beautiful. I'm 'bout t'say, I'd love to stare at your curves the whole night." A whiny male voice declared behind her.

She turned and gave her driest blank stare to a leather clad stick of a man who came up three inches short of Dia's height.

He rubbed his hand over his slicked-back blond hair, apparently taking her glare as an invitation. "They call me Cray. As in Crazy. I'm 'bout t'say, you've got the prettiest backside of anyone at this party. Maybe one of the finest I've ever seen with my own two eyes."

She sustained the blank stare for another ten seconds then went back to pretending to check her phone.

He didn't take that hint either. "That's a compliment. Tracy over there has a fine backside, I'm 'bout t'say, but it's too big for my dispositions. Yours is just right. Not all bumpy, but a padded, comfortable pillow."

He continued talking. She tried her best not to listen but had a difficult time because after she noticed Cray's "I'm 'bout t'say" speech dysfluency she couldn't unhear it. The phone wasn't working as a hint. However Cray's attention helped her blend, so she let him continue explaining the superiority of her body parts interspersed with his life story. When he wasn't looking she checked the bedroom door to ensure the coast was still clear.

"...I'm 'bout t'say, I knew this girl in one of those towns in Ohio or Kansas that ate a Quarter Pounder with Cheese in three bites..."

There was still no sign of Bride. Dia went over in her mind the steps she had told him to follow; open the junction box with the flat head, pop the right side of the board up, use a knife to break the solder around the USB port, disconnect the USB wifi card, use the snips to—"...I'm 'bout t'say, I bet you've got over-symmetrical kneecaps..."

Damn it. Where was he?

"...I got two lobes in my brain, too. One's Mexican-Muslim-American—"

"Mexican-American," a woman's voice from inside the party corrected him.

"...I'm 'bout t'say, Mexican-American and the other lobe is Atlantean."

He had Dia's attention again. She looked up. "You're from Atlantis?"

"No, silly girl. Atlanta."

"Atlanta is a country now?"

"What?"

"Move on, Cray," Dia said turning from him, "You've struck out here."

"Why you little bitch..." Cray as in Crazy boiled with anger.

"Whoa. Whoa. Calm down." She faced him again and calmly patted his chest. "I'm doing you a favor here, Cray. You're getting nowhere with me today. I'm telling you to focus your two lobes on one of the other well-formed women at this party even if she has an incorrectly sized backside. You and I, Cray, we are incompatible. You need to focus your charms on someone more..." She searched for a civil word for low intelligence.

"Compatible?" he said.

"Exactly."

She started to tend to her phone again. Astonishingly, Cray was thanking her for her advice when she noticed the bedroom door was open. Two dirty-blonde biker girls, perhaps sisters, were pulling a man by the arms into the room. The man, a large burly biker in a leather vest sporting the colors of the Knights of Freedom, put up a show of resistance.

Dia cursed and scrambled to get her phone back open. She had instinctively locked it when she let Cray down easy. Damned phone wouldn't take her thumbprint. After the fourth try it asked for her passcode. She tried to type her code, "BTb0op/7917+", but her speeding thumbs had on at least one character missed their mark. She cursed again. Dia drew in half a breath and attempted the passcode again, this time slower. The phone unlocked and Threema presented "Enter your passcode". She entered this passcode flawlessly, but cursed her paranoia anyway.

When she glanced up, the threesome were in the bedroom and one of the sisters was reaching for the door to swing it closed. Dia pecked a message on the phone as the phone and her fumbling thumbs managed to type "Dsnger" when an arm blocked the door from inside the room. It was Bride. He slipped out the door while graciously ceding the room to the trio and turning down the offer to make it four.

As Bride stepped in to the light, Dia saw he was filthy. Black dust and fiberglass coated him and his new clothes from sole to scalp, but he was carrying the node. Time to go.

Bride followed as Dia scatted down the stairs.

On the bottom stilts level, lit by a pair of floods near the stairs, a large group of bikers were on their way up. The front biker gentlemanly cleared the way for Dia. She gave him a "Thank you" and Bride nodded his appreciation. Dia snaked her way through the group out to the gravel lot. As Bride trailed, however, the ranks closed and an unseen hand snatched the circuit board from his grasp.

Startled, Bride spun to find a hairless bull terrier of a man clutching the board. An embroidered patch on a leather vest christened the man Toe. A second affiliated him with Sorrow's Horsemen. He held up the dusty piece of raw electronics high and examined it. "What have we here? And why did you steal it, Mr. Wannabe?"

Before Bride answered, Dia's voice shouted over the shoulders of the line of bikers that inserted themselves between Bride and the girl. "That's mine! Give it back!"

Dia assumed any confrontation left Bride and her defenseless. Bride held his ground, but two bikers behind him grabbed his arms and restrained him.

The larger of the two—a Hulk Hogan look-alike if not for the greasy, black hair—reached below Bride's vest and pulled the pistol from the small of his back. "The man's packin' a nine." Bride did not resist.

Toe's smooth head almost glowing from the back lighting, he spoke over the line bikers to Dia, "This is yours? I don't think so, girly. I don't think you two belong here. He—" Toe pointed at Bride, "—definitely doesn't. Pretty boy is no more a biker than I am a CEO." Turning to Bride, Toe continued, "What are you doing here, narc? And *why* have you stolen this..." Toe scrutinized the node again. "...thing?"

Bride surprised Dia by laying a few of his cards on the table. "I'm with Homeland Security and that device is a threat to—"

"Bullshit." Toe interrupted. "I think you're a narc and this has evidence or something on it." He turned to a smallish man who had apparently Single-White-Femaled Toe's look. "What do you think this is, Buff?" He Frisbee-tossed the node to the smaller man, who nearly dropped the bare circuit board.

After getting a better handle on it, Buff held the device up in to the light from the flood and inspected it. "It's a Raspberry Pi. It's a tiny, self-contained computer. You can get them from Amazon for around thirty bucks."

"Could it contain evidence for this narc?" Toe asked.

"Sure. It has an SD card though it seems to be glued in. Otherwise The Man here could've just popped that out instead of taking the whole gizmo. Or it might have been connected to microphones or cameras."

Dia slipped between the line of bikers blocking her and lunged to grab the node from Buff's hands. "That's mine, you smeghead."

Buff jumped back to avoid Dia and tossed the tiny computer across the lawn to a similarly vested biker. A game of keep-away ensued with Sorrow's Horsemen tossing the device over Dia's head across the overcast night's sky. The game ended with Dia on all fours on the rough ground and the Raspberry Pi back with Toe.

"Help her up." Toe ordered. "Narc or not, a girl shouldn't end up in the dirt." As two more of Sorrow's Horsemen helped

Dia from the ground, Toe handed the Pi to a Horseman with a patch that read "Jackal". "Take this to the campground, while we figure out what to do with our narcs."

"They're not narcs," a familiar voice said from behind the gathered crowd, "This girl helped me out. I don't think a narc would do that for me. Plus, I'm 'bout t'say, she's too pretty to be a narc."

"Cray, stay out off this," a woman's voice said. "This ain't your concern."

"All right then," Toe said turning back to Bride, "What is that gizmo, narc?"

Bride sighed. "As I was saying, I'm with Homeland Security and that device contains information that helps disseminate top secret national security information that, if released, would help our country's enemies. It was placed in this condo months ago by a person with nothing to do with bikers or anybody at this party."

The crowd waited as Toe considered the little computer in Jackal's hands before he looked back to Bride and said, "Bullshit." Back to Jackal, "Take that away and hide it."

The crowd split and let Jackal through like Moses at the Red Sea. After the crowd re-circled but had yet to refocus, before attention returned to him, Bride crossed his arms over his chest, grabbed the wrists of his captors, and burst forward, dragging them to the ground. The two oafs tumbled over the ground in Bride's wake. With his shoulder lowered, Bride prepared to play red rover with the line of partygoers on the street side of the crowd. Seeing Bride charge the group, all but one moved to the side leaving a stunned but solid member of Sorrow's Horsemen in Bride's path. The concrete block of a biker braced himself for the blow, but at the last second, Bride went low and rolled through an impressive set of cankles. The biker's face slammed hard in to the gravel. Bride rolled right back up to his feet and tore down the street after Jackal.

Dia, feeling vulnerable, attempted to blend back in to the crowd, when she heard a deep voice whisper in her ear, "I know who you are, Dia Reynolds." She pivoted to look, but could not figure out who had whispered. She nearly jumped when she felt a hand take her wrist and pull her back.

"Come on, beautiful. I'm 'bout t'say, we need to get you out of here."

20> Cray—as in Crazy

DIA SPUN TO FIND her shiny-armored knight was none other than Cray—as in Crazy. The indelible Cray led her through the shadowy yard to a line of motorcycles. The pair came to a flame-red three-wheeler with its wide dune buggy wheels on the back end. Cray mounted the contraption, turned a key to fire up the raucous engine and beckoned Dia, "Get on."

Not sure why, Dia straddled the seat behind him.

As they pulled out onto the dark street, they saw Bride under a streetlight a block or so down. He was acting as matador as Jackal toyed with Bride by riding fast back and forth dangling the Raspberry Pi out as a taunt as he sped past. Bride was receiving no luck grabbing the node out of the biker's grasp. The scene paralleled a bully taunting nerd over a pocket calculator.

Except, Dia thought, Henry Bride was doing this for her. It was her calculator.

"That your boyfriend?" Cray asked Dia, shouting over the continuous rumble of the Harley-Volkswagen amalgamation's motor.

For an instant, Dia wasn't sure what to say, watching Bride again lunge to snatch the little computer. Again he failed.

"For all practical purposes."

"I get it," Cray said.

Jackal grinned widely when he noticed Cray and Dia sauntering toward him. He stopped his Harley a half block beyond Bride. Cray passed Bride and pulled his amalgam alongside but facing opposite to Jackal's fat-tired street hog.

"All right, Jackal, give the girl the thingy. I'm 'bout t'say, this isn't funny any more."

Jackal laughed, tucked the resin-covered Pi in to his vest, and said, "Tell you what, Cray. You catch me, you can have it." With that, Jackal gunned his Harley and squeezed the fat rear tire as he tore off down the street, barely swerving to miss a dodging Bride before turning west.

Cray looked back to Dia and said, "Hang on tight, sweet bottom." Cray turned the ape-hanger handlebars full to the right side and cranked the throttle handle all the way forward. The broad track tires wailed against the asphalt and vomited rocks and smoke as the trike rotated in place until it had carried out a complete 180-degree turn. With a lurch the twin rear tires gripped the pavement and shot Cray, Dia, and the trike forward like a missile. Despite the tall seat back behind her Dia clung to Cray's thin torso as tightly as she could. Before she knew it, they had shot past Bride and turned to follow Jackal down the side street. They arrived at the ninety-degree turn just in time to see Jackal winding through the road's next curve past a wooden railing. The trike's gears kicked again, and it again propelled them faster down the residential drive. The municipal road narrowed after the turn and the trike was forced onto the dirt to dodge an oncoming car. They continued to follow Jackal around winding corners and through the back streets lined with North Myrtle Beach's vacation condos. Then they found themselves behind the glass and concrete towers of the shore's main drag. Finally they turned south on South Ocean Boulevard where heavier traffic crept under the glow of the hotel signs.

Once out on the four-lane boulevard, Jackal held a decided advantage as his two-wheeled cycle cut between the slow-moving cars leisurely cruising by the Atlantic. As luck would have it, the boulevard's late-hour traffic thinned enough for Cray to illegally pass the vacationers' automobiles in the oncoming lanes, so they didn't surrender too much distance. It didn't sit well with Dia when they barreled head on toward a large

SUV with an inner tube tied to its roof. She tightly closed her eyes, braced for impact, and again reassessed the sanity of riding two up with a stranger named Cray, as in Crazy. With the SUV's horn blaring, Dia sensed the trike's wide track tires kick back to the right.

With one eye re-opened, Dia discovered that while back on the correct side of the roadway, Cray had squeezed the trike within inches of a hatchback to the front and a family sedan behind them. The instant a break presented in northbound traffic, Cray swung out into the oncoming lanes again and gunned the thundering three-wheeled beast.

"Cray," she yelled over his shoulder, "It's more important I stay alive than we get that gizmo. Can we not play chicken with the tourists?"

"Don't fret, beautiful," the diminutive biker shouted back, "I won't let anything happen to you. I'm 'bout t'say, we'll catch him for certain." He removed one hand from the high-rise handlebars and patted the gas tank. "This baby's sporting the power plant from a 1962 Chevy Greenbriar pickup truck. He ain't getting away."

"Two hands!" she shouted. "Two hands on the bars."

He laughed, placing his hand back on the handlebars' grip. "Ain't you precious."

Dia spotted Jackal's Harley ahead. Apparently he wanted to toy with them further so had slowed enough for the pair on the trike to catch up. When Jackal peered back and saw the Crazy train gaining ground he cut across the road to the left. A startled father in a minivan was forced to grind its ABS brakes to a stop to avoid the motorcycle when it sliced through the oncoming traffic. Then the Harley disappeared between two of the high-rise beachfront hotels.

"Why is he pulling in to a parking lot?" Dia asked.

"I know where he's going. I hope you brought your bikini, I'm 'bout t'say, we're going to the beach."

Cray was right. Jackal had crossed through an unlit sand-covered parking lot. He rode between a pair of metal poles where a chain or cable barrier should have hung, past the rolling dunes, and straight out onto the beach.

/ / / /

Henry Bride walked alone in the street from where he tried chasing Jackal, Dia, and the man on the trike. A few taunters who had laughed at him when Jackal played his game of keep-away still sat on the side of the street.

"You better not think about going back to the party, narc," one taunter yelled.

"You'll get your ass kicked for sure," called another.

But for the most part the crowd near the condo ignored him. As he headed back toward the party, he found a group of women had taken over the second level balcony and took turns flashing their breasts at the crowds below. Each met with a thunderous applause and the one on the balcony encouraged the crowd and scored the levels of the cheers to decide who had the best breasts. As he got closer, he noticed that man was Boo, the biker who had invited them to the party.

The distraction proved ideal for Bride. It would allow him to get to his Harley. As he approached the corner of the open lot where he had parked he could swear Boo looked at him and bowed. Bride returned a small acknowledging salute. He was ready to slip out peacefully until he spotted that member of Sorrow's Horsemen who some might say resembled Hulk Hogan with black hair. The thug was alone and headed toward the back of the property. Spotting a Springfield XD Mod.2 tucked in the biker's belt, Bride increased his pace, quietly pursuing until close enough to make his move. Once directly behind, he wrapped his left arm around the man's thick neck. With his right he gripped the pistol, slid his finger on the trigger, and angled the barrel so it buried itself between the man's butt cheeks.

"You took my gun," Bride said into the large man's ear. "I'd like to take it back quietly, but if you'd prefer to make a fuss, this gun here might join in and be louder. Now I'm sure that would bring your entire gang down on me. But the angle my gun is at, they'll be picking up the parts from where your ass blew out of your genitals onto the dirt."

"Shit, brother," the trembling man said. "Take it. Just take the gun. I don't need it that bad."

"Perfect, your best bet is to rejoin the party and pretend this never happened."

"I'm cool with that." The man shook. "Nothing happened."

Bride let the biker go. He didn't trust him, but as long as he said nothing in the next thirty seconds, time for Bride to get to his Harley and ride away, it would be fine.

When dark Hulk Hogan reached the underside of the condo, Bride went for his bike. He was disappointed that Dia's Harley was still there; he should have insisted on one bike; now they'll have to come back for it later. But the immediate worry, where was Dia? Based on the sounds he heard walking back he guessed they ended up on South Ocean Boulevard. Those sounds, however, might be any of the thousands of motorcycles gathered in Myrtle Beach for Bike Week. He started up his Harley Fat Bob and decided that was the best place to start.

As he pulled off of Hillside Drive someone threw a beer bottle toward him and yelled, "Don't come back, narc!"

Good riddance, he thought.

When he rolled on to Ocean, he saw nothing. No sign of Dia. No sign of Jackal. No sign of that custom-built trike. He didn't imagine it would be easy, but he also didn't know where to go from here. At that moment at the next intersection a teenager in only a swimsuit and sandals ran across the street against the lights, nearly getting hit by a taxi. Two seconds later, three more teens sprinted across the boulevard with no regard for their safety. Five more kids on the shoulder of Ocean anxiously awaited a break in traffic to make the run. When the next one bolted Bride followed his path. He cut through between the hotels and headed toward the beach. He observed the kid climb over the sand dunes and toward some kind of lights moving around beyond the dunes. Something was happening on the beach.

After the next ocean-side building Bride turned his bike seaward, jumped the curb, and rode on a walking path that led to the beach. As he passed by the hotels, the night grew darker. Unlike the streets, there were nearly no artificial lights on the beach. He switched the headlight to high beams and lit up the wooden stairs that led to a raised walkway over the dunes. Bride stood on the foot pegs and pulled up on the handlebars to coax the motorcycle into climbing the weathered wooden steps.

Once up on the raised walkway he recognized what the fuss was. Two cycles, one a straight Harley and one a three-wheeler, raced through the night across the dark sand at the ocean's edge. Crowds gathered on the walkways and balconies up and down the ocean to watch the nighttime excitement on the beach. The two headlights glistened on the wet sand as they approached from the north. Judging by the trails they illuminated, this wasn't their first time over this stretch of beach.

Bride tried to time his move. He waited. When the lead cycle was a couple of buildings away, he set his Harley forward and rode the bounces of the stairway down. He had hoped to come out ahead or at least even with the front cycle, but his rear wheel spun in the loose sand at the bottom of the steps. Now he was behind the leader but ahead of the trike. With the throttle full open, sand spat out rearward. Finally, the tire gripped in to solid footing. He accelerated on to the beach, but before he got up to speed, the trike blew past. He looked over at the tiny man hanging from the handle bars of the massive bike. The trike's diminutive driver didn't pay heed but clinging tightly to the rider's back, Dia gave Bride a look. He couldn't decide if it was grin or grimace.

As the tires reached on the hard wet sand, the bike sped forward and kept pace with the two cycles ahead. Bride watched the front bike and the trike weave down the beach. *Try to keep as straight of a line as possible*, Bride thought. This plan was slowly working; he gained ground until his front wheel dropped into a rut caused by one of the vehicles ahead. The wheel pulled toward the breaking surf and as Bride steered out of the track the wheel dug deeper into the sand. The Harley nearly went over, but Bride turned the other way into the rut. The front wheel crossed and jumped out of the rut, but the rear wheel didn't seem to want to follow. He cut the front wheel back to the right. With his left boot planted in the sand, the bike drifted sideways. The rear wheel spat sand again and the front cut trough a crashing wave. He pushed up with his leg and let the bike pull itself back upright as now both wheels split the three-inch-deep ocean water. The Harley was back up, but he had lost more distance to the two cycles. He wondered if he could ever catch up.

From his trailing position Bride saw the trike pull even and its rider attempted to kick at the other man's bike. The short legs barely extended past the trike's wide wheels, but with each kick the motorcyclist weaved right and the trike followed him over. With the motorcycle being nudged over toward the looser sand, the biker took a chance and slid his bike sideways and then jumping it back up turned around. Now its headlight headed straight toward Bride.

This was his chance, but he had to act quickly. Before the other motorcycle sped past, Bride duplicated the other rider's maneuver, power sliding to a near stop then kicking the bike back up and reversing direction. His timing was better this time. He ended shore side, ahead of the other cycle, but by the time he was up to speed he ran neck and neck with the other rider. As he expected, it was Jackal. The Sorrow's Horseman looked to Bride and flashed a wide, mischievous smile.

The two Harleys raced back up the beach. Each one tried to keep top speed until the beach got too rough from either the surf or the earlier tracks in the sand. Jackal was the superior rider, cutting over the bumpy areas of beach with more grace and speed than Bride. By the time they arrived back to where Bride had joined the chase Jackal had pulled ahead. This was much to the delight of the gathered crowd on the beach who waved towels and tee shirts as the bikes flew by. Bride's best hope seemed to be just don't lose him. But the Grand Strand stretched sixty miles, and he had no idea how much was left. The long race up the beach was taking its toll on Bride's body. His arms and legs burned like after a workout at the gym. He was exhausted and beaten about the backside. His mind wondered how long they could go with Jackal having pulled ahead by about ten lengths. Instinctively, Bride looked to his speedometer—112MPH. This was insane, but he couldn't let Jackal disappear with the node. Waved on by more onlookers Bride bore down and gave the throttle another twist.

Over the next set of bumps in the beach, Bride just prayed, kept the throttle full, swore repeatedly, and barely kept the Harley upright. He had to catch his breath after the risky maneuver, but he'd gained about four lengths on Jackal, who now cut his cycle in precariously to the waves. Bride kept just shore-side of Jackal's path. This section of beach seemed to be darker. The lights of North Myrtle Beach shrank in his rearview—the headlight of the trike had fallen well back. Bride now fully relied on the two motorcycles' headlights and the dim glow of the three-quarter moon that penetrated the covering of clouds.

Suddenly a pier in front of them with its thick trunks jotting down into the sand came into view. Not knowing what the pylons would do to the sand beneath Bride decided he needed to play this safe; he slowed his bike rather than crash into two-foot thick round timbers. Jackal kept his throttle open, looking back over his shoulder apparently to confirm what his rear-view mirror told him. He was laughing. Bride almost believed he could recognize the cackle he remembered from back on the street. Jackal shot through the pier's pylons without slowing. Bride swore again; the man was getting away.

But timed right with Bride's thought of defeat, Jackal's front tire dug in to a patch of loose sand and pounds of steel went tumbling. The Harley spun end over end, smashing hard into a pylon. The bike shattered, and the pylon splintered at the point of impact, but what happened to Jackal? Bride stopped his Harley just short of the pier, dismounted, and ran under the pier to find the man he was chasing. Bride's immediate concern was Jackal's well being after the man viciously crashing his motorcycle at speeds at times in excess of 100 miles per hour.

When Bride stepped through to the far side, and the trike pulled up and parked near his bike. Had he killed this man? But his thoughts were broken when he heard that same laugh— albeit with an obvious pained strain. He ran toward the cackle and found Jackal lying on his back cringing and laughing.

"That shit was wicked awesome." Jackal said.

"Are you all right?" Bride asked.

"Hell no. My leg is broken to all fuck, but I'll live to ride again." He laughed again.

Dia and the trike's driver ran up to where Bride knelt over Jackal.

"Wow," Dia said. "I can't believe he's not dead."

Bride looked up to her and read the concern on her face. She turned her head to Bride and gave him a hint of a smile.

The trike's driver spoke. "C'mon Jackal, I'm 'bout t'say, a deal's a deal. Give her back her dingus."

"Henry, this is my friend Cray." Dia said, "As in Crazy."

21> **"I Can't"**

IN THE STILL-DARK MORNING Dia and Bride
returned to their North Myrtle Beach condo. After locking and
barring the front entrance, Bride excused himself. He was
exhausted, and he needed a shower to wash the embedded
sand, salt, and microscopic shards of fiberglass from his
pores. After the night's events, he didn't relish leaving Dia
alone again. Cray had been remarkably understanding
when they retook the "dingus" and left him to wait for an
ambulance with Jackal. To Jackal, the whole ordeal was a
game. He laughed in pain and recounted various events
of the chase. He didn't act distressed about his shattered
leg. Bride and Dia retrieved her 883 from the dwindling
party without incident, but she appeared flustered by the
evening's events. The prolonged chase had drained her as
much as Bride. He wasn't sure what changed, perhaps she
was merely tired, but she seemed vulnerable. Or perhaps she
was affected by him leaving her alone to chase Jackal and
the node. He yearned to sit with her and hold her and make
certain she was all right, but he was outright filthy. Besides,
he thought, his bedroom and bath were at the front of the
suite. And with the replacement Master Lock security bar
wedging the front door hard shut and tape over the peep hole,
potential intruders would find it significantly difficult to gain
entry. Bride should be suitably warned should anyone make
a serious entry attempt. Plus, Dia also expressed a desire to
bathe and retreated to the master bedroom. The Jacuzzi in

the bedroom would presumably occupy her for near an hour, then she would retire to bed.

Bride took twenty minutes to clean the XD Mod.2 first. As filthy as he was, the salt and sand wouldn't hurt him as much as it would gunmetal. Afterward in his bathroom, Bride stripped off the dirty, itchy biker clothes and headed for the shower. With the doors to the bedroom and the shared area left open so he could keep an eye out, he entered the broad, glass-doored shower. Impulsively, he carried the firearm in with him and set it on the soap holder. An instructor taught Bride early in his career if there was any potential danger, then "shitter, shower, or bed, the gun stays with you. A little water won't hurt it."

A quarter hour of scrubbing and he no longer felt the fiberglass cutting. At that point he indulged himself under the shower's scorching stream. After five minutes of hot bliss, he realized he was not alone. He could see the outline of a person through the steamed glass. He reached for his gun and swung the fogged door open. In the center of the bathroom, standing nude with an impish smile, was Dia.

"I wanted to thank you for helping me," she purred.

He left the gun in the shelf in the shower. No need to frighten the girl.

After a silent pause in time, a likewise nude, dripping-wet Bride stepped from the stall and inhaled deep through his nose. He needed extra energy to say what he was about to say, but with the breath came in her luscious scent.

"I'm sorry, Dia. I can't." He regretted the words before they escaped his mouth. "As much as I'd love to and as much as I'll dream of what could've been tonight, it would compromise my protecting you. It would void my security clearance and end my career."

With only the sound of water dripping on tile and the distant, constant drone of the Atlantic's waves, the potential lovers stood naked for a moment with no foreseeable end. She was beautiful and intriguing, but Bride dare not gaze beyond her soulful eyes. If he dared to adventure past them, he might just throw away his career in the Department of Homeland Security, if he hadn't already. If his eyes wandered to her body, he risked them falling into each other's arms. Did he possess the willpower to resist the touch of her smooth, well-tanned skin? As their gaze remained locked, tears welled in those beautiful eyes. "You don't want me?"

Half his mind struggled for an answer. The other half already had his tongue exploring the soft contours where her side met her pert, young breast. His hand—the hand that just held his gun—journeyed the situate skin from the thin, yet powerful thigh to the tantalizing hip and around to the well-domed bottom. Each stop along the way a contrast of delicate and vigorous.

"Dia, that's not it at all," he said, the logical side of his brain narrowly winning the moment from the easily obtainable fantasy. "You're burned. I can only help you as long as I can plausibly say I'm doing it for national security. If we..." he paused to find a polite phrase, "...get involved then my motivations would clearly be to help a fugitive—a possible traitor. That's why I couldn't help you flee to Canada. It's in your best interests that I help you defuse your situation. At some point, I'll need my clearance to help you."

"What happens when my interests and America's interest no longer align? What happens to me then?" she asked, her words at conflict with the sight of her naked, sexual heat.

"I don't know. I haven't thought about it. But I don't think that will happen, at least until someone gets the password to your file."

Realization of the significance of the last phrase swept over Dia's face. She tilted her head to the floor and weighed its implications. Bride mistakenly exploited the moment for a full visual exploration of Dia's glory. A second tattoo caught his eye first, a white diamond over a red slash on exhibit off center, just below her belt line. A silver dongle of jewelry swung in the folds of her bare womanhood. But her natural beauty was what most excited him, her subtle curves hour-glassing between her small but round breasts and those dangerous hips that broaden her frame just enough. She was exquisite. He fought off the fantasy to try to hide his attraction before she looked up.

But she didn't look up. With tears streaming over her cheeks, Dia turned and bolted from the room. Bride nearly chased after her, but she had turned left, she hadn't run from the condo. Instead Bride entered his own bedroom and quickly dressed, donning a clean pair of Levi's and a plain white, fitted tee-shirt. After he fixed his still wet hair with his fingers, he headed through the condo's main room to Dia's door. Knocking lightly he called to her, "Dia?"

No answer.

He knocked again before trying the door. It was unlocked, but Dia wasn't inside. Neither was she in her bath area, which was open to the bedroom except the private commode. He stopped. There was movement outside on the balcony. He peaked through the curtains. She was leaning against the rail, staring blankly out to the pre-dawn Atlantic sky wearing only his extra "Bike Week" tee. He passed through the main room and out the sliding glass door to a small concrete balcony that cleverly gave every condo in the tower an ocean view.

Without facing him she said, "I'm an idiot."

"I wouldn't say that," Bride said. Then, "Unless you're talking about the view you're giving everyone on the lower floors and pool deck."

It took a second for it to register what he meant. Then it dawned on her. She quickly tucked the front of the tee between her legs and stepped away from the balcony's edge. As she did so, the plate-glass window behind her cracked into a million connected cubes centering on a new hole about four feet off the floor. A fraction of a second later, the distant pop of rifle fire caught up to the bullet that had bored the hole through the glass. From Dia's perspective the scene must have been chaos, but Henry Bride instantly recognized the danger. Prior to the second shot plunging in to the concrete behind Dia, Bride commanded, "Inside now!" Tiny chunks of concrete flew from the wall as he grabbed her by the arm and yanked her through the open doorway. He dove to the floor and pulled her on top of him.

He rolled over atop of Dia and kicked the floor lamp—the only light on in the room—breaking its bulb as it hit the wall. His right hand went to his belt for his gun. It wasn't there. He cursed. The XD was in the shower, idiot, on the opposite end of the suite. But the front of the condo presented a second problem. A banging and rattling resounded from the front door; someone was attempting to break through. "Stay down. Get to the kitchen," he ordered as he regained his feet and ran toward the front. There's no way they were getting through the front door with the heavy-duty jam installed.

But before he reached the front hall, a crash of glass came from inside the front bedroom. It made sense. The condos' rear balconies were private and disconnected, but the fronts opened to a shared balcony that doubled as the hallway to the elevator and stairs. And the front bedroom's window was right next to the door on the front balcony. A second crash of glass told Bride the front window's glass wasn't so easy to shatter. He forewent the gun for time's sake and entered the bedroom. The curtains hung closed as he left them, but small shards of glass sprinkled the floor and his feet were bare. As he entered the bedroom, a bulk came through the window and was fighting through the curtains.

He regretted not retrieving the gun more as the expanding hump in the curtains grew. So much always keeping your gun with you.

The rustling curtain begot a behemoth in black fatigues and a leather jacket. The intruder was six foot six or more of that Brian Dennehey kind of solid. An over taut nylon stocking over his medicine ball head failed to hide the ugly, scarred bull terrier of a face beneath it. One cinder-block fist gripped a dented aluminum bat halfway up the handle. The giant quickly closed ground on Bride and wound back the bat to prepare for the assault. *Should have gone for the gun.* With nothing else to defend himself, Bride yanked the top drawer from the dresser behind him. Pillowcases dropped to the floor from inside as he clutched the wooden box high as a shield. The brute's bat came down hard and struck the drawer. The wooden drawer rang like a drum and its wood dented. But the structure held. Let's hear it for hotel-grade furniture. The next swing came knee-level, but Bride once again positioned the container in its path. The drawer held but for how long. As well as it performed defending, a simple wooden box doesn't make a good offensive weapon. To add to Bride's troubles, a second intruder—this one thankfully smaller—climbed in through the window. This second man, also in black, reminded Bride of a pre-Mellencamp Johnny Cougar with a whiplash sneer. This one hadn't bothered with the stocking, but was wearing Chuck Taylor High Tops, one red and one white.

With his attention on the new man and his odd footwear, Bride nearly missed the immediate threat. The giant's muscles ballooned as he reared back for another high attack, but as the bat came down toward him Bride caught the glint of aluminum. He dropped to a squat and jabbed the drawer over his head to deflect the oncoming blow. This time the wood cracked with a rapid and deafening burst of snaps. He saved himself again and detected an opportunity to counter. Fortunate timing too, the drawer had little structure remaining. The agent spun on one foot, extended the other, and swept the leading leg of the oversized attacker. It was like kicking down a tree. Bride's leg stopped dead against brute's. The maneuver accomplished little but to tap the giant slightly off kilter. Not the outcome he hoped for, but it was enough of a win for Bride to stay on offense. Replanting his foot, he pushed up and forward, the battered drawer leading the way, into the shaken stance of the brute. Further staggered, the brute stepped backwards in to the path of the newcomer who tumbled over and then behind the bed, the multi-colored shoes sticking up from behind. But the big man stayed on his feet.

"Hey! Watch yourself, Rock," the little man shouted at his partner. "I'm trying to help you out."

Bride kept pushing, but the man called Rock was now square and would not budge any further.

"Damn," Bride said. "The bigger they are; the harder they are to knock down."

Rock dropped the bat behind him and clutched his huge hands around the sides of Bride's drawer. The brute thrust the wooden box down on Bride in a lop-sided test of vigor. Bride tried to stay between the intruders and Dia, but at this rate these bastards soon will step over his beaten body. *Go for the gun.* Rather than foolishly trying to hold against Rock crushing downward, Bride released the drawer and scrambled from below the combined weight and strength of the attacking brute. It nearly worked. Rock came crashing down with the wooden drawer on to the floor. The box disintegrated in to a pile of splinters, ending its valiant I-think-I-can effort. But Bride's foot hadn't cleared. An edge of the remainder of the drawer, *his* drawer, caught his Achilles tendon. A bolt of pain shot up his leg, and Bride landed flat on the floor, barely leading Rock's splayed body and the kindling remains of the drawer. Bride's surprise maneuver finally felled the giant. For the negatives, Rock now lay atop of Bride's legs, and the lesser interloper, with bat in hand, was climbing over the bed toward them. Bride tried to churn his legs, striving to scramble from beneath the giant, but the injured leg would not cooperate. Instead his arms fought to drag him forward across the carpeted floor.

After an eternity of a second, the uninjured leg popped free. Without hesitation Bride crushed his free bare heel in to Rock's left eye socket. Something crunched.

Rock swore—loudly and repeatedly. The brute's gargantuan hands grasped the damaged eye as he rolled off Bride. The lame leg free, Bride clambered to his hands and knees. He was out from under the boulder of a man named Rock, but he lost track of Rock's partner, who Bride had mentally dubbed "Roll".

Roll appeared again, coming over top of his downed partner, bat clenched two-handed over his head. Bride dove back to the floor with what might his legs could muster but not quick

enough to avoid the vicious downswing. It was not far enough.
The strike landed square on Bride's spine. Bride screamed. The
hit stung like a spike to the nerve, but was less deadly than the
head blow Roll had aimed for. Instinctively Bride crawled from
the new attacker. Roll stepped the red shoe over his partner
and prepared to continue the beating. But Bride had one thing
going for him: the pain in his back replaced the pain in his leg,
and the new pain didn't hinder his motion. When Roll stepped
over him for another swing. Bride turned over to fight, tangling
his legs with Roll's as he did, and he was in position to take
down the aggressor. His strong leg hooked around the tops
of Roll's high tops. A quick sweep pulled Roll off his feet and
sent him falling atop his rising partner. Rock rose from the
floor, his massive body seemingly expanding from the ground
as he stood. His smaller partner tumbled heels-over-head off
the giant's back, but Rock took no notice.

"Now I'm going to kill you, little man." Rock said to Bride,
his left eye shut and bleeding.

"What were you planning to do before?"

The question appeared to confuse the giant, and the
momentary lapse gave Bride time to get to his feet and hobble
to the bathroom door. Bride entered the washroom ahead of
Rock. But the giant lumbered in behind, caught up, and grabbed
Bride's neck and the waist of his jeans. The brute effortlessly
lifted Bride off the tile like a sack of potatoes. He reared Bride
back and tossed him across the bathroom headlong toward the
glass wall of the shower. Bride had only enough time to contort
so his shoulder, rather than his head, connected with the glass
first. He hit the safety glass hard with a thud and bounced off,
splatting onto the marble tile floor. Amazingly, for a partial
second the glass held. But with a tick then a crash, the glass
wall exploded in to thousands of sparkly cubes, showering
Bride in the tiny diced glass pieces.

He looked to Rock to watch for the one-eyed brute's next
move, but Rock's eye wasn't on Bride. It focused on the shower—
and the gun. Bride turned to see the XD mod.2 sitting on the

shampoo shelf where he had left it. Both recognized the need to get to the gun first. Bride had about a third of the distance, but was barefoot in a puddle of glass cubes. Rock's advantages were being upright and wearing heavy-duty boots. At the same instant, both men started toward the gun. Bride could barely move at all as his arms and legs, which battled to propel him, mostly shifted about the tiny glass pieces. Rock strode forward and closed half the distance before Bride moved an inch. His feet sacrificed to the glass, Bride placed the ball of his feet on a layer of glass. He stretched himself to grab a towel from the rack and throw it over the floor in front of him. Now he could get traction, but Rock caught up with momentum. Bride stood, but Rock was already reaching for the weapon. Before the giant could grab the gun, however, Rock's traction failed as his back boot slid rearward on the granules of glass. Bride thought he could hear the giant's groin tear as the tree trunk legs went in to an unnatural split.

Damn the towel. Bride had a better, clearer path to the gun. Bride grabbed the giant's shirt and pulled himself atop the downed man. He rolled his body over the big man's back, Rock letting out a roaring scream as Bride's weight forced a deeper split. Bride spun off in to a stand, nabbed the gun, and cocked the slide, more for effect than to load the chamber.

Supported in the corner of the shower with the 9mm's barrel pressed against the nape of Rock's neck, Bride barked, "Out!"

The giant tried to crawl back and away when a gun shot rang from the other room followed by Roll swearing, "Watch it, you crazy bitch!"

Dia was in trouble, but, for now, holding her own.

"Go!" Bride ordered Rock who slowly, painfully stood, raised his hands, and backed out. "Run!" That command sunk into the big thug's thick skull and he twisted and painfully thundered back through the bedroom.

From the bedroom door Bride saw Rock squeeze out the shattered window he'd entered. He had to trust that the big man wouldn't return. He sprinted through the condo's common area to find a standoff in Dia's bedroom, Dia taking cover in the hot tub, Roll hiding behind the bed.

Bride knew time was short. If they hadn't been already, once Dia fired that gun, the police would be on their way. Once he needed to talk to anyone official, his plans would fall in to a bureaucratic quagmire. He and Dia needed to get out fast, but first Roll had to go. He'd love to interrogate the intruder, but there was no time. With a step halfway into the room, Bride aimed the 9mm at Roll and said, "I let your partner live. If you'd like the same courtesy drop whatever weapon you have and go now."

Roll seemed to contemplate the offer before he said, "If I stand up, the bitch will shoot me."

"That's true. I will." Dia said, her voice echoing from the hot tub.

"D..." Bride stopped himself before he said her name, nearly making the same mistake that Roll had with his partner. "Don't shoot him unless he passes the door, all right?"

"Why?" She asked.

"I'm not cleaning up another body." The word "another" was for Roll's benefit, to let him infer that at least one of these two had already been killed.

"Fair play," Dia said. "He can go. One toe past the door—or if he calls me 'bitch' again—and he gets a new hole."

"That a deal, fella?" Bride asked.

"Yeah. I'm in." Roll answered before he took a deep breath and bolted for the door where Bride stood.

Bride backed off and let Roll pass. The final trespasser darted for the front door but failed to notice the jam, so the door would not open.

"Out the way you came in," Bride ordered.

Roll doubled back, moving the mismatched Converses at an impressive speed, and scurried out the front bedroom's window.

After Bride made sure the condo was clear, Dia came in to the common area, still carrying Grits' pistol. "They gone?" she asked.

"Yeah. They've left the condo."

"He tried to take the node."

"What?"

"Yeah, I was hiding in the tub. And the punk didn't see me, and he started to go through my bag on the nightstand. He pulled out the node and said, 'This'll have to do.' That's when I shot at him and he dropped the node and jumped behind the bed. Do you think he wasn't, maybe ... he wasn't trying to kill me?"

"Not sure. They didn't bring in guns, but maybe..." He stopped not sure what the intruders plans were. "Get your stuff together. We need to leave. There's no telling where these guys are outside. So we need to go as soon as the police arrive at the resort, but before they get up here."

"Why wait for the police?"

"They'll drive away our unwelcome guests and hopefully the snipers," he said.

"There's more than one sniper?"

"We have to assume so."

/ / / /

"I don't recollect what happened to her after that, I'm 'bout t'say, but I do know that woman was supposed to be the love of my life. That boyfriend of hers sure is lucky," Cray told the government agent.

"Boyfriend?" Liptmann asked, using his notebook to help shield his eyes from North Myrtle Beach's undiluted sunlight.

"Yeah, a right handsome dude, I'm 'bout t'say, if that's your type. Not that I'm implying anything about your sexual references. But I'm not blaming the girl. My friend, Boots, she said this fed was smokin' hot. Otherwise, we would probably have hooked up, me and the twinkie. I could tell she would've gone off the rails on the Crazy train, I'm 'bout t'say."

"The 'boyfriend' was a federal agent?" This confused Liptmann, but he tried to pick the pertinent information from the biker's ramblings.

"The guy said so after Toe snatched his doo-ma-thingy pie. I'm 'bout t'say, he said the thing had lasers or something that was going to stop a huge computer attack on the national secret-y.

Then Toe tossed the thingy around to his boys, The Sorrow's Horsemen, and Jackal took it on his Hog. That's when me, the sweet honey, and my trike ended up moto-chasing Jackal out on the beach. And we about caught Jackal when, I'm 'bout t'say, he hit that peer full speed and tumbled all over the sand. Then the Betty and her beau snatched back their thingy, and I stayed here and made sure Jackal didn't count worms or nothing. It reminded me of that movie with that guy from *Wings*, the one with the airplane. I'm 'bout t'say, that was the third funniest movie I'd ever seen in the theater. Not as funny as—"

"Thank you, Mister Crayton," Liptmann interrupted.

"I'm 'bout t'say, I told you, Mister Lips man, you can call me Cray, everybody does. Even my Momma calls me Cray, except at Nana's house. At Nana's everyone calls me Horrace."

"Yes, well, thank you, er…" Liptmann refused to call the man "Cray" so he let the statement stand. "I'll get back to you if I have any more questions."

Liptmann walked back up the peer toward his car. Horace Crayton's story fit with the little information the other witnesses recalled. The story matched the account of Jackson Lawrence, AKA Jackal, given to Liptmann in the biker's hospital room. Both men claimed the unknown individual with Dia Reynolds was a federal agent. The question was who? He obtained digital footage from the Wyndham's front desk security cameras. Liptmann now had his forensic team coming in to examine the Wyndham condo that had taken so much damage. Hopefully the local police did not contaminate the scene.

He stopped on the wooden steps leading from the fishing pier to use his phone.

It took one ring for the line to be answered. "Franco."

"William, it's Robert. Subject one was here in Myrtle Beach and she may have had a federal agent with her. Can you quietly put out feelers? Maybe another agency has recruited Dia Reynolds to their payroll. Or perhaps someone's one step ahead of us. I have video footage. I've sent it to you. Try to discover who this 'agent' is."

"Will do," Franco said. "Are you coming back home?"

"Not yet. I need to track where they fled from here. I'm checking the local airports next."

"Let me know if you—"

A voice coming from behind Liptmann drowned out the phone's speaker.

"Mister Lips man. Mister Lips man."

Liptmann turned to see Horrace Crayton running toward him.

"Yes, Mister Cray..."

"I just remembered something I didn't tell you earlier, I'm 'bout t'say."

"What is it?"

"This honey had the sweetest, tightest caboose you'll ever behold on a woman. Grade-A premium."

Liptmann sighed, "Thank you for your added information, I'm sure that'll help us crack the case."

"IT'S NOT HERE."

"What?" Bride said, standing sentry at the doorway just inside one of the entry-level rooms of the Luxor Las Vegas ready to alert the return of the room's legitimate tenants.

"It's not here," Dia Reynolds repeated.

Bride left his post by the entrance and walked toward the expansive angled window looking out of the glass pyramid hotel and casino. He joined Dia in the hotel room. The white casing from the air conditioner lay in the floor's center where he earlier helped her haul it. A separate sheet metal panel from the A/C's back rested on the carpet near the casing.

Dejected, Dia sat vulgarly cross-legged on the floor. The posh red dress was hiked up to her upper thighs; Bride assumed for comfort.

"What do we do now?" she asked.

After escaping the Wyndham towers back in North Myrtle Beach, Dia revealed the final computer node location was in Las Vegas. They grabbed a taxi from the resort next door and took it to the airport. From there they booked a flight to Las Vegas with a layover in Atlanta. The forged drivers' IDs and debit cards Krystal overnighted in her "care package" had done their jobs. The debit cards paid for the trip and a suitcase to check with equipment not suitable for carry-on. Their new IDs allowed them to breeze through the TSA at Myrtle Beach International Airport. Dia's ID listed her as Kay Diana Cochrin and Bride's used the alias Paul Henry Koler. Krystal's middle-name trick was clever. Knowing Dia lacked field experience, Krystal matched their middle names near to their true names so they had a natural out for slip-ups. The seven-hour flight to Vegas passed with surprisingly little discussion and no hiccups.

After landing in Vegas in the late afternoon they checked into The Diamond Inn. Bride intended to stay at the Motel 8, but Dia found it serendipitous that she shared names with the pre-World War II hotel. Once checked in, Dia divulged to Bride the node's location, a hotel room at the Luxor. Still she declined to divulge which one.

Only at arrival to room 10152 did Dia say, "This one."

Dia extricated equipment from her bag and stooped to attack the magnetic-strip card reader lock. Before she could start Bride stopped her.

"Wait." Bride stuck his eye to the door's peephole for an overly distorted view inside the room. Though he could discern no details peering backward through the looking glass, he had what he required.

"Someone is moving inside," he said. "We need to wait."

"Dinner then?" she asked.

Bride took the opportunity of her kneeling to pluck a hair from her scalp.

"Ow. What the hells?" she protested as she rose.

Bride licked the hair and stuck it across the door and jam. The near-invisible hair would help signal if the door had been opened when they return.

"Dinner sounds like a fine idea," he said.

"All right, but you're taking me someplace nice." She stood, and they walked to the Luxor's elevators. "Someplace with a dress code that won't approve of this." She gestured to their clothes, the same clothes they'd worn since leaving their Myrtle Beach condo without time to worry about changing. Bride wore jeans, loafers, and a plain white tee; Dia sported the over-sized "Bike Week" tee, her white boots, and the jeans shorts she had donned in the rush.

"Are we going back to our hotel to change?"

"No, idiot." She took his arm. "You are going to buy me a dress."

"Well, it's the least I can do," Bride said, not bringing up everything he had done for her already.

Fortunately, the Luxor connected to a small shopping mall. The Shoppes at Mandalay Place lived inside an enclosed skyway that joined the glass pyramid to the Mandalay Bay hotel and casino tower. A variety of events occurred since Bride consented to Krystal Carrie's "mission," but Bride honestly felt dress shopping would be the last burden he would have to endure. But first they found Elton's, an upscale men's clothing store. Dia stormed in and jauntily picked a gray blazer, a lavender dress shirt, and black trousers off the rack. The salesman eyed Bride up and down and substituted the identical pieces but in what he termed "a more appropriate size." Within fifteen minutes of entering the store, Bride emerged from the dressing room in the suit and stocking feet to ask for Dia's approval.

She proclaimed, "We'll take it, he'll wear it as is," and handed him new black dress shoes and a basic black tie with subtle pinstripes. "Put these on and pay the man. When you're done, I'll be across the hall in Fashion 101."

Dia bounded across the mall as the cash register rang up well into the triple digits. Bride sighed and handed the salesperson the Paul Koler debit card. He wondered how much funds Sunshine had put onto the card. They had spent over a thousand dollars between the airline tickets, the taxi, and the budget motel. Happily, the card reader displayed "Approved" on its blue LED screen.

Before joining Dia, Bride found an ATM, withdrew money to cover dinner, and checked his balance. The account currently held over three thousand dollars. He wondered about the money's source. Was this Sunshine's personal funds, or had she somehow made this mission official? Or perhaps it was obtained in a darker way. However the capital ended up in the account, Bride now felt guilty spending it.

Bride forgot the guilt when he stepped into Fashion 101 to see Dia facing a full length mirror in an exquisite ankle-length, deep red dress. Even with the tags still hanging from the garment, the sight was striking. She was gorgeous. The crimson satin surrendered to her graceful curves and blazed in harmony with the color of her hair and arm tattoo.

Dia watched him standing there, whirled, and shot him a smile. "What do you think?"

Bride pulled out his wallet, slipped out the Koler Visa and handed it to the saleswoman. "We'll take it, she'll wear it as is."

While Bride waited patiently at the register, Dia brought up a simple, low-heeled pair of strappy sandals to add to the purchase. The full bill ran near two-hundred dollars. No complaints from Bride.

They agreed on Lupo at the Mandalay Bay for dinner. Lupo was a Wolfgang Puck restaurant, something neither had tried. Even though it was later in the evening, there was a long wait for a table.

They agreed to share the *Bistecca alla Fiorentina* for Two, medium-rare. After the steak arrived, Bride explained he always ordered his steaks medium-rare unless he can establish the chef takes the proper philosophy for preparing a steak rare. "Bloody, but warm," Bride said. "None of this cold in the middle stuff."

Dia laughed. "You remind me of my friend, Alec." She went quiet and sullen for a moment before changing the subject. "How'd you end up with Homeland?"

"That's an uncomplicated story. I was recruited directly from the Navy," Bride said, simplifying his history. "The real question is how a sixteen-year-old girl decided to hack an al Qaeda server?"

"Oh. You know about that." Dia smiled, either proud of her accomplishment or flattered Bride knew the story. "I had two major reasons. First, it was the challenge. As a hacking nerd, I wanted something challenging. But I was a proper, law-abiding kid who even refused to illegally download music. Hacking bad guys was a challenge that fit my moral code.

"Then there's my father. Dad was career Army, stationed intermittently in the Middle-East. So for him, and for me as his daughter, the World's villains were al Qaeda. One thing led to another, and I needed somewhere to send the information I was digging up. So I 'obtained' the NSA director's private email and forwarded what I found to him, whenever I found something."

"Impressive," Bride said, after finishing chewing a bite of steak.

"I'm going to miss it," she said, "catching bad guys."

"You could always continue to email the director," Bride suggested almost making her spit-take her wine.

"I don't know how well that'd go over," she laughed.

After a bit more small talk, they finished by sharing dessert, a *Crostata di Mela*. Dia declaring her love of caramel and apples.

"We should go," he said. "We need to check if the room is empty yet."

"It's not." She glanced at her phone below the table.

"How are you so sure?"

"While you were doing your little spy trick with the hair, I planted a motion-activated camera on the ledge. It buzzes whenever anything moves nearby. So far we had four guests walk by and a porter. No one has opened the door yet."

Bride laughed silently. "So since we apparently have time, tell me what's stopping someone from brute force attacking your password on this file?"

"I can't give you my trade secrets. What if you're not the spy I thought you were?" she laughed.

"Seriously, you don't need to spell out the details. But I would prefer to know, in case..." He didn't want to spell out the cases. "What's stopping a brute force attack your password on this file?" Bride repeated.

"It'll never work." She smiled. "My password is 2048 characters of seemingly randomness."

"Seemingly?"

"Yeah," she appeared excited to explain, "I took a book passage—I'm not telling you which one—and I hashed it ten thousand times with a shorter key. I added a PIN for good measure. Bam! The strongest password you'll probably ever encounter."

"So your password of epic awesomeness only sees the light of day if you die? Anyone who wants your software bundle..."

"Yeah, yeah, I remember. I suppose if someone did a right good job of faking my death that'd do the trick as well, but they'd need access to a node."

"Do you mind assuring me that won't happen?"

She didn't answer. Instead she looked down at her phone and said, "We're clear. They've left the room."

She wiped her mouth with her napkin and stood. Bride followed leaving the server a handsome cash tip.

They headed back to the Luxor through the mall bridge. The shops had all closed and rolled their gates down for the night, though some restaurants remained open.

After entering the odd-shaped space of the Luxor's interior, with its Egyptian-themed buildings, Bride felt daunted. He and Dia walked directly under the peak, while crossing to the far side elevators. Night or day, inside the Luxor pyramid there existed continually dark and foreboding ambience. The dimly lit atrium level brimmed with show theaters, storefronts, and exhibitions illuminated for the perpetual artificial night. Despite the floor's attractions, one found his eyes rapidly climbing to the drowning sight of the hotel's diminishing balconies. But most disquieting about the scene was the colossal atrium's acoustics. The vast open space swallowed all sounds and reverberated them back from every direction. When combined with the whir of the pyramid's huge vortex fans, there existed a sustained anti-buzz.

They passed the Luxor elevators near the mall because Bride insisted on an overview of room 10152 and floor 10 to reconnoiter the area before heading up. It didn't help much; they could only tell there might be someone walking along floor ten by a moving shadow. Of course, that assumes Bride counted the level numbers correctly.

"Someone might still be inside," he whispered, though not sure why except the pyramid setting seemed to demand it.

After checking her phone, she said, "Not according to my camera."

"I thought you were forgoing that phone for fear of being tracked."

"Yeah, but I'm running totally off wifi, and I've popped out the SIM and randomized my MAC address."

"All right." He comprehended her words but wasn't sure if her action was enough or overkill.

The elevator opened to what-seemed a welcome bit of normal. They stepped into the enclosed car. Dia poked her magic box in the card scanner to access to the tenth floor again. The elevator then extraordinarily climbed the pyramid's interior at its thirty-nine degree angle.

After the ornate, gold doors opened, they traced the hall back to room 10152. As she approached the door, Dia called attention to the white puck-shaped camera stuck to the concrete railing.

Bride examined the door. The hair strand was missing, and this time he saw no movement in the peep hole.

"No hair," he said.

"Oooo…" she replied sarcastically.

Dia approached the door's lock, shooed Bride to the side, glanced around, hiked up her dress, and knelt into a Tony Peña-esque stance. She worked with her miniature black device in front of the electronic lock until, after thirty seconds, the door handle beeped and a green LED lit. The handle turned, but before she could unseal the doorway, it was Bride's turn to shoo her aside.

He gently cracked the entrance open and peered into the unoccupied 420-square-foot Pyramid Deluxe Queen Room. So far, so good. He stepped in, unholstering the XD Mod.2 only after clearing the doorway. It was probably a dumb move. Whoever rented the room played no part in Dia's drama. It would be an easy lie if caught in the chamber unarmed, but Bride felt better with the gun out.

Dia waited inside the entry hall while he cleared the entire room.

Bride returned to her. "All clear. Where's your gizmo?"

Dia entered and marched straight to the wall-mounted air conditioner unit near the slanted window overlooking the Sphinx that endlessly guarded the front of the Egyptian-themed hotel.

"Help me pull the cover off," she commanded.

After muscling the metal cover off its snug spot. Bride returned to the entry to stand watch until Dia cried out, "It's not here."

They had a problem. The node was gone.

"Are you positive we're in the correct room?" Bride asked. "These rooms can all look alike."

"Yes, I'm sure."

"Maybe they switched out A/C units."

"No, this one has my mark."

Dia pointed to the corner of the panel on the floor. There, neatly etched in the metal, Bride found the less-than X greater-than symbols that she had signed her "out" letter.

"What do we do now?" she said. "I don't know where to start looking."

Bride realized they had more immediate issues. At this point, whoever removed the node might assume they had come to retrieve it. Likely they would be watching room 10152, perhaps with their own camera hidden in the hallway or in the room itself.

"We need to go," Bride said. "Help me put the front panel back on."

"Let me put the guts back in."

"No time, toss it inside so no one notices. We're blown. We need to move," he reiterated for emphasis.

They pushed the pieces Dia removed inside and dropped on the panel. Bride kicked the dust bunnies fallen from inside the A/C unit under the bed as Dia collected her tools.

Determined not to be cornered in another hotel room, Bride checked through the peephole into the pyramid's vast concrete interior.

"Have you learned nothing?" Dia asked stepping up from behind.

With the remote camera app open on her phone again, she swiped her thumb on the screen and rotated the camera view off the doorway. It now focused down the hall and ledge toward the northern elevators. As he worried, a wiry yet sturdy stranger in a Brunswick green jacket loitered near the elevator.

"He's one." Bride said.

She spun the remote camera to the extended hall's opposite direction.

"There's another," he said as a second, beefier man in a burgundy dress shirt came to view. "They're waiting for us."

"How do we get past them?" Dia asked.

"Room service," he smiled. After finding the menu lying on the end table, Bride sat on the bed and picked up handset of the hotel's internal phone.

She raised an eyebrow quizzically.

He punched the number series for room service. After one ring, a woman's deep voice answered.

"Can I get an order of..." His finger sought an item he suspected was pre-made. "...the cheese platter. And tell the porter there's a twenty dollar tip if it's here in five minutes."

The bedroom remained silent while they watched the two loitering individuals on the smartphone's screen.

"What's our plan?" Dia asked.

"Still working that out," Bride said, "but it involves a distraction and a witness. Room service gives us both."

"We smash the window and sled a mattress down the surface of the pyramid," Dia suggested.

He stared at her quizzically.

"What?" she said.

"I like your thinking, but beside the problem of us dying at the bottom, I don't imagine we wish to draw that kind of attention to ourselves."

Four minutes and fifty seconds after Bride's call, Dia's smartphone screen pictured a dainty female porter. She was around Dia's size, and sprinted down the hallway holding a plate of cheese overhead. The loitering goon in the green jacket at the hall's end was flabbergasted.

"Get ready," Bride said.

On cue came a knock followed by a "room service" announcement.

Bride swung open the door to the smiling porter. She was pretty and young, perhaps twenty, with curly jet hair and bright brandy eyes that shined as innocent as a teddy bear.

"Your cheese plate, sir."

"Can you set it on the table?"

"Yes, sir."

He stepped aside permitting her in. As she placed the wide dish on the breakfast table and efficiently removed the plastic wrapping, Bride wrote two brief notes on Luxor stationary. The first he laid near to the cheese plate. It read, "Thank you for staying at the Luxor." The second he folded in half and handed to the porter along with her tip. While waiting, Dia leaned against the wall and watched the screen of her phone.

"Here's the twenty you earned," Bride said, "but can you do us a favor? My friend is waiting for us by the elevator. You may have passed him on the way up. He's wearing a green jacket. There's a second twenty if you could pass this note to him."

"Oh, I saw him. That'll be no problem, sir. I'd be happy to."

He handed the porter a second twenty-dollar bill and showed her to the door.

At the doorway the porter said, "If you need anything else Mr. Kelby, my name is Camilla."

"I'll be sure to request you, Camilla. Thank you."

Bride held the exit cracked open after letting Camilla out. He motioned for Dia to come. She grabbed a slice of cheese, popped it in her mouth, and joined him at the door.

"Signal me when the porter is halfway to the elevators."

"Sure thing," she said, her mouth half-closed as she chewed.

Dia swallowed and said, "She's halfway."

"Let's go," he said opening the wooden door and following Camilla down the hallway.

Dia palmed her wifi camera on her way out, and the two marched down the hall overlooking the Luxor's grand atrium.

As Bride expected both loiterers started moving toward them the moment Bride and Dia exited the room.

"Keep moving." Bride said to Dia. "Don't worry about them yet."

"Are these guys assassins or are they government?" She asked.

"I'm hoping assassins. If they are government men, they won't have any qualms about arresting you with a witness. With assassins, it'll hopefully give them pause."

Over his shoulder, Bride noticed the burgundy-shirted bruiser behind them had sped up. Bride, in turn, increased his pace. Which led the antagonist ahead to follow suit until he reached Camilla who surprised him by blocking his way.

Bride slipped off his tie while Camilla handed the man his folded note and explained that it was for him. The confused man read the note that Bride had written, "The contract is off. You can let the girl go." Bride coyly wrapped the tie around his right hand.

As Bride and Dia approached the pair in the hallway, Camilla stood at ease in front of the unfamiliar adversary, waiting to be dismissed or, perhaps, for another tip. The green-jacketed man, visibly perplexed, looked over Camilla's head at Dia. Bride thought his absurd ploy might indeed work. Then the fellow's face shifted to express clarity. Shoving Camilla aside, he stepped over the porter's legs as she tumbled to the carpet. He reached into the green jacket and drew out a handgun, complete with a sound suppressor attached to its barrel.

But Bride closed distance. He raised his fists, connected by the tie, and swept the pistol upward. Bride spun himself and the man around in opposite directions. This maneuver wrapped the tie so it completely encircled the man's wrist and yanked it up into his face. The tie's remainder wound snugly around his neck. In less time than it took Green Jacket to unholster his gun and attempt to fire on Dia, Bride managed to bind the man into a choke hold, tie up the gunman's pistol hand, and end with Green Jacket between him and his approaching partner in the burgundy shirt.

Dia scrambled to Camilla and helped the porter to her feet, the two women crouching low as they ran toward the elevators and stairs.

Green Jacket flailed his free left arm about, frantically clutching at anything to help break Bride's hold around his neck. Somehow in the struggle's chaos the pistol fired. Then again, and again. Despite the suppressor, the shots, which originated only inches away from Bride's and Green Jacket's right ears, were deafening. Bride instinctively swung his head from the gunfire. Someone somewhere inside the vast pyramid screamed, but Bride could scarcely hear the sound over the high-pitched ringing in his left ear. His right ear heard nothing. Green Jacket chose the wrong gun for a suppressor. If you truly want silent gunshots, it's never going to happen. The term "silencer" is a fallacy. While "suppressor" is a more suitable term, the device does surprisingly little suppressing unless its bullet travels under sonic speeds. Otherwise, the bullet's miniature sonic boom is virtually as intense as the original gunpowder explosion inside the shell. The bullets from Green Jacket's 9mm created sonic booms loud enough to cause at least temporary hearing impairment. And now the plaster dust fell onto Bride's scalp from the spot on the ceiling where the bullets struck.

By the time Bride regained his equilibrium, Burgundy Shirt was barely one door away, closing fast, and drawing his own gun. Surely the police will be called. Time to get out fast.

Burgundy stopped short, five yards away, and leveled his gun at Bride through Green Jacket.

"Let him go," Burgundy barked authoritatively.

Who were these guys? Bride had assumed assassins, but Burgundy behaved like a cop. The stance, the command, even the expression on his face said police training, but he hadn't identified himself. Bride figured one of two possibilities: ex-cop assassin or NSA. Burgundy's face said cop or ex-cop. The tall forehead domed at the top to a semicircular widow's peak. His beady, undersized eyes burned intensely over his wide cheeks and jaw. The nose was thin and childlike. Cop, right? Not "everyman" enough for a fed. Neither way didn't fit the model of a rogue assassin. But neither had the killers they previously encountered.

While the standoff continued Green Jacket grew weak in the knees. *Crap, he's going to pass out.* Bride loosened his strangle hold. Green Jacket may have been the sole thing stopping Bride from being shot.

After considering his limited options, Bride's left hand released the tie and hooked under Green Jacket's arm to support and hold the full-sized man. His right hand wrapped the tie once more around Green Jacket's wrist, looping it through itself, praying the rudimentary knot would hold. He grasped the loose end of the tie and yanked it down, slamming Green Jacket's hand hard into the metal railing. Part one of the plan worked, Green Jacket dropped the semi-automatic pistol. The weapon fell the eight stories toward the atrium below. Bride hoped the gun would land atop one of the Luxor's many indoor buildings instead of to the floor, but with no control over that, he cleared it from his thoughts. He wound the tie's long tail around the railing and looped it into the best knot one hand could muster.

Burgundy half-stepped forward. "You're not getting out of this, Bride," he said. "Let Sutter go, and we'll go easy on you."

Definitely cop blood. Bride's course of action should work, theoretically anyway. The physics were a deal more uncertain. To hell with it. He'd already wasted too much time here.

He spoke into Sutter's left ear, "Grab hold."

"What?" The command seemed to confuse Sutter's mind, but his hand grabbed the rail tight.

Bride reached his own hand under the green jacket's waist, clutched Sutter's belt, and hoisted two-hundred pound man up and over the railing into the Luxor's abyss. Without waiting to see his results, Bride tore a mad dash toward the elevators. This instance he definitely heard the screaming, but was pleased to note Dia and Camilla were no longer in the corridor. Upon reaching the end of the hall, he glanced back to see Burgundy struggle to pull Green Jacket—Sutter—back over the rail.

Bride was thankful the silk tie held, and that Burgundy appreciated his partner enough to save the man rather than chase the bounty. The last-ditch maneuver bought time for escape, but when Bride stepped into the stairway, there was no sign of Dia.

"Shit."

"MR. KELBY, is he your boyfriend? Or husband?"

Dia stood watch near the doorway inside the maintenance closet, hoping the Vegas hotel's hall outside would stay clear when the elevator arrived. She realized the petite porter had asked a question.

"What? Who?"

"Mr. Kelby. The gentleman who ordered the cheese platter. Is he your man?"

Mr. Kelby must be who actually rented room 10152. The porter believed Bride was this Mr. Kelby. Wanting no part of this conversation Dia said, "No."

"Why not? He's hot."

Great, Dia thought, *I'm running for my life and I'm stuck in a closet with a woman determined to fail the Bechdel test.* After a measured breath, Dia appreciated she wasn't acting fair. She and this porter may have saved each other's lives; Dia by helping the porter up and away from the mêlée, the porter by diverting them from the stairs to the service areas where, hopefully, those assassins couldn't follow.

Dia faced the porter and smiled. "What's your name?"

"My name is Camilla," the porter said.

"How long do these elevators usually take, Camilla?"

"They're awfully slow," Camilla said. "I had to run that cheese plate to your suite because the elevator took so long. Don't tell, Mr. Kelby, but it took a little over five minutes."

"Mum's the word." Dia continued listening for the elevator.

"So if Mr. Kelby isn't your man, what is he?"

Dia again wondered that herself. "I suppose you could say he's my bodyguard."

"Really?" Camilla seemed excited now then sheepishly asked, "Are you famous?"

"Could be. 'Infamous' might be a better word."

"Huh." Camilla seemed bewildered by the claim. "Have you noticed that Mr. Kelby looks like Johannes Huebl?"

"I don't know who that is."

"Johannes Huebl. He's this hot German model, and he's married to Olivia Palermo."

"I don't know that person either."

"She was on that TV show *The City*. She was the one who—"

Bing.

"The elevator's here," Dia happily interrupted.

Peeking her head into the hall, she scanned the elevator car. Both empty.

"Let's go," Dia said, swinging open the maintenance closet door and hurrying across to the waiting elevator. Camilla trailed directly behind. Once inside the ornate elevator car Dia flattened herself to the side wall so passers-by couldn't see her. Of course the mirrored rear wall didn't help matters. Camilla used her master key and pressed and held the kitchen level button and the close door button.

"Thank you, Camilla." Dia said. "You are truly a lifesaver."

"I didn't get your name," Camilla said.

Dia smiled. Man crazy or not, Dia had started liking this young woman. "My name is..." Dia caught herself and remembered Bride's instructions. "...Kay."

"That's a pretty name." Camilla smiled back wickedly showing a set of cute little chiclet teeth.

"Listen, Camilla, I need another favor from you. I need clothes. Those men, they're trying to kill me, and unfortunately this dress is almost literally a red flag. I have an extra outfit with Mandalay Bay's guest services, but I'm afraid they've seen me in those clothes as well. Can I—"

"Don't sweat it, girl," Camilla interrupted with a sly wink. "I have an outfit in my locker. You can have it."

"I can give you money," Dia offered.

"I said don't sweat it." Camilla smiled again.

The elevator's doors opened onto the service level, and in contrast to upstairs with its elaborate Egyptian façade, this level was plain and stark and lit fluorescently.

"Wait a second," Camilla directed. "I can't have you down here. I need to make sure no one sees you."

Camilla pranced ahead, looked around a bend, then waved Dia to follow.

Camilla whispered, "Walk like you belong here. There are cameras everywhere." The two women progressed down the concrete corridor like coworkers, though one wore a floor length red dress. Camilla brought her to a doorway marked "staff locker room – women". She cracked open the entrance and peeked in, then grabbed Dia's hand and led her new acquaintance inside.

"No one comes in here except near shift change." Camilla said. "We should be safe for a while. My locker's over here."

Camilla ushered Dia to the third row of metal lockers in the second aisle, dialed a three-number combination, and swung open the sheet-metal door. She handed Dia a scant pair of purple denim short-shorts and a matching flowered halter top. The outfit was skimpier than Dia was accustomed, but this was Vegas; it was near 2:00 am and the temperature may still be in the eighties outside. You can't fault a girl for trying to stay cool.

"It's a shame you can't still wear that dress," Camilla said. "You look amazing in it."

"Do you want it?" Dia asked.

Camilla blushed. "No. That's too much."

"Seriously, it's the least I can do." Dia slipped the dress up and over her head. Dia now stood nude in front of Camilla, save the red lace panties, and tried to hand her the garment.

Camilla's face grew flushed red. "Oh," she said, looking Dia up and down before turning her back to her. "I'm sorry, Kay." Camilla shook. "I should have told you. I like girls."

"Oh." This time Dia said it. The moment filled with an awkward silence. She rethought their entire conversation. Camilla hadn't really been talking about Bride at all. She was inquiring coyly about Dia's availability and sexual orientation.

Dia hopped into the shorts and slithered into the cotton halter-top. "That's all right, Camilla. That's not me, but I wouldn't hold it against anyone." Dia turned around and crossed her arms over her breasts and said, "Can you tie me?"

Camilla turned back to Dia and grabbed the halter-top's loose strings and knotted them in the center of Dia's back.

"Thanks." As she spoke, Dia saw her reflection in a mirror. The clothes looked nice—importantly they weren't like anything she would ordinarily wear—but it was nevertheless clearly her. She scowled.

"What's wrong?" Camilla asked. "I think you look pretty, although you'd look amazing in anything."

Dia could grow accustom to the friendly porter's compliments. It was an odd sensation. Dia had been told by many women that she was attractive, but knowing Camilla desired her sexually made Dia trust the woman's flattery. It made her feel warm.

But Dia remembered what caused her to frown. "It's not that. I love the outfit..." She didn't love it, but close enough. "...it's just that it's not much of a disguise. I'm regretting this tattoo right now."

Camilla remained silent for a moment, then, "I have an idea. Follow me."

With the dress staying in Camilla's locker, they returned to the painted concrete hallways of the Luxor's basement. Camilla led Dia through a maze of corridors until they reached a passage with the hotel's ornate, carpeted floors. They climbed a flight of stairs, passed through a black curtain, and approached a door with an emblem of a stickman with crazy wavy hair on it. Camilla knocked.

"Scott? Are you in there?" Camilla called softly through the door.

After hearing movement inside, Camilla leaned in to listen. The door suddenly thrust open. There, in the doorway, stood a shocking sight of a human being with curly, flame-red hair and penetrating eyes intensified by dark makeup.

"Camilla! Hey, how's it going? And who's this?" The stranger talked fast, almost frantically.

"Hi, Scott." Camilla said. "This is my friend, Kay. She really needs our help."

"Sure. Come in. Excuse the mess. Any friend of Cam's is probably pure trouble. What do you need? Are you going to make trouble? If so, I'm in."

They stepped into what Dia assumed was Scott's dressing room that resembled a dark man-cave. Mirrors covered the opposite wall floor to ceiling. The other surfaces were painted orange and black and covered in guitars, nunchaku, signs, posters with Scott's face, and other miscellaneous memorabilia.

Dia busied herself looking around the place. Her gaze caught on a Cabbage Patch Kid doll with an identical red mop of hair and angry eyebrows.

Meanwhile Camilla said, "Kay needs cover makeup and a wig."

Scott looked flabbergasted. "What? Why would I have cover makeup? A wig? Sure, I get that, hide these sexy locks from the under-eighteen kiddies, but cover—"

"Scott," Camilla berated him.

"Yeah." Scott rolled his eyes dejected. "I've got cover makeup."

Scott walked over to a large makeup table against the far mirrored wall. He searched through the drawers and pulled out a half-used tube of Dermablend Leg & Body Cover and handed it to Camilla.

Camilla took Dia by the shoulders and steered her into the makeup chair and thanked Scott for helping out. Scott said he would borrow a wig from one of "the girls".

"Sit down, honey. We'll get that tatt covered."

After several minutes the cover up satisfied Camilla, and Scott returned wearing a long wig with straight raven hair. The red curls shot wildly from the sides. He also wore a large plastic buttocks. Scott puckered his lips and said, "Am I more a Kim or a Khloé?"

Both ladies giggled. Scott removed the dark wig and asked, "Will this do?"

"It should." Dia said, slipping the wig on and adjusting faux hair in the mirror. Once straightened, Dia witnessed another person returning her gaze in the mirror. "It's perfect. Thank you, Scott."

"Oh, she speaks?" Scott said to Camilla. "Darned, I thought you had met the ideal girlfriend."

Dia laughed again, but Camilla merely smiled and blushed. Dia looked at Camilla. This young woman entered her life less than a half-hour ago and Dia already felt like they were friends, though possibly to Camilla's chagrin. Dia knew she would soon walk out of Camilla's life and wondered if that's what it was like living in Las Vegas, or any vacation town. Strangers must filter into the residents' lives daily. New people, temporary friends. It was sad, and Camilla attempted to will a smile onto her anguished face. Dia sensed they were about to say goodbye, probably forever.

She thanked Scott again by giving him a hug.

While embraced Scott said, "You can touch my butt if you want."

Dia released him, shocked until she realized he still wore the plastic buttocks. Then she laughed through her sadness.

Dia faced Camilla, not knowing what to say. She struggled to cobble together something meaningful. "Listen, I want..."

When Dia hesitated Camilla grabbed her, pulled their taut bodies together, and kissed her firm on the lips. Dia's eyes shot open. She was astonished, but she let it happen. After a dizzying ten seconds, Camilla released her and said, "You don't have to say anything. Just go. I'll think about you."

Dia muttered, "Bye," then turned and walked out the door.

In the hallway she overheard, "That was hot, Cam."

"Shut up, Scotty."

Dia stopped, drew a deep breath, and refocused. What to do now? Find Bride? Go back to the Diamond Inn? Lie low? She pulled her bag back high on her shoulder and searched for an exit. No, she needed to find Bride. If he made it. What if he hadn't made it? What if he'd died? She didn't want to believe this man who helped her lay dead in the hallway above, so rather she asked herself, *what if I'm alone now?*

Dia wandered aimlessly through the Luxor's sub-basement corridors, struggling to decide her next move. No ideas came to mind. She was too upset. What had become of Agent Bride?

Eventually, she stumbled into the stairway and headed upward, climbing to the atrium level for a look up to the open hallway. Taking another long breath, she remembered her disguise, and stormed out on to the Luxor's atrium posing as a novice sightseer on her first excursion to Las Vegas. Dia checked out everything, the shops, the lush Egyptian decor, the elaborate food court, the multiple theaters, a poster for a show called "Carrot Top" with Scott's photograph. *Weird.* Then she stood directly below the pyramid's apex and peered around the various levels of the ziggurat-shaped hotel, because that's what a tourist would do. Then she noticed the police. Up on the tenth floor, two law enforcement officers were examining the scene. *Not good.*

Dia felt comfortable in the scene for a brief minute. That's what a tourist would do. A tourist wouldn't be investigating Bride's death. Maybe it was an assassin, the green jacketed man or the one in the burgundy shirt. Perhaps both. Dia's spirit sank when the individual in the green jacket, now wearing a shoulder sling, walked over to a police officer and conversed. *Oh hells.* She had to go up there. She had to know.

First, she found the ladies' lavatory. Empty. She faced the mirror and again reassured herself the woman in the reflection did not resemble her. No one would recognize her. She would do it. After establishing a sufficient back story in her mind, she exited the restroom and located another bank of inclined elevators on the far side of the pyramid. It would involve more walking but she'd rather not enter next to the crime scene. She expected they wouldn't let her turn the corner near where the police had gathered. When the elevator arrived, she boarded with a sweet elderly couple. She pushed ten on the panel then spoke to the woman, turning on her character, "'scuse me. Ya gots any gum?"

The old woman glared at her for a second, then surprisingly reached into her handbag, pulled out a half pack of Juicy Fruit, and handed Dia a stick.

"Thanks," Dia said. "You're an angel."

Dia unwrapped the gum, popped it in her mouth, and chewed with her mouth open. The act was too overt, so she closed her mouth and just chewed obviously.

The elevator doors opened for floor ten. Dia stepped out. After the doors shut, Dia withdrew her phone, brought it to her ear, and conversed to an imaginary BFF while walking the hallway bragging about vacationing in a swank hotel. Dia wanted to travel the added distance. By starting on the pyramid's far side, she viewed the scene from more angles.

"Nah, girl. I'm at the Luxor, the King Tut casino place."

Pause.

"Steve's at the MGM Grand. I dunno why they didn't put us in the same hotel, but you can get mosts way there on the monorail."

Pause.

"Yeah, a monorail like Disney-frickin'-World."

Pause.

"Nah, they don't have no Disney in Vegas. If they did, it'd be like Mickey playing slots with hookers." Dia laughed.

Pause.

"I like Goofy best. Or the Tasmanian Devil."

She reached the next corner.

"Yeah, Taz is Disney. He was in that one with Donald."

She walked past the next banks of elevators.

"Oh damn. Yer right, girl, that was Daffy. I get them two ducks messed up."

At the hallway's corner, she arrived where a modest gathering of police officers had amassed.

"Was that Donald or Daffy with the Martian with the Q-38 space modulator?"

A stout uniformed police officer stuck out his arm and stopped Dia from advancing down the hall.

"'scuse me. I gotta talk to dis cop." She cupped her palm over the microphone, but left the phone on her ear. "Can I get through?"

"I'm sorry, ma'am, you have to go around."

Dia attempted to gaze down the open passage into the crime scene. No body, but she did notice the fellow in the burgundy shirt.

Dia asked, "Someone die?"

The police officer smiled. "Nothing like that ma'am. Someone just thought it would be funny to fire a gun in the hotel."

She breathed easier. Unless the officer was covering things up, Bride was alive.

"My room's just around the next corner," she declared, "can I get through soon?"

"We will be a while," he said. "Your best bet is to go around."

"Damn," she said. "A'ight then. Thanks anyways." Dia returned to her phone and resumed the phony conversation. "Yeah, girl, I thinks someone tried to pop someone inside the hotel." She spun to leave and almost bumped straight into a man approaching behind her.

"'scuse—" Dia froze. She promptly identified the austere face on the shaven head. She had witnessed that face speaking to Thorenus in the Fort Meade headquarters. Her heart momentarily stopped. Dia was busted.

But he barely looked her direction. Instead he stared down the hall. "No, excuse me. I wasn't watching where I was going."

She recovered. "Yeah, well try looking next time." She scurried away.

/ / / /

Emerson Kosma soldered the final wire then tested the servos by twisting the left joystick on his radio controller. Just as he planned, the Surface RT tablet arose from lying prone on the back of the disk-shaped Roomba to a vertical position. The miniature camera rose with the tablet but maintained its direction as directly forward. The hacked together contraption worked. So far anyway. Koz still needed to program its multiple automatic functions, but the beta of his remote presence robot had all of its remote functions.

"Hell yeah!" he yelled, although no one was there to hear it.

It was time to put Kozbot 12 through its paces, but first a little celebration. He reached under his workbench to the dorm refrigerator and pulled out a cold IPA. He popped the top with the bottle opener mounted on the bench's corner and drank a healthy swig of the local microbrew.

Time to test. He lifted Kozbot 12 off the crowded bench and placed it onto the floor. He grabbed the Walkera DEVO F12E 2.4GHz remote and looped its strap around his neck, adjusted the remote's sunshade on the first-person-view monitor, and pushed the right joystick forward. Kozbot 12 whirred forward and set about performing tricks at the whim of Koz's joystick.

"Hot damn." Koz said. "Go Twelve, go."

He took another sip of his beer and was ready to run Twelve through an obstacle course when a knock came from his front door.

"What the...? Another tenant let someone past the front door." Koz said to Twelve.

Twelve scooted back and forth in what appeared to be enthusiasm. In truth, the robot was simply reacting to the movements of Koz's fingers on the joystick.

"Go see who it is, Twelve."

Twelve zoomed under the workshop's plastic shroud and weaved under the rows of shelves, gathering hidden dust bunnies in its swirling brushes along the path. When Twelve reached the front door the screen and camera tilted up and Koz's face appeared on the screen.

"Who is it?" Koz asked through the mechanical pet's internal speaker.

"We're here to speak to Emerson Kosma," a man's voice said through the door.

Koz silently cursed that the diminutive robot couldn't access the peephole or the door's camera.

"He's not here right now. Can you try later?" Koz said through the robot.

"Who am I talking to?" the voice asked.

"I'm merely the house robot. You'll have to come back later." The little robot waited by the entrance and picked up the sound of someone leaving.

"What was that about, Twelve?" Koz said before lowering the robot's 10.6-inch screen and directing it through another series of shelves and boxes back to the workshop.

"That was weird, Twelve." Koz said, stooping to tinker with the screen's pivot joint. It hadn't raised as smoothly as Koz expected. He was spritzing the joint with Teflon lubricant when he heard a thud coming from his storage area.

"What was that, Twelve?"

Twelve raised its screen slightly then lowered it again. The intention was to mimic a shoulder shrug, but the movement manifested more like a glitch. Koz frowned and made a mental note. *Try a different shrug gesture next time.*

"Go see what that was."

Twelve rocked with a short back and forth movement then jetted off under the shop dust curtain once more.

Koz stayed transfixed to the monitor as his robot scout explored the cavernous loft. The bot charted yet another course through shelves and furniture. The screen image bumped up and down as Twelve jumped the threshold between the storage room's linoleum onto the media area's hardwood.

Mental note: image stabilization.

Twelve's webcam scanned around the dark room across the action figure collection and prop displays. The picture grew grainy and the compression boxes were now obvious as the cheap camera attempted to adjust for the dark.

Mental note: Better night vision, maybe infrared.

Something was on the media couch. Some sort of mass protruded from the couch's top. *It's doubtlessly a pillow.* Koz thought, but he directed Twelve to roll under the couch to check. The bot found dust bunnies, coins, and wayward Cheetos under the furniture, but for some reason Koz decided not to start the robot's vacuum.

Mental note: Clean under the couch.

The robot emerged from the couch's front side and the camera re-adjusted for the improved lighting conditions. When finally refocused, Koz's monitor had filled with a pair of Chuck Taylor Converse All Star High Tops, one red and one white. WTF? Someone was in the apartment. The basketball shoes' owner stood from the couch then knelt to address Twelve's camera. Koz tilted the screen up, leaving the robot's built-in display off.

A slick, smooth face appeared on remote's display.

"Hello, Mr. Kosma." the handsome intruder said into the camera. "I expect you may know a password that someone wants really badly. My friend and I are here to get it from you."

"Friend?" Koz said, not intending to transmit.

"I'm speaking of the giant fellow behind you."

/ / / /

Henry Bride sat at the Eyecandy Lounge & Bar in the center of the Mandalay Bay casino's floor. He nursed the Dark and Stormy cocktail, easy on rum, that he had ordered fifteen minutes hence. From his stool he could observe both passages through the casino from the Luxor whether coming in through the Shoppes or from the monorail. He figured Dia would ultimately come through the casino, assuming she hadn't been caught. Whether heading to the Mandalay Bay guest services to pick up their checked luggage or cutting an indoor path back to the Diamond Inn, Bride would be able to spot Dia. It wasn't a sure bet she'd come through, but it was the most favorable odds he'd get. Las Vegas had no sure bets.

The lounge likewise provided safety from the two fellows Bride clashed with on the Luxor's tenth floor. If they searched the Mandalay Bay, from his position, he should spot them first, and the bar offered over a dozen possible exits plotted from the casino.

His biggest concern, however, was Dia Reynolds. He couldn't believe he lost his one responsibility. He allowed himself a four-hour time limit before he departed the gambling den and returned to the Diamond Inn; She may have taken a different route back to their hotel. His plan was to stay an hour at the bar unless he gained a reason to stay longer. He might chat up one of the women (he assumed they were call girls) that kept propositioning him as he drank. But barring that he would move to a well-placed slot machine and try to break even while he kept his eyes out for the woman put in his charge.

"Buy a gal a drink, hottie?" a short black-haired woman sitting on the stool next to his said.

Bride gave her a quick glance. "No, thank you."

"Maybe something with Pearl vodka," the woman said lowering her sunglasses.

He smiled then studied her again, this time with recognition. "I'd love to."

He took her arm, picked up his jacket, and they promptly left the casino.

24> The Backup Plan

THREE AM AND CLARENCE AXEWORTHY was running on thirteen minutes of sleep. Not by choice. It was never by choice. How much sleep had he gotten this month? His expansive bedroom was softly lit and quiet to promote repose, and he had banished the woman to her keep. Sometimes sex helped him sleep, but not tonight. Perhaps he should summon her for another round. He didn't especially have the energy, and since Lloyd hadn't offered a satisfactory replacement, this woman didn't possess the energy to properly perform the toils herself.

For now, Axeworthy decided to focus on business. He collected his laptop off the nightstand, propped himself up in the bed, crossed his legs, and placed the machine across the lap of his white silk pajamas. The system woke from sleep when the lid opened and unlocked instantly, thanks to his subcutaneous NFC chip. He launched the Mattermost application and checked his recent messages. There were seventeen.

He reviewed the top message thread concerning network router hacking. He grimaced when he found minimal progress from his team. They discovered an exploit in an additional router model, but it could only be executed from inside the local area network. All efforts for accessing from outside the network had proved failures. Even the supposed zero-day exploit bought and paid dearly for proved to be a dud, having been already patched by automatic firmware updates. The team traced a smattering of vulnerable routers on the web, but only routers updated from factory defaults but not entirely up-to-date.

Depressing.

Another priority thread from Kenneth reported from Asheville that he and Rock had confronted Emerson Kosma as instructed. After interrogation, they were thoroughly convinced the hacker had no access to the NSA files' password. Emerson Kosma was eliminated.

Axeworthy knew Dia Reynolds had been revisiting places she had vacationed or visited in the last year—presumably to deactivate her nodes. Axeworthy had at least a partial list of those places thanks to a couple of rather talented data-mining hackers borrowed from IPvØ, but his "freelancers" had remained a step behind her.

More depressing.

Axeworthy checked the next message thread. His eyes lit up. Finally, reasonably good news. Steven had posted a message received from a hitman who went by QMark.

```
Spotted target in Las Vegas. Unable to engage
since feds were everywhere. Backing out for now.
Before target arrived, was able to find and
remove target's "node" from its hiding place.
Have node on person and willing to sell if
amicable price can be met.
- QMark
```

Steven updated the thread periodically with miscellaneous information concerning the brief negotiations. Ultimately, the hitman, QMark, agreed on a reasonable price. Steven transferred the Bitcoin to QMark's account and traveled to retrieve the unit from an MGM Grand concierge in Las Vegas.

Axeworthy was now excited. He stood, flicked his wrist, and spoke to the subtle chirp from the bedchamber's speakers, "Call Steven."

The room responded, "Calling Steven Burgess."

He paced the hardwood floor while the phone line played through the bedroom's built-in speakers. After two rings the call was answered.

"Hello." Steven's voice was groggy, but Axeworthy could hear a car engine.

"Steven, it's Clarence Axeworthy. I want that node here. How soon can you have it here?"

"I'm in route to Yuma. I can be there in..." There was a pause while Steven's GPS recalculated his route. "...two-and-a-half to three hours."

"That's perfect. Also I want you to plant a news story." Axeworthy spelled out details of the story before disconnecting the call.

Axeworthy continued pacing. He was wide awake and knew he wouldn't sleep tonight. For an instant he considered trying anyway before giving up. Instead he flicked his wrist and said, "Sex now."

The room once again answered, "Unlocking the woman's chamber and summoning her to the master bedroom."

/ / / /

Robert Liptmann pushed his eyeglasses back up his nose as he watched Anthony Thorenus exit the National Security Agency headquarters in Fort Meade. The deputy director was heading for his Town Car. Time to pounce.

Liptmann timed his exit from his Oldsmobile so he would just beat Thorenus to the director's driver side door. Liptmann had flown back from Vegas to update his boss, but used the trip as an opportunity to squeeze more clarity from Thorenus.

As expected, Thorenus first went to the rear of the Lincoln and placed his leather briefcase inside the trunk. When he slammed the trunk lid shut, he was visibly startled to discover the bald little investigator hovering by his driver's door.

"Deputy Thorenus, may I have a word?" Liptmann asked.

"I don't have time right now, Colonel Liptmann," Thorenus said. "I'm afraid I'm expected at the State Department in under an hour."

"If I misled you, I'm sorry, but my request was just a courtesy. I truly must insist." Liptmann refused to budge from his position that blocked Thorenus entering his vehicle.

"Fine." Thorenus relented, stepping back and yielding Liptmann the ground. "But can we make it quick?"

Liptmann ignored the request. "What duties did you assign to Alec Holloway about project Wonderbread?"

"Is this a trap?" Thorenus's head shook minutely. The director was more irritated and nervous than he wanted to show. "You know I can't discuss employee duties outside secure areas, even deceased employees."

"I'm sad to say you're not permitted to communicate who is or has been an employee outside the secure zone, but I'm afraid you just did. And I had inquired about a project called Wonderbread, not a current or former operation of your agency."

Thorenus seemed to search for a path out of the web of semantics that Liptmann spun. "Whether a project is of the agency or not, I cannot discuss this."

"Perhaps you can tell me, who else was involved in Wonderbread beside yourself, Alec Holloway, and Dia Reynolds?"

Thorenus was perspiring. "Look, Liptmann, I don't know what you are talking about. I must get to my meeting at the Department of Defense. Are you going to let me access to my car or not?"

"Yes, but consider two factors. I'm about to bring in Dia Reynolds, and I'm sure her story about Wonderbread will be a compelling one. And the White House is not happy about Project Wonderbread."

Liptmann's name drop of the White House produced a visible flinch in Thorenus's shoulders. It had been a complete bluff on Liptmann's part, but he suspected that Dia Reynolds had conveyed a message by posting her files on whitehouse.gov.

Liptmann stepped back and allowed Thorenus to enter his car.

"Oh, one more point, Deputy," Liptmann said, "your meeting was at the State Department."

25> "You're Dead."

EVERY TOURIST DESTINATION AIRPORT Henry Bride had visited followed the same routine. Throngs of arriving travelers filed through the terminals in spurts, eager to begin their vacations or conventions. In contrast, tired, sweaty departing travelers crowded the bars, shops, and seating areas awaiting their flights back to the real world. The difference between other destination airports and Las Vegas' McCarran International Airport, as with everything Vegas, was gambling.

McCarran set aside areas, both inside and outside the secure zone, with banks of vibrant slot and video poker machines. Consistent with Bride's prior visits to McCarran, these areas were sparsely populated. A handful of desperate gamblers sought one final score before jetting back to their home cities where gambling was illegal or sparse. The occasional arriving tourist would stop by these machines as though stirred to surrender his or her first dollar on Nevada soil.

Bride occupied his time sitting at their gate fascinating himself with the contrast in manner between the arriving players and those departing. The arriving seemed excited to lose, shouting groans of joyous disappointment as they each apparently barely lost. The departing languished while feeding their wages into the apparatuses with poor expectations and the narrowest shred of hope to strike a jackpot to at least break even.

Bride mindlessly focused on one particular departing player. Bleach blonde and permed, the woman insert a quarter, depressed the button, and waited while the wheels narrowly missed the elusive jackpot. She then repeated the process. As he spied, Bride guessed the lady's story. A divorced mother of two teenagers, perhaps living in the Midwest—Illinois or Indiana—she had lost most of her vacation money gambling. The rest she had spent on buffets, a mid-range hotel, and keepsakes to show off at the department store where she served as a mid-level manager. Bride put her gambling losses at $2,000—plus or minus $500—and climbing a quarter at a time. Not counting the clothes, food, and lodging, Bride's Vegas losses totaled three dollars, and that was to a vending machine that refused to discharge a Pepsi. He had learned much about gambling over the years, chiefly that he could not afford it, and he refused to gamble against a machine. To his mind it would be easy enough to program these video gambling devices to only payout a small percentage to each bettor.

Bored with his Midwest divorcée, Bride returned his attention to Dia, who thankfully had returned to coding on her laptop. He didn't understand a word, but he knew a plan was now in place. He was worried about Dia, more so now than before that moment back at the Diamond Inn, when for the first time this week Bride's phone rang.

"What happened?" the panicked voice of Krystal Carrie had asked before Bride could utter, "Hello."

"We're outside Vegas in a little hotel," he said, trying to figure out what Sunshine was asking.

"We?" Sunshine asked. "Who's with you?"

"Dia—and a friend may join us."

"Dia's alive?" She sounded surprised.

"Yes."

"The news says she's dead."

"What?" He turned to Dia. "Dia, call up the news. Sunshine, I'm putting you on speaker."

"Hey D. My fellow treating you right?"

"Yeah." Dia seemed reluctant to speak, but also perked up upon hearing her friend's voice. "I don't know what I would have done without him. I'd be at least twice dead."

"You're once dead according to news reports."

Dia sat on the bed's edge with her laptop beside her. She launched her self-customized Firefox/Tor browser and dug through CNN.com until she found the story.

Body of NSA Deserter Found in Michigan.

"Motherfff..." Dia said, clicking on the story.

```
GRAND MARAIS, MICHIGAN - The body of alleged
NSA deserter Diamond Reynolds was identified
after it was discovered in a vacant house
outside Grand Marais, Michigan, a small town
in Michigan's Upper Peninsula on Lake Superior.
Reynolds reportedly worked as a consultant
programmer for the NSA. She is alleged to be
the NSA staff member who famously announced her
intent to desert on the dark web late last week…
```

Dia did not continue reading.

"I'm having a real Sarah Connor moment," she said. "They're trying to trigger the password release."

"Will that work?" Sunshine asked via the phone.

"Not CNN." Dia quickly typed a different URL into the browser's address field. After the page loaded, she scanned it. "Nothing's on democratandchronicle.com yet. That's the paper in Rochester, New York, and it's the main trigger of the last node. If my name appears, along with certain keywords, the node will release the password. It checks twice daily, so depending on when the story goes live we'll have anywhere from zero to twelve hours to shut it down. But more importantly what's this 'consultant' crap? I wasn't a consultant. I was..."

Bride ignored Dia's complaining and explained to Sunshine about the nodes, how they work and how he and Dia have disabled two of the three nodes.

"*Keep reading, D,*" Sunshine said, a serious tone evident in her voice.

"Why?" Dia had a hesitant quiver in the question.

"*Just read it.*"

Dia found the part Sunshine wanted her to see.

```
...coming mere days after Diamond Reynolds'
sister, Ruby Greer nee Reynolds, died from
injuries sustained in a one car accident near
the township of Kinross, Michigan.
```

Dia sat frozen. Her eyes still aimed at the screen, but looked right through it as tears welled at their corners. She began to hyperventilate.

Bride knew immediately what she had read and the pang of guilt jabbed at his side. He had known but had not told her about her sister. In the front of his mind, Bride assumed Dia knew her sister's fate, but deep down he was aware she had not acted like someone who had recently lost a loved one. At this point he felt it best to continue to feign ignorance. "Dia, what is it?"

"Ruby... My sister, Ruby, is d-dead?"

After a long pause, Sunshine said solemnly through the phone, "*I'm afraid it's true, darling. I've confirmed it myself with the hospital.*"

"This is my fault," Dia confessed, the tears now soaking her cheeks.

Bride sat down next to her on the bed and put his arms around the grieving sister. The room was silent for nearly ten minutes, Bride just holding Dia as she cried. Sunshine patiently waited quietly on the line while Dia processed the shock of the news.

Finally, Dia released herself from Bride's arms, wiped the tears from her face, and with quivering voice said, "Well, what do we do next?"

"*You sure you're up for it?*" Sunshine asked. "*Perhaps Bride and I should take it from here.*"

"No. I have to—" Dia tried to fight the grief, but she broke down again.

"No," Bride consoled. "You're in no mind right now. Don't worry about what's next. Sunshine and I will figure out the next move. You get some rest and take some time. We'll work it out."

He told Sunshine he would call her back, and then held Dia again. This time she held him back. Eventually she fell asleep, crying in his arms. Gently he took of her shoes and tucked her into the bedding still clothed. Once satisfied Dia was fast asleep, Bride picked up his phone, stepped out onto the motel's balcony and called Krystal Carrie back.

Sunshine answered with *"How's she doing?"*

"Not good, but she's asleep now. That was news she didn't need to hear right now." Bride said.

"Better now than later."

Sunshine was right. Bride didn't know what the future held for them, but this journey would get worse before it got better.

"When can you collect the last node?" Sunshine asked.

"It's gone. The remaining node has disappeared." Bride said. "Dia placed it here in Vegas, but it's gone."

"What?" Krystal said. *"Where'd it go?"*

"That's the trouble, She said she built the damned thing to be untraceable."

"Well, shit. She'd know how to do that better than anyone." Sunshine paused. *"Start from the beginning, tell me everything you two have been up to. Maybe something will help me figure this out."*

For the next hour, Bride stood in the dry night air of Vegas and walked her through everything he and Dia had been through since Michigan. Krystal asked some detailed questions about the nodes they did find, and, while Bride did his best, he felt woefully uninformed about the subject. After finally finishing up the details of Bride losing Dia in the Luxor, he asked, "Did any of that help?"

"Still processing."

He hung silently on the phone for several minutes, letting her "process". However long it took, she would be the next one to talk.

Finally, *"I suppose we could try a Freedom Hosting trap variation?"*

"Freedom Host ... what?"

A moment later, a dry voice behind him said, "Won't work. The Freedom Hosting trap relied on zero day vulnerabilities in Firefox and JavaScript."

He turned to see Dia standing in the doorway. He wanted to celebrate her return. He wanted to give the biggest grin of his life that Dia had returned, but he sucked back his expression when he saw her solemn, almost emotionless face.

Dia continued, "Mozilla patched those zero days and by default the node doesn't launch a browser; it scans pure HTML. There's no JavaScript to be hacked."

"Don't tell me. Here—" Bride put the phone back on speaker and held it out in front of her. Dia repeated what she had told Bride, but finished with, "But..."

"*But what?*" Sunshine asked.

"But the node has an integrated JavaScript parser installed and it will run through a Chromium browser which it would launch if democratandchronicle.com presented a subscription logon requiring JavaScript."

"*I don't get it.*"

"Hang on," Bride interrupted. "Let's take this back inside." He led Dia back into the room and set the phone back on the table. "*You were saying?*"

"The D & C doesn't require a subscription," Dia explained, "but the second node checked a server that did. It needed JavaScript to gain access to its appointed server. The same source code exists in all three nodes. So if..." Dia dove into deep contemplation again, but it seemed, for now anyway, her mind was back on track.

Sunshine picked up on Dia's idea. "*If democratandchronicle. com presented a logon, the node would use JavaScript.*"

"Yes." Dia leaned forward and showed a hint of energy. "We'll need a JavaScript-related vulnerability in Chromium."

"*What versions of Chromium, JavaScript, and Linux does the node run?*" Sunshine asked, and the conversation sunk to depths beyond Bride's computer knowledge. Eventually, he returned to cleaning his guns and preparing equipment.

"Mister Bride? Are you paying attention?" Sunshine's voice barked from the phone.

"Yes," Bride lied. "What do you need?"

Sunshine answered, "We're going to spoof the Democrat and Chronicle and create a subscription-only page."

"Why, may I ask?"

"The node'll need to execute JavaScript to log in." Dia explained in a monotone. "We'll use JavaScript code that will make the node relinquish its IP address. This assumes the node is online."

Sunshine continued the explanation, "If we do this right, from the point the node attempts to sign in we'll have twelve hours to travel to the node's location to shut it down. Unfortunately, it might be anywhere."

"So we may need to travel to rural Indonesia in twelve hours?" Bride asked.

"Yeah, I suppose so," Dia said.

"If this works." Sunshine added.

"How big is that 'if?'" he asked.

"It's a healthy-sized 'if,'" Sunshine said.

"Why twelve hours?" Bride asked.

The two women paused before answering. Bride assumed they were dumbing it down for him.

Dia finally spoke up, "After the node attempts to log in and fails, the next cycle, twelve hours later, it will switch to its backup site."

"And what's its backup site?"

"That's the trouble. I don't remember. It might be cnn.com or another site that's carrying the fake story. One node had CNN as its backup."

Bride contemplated her explanation. "So there's a thirty-three percent chance that the node will determine you're dead and release the password?"

"Fifty percent," Dia said. "The Myrtle Beach node had CNN as its primary check. That means Vegas or North Carolina used CNN as the secondary site."

"Can you put your solution online from the airport?"

Dia went quiet in thought.

"Dia?" Bride prodded her.

"Oh..." she said, shaking away the malaise. "Yeah. I think so."

"That's good," Bride said. "We'll buy the cheapest tickets to at least be past security before we unleash your idea. Pack your equipment, Dia. We'll get a taxi. Sunshine, buy us some cheap tickets—any tickets—flying out from McCarran International and forward them to my phone.

"I will," Sunshine said, "but I'm going to the airport, too. I'm back in DC and the node may be closer to me. If it's on the East Coast, I could reach it first."

Bride said, "Sunshine, please, I can't have you involved. What happens if you arrive at the node first?"

"Same as you. If you're first—wing it."

"I suppose I can't argue with that logic," Bride said.

Dia spoke up. "If we're doing this, we need to leave now. CNN is already reporting me dead, the D & C may follow suit shortly. We need to beat them to it."

"Sunshine, I'll call you before we pull the trigger. Take care."

"You too. Agent Bride. Take care of my girl."

"I will," Bride said, hanging up the phone.

"Will you tell her where the node is?" Dia asked.

"Only if there's no possibility we arrive first."

"What if neither of us can arrive on time? What if it's in Indonesia?"

"Then I'll make phone calls to the CIA or FBI, whichever is appropriate. At that point, Dia, you'll have to surrender yourself."

She didn't speak. He hoped she was churning the situation through her incredible mind. He knew she'd have to agree. If it comes to that situation she'd be compelled to face the consequences to help dismantle the thing. If she ran, she'd risk a greater probability of treason charges. Chances were there would be treason charges either way, but she'd be offered a better plea bargain if she helped.

"We're overdue some luck, Dia," he said, derailing her train of thought. "So let's plan on reaching the node in time."

A brief cab ride and a thankfully undramatic foray through TSA screening had Dia and Bride at Gate B12 in Terminal One. There Dia set the plan in motion on her laptop. While she was still obviously sad, Bride could tell she was pleased to have the distraction. Next to her, Bride sat reading a Michael Connelly novel purchased from the gift shop along with snacks and drinks.

After twenty minutes of working—with Crystal's help in DC via Threema—Dia said, "All right, we're live. The code is set. The fake login page is online. Now we wait for the node to find it." Dia glanced to Bride who was listening but intensely watching passengers deplane Southwest flight 470 through the gate. Curious, she asked, "Why are we here?"

"It's the plan," Bride said. "From the airport we can hop any—"

Dia interrupted. "No. Why are we at this gate?"

"Oh. We're meeting someone."

"Who?" she asked.

"Here he is."

Bride stood and met a solidly built black man of military bearing. He appeared comfortable in black fatigues. The two men greeted with what Dia would call a 'bro hug'. He brought the man over to Dia. "Kay Cochrin," Bride used the name on Dia's identification, "this is Sergeant Gordon Greene, U.S. Army Reserves. If he agrees, he'll be helping us today."

Dia sat down her laptop in the next chair and stood to greet the affable man.

"Nice to meet you, Miss Cochrin." He gently shook her hand with both of his. "And of course I'll agree, Henry. Anything I can do to help my friend."

Bride frowned and searched for an airport-safe way of saying what he needed to say. "Helping us could be seen as betraying your weekend employer."

Greene hesitated to be sure he understood. "But would I actually be?"

"No. By my thinking, we'd be helping." Bride said.

"That's fine now, but you'll have some explaining to do later."

At that instant, Dia's laptop chirped. Dia's eyes studied the machine with dread. Bride watched her. From her expression Bride could tell she understood the beep's true meaning. It meant the node was active and the direction of her life depended on the words displayed on the computer's screen.

"What does it say?" Bride's voice was calm and serious.

She didn't move.

"Dia," he whispered.

She returned from her thoughts. She sat, placed the laptop in her lap, drew a deep breath, and plugged the IP's four numbers into a trace route utility. They watched as vector lines drew a simple route on a map starting from their location through a few hops to Yuma, Arizona, then ending with a question mark.

"Damn." She swore. "It's behind a VPN."

"I know VPN stands for virtual private network, but what does that mean?" Greene, who stationed himself behind her chair, asked.

"It means," she explained, "essentially the machine is acting as if it's connected to the local network in Arizona but, in reality, it could be anywhere in the world. But this should have worked. Even through a VPN, this app should reveal the final location where the VPN's tunnel entered the internet. The node apparently isn't on the internet until Yuma."

Bride hadn't paid close attention, instead he perused a travel website on his phone. "There's no direct flight to Yuma. There's a flight connecting through Phoenix in three hours," he said. "I'll book us three seats."

"It's only a four hour drive to Yuma from Vegas," Greene said. "I've made the drive before. I've a friend near Yuma."

"That's a better plan. We'll rent a car. Good thing I insisted we come to the airport."

"It's not in Yuma," Dia said. "The node is on a non-TCP-IP network. It's using an unknown protocol."

"Can you trace where it actually is?" Bride asked.

"No, but if that's where the node is tunneling to connect with the internet, we may be able to stop it or slow it down from there. Or possibly figure out where it actually is."

"Hang on. Someone give me the pigs and bunnies version," Greene said.

Dia and Bride froze, then slowly rotated their heads to glare quizzically at Greene.

Greene stared them down. "You know. How would Mr. Pig puppet and Mrs. Bunny puppet explain this to the kindergarteners?"

"Yes," Bride said gathering his thoughts. "We're going to Yuma, Arizona, to stop a thingy from releasing bad stuff on to the internet."

"Why didn't you say so?"

three: denial of service

26> Three to Yuma

BRIDE DROVE THROUGH THE NIGHT in the white Jeep Renegade they had rented from National back at the Las Vegas airport. Greene sat shotgun, and Dia sat quietly in the backseat, laptop open next to her. Bride kept an eye on her in the rearview mirror. She did some work on her computer, but mostly she stared out the window at the desert night. Over the first part of the drive, Bride explained to Greene what Dia's situation was, leaving out anything about Dia's sister. After Bride had completed the story, Greene turned in his chair, looked back at Dia, and playfully chided, "You've been a bad girl, little missy."

Dia stopped gazing through the window long enough to shoot one of those "whatever" evil looks toward Greene. Greene turned back to Bride and said, "I'm in. What's our plan?"

Dia had narrowed the location to the headquarters of Axeworthy Internet Security, just northwest of Yuma.

This revelation saddened Dia further. "Axeworthy offers a VPN service, so we could be talking about any one of their customers anywhere in the world. But the IP is not the same as what's listed to the VPN service. We may be talking about someone internal. Fingers crossed, we may be heading to the right place after all."

With some prodding by Bride and the use of a burner hotspot, Dia researched Axeworthy Internet Security's Yuma headquarters. She explained that they would have to enter Axeworthy's network center.

"If we can get hooked into their main network, I should be able to map their network," she explained. "If so, then I can trace the location of the last node. Or at least figure out how this strange protocol works. I'm reprogramming the first node to run the trace and hijack democratandchronicle.com for everyone on its LAN." She held up the first node. "We plug this thing in to their router via ethernet, and it'll break into their network. Then I'll be able to do all the magic remotely."

"Do you understand any of this?" Greene asked Bride.

"Enough to agree," Bride said. He then asked Dia, "So we just need to plug it into any ethernet port?"

Dia hemmed and hawed a bit, "Well, our best bet is to get this hooked up as close as possible to the main router. Otherwise the spoofing and tracing may not cover the whole system. You'll have to figure out how to get it in there after I finish coding this. If I don't get this right, we're screwed. There's no time to beta test."

Greene, "There's going to be a test?"

Dia dug into her code while Bride and Greene discussed plans. After roughing out an idea Greene declared, "We're going to need more firepower. My friend, Doc, in Yuma would be able to supply us with what we'll need. I'm going to call him."

"Hey!" Dia chimed in from the back seat.

"She doesn't trust phones," Bride explained.

Greene turned around to Dia in the back seat. "Well, it's nighttime, so smoke signals won't work."

She gave Greene *the face* again.

"I don't think she likes me." Greene said. "I'm a nice guy. She should like me." He turned back to her. Slowly and deliberately, as if speaking to a small child, Greene said, "You should like me. I'm the nice man who's helping you not die."

Bride didn't want to get involved in this right now. He was about to speak up when Dia said, "Unlock your phone and give it to me."

Reluctantly Greene did as ordered. "What's she going to do to my phone?"

"I don't know," Bride said. "She did something to mine as well."

"I like that phone. I still have seven months of payments on that phone." Back to Dia, "Don't break my phone, please."

Dia handed the phone back to Greene. "You're good now."

"What'd you do?"

"I put in a different SIM card so it now uses a different number. No one can trace your number now."

Greene protested, "But if Doc doesn't see it's me calling he's not going to answer the call in the middle of the night."

"It'll spoof Caller ID with your old number. He'll think it's you calling."

"But will it be me calling?"

"Yes, but not your number. But he'll think it is. Do you get it now?"

"I don't want to say," Greene mumbled. "Can I dial now?"

"Yes."

"What number do I call?"

"The same number. I didn't do anything to his phone."

"Just checking."

After the arrangements were done, the three rode down the highway in silence, Bride's mind getting lost in the hypnotic randomness of the headlights of the car's traveling north. He was happy to see Dia finally falling to sleep.

He assumed his friend in the front seat was falling asleep too when, after a few more miles, Greene leaned around and checked on Dia in the back seat. After seeing her sleeping, he seemed to contemplate, eventually saying, "Just tell me one thing, Bride. What the hell are you doing?"

Confused, Bride started to explain Dia's situation again, "Like I said, Dia is running—"

"No, no, no. I get what you're doing for her. What are *you* doing? And why are you doing this? This can't look good to your superiors."

"It's the right thing," Bride said.

"Bullshit." Greene looked him in the eyes. "What the hell is going on with you to get you mixed up in this girl's mess?"

At first Bride didn't answer, staring out at the road as if the asphalt had the answer. Finally he said, "Well..." He paused, deciding whether he wanted to say it out loud. "Do you remember a twenty-year-old black kid that was shot by Homeland Security agents in DC a couple weeks back?"

"Yeah?"

"I was the one who shot him."

"Damn... That was you?" Greene asked.

"Yeah," Bride said with a crack in his voice. "I shot that kid. I took away that Garrett Jackson's life. He had made some wrong choices, but did he deserve to die?"

"Nah. That's crap. I read about this. The so-called kid was a terrorist. I read this. You didn't take away Garrett Jackson's life. ISIS, al Qaeda, or whatever radical nut bags converted him to hate, took Garrett Jackson's life and stole his promise. You, my friend, killed Abu Bakr Hamed, the crazy puke out to destroy our country and any other country that doesn't agree with the bastardized religion his new friends have burnt into his brain. You can't hold yourself responsible."

"I know all that, but it still doesn't sit right."

Greene thought a moment before asking, "I'll tell you what to do. Send his mother flowers anonymously, get over your sad sack self, and let's help this woman asleep behind me without doing something that would ruin your career."

Bride looked at Greene with an expression that said, "Really?"

Greene sighed. "How deep are you in this thing with Miss 'No Phones' there in the back seat?"

"Deep enough."

"Well," Greene added, "at least let's not get caught. Deal?"

"Deal."

IT WAS THE DAWN of a relatively cool day in Yuma, Arizona. Dia Reynolds put her eye to the scope of the high-powered rifle. She took a moment and focused the blood red crosshairs on the North Second Avenue gate of the Axeworthy Internet Security complex. She lay prone on the ground, concealed in a narrow grove of trees inside the Yuma Quartermaster Depot State Historic Park which sat across the Main Yuma Canal from Axeworthy. A half hour earlier, under the light of the setting full moon, Henry Bride jogged past the gate and secured her NFC hijack device to its card reader. Since then the sun had cracked the east horizon, blasting its light through Dia's hiding space.

"Still no love," she uttered in to the microphone of her earbuds that connected to her phone. The phrase signaled her cohorts that so far no car had used the front gate.

"Remind me again, why does she get the Winchester .308?" Greene's voice reverberated in the tiny earbud speakers in Dia's ears. *"You're a sharpshooter. I taught shooting at Fort Dix. She's a skater girl."*

"You and I are going inside," Bride's voice replied. *"We need her and the .308 outside."*

"And she *can* hear you," Dia's retorted. She wanted to go in. It made sense for her to be on scene. But Bride had explained the risks. If Dia gets caught inside, it's all over. If arrested—or killed—it would be all for naught. The final node would surrender her password exposing the NSA software to the world, and she would be dead or in prison awaiting treason charges. Reluctantly she conceded.

Bride hadn't said it, but Dia also thought Bride wanted her out here because, since hearing the news about her sister, Dia's head hadn't been in the game. She had been zoning out, and having a hard time concentrating. Bride was right. If she zoned out while breaking and entering it would be fatal to the plan.

Though until now she hadn't realized that if she were caught here, on public land, with this high-powered sniper rifle, the same troubles would arise.

Greene's voice broke in again. *"And why is the black guy posing as a landscaper and the white guy posing as a software engineer? This seems like racial profiling."*

At the nearby side of the complex, Dia's scope found Greene holding a rake and wearing deep blue coveralls and a khaki, wide-brimmed hat. He was raking at rocks near the vent that stuck out from the ground near a small rear building.

"Hush," Bride's voice said. *"It's too late to trade now."*

The scope drifted back to the parking lot's primary entrance. A silver BMW pulled on to North Second and headed for the gate.

"We may have love," Dia said.

The window of the BMW rolled down and an arm emerged brandishing a square of plastic at the keypad. The gate rose and allowed the BMW to enter.

Dia spoke again, "We have love."

After following the BMW to its parking spot, her scope shifted west to North Fourth Avenue and found Bride in the rented Jeep heading south. She observed the progress as the Renegade rounded the Axeworthy Complex on West First Street and on to the entrance on North Second. During planning, Bride had concluded they didn't have time's luxury to wait for the following night for this break-in. She and Greene agreed. Those with the node might post the false obituary at any point. There was no waiting. At least it was Sunday and the complex that housed Axeworthy Internet Security Headquarters, judging by its rear parking lot, was nearly empty. Unfortunately Sunday also meant closed buildings. A deliveryman or repairman ruse was out. On Sundays those tricks wouldn't fly.

Checking the rear side of the compound again, she no longer saw Gordon Greene, but she knew he should now be attempting his entry. Dia didn't know what to make of Greene. It seemed curious that Bride brought him into this mission when Crystal had brought in Bride. And then there was Marine Sergeant Corey "Doc" Martins. Doc was Greene's friend in Yuma. From Doc they had obtained many of the hard supplies they carried, including the massive rifle that Dia now aimed into the software company's complex. She didn't like that she had to trust her life to people who would be blocked from seeing her posts on Facebook.

The scope slid back to the compound gate where the morning New Mexico sun glared from the bleached asphalt. She followed the Jeep as it pulled up to the gate at the entrance to the complex. His arm emerged from the window and reached under the keypad. He detached her NFC device—the same one she employed on the hotel doors of the Luxor—and waved it at the keypad.

As she expected, the gates opened for the device's captured NFC code.

"The Beemer drove to the east end of the lot," she said.

The Jeep pulled through the gate and headed to the west end of the lot.

She recalled the Google maps satellite view of the compound. It showed the compound consisted of four buildings, three central buildings and a fourth, smaller building at the far west end of the compound near where Greene had been. The main three rectangular buildings and their enclosed connecting walkways formed a stretched International Harvester logo. The largest and center building, the "I", doubled the height of the neighboring two. The exception was a modest one story cube that seemed to be tacked on to the relatively new complex. But it seemed this structure connected to the west building through an underground tunnel, at least if the line of vents protruding through the manicured grounds told the story Bride thought they did.

The Jeep drove toward the one building of the complex not part of Axeworthy's headquarters. A Wikipedia entry said a local construction firm built the complex in 2008. At that time, a press release touted two outer buildings as "spurring innovation in Yuma" by attracting various tech start-ups to the border city. But, to date only two startups resided in the Axeworthy Complex. Both shared segments of the east building. The west building housed overflow from the continually-growing Axeworthy Internet Security Corporation, also known as AXIS Corp. The center building, AXIS's main office, stood five stories tall—six if including the square, roof-level penthouse at the rear. It wasn't what Dia considered tall, but its seventy-one feet was sufficient to establish it as the third tallest structure in Yuma.

The Jeep pulled into one of the parking spots in a small section reserved for Hola IoT. She watched Bride step from the Jeep in a different outfit than he sported when he'd planted the NFC device at the gate earlier.

Created during a stop at one of Yuma's 24-hour Walmarts, the current disguise was of a young, hip programmer in Yuma. Dia chose the clothes based on Instagram in the accounts of various Axeworthy employees. It consisted of a faint blue plaid short-sleeve button-up over a heather gray tee posthumously promoting Nirvana, cargo shorts, and cheap navy blue boat shoes. Bride added a pair of knock-off Ray-Bans.

Already in character, Bride acted as a hurried software technician might behave. He took three strides from the Jeep, paused, and patted the pockets of his deep gray cargo shorts as if he overlooked something. He ambled back to the Jeep and fetched a laptop bag similar to Dia's from the Jeep's back seat. The guise was now complete.

With the bag over his shoulder, Bride rushed for the door. Once at the door he again waved Dia's NFC device, this time at a sensor pad mounted on a pole near the glass door entrance to the east building. Instead of entering, Bride stood in place, his back to Dia's position, and tried again.

"It didn't work," the tinny voice of Bride said. "It just buzzed, and the light is flashing red."

"Try again," she encouraged.

He tried again, and the pad rejected him again. "It's not working."

"Are you holding it the way I showed you?" Dia asked.

"Yes." Despite his assurance, she watched Bride check the gadget's position in his palm.

"Sorry," Dia said. "It may be as straightforward as our target doesn't have access to this building. Or it could be a system update, which means we may need to wire in a Tastic Printed Circuit Board with vampire leads into—"

"That's not helping," Bride broke in and she noticed he tried to swipe the pad again.

"Gray Octopus, you have a patrol coming," Greene's voice sounded.

Bride's bitter curse burnt through the airways.

"Language, Gray Octopus." Greene said. "There are children on this channel."

Dia ignored Greene's dig. It was all she could do to stay concentrating. She swept the scope back and forth until she caught sight of the guard inside the glass walkway connecting the center and south buildings. He scampered over the marble strip on the floor between a dozen or so round tables and chairs. The space was probably a communal lunch area and maybe an alternate place for the employees to work or meet. She centered the scope on the pear-shaped guard. The man was in no rush.

"I see him. Do you want me to take him out if he gets too close to you?" she asked.

"No!" Bride was emphatic. "Definitely not. We're talking about a simple security guard. He's a guy working weekends for a software company. This man is not a henchman of an evil organization. He's earning a living, probably has a family, and is not privy to the nefarious plans of the company."

Dia watched the guard scurry closer. Bride was correct. With his white hair and sunken eyes, this guy could have been age seventy. She had become overly excited. This was not *Ocean's Eleven* or *Mission: Impossible.* Her weapon and her cohorts were overkill for what should be a straightforward social engineered breaking and entering.

"*I'm feeling great about this,*" Greene voice said, the sarcasm clear even remotely.

Bride replied, "*Do you have a better plan, Red Pelican?*"

Greene replied, "*I don't have a better plan. I just don't like this one.*"

"*All right, I'll give. What's wrong with this plan?*"

"*Too much tic and tac,*" Greene said. "*Not enough toe.*"

Having lost the guard when he entered the east building, Dia shifted the scope back to Bride, who had turned from the glass and seemed to sigh. After a second he rotated back and immediately resumed character. Bride's body language feigned relief at finally seeing someone and waved toward the guard that had appeared in the main hallway.

Bride waited for a painful stretch of time as the ancient guard slow-shuffled toward the entrance. After a small eternity, the guard arrived at the inner door. Dia could read the guard's lips saying, "Can I help you?"

Bride pulled his earpiece from its place, cupped a hand to that ear, and gestured that he couldn't hear the guard.

The guard repeated, "Can I help you?"

She guessed Bride understood the guard—through lip reading or simply by the muted sound through the glass. But Bride pointed to his ear and again miming that he still couldn't understand.

At last, doubtlessly out of sheer frustration, the guard clicked open the inner door and came just inches from the exterior glass entrance. He said, this time loud enough for Bride's microphone to pick up the sound and transmit it to Dia, "*Can I help you?*"

"*Yeah.*" Bride said with enthusiasm. "*My card isn't working.*" He held up a blank plastic card.

The guard stared at him skeptically. "*That's not our badge.*" The muffled voice in her ear was bizarrely out of sync with the guard's lip movements.

Bride studied the white, plastic rectangle and held it up again. *This is what they gave me. Can you possibly see if Bradley is here? Bradley Grey with Hola IoT. He's supposed to meet me here, though I didn't see his car.*

"I don't think anyone is up there. I was just on the second floor," the guard lied.

"Shit." Bride shook his head. *"Look, someone discovered a vulnerability in our latest dimmer switches. I need to get up there and patch the code before the world knows our switches will fork over people's wifi passwords if you just ask them nicely. It's all just frakked."*

It took Dia a half second to realize Bride had just said the code word. She was up. Her heart immediately raced, going completely against what Greene had earlier explained about the details of firing the great rifle. She had explained to him that she had shot rifles before, but Greene had insisted on walking her through how to shoot the beast of a gun anyway. Now she felt she was failing him. *Calm yourself, Ducky,* the voice in her head said. *Don't blow this.* She drew a deep breath, exhaled, drew another, and steeled her nerves. She refocused the scope on the center of a window in the middle of the second floor of the main building. *Breathe.* She took a moment to be certain her target room was still unoccupied. *You're fine. It's nearly literally the broadside of a barn.* She exhaled, and in the pause between heartbeats, she pulled the trigger.

/ / / /

The security guard was struggling to explain building policy to Bride when the fourth story window in center building shattered. The thunderous roar of the glass crashing into the ground combined with the echo of gunfire. Seconds later, alarms bellowed. He watched the portly guard turn his vast body toward the origin of the clamor and started to scurry off. Bride stepped to the glass and banged his palms on the pane. When the guard twisted his head back, Bride held his palms skyward in a have-a-heart gesture.

The old guard rolled his eyes, but returned to the lobby and pushed the release to let Bride enter the building. As he stepped in Bride replaced his earpiece, deadening the alarms' klaxons. He shouted his gratitude to the watchman who sauntered off around the corner toward the connecting passageway to investigate the disturbance.

Dia's exhilarated voice sounded in the earpiece, "*Fuu...*" Her heavy breathing reverberated into her microphone. "*Oh hells, that was...*" She almost sounded as if she were crying. She had done well. Bride hadn't been pleased with her codeword of "Frakked," but it did the job. By the plan, however, Dia should already have stashed the rifle and be on the move from her hidden position in the grove across the irrigation canal.

"Pink Dog," Bride said, "are you all right?"

"*I'm... I'm fine.*" It was evident she wasn't. "*I'm fine.*" She whooped almost in harmony with the alarms. "*That... That was intense. I think I peed myself.*"

"Pink Dog," Bride spoke calmly and only loud enough to be heard over the wailing as he strode the marble floors of the easternmost building, "follow the plan."

"*Shit,*" she swore. "*Yeah, I'm going. I'm going.*"

By now Greene should have entered or at least be attempting to enter the west building. It took a while, but as soon as the guard disappeared from sight around the corner, Bride followed into the walkway to the center building.

"Red Pelican." Bride noted that he would choose the code words in the future. "Where are you now?"

"*I'm in west, Gray Octopus,*" Greene's voice replied. "*Designated rendezvous major is on.*"

Step one completed. He and Greene both were inside in the tech company's complex, but they needed to reach Axeworthy's center building.

Bride casually crossed through the café in the broad walkway and arrived at the sliding glass door at the end where another sensor pad on a pole confronted him.

"I have another pad. Should I try your gizmo again?"

"*Same model as before?*" Dia's panting voice asked.

"Looks like it."

"Then no. Give me a minute to reach my position and I'll dig into it."

"I don't have a minute. The police will be on their way and I'm in the open here."

He wasn't joking. Sixteen-foot-high sheets of glass made up the sides of the passage. It was like a fish tank. Anyone watching from the lower levels of the central or east buildings or West First Street would have an open view of Bride standing at the entrance.

"Well, if you try the NFC cloner again," Dia said through the gasping—she was undoubtedly still running—*"it might set off more alarms. So hush until I can get in position and google your butt out of a jam."*

Greene chimed in. *"May I recommend you don't use that phrase for a Google image search?"*

Bride ignored the quip and stood figuratively naked waiting for Dia to arrive at her next position under the canal bridge and hopefully provide his next move. He glanced around and concluded his best course of action was to sit at the nearest round table and feign working. So he pulled out a metal chair, laid his equipment bag on the tabletop, and sat down. He burrowed into the attaché case and realized the flaw in this plan is he had no laptop computer to make this ruse believable. He checked the case and withdrew any random object a programmer might reasonably need.

A charger cable, an ethernet cable and the power block for the Raspberry Pi node cluttered the table. He was shuffling the mixed components to appear busy when finally Dia chimed in his ear. *"Okay, no guarantees, but you'll need to pop the lid off the keypad. Carefully. But you should be able to open the lid half an inch with a screwdriver or a knife. Again, be careful. Too far and the wrong wire breaks..."*

Bride was repacking the bag when he sighted a small metal flap in the center of the tabletop. Lifting it up he discovered it possessed outlets for AC power, USB-A, and ethernet.

"Hey, before we try that, there's an ethernet connection here."

"What? There is?" Dia's voice sounded puzzled. *"Excellent. We could use that. Anyway it's worth a try. Do you remember what to do?"*

"Yes." He reached back into the bag, drew out the cigarette-lighter-sized Edimax N150 Wireless Personal Hotspot & Travel Router Dia had set up for this procedure. He connected its ethernet cord in to its outlet inside the flap and plugged the USB connection straight into its USB outlet for power. He tucked the extra slack of the six-foot ethernet cable into a thin slot inside the table and closed the lid. The setup would be found the next time someone wanted to use the table's services, but until then it was virtually invisible.

"Okay," Bride said, "it's hooked in, and hidden."

"*Great. Give me a tick. I'm attempting to connect.*" Dia said.

Bride sat like he was expecting for someone to join him for a business meeting. It fit his story to the security guard, but he wasn't happy. Hopefully this works from here. He doubted he could find a better place to connect, and the router's signal didn't need to reach Dia. It only needed to reach the wifi extender inside the Jeep.

"*Good news/bad news,*" Dia sounded in his ear again.

"Bad news first," Bride decreed. He had a rule: Always take the bad news up front. Bad news requires action and at the least one could start to think through the trouble.

"*I'm connected to the router, but we're going to need to go deeper in to their network to trace the last node.*"

"What's our good news?"

"*Nuqu is already installing on the router.*"

"That's good, right?" Bride asked. During the road journey from Vegas, Dia had explained about this Israeli spyware that attacked anti-virus companies. She expected to find the Stuxnet and Duqu related malware on Axeworthy's systems. Nuqu was her in, she had said. It would provide the exploit needed to crack in to the AXIS system. The explanation then turned technical and lost Bride and Greene in the minutia, but she maintained that she could utilize this great "super spyware" to break into Axeworthy's internal systems.

"*I told you this earlier. Nuqu puts a backdoor in to the local network I can use to get in. It—*"

Bride cut her off. "Without the particulars, what's it do for us?"

"It means I think I can relay into their security system from here."

Greene's voice chimed in, "That's good because I'm stuck outside the center building here as well."

"What's your position, Red Pelican?" Bride asked, struggling to ignore the blaring alarms, but they were bringing on a headache. *Note: Sound cancelling earbuds.*

"In an underground passage below the walkway between west and central. I'm just outside—"

"Holy hells!" Dia interrupted. "Nuqu is outstanding in the real world. Much cooler than in the lab. Isaac, you little genius."

Greene: "I don't get it. How does a virus infect this place? I thought this place was anti-virus. And who's this Isaac?"

She attempted to explain again, "Nuqu is Israel's ultra-sophisticated spyware. We don't know what they were using it for, but we presume Israel uses it to spy on the anti-virus companies like its predecessor, Duqu. Isaac is the codename of the Unit 8200's main programmer. Unit 8200 is Israel's Central Collection Unit of the Intelligence Corps."

"And we're letting it infect us?" Bride asked.

"Yeah, Nuqu is mainly a monitoring protocol. After it installs, it hides in spaces anti-virus programs don't even know to check, like the gaps between sectors of hard drives and controller chips. It only reports back what it finds when some master controller pings it."

"How's this not bad?"

"It only reports to Israel. If it weren't invisible to the company, it wouldn't be here. And I know its secrets. I've studied this beast. And I'm going to piggy back into AxIS's system using Nuqu's control structure." She paused. "So give me a minute and I'll get you boys in."

Bride complained, "Naked here."

Greene added, "Bored here. And annoyed by the alarms."

"If anyone comes by, look mean. That'll scare 'em away." Bride said.

"I don't do mean," Greene said seriously. "I do crazy."

"Even better." Bride laughed. Then to Dia, "Can we hurry it up here?"

"*Yeah, yeah.*" Dia seemed to dismiss them.

While waiting, he witnessed a white and black Yuma police SUV drive past the window on First Street—lights on but no sirens he could hear. The sirens could be drowned out by the alarms' klaxons. He stayed calm, repacked everything back into the bag, and acted as if he were just moving locations.

Then, "*Okay, just about there. Prepare to move.*"

Bride did as instructed. As he stood and slung the bag over his shoulder, the twin glass doors to the center building drew open and the alarms blissfully fell silent.

Before Bride could, Greene declared, "*I'm in.*"

28> The Hot Aisle

THE PASSAGE INTO THE HEART of Axeworthy's Yuma headquarters was relatively straightforward. The organization's website even provided a virtual 360-degree tour of the company's offices. As planned, Bride met Greene in the central stairway just inside the first floor access.

"Nice to see you, Red Pelican." Bride said to his friend and coconspirator.

"What took you so long, Gray Octopus?" Greene retorted. "Where now?"

Bride pointed up. "Four." After that the pair communicated with hand signals.

Greene climbed the steep concrete stairs with speed and stealth. Bride followed directly behind. Upon reaching the fourth floor, Greene stopped shy of the doorway. Bride signaled to wait. He removed Dia's NFC gadget from his pocket and waved it near the keypad by the sealed entrance. With a friendly chirp and accompanying green LED the door unlocked. Bride carefully cracked open the heavy fire door, peered through, and observed a wide-open low-walled cubicle space. In the extensive office's center, enclosed within three glass walls, stood the server racks, their target. So far, so good. But at the floor's distant end Bride spotted trouble; two guards, two police officers, and an employee in plain clothes, possibly the driver of the BMW. The group inspected the vast hole where the floor-to-ceiling plate-glass window had shattered. *Great!* Dia's shot hit two stories too high.

Bride signaled to Greene that five individuals were inside the office and gathered at the far end.

Staying low Bride and Greene slipped quietly into the low maze of cubicles, careful not to allow the latch click when it closed behind them.

Huddled in a vacant cubicle, Bride gestured for Greene to remain here and keep an eye on the five people.

Greene affirmed with a curt nod and withdrew his burner phone, shaking it toward Bride.

Bride understood. Greene could text him if anything happened. With his earbuds in and accessibility set to read notifications, Bride would hear Greene's silent messages. He gave Greene an optimistic thumbs up and ventured from their safe cubicle.

Crouched and moving cubicle to cubicle, Bride wound a path toward the fourth floor's center. Upon arrival at the server room, he found two doors. A wide glass door leading into glass enclosure that housed the front side of the server racks and a narrow solid padded door that presumably led to the server backs. The latter was where Bride needed to go, but there was no crossing the open hallway without risking being observed by the group lingering near the missing window.

Bride withdrew his burner phone and typed into the secure messaging app:

```
need distraction
```

"I'm on it," the digital voice in his ear replied. He was relieved until a glance at his screen indicated Dia had responded, not Greene as expected.

He frantically tried thumb-typing a reply when again came the crash of shattering glass followed by the trailing pop of a gunshot.

"What the hell?" the junior guard yelled.

"Did you see that?" a woman's voice questioned, presumably a police officer. "I'll call it in." Then, "Dispatch, 10-32, we have an active shooter downtown near the Axeworthy complex."

Red Pelican, go help her.

RED PELICAN> On it.

The surprising distraction worked. The police and guards scurried away with the elder guard leading the worker away from the open window. But at what cost? Dia was supposed to conceal the rifle after the original shooting of the window. She was apparently running about outside hauling the huge rifle, daring to be caught. They should have waited. He understood this plan wasn't perfect when he hatched it. Who was he kidding? It was a terrible plan. A high-powered rifle as a distraction—terrible. But they hadn't the time to plot anything different. At least he should have taken the time to be certain everyone was clear on their respective roles. The plan had turned to shit. The plan was shit.

He hid motionless under the cubicle's desk taking a breather to think. What next? Complete his portion of the plan or leave with Greene and help Dia? That would involve devising an entirely new plan, wasting effort and the time they didn't have. The situation backed him into the proverbial corner. A new plan takes time. Time and ideas were commodities not available. He had to finish what they started here.

This better work. From the cubicle's underside Bride saw his way clear. He slowly duck-walked to the narrow entrance and leaned against the glass. The NFC cloner in hand, he waved Dia's magic black box over the padded door's sensor. The lock clicked open.

Bride eased open the padded entrance and the rush of hot air assaulted him immediately though he stood feet from the door. He drew a last breath of cool air and rolled into the aptly named hot aisle. Dia's advice had been to leave the door open—that's what IT workers in the hot aisle do—but it left too much risk of discovery. The roar of the rushing air calmed when he snapped the door shut, but the narrow technology aisle was still uncomfortably loud.

Within seconds, perspiration trickled from his brow. On a rack pillar hung a "Welcome to Yuma" thermometer. It read 125°F, eight degrees hotter than the OSHA limit permitted for such a working location. He removed his outer, button-up shirt and used its cotton fabric to mop the sweat from his forehead.

"Where do I hook this up now?" he whispered into his microphone. But no response came. The only sound was the unceasing thunder of the enormous fans' airstreams. The fans circulated the torrid atmosphere away from the servers and up a hot-air chimney to return to overworked air conditioner units cooling the outer server room. His sweat-wet hand slipped the phone from his pocket and checked its screen—no signal. Dia may have warned him about this. She had mentioned "air gaps" and "Faraday cages". He'd have to recall her instructions from memory. Apparently even he required added time to complete his share of this terrible plan.

What was first? Locate the primary router's aft access, the box with the most cables running to it. This was easy. A hundred blue wires led to one component on the server wall. *Jesus, it's hot.*

Next, locate a nearby place to conceal what Dia had re-dubbed "the counter-node". He started by searching low. If someone was to find the counter-node, they wouldn't do it walking past. He found an appropriate location on the shelf's underside and peeled off the device's self-sticking backing Dia had placed on the surface of the device. With his back laid on the grated floor—where it was mercifully a few degrees cooler—he reached under and stuck the device to the shelf's bottom.

The home-brew device offered two power options; power adapter or USB. Bride recognized he should have attached the counter-node's wires before installing it in such a hard-to-reach cavity. A nearby server box offered an available USB-A port. He'd tap power there but fumbled to plug the other end into the Raspberry Pi's power input. For network connection, he snaked a similarly blue three-meter ethernet cable from the counter-node to the router. It was not perfect. The plug ends didn't match what was already there, and the wire's royal blue was a marginally different hue, but it didn't draw undue attention to itself. With sweat rolling down his brow, he re-examined the counter-node; its power indicator LED lit green. Things appeared to work.

While preparing to rise from the floor grates, he recalled the next step; he needed to cycle the primary router's power. Dia explained AXIS's routers possessed a flaw. The industrial routers required a short time to launch their operating software from their firmware after booting, and until they did, the router acted as a basic network switch. This meant for several seconds the hardware gave hard-wired connected devices full access to its system before the hardware firewall launched. That, Dia said, was the counter-node's in onto Axeworthy's network, circumventing all walls of protection the network device offered once fully booted. The trouble was this involved shutting down the system for roughly a minute. And it meant an Axeworthy IT professional would later check the network's appliances, offering a possibility to discover the planted Raspberry Pi. But that risk needed to be taken.

The original plan called for Greene to shut off the entire center building's electricity while Bride cycled the router's power inside the uninterruptible power supply, AKA the battery backup. The blackout would function as a smoke screen to their subterfuge. Without the building-wide power outage Bride would simply unplug the router and pray the counter-node wouldn't be exposed.

Bride attempted to trace the router's power cord to the battery backup, but it seemed every apparatus's power cables intertwined in an impossible to follow jumble. Each cable's plug was tagged, but that proved unhelpful since each tag only offered its corresponding equipment's model number, which meant nothing to Bride. *Idiot.* After repeatedly attempting to follow the cable, he realized both ends of the router's power cable were removable. He unplugged the power cord from the back of the router, waited the magic ten seconds, then re-plugged the cord. He had to trust that it worked. Only Dia had the ability to check.

When he stood, he left a field of perspiration from his back on the floor grating, and he hoped it would evaporate quickly. He took comfort that the shape was already rapidly shrinking. His work here was done.

Bride peeked between the slender air spaces surrounding the racked servers' aluminum cooling fins, out through the glass, and into the open office. It was tough to determine, but the outside floor appeared empty. Unfortunately, Bride didn't have a clear view. *Hell.* This must be what hell feels like. Everyone had exited the floor before he entered the hot aisle. One more peek the opposite direction and... *Damn!* He spotted the police woman. She stood overlooking the waterway through the missing window and speaking on her radio. Brave, since she understood there was an active shooter. Or did that suggest they had spotted Dia? Perhaps they didn't understand what broke the window. Or maybe caught her? *Damn it, Dia.*

He concluded he couldn't help Dia now. If he departed this corridor, he would be arrested immediately and then he could do nothing to help Dia Reynolds. So his greatest immediate problem was the heat. His overheated body dripped with sweat. Perspiration soaked his tee shirt, his shorts, even his socks. His mind felt faint. In the Navy, he had spent an extended tour in the desert. He understood what to do there. He had prepared for the desert's high-temperatures. This heat wasn't as terrible, but it would still kill an average person. Bad planning seemed to mark the entire day. To bide his time, he sat on the uncomfortable floor resting his shoulders against the padded door. This heat wouldn't kill him. He would bail out and give up before the heat overcame him, but how long to wait? When would he surrender? A ball of sweat gathered on the tip of his nose. The thermometer must be wrong.

After another five minutes of grueling heat, he checked again. Everything was clear. From his vantage point he saw neither the police officers, the two guards, nor the other man.

Bride panned side to side, trying to peek through every tiny gap between the rack-mounted computer hardware, but found no movement or signs of life. He waited for further signs, but the hot aisle was brutal. His tee shirt was now drenched with sweat.

He needed Greene here. He needed to be sure his exit path was clear.

With no such luxury, Bride prayed, swung open the padded door, and mercifully stepped from the hot aisle into the main office. His body still overheated, he considered the glass door. It would be as cold in there as it was hot in the hot aisle. With a wave of the NFC device, he opened the glass doorway and let the near frigid air flow from the room over his sweat-soaked clothes and skin. The cool aisle's frigid air was bliss on his heated skin, but it quickly grew uncomfortable. Time to get out.

Bride shut the glass door, but as he did he recognized, through the glass chamber, the fifth man, the worker, staring straight at Bride.

His barely audible voice said, "Hey, what are you doing in there?"

"Leaving," Bride said and bolted toward the stairway exit. Before reaching the stairs, however, Bride overheard the worker calling security. No turning back, Bride pushed through the stairway door and scurried down the steps in practically a controlled fall. *Get out fast.*

After exiting the stairwell on the ground floor, Bride reverse-traced his steps through the walkway and out the east building. As he sprinted for the Jeep, he pressed the unlock button on the key fob. Before he arrived at the Jeep, the voice of the old guard yelled out, "Stop!" But Bride wasn't stopping. He jumped into the Renegade, fired the engine, mashed the gear lever into drive, and floored the accelerator toward the parking lot exit.

Bride attempted to achieve that subtle distinction of speeding away without drawing the attention of the circling police cruisers. He had driven the rental Jeep Renegade completely around the block-long Axeworthy complex and traveled north over the canal on Third Street. With an eye out for Dia and

Greene, Bride's best play was to pull into the state park's parking lot, where they had left Dia, and pretend to wait for the museum to open. He prayed the old security guard hadn't had time to talk to the police. While turning onto the lot, he caught sight of two uniformed officers standing by a police cruiser, interviewing Dia. The young hacker didn't appear to be under arrest. Score one in the plus column. He slowed the Renegade, wondering if he should stay clear or...

Before given the chance to consider his options, Dia turned to him, smiled, and waved him over. He eased the Jeep into an open spot near the police cruiser. Lowering the passenger-side window, he spoke across the vehicle. "What's happening?"

Dia took the lead. "Oh my God, Paul. These officers are telling me that a crazed black man shot out the windows of that office building over there."

"That's terrible," Bride said, feigning shock. "Anybody hurt?"

Dia turned to one officer and gave him the floor.

"No, sir," the taller officer said. "Thankfully, the floors were clear where the windows were broken. We believe it's simple vandalism. Perhaps a manner of protest. You two should leave the area though. Unless you noticed anything, Mister..."

"Koler. It's Paul Koler. And no, I saw nothing. But yeah, leaving sounds like an excellent idea."

Dia said, "Well, thank you gentlemen for your service. My fiancé and I always back the boys in blue. Good luck with your shooter." She stepped toward the Jeep.

"Miss Cochrin?" the officer said, stopping Dia in her tracks.

To Bride's sense she turned a beat too slow.

"Yes?" she asked.

"Your driver's license." He held out the falsified driver's license, which had passed muster with Yuma's finest. Bride reminded himself to compliment his paper guy in Georgetown.

"Oh." She smiled. "Thank you. I guess I'll be needing that."

She collected the license from his hand then removed the wallet from her bag and slid the ID into its proper place. *Nice touch, Dia.* Other than the slight delayed reaction when the officer called her back she played the whole scene cool. Her undercover work had improved.

After stepping up into the Jeep, she wished luck to the Yuma police officers again and closed the door. Bride shifted the vehicle into reverse, backed from his parking spot, and casually drove out of the lot northward.

Once clear Bride asked, "Where's Gordon?"

Dia's façade dropped like an anvil. "Hells, Bride, they arrested him. I didn't know what else to do. I was hiding under the bridge with the rifle and police were swarming everywhere. Suddenly, there's Greene behind me, and I about punched him. I didn't expect to see him there." Dia was speaking a mile a minute, as if she had controlled her adrenaline but suddenly it all gushed free.

"Slow down, Dia. They arrested Greene?"

"Yeah." She slowed, but still breathed rapidly. "Greene took the rifle, Bride. He insisted. He took the rifle and ordered me to go." She repeated herself as if it would help better explain things. "I left him there under the bridge and I did what he told me. I walked up the trail like nothing was happening. They, the police, pulled me aside up onto the parking lot. They told me to stay down behind the squad car, and that an active shooter was in the vicinity. Just after that, Greene surrendered to them. When they brought him up, he was acting crazy, saying all sorts of things like, 'This is still America!' and 'Ferguson! Ferguson!' I don't know what got into him."

Bride had to laugh.

He pictured Greene going wild eyed and doing his crazy man routine. He'd seen it before. One night after fencing, five punk teenagers decided they wanted to show how tough they were. They started to give Greene trouble. Bride saw the scene play out outside the window. The five boys surrounded Greene. Bride knew Greene probably could wipe the floor with the lot of them, but rather than fight, Greene's eyes went wide and sideways and he began yelling. "Y'all are just peon tools of the overlord!" and, "You've got chips in your cerebellums!" The teenagers ran from him without him touching a single one.

"So what's our next move?" Dia asked. "Do we bust Greene out of jail?"

"No," Bride said sternly. "Top priority is finding that last node."

Dia reached between her legs to her bag sitting on the floorboard and pulled her well-beaten laptop from its bag. She crossed her legs on the passenger seat and tugged her shoulder strap to get more comfortable. With the no-name computer perched on her thighs, she pried open its screen and the display lit up. Through the corner of his eye Bride could make out a map on the laptop's screen.

"I have something already," she said. "If it's right."

"Yeah?" Bride asked, egging her on.

"You ever hear of the Salton Sea?"

"Yes." Bride looked at her quizzically. "That's where we're going?"

"Apparently. I've never heard of it. Is it some sort of resort area?"

"Used to be."

/ / / /

"Two police officers identified Miss Reynolds and the Jeep they rented in Vegas," Charles Watts said to Robert Liptmann. Watts trailed his boss as he power-walked across the tarmac from the C-9B Skytrain II at the Marine Corps Air Station Yuma.

"Well, hello to you too, Charles," Liptmann said. "My trip back to DC was fruitful. Thank you for asking."

"Sorry, sir." Watts said. "I assumed you'd prefer to be advised on Dia Reynolds as soon as you landed."

Watts was a good man. This was the third time Liptmann had used him and his partner, Sutter, to assist in an investigation. Both proved efficient and thought like police investigators. This mission Liptmann had requested the duo because their conventional minds complimented his rather unconventional methods. And they both excelled at the more physical aspects of police work, something outside Liptmann's scope. Though they were made fools of at the Luxor in Las Vegas by the subject now identified by fingerprints as DHS Agent Henry Bride.

"Do we have an idea where Miss Reynolds was heading?" Liptmann asked.

"Better than that, we have her precise location. Turns out their rented Jeep has a GPS tracker. She's not as clever as we'd believed."

"Well, spill the beans, Watts. Where are they?"

Watts smiled and checked his smartphone's screen. "They are currently driving west on US-50 toward Reno."

Liptmann laughed under his breath. "You've been duped, Mister Watts. I've seen that route before from Miss Reynolds. And it is confirmed phony."

"Well, we've lost them again." Watts shoulders slumped when he frowned. "But we do have the guy who shot up the Axeworthy complex, one Sergeant Gordon Greene. We've brought him here. He's Army Reserves, but since giving up on his crazy act, he's only provided us name rank and serial number. He's demanding a lawyer."

"Did he get him one?" Liptmann asked.

"No, he's asking for a particular lawyer, a guy named Burger."

"Hamilton Burger?"

"Yeah, you heard of him?" Watts asked. "We haven't been able to find him."

"You'll find Sergeant Greene is still doing his crazy act, and you need to watch more old television shows. Or at least search for people using Google rather than phone listings"

Watts simply nodded in acknowledgment.

Liptmann continued, "So any theories on why the strange attack on Axeworthy Internet Security?"

"No, sir. It seems to be straight out of left field."

"Get me everything on the company and the CEO...What's his name? Carleton Axeworthy?"

"Clarence."

"Right. I want everything on him as well."

29> The Dying Sea

BRIDE GRIPPED THE BINOCULARS steady despite the rocking ski boat under foot. Only the edge details of the lonely sea's shoreline were visible thanks to the full moon's faint radiance. Bride and his two boatmates approached the modern beachfront mansion by sea, but with its glass walls agape toward the watery expanse, every other direction offered better cover. No other boats floated this night on the dying sea's pungent water and Axeworthy's estate was the sole structure along the near shoreline emitting light. Inside the field glasses Bride could detect the silhouettes of the houses' and marinas' skeletons, structural ghosts from the desert coast's raucous heyday.

But tonight's primary focus was that solitary edifice of concrete and exotic woods. Reminiscent of Frank Lloyd Wright's Fallingwater. The beach house's structure appeared unsteady, like a great stack of concrete blocks. Each block haphazardly arranged with its glass face open toward the sea. The tallest and narrowest block, the master bedroom, sat perched atop the pile on the right and appeared to hover over the water.

"You lookin' at the Axeworthy place?" Matyas Pataki asked. Pataki was the old fifteen-foot powerboat's owner and the first person Dia and Bride met after their Jeep entered the strange, apocalyptic-like community of Bombay Beach. The motorboat was a living relic of the 'Seventies, possibly earlier, and had been patched together with fiberglass and hand-painted brick red. Pataki, himself, was a relic of still earlier times. A refugee of the 1956 Hungarian Revolution, eight-year-old Matyas and his parents first found their way to Bombay Beach in 1960 and he had remained there ever since. Handsome, but scarred, the Hungarian survivor had lost two fingers and an earlobe to the revolution. When Bride asked him where one could charter a boat, Pataki explained nowhere on the sea rented any boats except kayaks. But he volunteered to transport the couple on his boat. Over Pataki's mild protests, Bride paid the expatriate $250 to sail after sunset.

Earlier, before making the arrangement, Bride and Dia drove past Axeworthy's modern monolith four times along Highway 111, twice stopping to scope the property through the binoculars. But from land, good views were sparse. The only windows on the land sides of the dwelling were thin horizontal slits near roof level. Axeworthy wanted no one viewing inside. He wanted no one entering either; an eight-foot concrete wall encircled the grounds. Bride decided the property's layout necessitated viewing the house and grounds from the sea. They discovered photographic references to its inside layout online, thanks to a feature in Architectural Digest, but needed to survey inside for the photographs to make sense. That's when they drove back to Bombay Beach, the last hint of civilization encountered while driving north.

"Yeah," Bride replied. "What can you tell us about Axeworthy's house?"

"As far as I remember it the only new building on the sea since the heyday, see? We all was hoping 'twas a sign of things to come, but ol' Clarence there, he built and hoped that no one else come to the sea and bother him. Dotty down there found out that Axeworthy put money to help those lobby against the reclamation project. It seem that Axeworthy move here just to watch the Salton Sea die."

Bride knew the Salton Sea's basic story, having some time back watched a History Channel documentary about the man-made disaster that created it.

As centuries changed from nineteenth to twentieth, California sought to adapt the desert into fertile land. So it diverted water from the Colorado River into the expansive dry lake bed in the southeastern territories of the state. The idea was to dig irrigation canals and allow growing crops on the then desert land that sat over 250 feet below sea level.

The ambitious plan worked for a time. But in 1905 Colorado River flooding cut further into the poorly designed irrigation canals of the newly renamed Imperial Valley, forging a new route for the river. For two years, the mighty Colorado's waters flowed uncontrolled into the wide Salton Basin, submerging the town of Salton and a nearby Native American settlement. The Salton Sea was born.

By the 1950s, the Salton Sea, still the world's largest accidental man-made body of water, became a popular resort destination. Dubbed the California Riviera, the vacation paradise was frequented by the likes of Frank Sinatra, the Marx Brothers, and the Beach Boys.

In the following decades, however, irrigation water continued flowing into the sea and escaped only through evaporation. The water escaped; the salt did not. Year after year, the sea's saline content grew exponentially until the levels became toxic to the fish stocked earlier to attract fishermen. The fish died in mass quantities, the salty water stank, and the vacationers traveled elsewhere. Only a few fish species survived to today. Tilapia still swim in schools of millions, but tens of thousands die each summer during stifling desert heat.

"Does Axeworthy get many visitors?" Bride asked, lowering the glasses.

"Don't right know." Pataki rubbed his gray, two-day whiskers. "I see a few cars go visit, but none too often, y'know. More lately. They drive in on one-eleven. But then, we probably not notice 'em if he threw a Woodstock party. I do remember he got an old Gypsy lady that work there for him. Irma. Met her once in Indio, but she didn't right want to talk to me, really. And that's funny 'cause all the ladies want to talk to Matyas."

Dia shot a skeptical sideways glance toward the old Hungarian sitting by the outboard Evinrude. It was her first show of pep in a while. She had rightfully acted depressed since learning of her sister's fate. And Bride guessed she wasn't happy Greene sacrificed himself for her.

"How close can we pass by the house?" Bride asked Pataki.

"Oh, you don't want go in near there. A couple of the black boys walk up there along the shore, so I hear, lookin' for junk, and Axeworthy plumb took a shot at them. Them boy's momma was plumb *mad.*" Pataki stretched the word "mad" to two syllables. "She used her welfare money to move them boys here from LA so the boys wouldn't be gettin' shot at. She go and get Mary, and Mary drive her up to the gate 'round front to complain to the man. And you know what this *görény* do? He tell her he gonna shoot at her too if she don't get off his property. Everybody pretty much leave him be after that. He's a black dog, that one."

"So his wall doesn't go to the water." Bride meant it as a statement, raising the glasses again to peer at the wall. He had blown the planning in Yuma; he would not do that again here.

"Don't know. I think the wall stop so he can't see it from his windows." Pataki said.

From what Bride viewed below the full moon's light, that seemed accurate. Bride examined the house. It was enormous, beyond 3,000 square feet, with its main living space on the upper levels. Axeworthy had either prepared for a flood, like those plaguing the sea in the 1970s, or he preferred a higher view of the water. The house's upper floors cantilevered out over the wall to nearly the water. A narrow wooden deck below the massive glass wall covered two floors of the home.

Dia disturbed the silence, asking languidly, "How does he get internet out here?"

"Oooooh," Pataki said smiling. "That been the one sweet part of him movin' shore side." Pataki said. "The phone company ran some high-speed cable for him. Now the Bombay Beach peoples get whatever speed internet they want. Me, I got the wifi now."

Bride contemplated his strategy. He assumed the house had an alarm. Even if triggered, how soon could the police respond and arrive at the remote house? Most troubling was the wall. Hard to tell by moonlight but the wall seemed to continue below the house's full width. But it was a plain wall, concrete or maybe adobe, with no spikes or razor wire atop it. Unless Pataki also owned a helicopter, there was no telling what waited within the wall's boundaries.

Bride considered asking Pataki to drop them along the shore south of Axeworthy's property, but decided the better tactic was driving the Jeep there instead. It would offer them a reliable escape method and would leave Pataki non-complicit in any laws broken.

"You seen enough, young man?" Pataki asked.

"Yes," Bride said, but again scanned the beach house. It was then Bride laid eyes on him. Standing behind the glass wall in what appeared to be the master bedroom, Clarence Axeworthy stared out toward his vast inland sea. "Hang on, I see him."

"What? Really?" Dia said. "Axeworthy is there?"

"We gonna want to go then." Pataki said. "We not gonna want to anger him."

"That's fine, Matyas," said Bride, but continued observing the man behind glass as Pataki started the boat's engine and swept a wide turn southward. Axeworthy continued gazing over his sea. Perhaps he contemplated the surrounding mountains in the moonlight, but there was something eerie about the way he stared into the darkness. Axeworthy wore his trademark black suit with the white shirt. Its priest collar was completed by a black square, just as in the publicity photos Bride viewed during their research. In the photos the style appeared eccentric; now, in person Bride regarded the style as that of a satanic priest. Bride's shoulders shivered as Axeworthy slipped from view. He realized one thing: this would be harder than he thought.

/ / / /

Clarence Axeworthy watched the tiny motorboat skim his sea northward. It was strange a boat would stop near his property, particularly this late at night. Fishermen perhaps, but he couldn't help thinking it was something else.

The boat had distracted him from his main task tonight, increasing the size of the IPvØ network. It was a delaying tactic. Hopefully, by showing a drastic increase in the network's size, he would finally have time to access the NSA router exploits. It had become clear he needed to bring the network closer to the size IPvØ community was demanding.

Of course, it seemed increasingly more that the underground hacker community was led by one man: Attila. Somehow in the past five years IPvØ evolved from the loosely associated collection of anonymous cyber-activists demanding less government and corporate involvement in the internet. The group used to be famous for its infighting, dissent, and intentional lack of leadership. In 2012, a handful of zerøs (their name for their members) took advantage of the leadership void and seized control of the group. One of those self-anointed zerøs was a person using the moniker Attila (signing posts as @π¡1å). Attila soon became the voice of the zerø leadership group. Some insiders wondered whether the other members of leadership still existed claiming Attila had risen to IPvØ's sole leader.

Many zerøs left IPvØ's ranks after the cyber-coup, but after a short, initial decline in membership, the hacktivist group increased its numbers over the past two years. Mainly the growth was attributed to defectors from other cyber-activist groups such as Anonymous. These neo-zerøs claimed IPvØ's focus as their primary reason for jumping ship.

Clarence Axeworthy himself was a neo-zerø joining the group in late 2013. Though Axeworthy's motive for joining IPvØ wasn't because of its focus; his reason was the group now had leadership positions he could strive for. After establishing himself in the group, Axeworthy, codename X∧$, contacted the IPvØ's leadership and offered the assets and connections of his company, Axeworthy Internet Security. To his surprise, Attila himself contacted him. Axeworthy and Attila formed a mutually beneficial arrangement. In the agreement Attila gained access to the network of AxIS's userbase; Axeworthy would be provided with money and men, in the form of some of the group's most loyal zerøs.

When Attila told Axeworthy of his newest plan to replace the internet's infrastructure with a new protocol designed by IPVØ, Axeworthy had to be part of it. Attila explained they had created new firmware code for utilizing home and business routers. This code bypassed the systems of the world's internet providers. Axeworthy was eager and presented a strategy to build this grid of routers to a large enough size to reroute web traffic away from traditional internet providers.

After receiving a substantial amount of cash, and adding more company men from IPVØ, Axeworthy realized he had vastly overpromised. AXIS had only installed the IPVØ firmware on a limited number of routers. And opportunities were vanishing daily. Software exploits carry a limited shelf life. Within days of a major exploit being discovered by the router's manufacturer, a patch to repairing it is released, and the exploit disappears. Current-generation routers offered two advantages Axeworthy's plan needed: direct unfiltered internet access and an install-base that rarely updates its firmware. The latter left exploits online for years after their patches were released. Unfortunately, the latest breed of router auto-updates, meaning the amount of exploitable routers will soon decrease. If IPVØ wishes to seize control of the internet with this protocol, it needed to be soon.

Axeworthy believed once IPVØ's new internet was online, people would voluntarily install the superior protocol. The trick would be to secretly create a large enough replacement network to be able to show the world its superiority.

With the boat travelling completely from view—it seemed to have gone ashore near Bombay Beach—Clarence Axeworthy decided he procrastinated enough.

"To your room, woman," he said to his slave who once again slept on his beddings. He had changed his mind about exchanging her after she showed more life in their subsequent sessions. She again immediately performed as ordered. He didn't want to train a new woman to that level of obedience while worrying about his current IPVØ problems.

Axeworthy exited the bedroom's main door while she exited through the less glamorous door in the boudoir's rear.

He descended the grand metal stairway, and crossed the great room to his home office, the lights following his path as he did. He entered his office, and the room switched to its nighttime work lighting scheme.

With a flick of his wrist, he commanded, "Call Steven."

The black curtains opened on the back wall revealing the bank of television screens it hid. The oversized center screen lit, showing a live view from the newest, private workspace in his company's Yuma headquarters.

"Hey, boss," Steven Burgess said from his desk centered on the screen.

"Are you the only one working?" Axeworthy inquired.

"Yeah, Warren and Chris gave up around ten-thirty. They'd been working since seven this morning, and with all the excitement in the main building, it's been a wickedly long day here."

The men IPVØ had provided had disappointed Axeworthy, but he decided not to dwell on it. He had Steven Burgess. Though not the most socially adept of the zerøs, Steven proved to be the brightest and hardest working.

"What's our progress?" Axeworthy asked.

"Well," Burgess said, "we haven't resolved the trigger for the defector's node yet, but we're still at it. And security-wise, that Pi is a frickin' tank so no luck cracking it."

"What about your modified Blind worm? What's the timing on releasing that?"

"We're going live today. We're using malvertising to kick start the launch," Steven told Axeworthy over the screen's speaker. "I've added a hook to Blind so it installs using the Angler exploit kit."

"How many systems would that effect?" Axeworthy inquired.

"Hard to say. We're sure to infect nearly every XP machine still surfing the web. Any that hit our injection ads, anyway.

Other machines, it'll depend on their versions of Flash and Java plug-ins. We've tested against all the competitors' current AV and anti-malware software and it busts through them all. They won't see it coming. Once on any machine it'll be relatively easy to inject other machines on their LANs."

"And the routers? How are we getting them?"

"There's the genius bit," Steven Burgess explained, "The worm will use the operating system to display a notification that the router firmware is out of date and instruct users to download the update. It's like what we did with the AXIS router firewall installer, except here they'll be directed to the router's actual firmware updates. When they download the legitimate firmware update, we replace it with our code."

"What if they don't install the firmware?"

"Then after four to sixteen days their computers will be actively attacked by the resurgence of the Blind worm. I hope they like Korn because that's what they'll hear until they install the Axeworthy Internet Security anti-virus suite."

"What percentage of routers on the 'net will we control?"

Steven pondered the math. "If all goes well? Five to ten."

Axeworthy sighed. That number fell well short of IPVØ's expectations, and he knew it. He didn't want to cross Attila, but he didn't think these numbers would satisfy the head of IPVØ. He needed the NSA exploits or he would fail in the hidden eyes of Attila.

"Very well, Steven. Launch the attack now. We'll build all the numbers we can until we gain access to the NSA code."

30> Bombay Beach

PATAKI CUT THE EVINRUDE ENGINE and floated the converted ski boat up the launch on its momentum. When they drew close enough Bride hopped overboard into the warm salt water and walked the old craft, guiding it onto its waiting trailer. Bride ignored the gathered crowd of a couple dozen, particularly the little bald man in the suit and glasses he had spotted previously in Las Vegas. Looking as out of place as a pigeon amongst the penguins, the government man stood alone, but his backup—the goons Bride had dubbed Burgundy and Green Jacket—awaited his orders just this side of the town's levee. That pair now wore more traditional, matching attire, with the one dubbed Green Jacket sporting a sling.

The Bombay Beach levee, a rectangular berm built to prevent the town's flooding, separated the town's two parts. Inside the embankment, where the roughly 300 residents of the nethermost community in America lived, was subject to the saline desert atmosphere's gradual erosion. Venturing beyond Bombay Beach's levee, where Bride, the government man, and the curious townsfolk presently waited, subjected to a post-apocalyptic dystopia. Skeletal homes and businesses lay in ruins. Decades-old debris rotted into the inanimate landscape. A battered metal trailer seemed to melt base-first into the acidic soil. But no eyes viewed the town's dimly lit, retrogressing charm. All eyes instead followed Bride and the short bald man in the suit.

Bride guessed the leader, silhouetted by the headlights of a dark-colored, late-model Chevy government special, was dismayed that Dia Reynolds wasn't with them. Surely the townsfolk disclosed that Pataki's boat left with a man and a woman. After spotting the new arrivals through his field glasses, Bride had Pataki slow so Dia could slip overboard near the campground north of town. Pataki said the water was shallow enough there to wade after a short swim.

Bride dawdled, assisting Pataki load the motorboat up onto the trailer attached to his rusted '70s era Ford Bronco. The outsider patiently waited while Pataki spouted orders to Bride and the agent obeyed. Two of the town's adolescents, welfare transplants from Los Angeles that Pataki called Ty and Lewis, helped as well. Burgundy approached the far side of the vessel, casually peered in, then shook his head toward the suited man. The town people loitered, clearly aware something out of the norm was happening in their sleepy waterfront burg but showing no grasp of the tense situation brewing.

After thanking Pataki, Bride decided the suited man had waited long enough. With fish bones and barnacle shells crunching under each step, Bride walked up to ten feet from the waiting man.

"Good evening, Agent Bride," the man said. "May I call you Henry?"

"I prefer Bride, if you don't mind."

"Yes... Mister Bride." He appeared uncomfortable with the irregularity of addressing Bride only by his surname. "My name is Colonel Robert Liptmann. I am investigating the situation in the National Security Agency as you have perhaps guessed."

Bride said nothing.

"I'm here concerning Dia Reynolds."

Again, Bride remained silent. He would let Liptmann offer the information for now. The village residents seemed to share the same idea.

"I know she is here. I understand she arrived with you. She needs to come in, Mister Bride," Liptmann said. "For her own good."

After further silent seconds of contemplation, Bride said, "Perhaps." He chose his next words carefully. "I believe it's in the nation's best interest for Miss Reynolds not to surrender." He wanted to add the word "yet", but didn't know how that word would affect Dia, who he assumed lurked just up the beach.

"This concerns you as well—and your friend Sergeant Gordon Greene. Your careers are in jeopardy, perhaps also your freedom. I don't wish it to come to that, Mister Bride. Perhaps we can find a scenario with no jail time for you or Sergeant Greene."

Bride noted that Liptmann had played a trump card; he knows about Greene. He may have even spoken to Greene in Yuma. But how many trump cards does he hold?

"What about Dia Reynolds?" Bride asked. "What happens to her?"

"That's beyond my scope, Mister Bride. Her trial may even elevate to a congressional level. I'm afraid I'm powerless to affect Miss Reynolds' fate. She will have to take her chances."

"That leaves me little leverage convincing her. Am I supposed to say, 'If you give yourself up I'm sure Congress will be fair, impartial, and without agenda'? That certainly wouldn't convince me."

Liptmann seemed to try to read Bride's thoughts. "I'm sorry. I've nothing to offer her other than to promise I will be fair in my investigation. At least that should help you understand I'm being straight with you, Mister Bride. In your position, you understand how the system operates. It would be pointless for me to feign hope. You would see through any subterfuge."

"Yes," Bride agreed. "We need a day. Back your people off. Give us twenty-four hours and I'll personally deliver her. We can prevent a possible national security situation with that time. Isn't that what your agency is supposed to do?"

Liptmann contemplated the offer. After a half-minute he appeared to reach a conclusion. He gestured Burgundy over to him and whispered into his ear. Burgundy shot him a questioning look, which Liptmann answered with a sly nod. Burgundy gestured his head to Green Jacket, and the two retreated over the levee.

Returning to face Bride, Liptmann finally spoke again. "You have your twenty-four hours, but inform Miss Reynolds that I know about Wonderbread. I have Thorenus' account of the story. Miss Reynolds may not wish to let his version of events go unchallenged. I personally would hate for my people to not hear her account. Currently, they only have one version to believe." Liptmann checked his watch and read the time out loud. "It's 11:17 right now. I will give you until midnight tomorrow night. That's beyond your twenty-four hours. I expect you to be here then." He reached in his pocket and pulled out a business card, stepped forward, and handed the card to Bride. "Or tell me where and I will meet you."

Bride examined the card. It was plain, white, and only contained a phone number centered in a black serif typeface. He weighed their situation. Only one road led from Bombay Beach. Bride had no guess to how many men Liptmann brought with him. He assumed more than two. Bride and Dia were mostly trapped here already. Agreeing would presumably grant them the freedom to do what was needed at Axeworthy's house. And if all proceeded smoothly, they could be done by morning, well short of the twenty-four-hour limit.

"What about Greene?" Bride asked. "I want you to make his troubles disappear. Everything he did was to protect the country."

"That I'm capable of doing, Mister Bride."

"Then you have a deal, Colonel Liptmann."

/ / / /

Dripping wet and coated in dust, Dia Reynolds returned to Bombay Beach walking the dirt road heading from the campground. Her whole manner exhibited her exhaustion. Bride longed to hug her to encourage her to not quit now, but he suspected they wouldn't both have time to wash.

"Girl," Gelli, a twenty-something LA transplant they met earlier, said to her, "you're needing a shower. I'll get you a towel."

Gelli was a radiant young woman. Bride noted everyone they'd met in Bombay Beach had been uncommonly friendly and curious though with a slight dose of healthy suspicion. Liptmann and his men had been gone for ten minutes, and most in town had retreated to their homes and trailers though a handful watched from their porches. Bride couldn't guess how much excitement the slowly rotting town of Bombay Beach had seen in recent years, but tonight's events seemed to have intrigued its citizenry.

"How are you doing?" Bride asked.

"I don't know. I only want this over."

"Soon, shortcake. Soon."

Whether from his promise of her ordeal ending soon or the pet name—something Bride hadn't intended—an unfinished smile invaded her otherwise weary face.

Bride continued, "I realize you're worn out, but I'll need you tonight. I spoke to the NSA investigator—"

"What?" She instantly changed from lethargic to angry.

Bride held out his hands in a "slow down" gesture.

"Let me finish. He was waiting here for us. That's who was on the beach, an NSA investigator, a man named Liptmann. He agreed to give us twenty-four hours. So he'll be out of our hair for now."

Dia was still freaked, but calmed slightly. "What then?"

"Then—" He paused. "Then I promised you'd surrender. That's our only choice."

Dia said nothing, but Bride followed her eyes scanning side to side as she processed this information. He didn't stop her. He wanted her to understand, to resolve everything in her head so she would accept they had only one course of action. In the meantime, Gelli returned with a towel and kindly offered Dia a shower. Dia walked off with the girl, leaving Bride alone in the street. He decided to recheck his equipment so headed for the Renegade.

"Your girl, she in trouble, huh?" Matyas Pataki's accented voice said.

Bride pivoted to discover Pataki standing behind a chain-link fence inside his hectic front yard, leaning on a washed-out palm tree.

"Yeah." Bride stopped, rested his elbows on the fence rail, and said, "She's in deep."

"Don't you go all worryin'. Things, they turn out fine, you see. Even for an ol' Hunky like me, things, they work out themselves. You just ponder our little town. This place here, it ought to be a ghost town by now, like them other forsaken resort towns along these shores. But us, we keep livin'. For ages we pretty much were all old timers here. But now, now we got the transplants, the city folks who come to Bombay Beach to escape big ol' Los Angeles. This is not what we expect or even wish for, but them young folks, they bring new life to Bombay Beach.

"That Gelli, she the sweet young *bombázó* your girl left with. She got two kids, one five and one three, a boy and a girl. She did not wantin' them growing up living with them gangs and the guns. So she packed them up and move them here. The fact 'bout Bombay Beach is, in this town you might find Hell or you might find paradise. Gelli there, she a good one. She see the paradise. Sure does. Gelli took up paintin' after she move here. She pretty good too. That girl, she find beauty in our decay, and she paint it. And she get driven up north on the weekends, and she sell her paintings. Now she happy and Bombay Beach have new life.

"Understand, young fellow, it all work out in the end. Your girl need faith and then choose the paradise."

"I hope you're right, Matyas," Bride said.

Twenty minutes later, while Bride fastened duct tape over the Jeep's taillights, a clean and freshly clothed Dia emerged from a trailer. She hugged Gelli and strolled up the moonlit lane with renewed bounce in her step. He couldn't fathom what caused her attitude change but was pleased to see her mood upbeat again.

He hoped to sit with her and explain the consequences of not surrendering to Liptmann. Sure, there were ways she might escape. The most straightforward was Pataki's boat—Highway 111 was likely watched if not blocked. But she needed to understand how everyone else would be hurt. Greene would face court-martial. Bride's career would be over and he'd likely serve prison time. Krystal Carrie—Sunshine—would likely face a similar fate. If she escaped the US, Dia's life would forever be changed. Like Snowden she could expect exile to a repressive country like Russia. Granted exile may be preferable to prison, but how much?

And there's Wonderbread, the mysterious codeword Liptmann had mentioned. Bride was clueless on the code's meaning, but he bet she knew.

Before he began his assertions, Dia approached him at the Jeep's tailgate, smiled, and said, "Are we ready to go?"

"Yup."

31> Seafront Villa

THE WHITE JEEP RENEGADE rolled lazily over the hard desert sand. The forsaken surface crunching under the tires sounded over the rumble of the 2.4L Tigershark I4 engine revving marginally over idle. It was 3:15 am, and they traveled scarcely faster than walking. But the point of bringing the Jeep wasn't for a quick trip to the house. It was for fast escape. Then he could utilize the headlights. Bride had steered the SUV off Highway 111's blacktop a quarter mile short of the property to avoid being detected from the property's few forward facing windows. The house's southern face was void of windows. That probably saved on air conditioning and obstructed the view of Bombay Beach, but it also created a blind area Bride planned to exploit. And provided an obvious location to hide the Jeep off the highway. The bright full moon didn't help, nor did the Jeep's white paint.

Upon reaching the beach's edge, still some four-hundred feet from the house, he pointed the vehicle's wheels back toward the highway, parked, and shut off the engine.

"We're doing this, right?" Dia asked, evidently for reassurance.

"Yes, we are." Bride exited the vehicle and softly closed the door behind him.

Dia followed suit.

After retrieving his equipment from the rear hatch, most purchased at Big 5 Sporting Goods in Yuma, they headed off along the beach toward Axeworthy's residence. A few steps on the shells and bones blanketing the beach and they discovered it quieter to walk slightly off the beach on the desert sand. So they continued that path until they arrived at the base of the wall.

Bride examined the concrete wall and the building's southern exposure, searching for motion detectors or flood lights. He found none.

"He's in there, right?" Dia whispered.

"I would bet on it," Bride whispered back.

"Great, then just like we planned?"

"Just like we planned."

Bride hugged the wall and stole a cursory glance around the property's backside. What he found was disappointing. While the wall's back opened under the house, it didn't open far. The seaside access to the building's ground level stood ten feet in and offered no windows or doors, only a single iron gate near where the wall and house connected. He lit his iProtec flashlight and shined it in, double-checking his findings. He sighed, running the light through the stilts along the underside of the upper floors jutting out over the beach, the second more than the first. Nothing again. His light doused, he again flattened himself against the outer wall.

Bride spelled it out quietly. "We have two choices: over the wall at the gate and hope for an obvious entry to the house from inside the compound or use the rope to climb to the terrace. I don't care for either choice. There's a chance of alarms and lights, either way. We go via the terrace and we're visible from nearly anywhere inside the house. But if we jump the wall, we risk dogs, guards, or who knows. What do you say?"

"I leave it to you."

"I say it's over the wall then."

"The wall it is." She smiled.

////

The bare concrete wall stood ten feet high at the solid iron gate, but Henry Bride scurried over its corner like a squirrel seeking a stash of acorns. By Dia's thinking, it would be easiest if Bride lifted her over and followed after her, but Bride insisted on entering first to "clear the way." Eleven seconds after Bride topped the wall, a nylon rope, looped at the end, flopped over its crest. Her turn. With left foot planted in the lasso, Dia tugged the rope, which pulled taut, and up and over she went. Bride caught her as she landed on the other side and Dia lingered in his welcome embrace for longer than the situation necessitated. He felt warm. She hadn't noticed that her skin caught the chill of the cool wind rolling over the mountains. With a head tip, he indicated *time to move*.

Dia pointed out a steel fire door set in the cement basement wall, questioning whether to enter. Bride shook his head and pointed his thumb upward toward the thick wooden stairs leading to the main floor. She agreed, but wondered if the beach house's network hub might sit beyond that doorway.

Bride released her and trotted silently up the stairs. Dia's footfalls followed, slower and noisier. *How does he do that?* Atop the first flight they discovered a closed entry leading into the building's main floor. A second flight continued to the top floor, but Bride stopped on this level. He tilted his head toward the door. They were breaking in here.

Standard-sized and fabricated of thick oak, the door contained a single, six-inch wide glass pane extending nearly floor to top, very much fitting the abode's modern esthetic. After a peek through, Bride knelt and magically produced lock picks from somewhere. He set to work on the deadbolt, which glowed blue like her friend Koz owned. The lock was bluetooth, but before she retrieved her equipment, Bride had solved the bolt's tumblers with his picks.

Before opening the entrance, they checked its metal jam for alarm triggers. They found none. This made sense. Modern alarm systems tended to rely on motion detectors rather than entry triggers; so no need for Dia's high-power magnets.

Bride gestured for her to look in, pointing to the far corner of the living room space. Dia's eyes spotted it, a miniature dome bulging from the wall, a motion detector, well, at least one of them. Using his palm as a basic diagram of the room, he pointed first to the far forward corner, then to the near corner. She understood; the great room likely hid two sensors, one in each forward corner. The sketch he'd drawn in the dirt back at Bombay Beach in mind, she knew Axeworthy's office resided at this level's far end, past the kitchen.

Bride clicked the door open a crack. No alarms. So far, so good. He zipped open his bag and withdrew two emergency blankets, passing her one. The blankets unfolded to their full four-and-a-half by seven feet. Bride held the corners up demonstrating the direction to hold hers. She mimicked his stance, holding her blanket below the top corners so its bottom wouldn't drag the ground. Lightly pushing open the door, they entered.

If anything alive outside the barrier of glass watched them she was certain they looked like fools sidestepping across the vast room holding silver blankets flat toward the far wall. But the blankets fooled the heat-detecting motion sensors, enabling them to pass slowly across the open-floor-plan main level. All was proceeding slowly, but well, until Bride's trailing foot snagged on an insignificant ripple in the hardwood flooring and tangled with Dia's lead leg. She tried to maintain her balance but ended up flopping side-first to the floor, losing her grasp on the blanket as she fell.

"Hells," she cursed under her breath. She had clocked her knee rather hard, but she had landed behind a sofa.

Dia shot an angry stare up at Bride, who still held up his blanket. He glared back with apologetic eyebrows. From behind the sofa, Dia's expression turned to worry. But thus far no alarms and no sounds of humanity. Carefully she lifted her cloak again and deliberately rose back to her feet. After a second, they continued. The dance progressed excruciatingly, but ultimately they arrived at the entrance to Axeworthy's home office.

The office sat closed and locked tight with the same smart deadbolt technology used on the beach house's outer door. *Weird.* Bride gave his blanket a little shake.

Dia stared at him quizzically.

He shook the blanket again with a tad more gusto and a bit of frustration on his face.

Now she understood him and nodded her head to let him know. She raised her blanket higher and stepped so it screened them both from the lone sensor scanning this quadrant of the room. And he knelt and started to work with the lock picks. The lock clicked open faster than the outer door had. Again he checked for sensors on the doorway and detected none.

The handle clicked, and he pushed it open an inch, repeating the procedure of the outer door. Except this door contained no glass. Blanket raised in front of him, Bride stepped in. Dia and her blanket followed.

Inside the immense office, Bride peeked around his blanket twice before lowering it and roughly folding it away. He returned it to his pack, closed the door, and re-locked the deadbolt.

The pair spoke in whispers.

"We're clear," Bride said, finally allowing Dia to lower her blanket. She hadn't realized how sore her arms were.

A check around revealed the glass-topped standing desk with its three stainless-steel pillars.

"Here it is. Man, this guy is rich." The screen lit up when she moved to behind the desk, and it offered a single word prompt.

Password:

Evidently they missed the computer's motion sensor.

Dia was ready. Once they knew the node was near the Salton Sea, they duck-duck-go-ed "Salton Sea Axeworthy" and found articles about Clarence Axeworthy's new house on the shore. The search didn't offer a virtual tour like the AXIS headquarters had, but it revealed articles with interior pictures. One article, from *Wired*, contained the fact that Clarence Axeworthy had a chip implanted in his wrist so the house's electronics always sensed his position on the property. The chip automatically unlocked doors, turned on lights, and granted him access to his computer.

She held out her hand and Bride handed her the pack. From inside she withdrew the cigarette-pack-sized signal booster and switched it on.

No love.

"You're sure he's in the house?" she asked.

"No, but I spotted him in this bedroom from the boat. Where else would he go?"

Dia didn't answer him. She was busy contemplating the problem, thinking about the house design. The structure was fabricated from concrete. Concrete means rebar, lots and lots of rebar. Essentially there was a steel mesh cage around them and another around the bedroom on the top level.

From her pack, she dug out a second signal booster, paired the two boosters' signal, then handed the new one to Bride.

"Take this to the bedroom and get it near Axeworthy," she said.

"What? I can't leave you here," Bride protested.

"You have to. I need to break into the network, and I'm not going to be able to crack the security master's password."

"Damn." Bride shook his head until he realized there was no choice. "All right, give me that thing."

He grabbed it from her hand that still held it out.

He recollected his blanket and walked to the door.

"Lock the door behind me." With that statement he raised the blanket and disappeared out the doorway.

32> **Bump in the Night**

IT SOUNDED LIKE A SIMPLE TASK, place the tiny signal extender near the sleeping Axeworthy. Dia explained this would unlock the tech giant's computer, allowing her to probe his local network and locate her final node. So far the most difficult part had been climbing the interior stairs backward with the unfurled blanket. At the top landing, he reached the master bedroom doorway and again encountered a smart deadbolt. Weird. Bride guessed the locks unbolted upon sensing the chip implanted in Axeworthy's arm was nearby. But why deadbolt interior doors?

He slipped his lock pick and tension wrench out again from the hollowed heel of his shoe. He crouched and tackled the new lock, working methodically so as to not wake Axeworthy with scratching sounds. *Click.* The lock succumbed to his tradecraft.

After abandoning the blanket on the landing, Bride nudged open the wooden door degree by degree. Only the low moon's glow escaping over the western mountains and filtering through the western glass wall lit the dark bedroom. Across the super-king mattress, Bride's eyes beheld the contours of a body lying motionless beneath the white silk sheets. With the signal booster slipped from pocket to hand, he moved in, still crouching, step after slow, deliberate step. Upon reaching the over-sized bed, cautiously he nestled the booster beneath the bed's frame and switched it on. The booster would receive the low-level transmission of Axeworthy's subdural chip and relay it to Dia's identical booster, which passed the signal to Axeworthy's office computer. Assuming all worked as planned. But before backing from the bedroom, he again observed the sleeping figure. Something was wrong. There, in the blue moonlight, radiant as the moon itself, was a small, firm, nude female breast.

It's not Axeworthy. *What now?*

He studied the half-covered nude woman in front of him. Her skin pale and even, her hair long and raven black, and her figure slender, almost cadaverous. Once sure she was breathing he reached back for the signal booster. But before his hand grasped the device again, banks of overhead recessed lights blazed on with a blinding intensity.

The girl jumped and propped up her nude frame with her weedy arms. At once, her sunken eyes found Bride's, but he failed to read her empty expression. Startled? Frightened? Perhaps, but not in the manner he'd imagine a woman who had just discovered a prowler in her bedroom would. The motionless eyes almost pleaded.

Then emanating from behind, a deep male voice spoke. "I'm guessing you are the one responsible for all my troubles this week."

Bride spun his head about, his pistol unholstering from its home in the small of his back. He—and the gun—located Clarence Axeworthy standing in an archway leading to a dressing room. The tech millionaire, wearing the same suit Bride earlier observed from the boat, held a hunting rifle close to his side, its barrel trained on Bride's center. Axeworthy studied the intruder and his pistol while ordering, "Woman, to your room."

The nude woman leapt from the bed, scurried across the firing lines of two gun barrels, and hastily scooped clothing from the floor. Then she bolted for the doorway set in the bedchamber's outer wall. In his peripheral sight, tight around her thin ankle, Bride spied an electronic ankle bracelet, like the kind worn by home-release prisoners.

As the heavy oak door shut behind the woman, Axeworthy spoke to Bride. "I assume you have come to kill me."

////

While waiting for Bride to place the signal booster, Dia searched the dark office. She discovered a bank of video screens behind curtains on the wall opposite the water. She uncovered hidden doors disguising filing cabinets that were mostly empty, locked, or uninteresting. And she found a concealed bar stocked with various Irish and Canadian whiskies. But she found no wires, plugs, or outlets of any kind save the empty three-pronged electrical outlets every twelve feet along the walls. She also detected no active wifi signal. Strange, but with Axeworthy experimenting with alternate networking executions that might not mean an irregular manner of radio networking couldn't be in place.

A scrutiny of the glass-topped desk found nothing but a mechanical keyboard and a 30-inch flat-panel screen attached to the stainless-steel pillar through the glass. When she found nothing extra of value, she pulled up the chair, and the desk lowered to sitting level—well, sitting level for someone much taller. Her arms needed to extend upward to reach the keyboard.

As she grew bored, she pondered cracking the password. But then an overhead recessed light faded on and the computer monitor blinked to life displaying a blue-themed GUI desktop.

"Good job, Bride," she whispered, and she delved into the machine's settings. For its operating system it used a custom build of BSD. The first item she noted was the network was ethernet. With a tad more investigation, Dia found what she sought: the node. The node somehow was wired to the network, attached to the same router as this computer. Excellent. She next needed to find that router. Of course, she didn't truly know where this computer's CPU lived, but she suspected the lower floor. The burning question was: should she wait here for Bride? No, she decided. She had the information she needed. Bride would probably meet her on his way back.

After closing every window opened on the desktop, Dia switched off her signal booster. The light faded. The screen at once returned to its simple password prompt.

With her blanket ready, she stepped back into the beach home's common space. But she was surprised not to see Bride on her slow shuffle across to their original entrance. As she approached, there, atop the open stairway, she noticed a corner of Bride's blanket dangling between the treads. Did he not understand he just needed to leave his signal booster in the room? *Come on, Bride, let's go.* She warily opened the outer door, stepped outside, and carefully pulled it closed behind her.

While refolding her blanket, Dia spotted someone stirring at the bottom of the outer stairs. She froze, staring down at the woman wearing only a white tee-shirt, herself frozen midway into the act of pulling on a pair of shorts.

Neither woman stirred for a good fifteen seconds. Feeling more exposed than the woman below who proved she "went commando," Dia raised an index finger to her lips and mimed a "ssshhh". The woman returned a tiny nod, but otherwise stood motionless. Dia lowered her arm to the stair rail and took a step down toward the still-motionless woman. Dia continued calmly as the woman only stared. Near the bottom, Dia whispered, "You can pull your pants up."

The woman nodded again, but remained frozen and exposed.

Dia mimed pulling up pants and finally the stranger raised the shorts and buttoned them. Only then did Dia notice how thin her body was, the tiny shorts fitting loosely around the rail of a waist. Dia paced the final steps. The slender young woman stood erect, four to five inches taller than Dia, but Dia bet she outweighed her by twenty pounds.

"What's your name?" Dia asked.

The woman's mouth animated, opening and closing, but with no words sounding. Until finally she uttered, "Woman."

33> Facing Evil

"Put down the gun," Axeworthy commanded. "You're in my house. I have the right to shoot you within my residence, and it only means I'll need to spend the morning talking to the state police."

Bride ignored the order, keeping the XD Mod.2 aimed square at the millionaire's chest.

Axeworthy twitched his right arm then said to no one in particular, "Call Chip."

Evidently microphones and speakers were hidden throughout the room as the air rang, though Bride couldn't detect from where.

A groggy voice followed three rings. "Yeah, boss. What do you need?"

"I've caught an intruder. I believe you know him. Come to my bedroom."

"On my way."

/ / / /

"Your name is 'Woman'?" Dia asked, speaking low.

"That's what he calls me," Woman replied.

Dia was sickened. "Who are you?"

"I'm nobody." Woman hung her head in shame, her dark hair hiding her porcelain face. "I just try to please Mister Axeworthy."

"Nonsense." As Dia grew angrier, her voice increased its volume. "How long have you been here?"

"I don't know. There aren't no seasons here."

"Oh, the hells." Dia placed her arm around Woman's shoulder, but when she flinched at her touch, Dia backed away.

"Look," Dia said, "my friend and I are here … running an important errand. As soon as we're finished you're leaving with us. Okay?"

"I can't leave. He'll kill me." Tears poured from Woman's eyes, but her face stayed emotionless.

Dia struggled to hold strong, but a tear fell from her eye as well. "No, no, sweetheart, my friend is with the federal government. In fact, his branch deals with these situations." Dia wanted to ask questions like "What have they done to you?" or "How old were you when you were taken?" but for now she simply asked, "Before they called you 'Woman', what was your name?"

"Girl."

Choked up, Dia managed to ask, "And before that?"

With the sweetest voice Dia ever beheld from an adult's mouth, Woman said, "When I was a little girl, people called me Ruby."

"Ruby?" The name hit Dia like a Mack truck. Why? Why did she have her sister's name? Thus far, Dia had mostly controlled her emotions, but she could no longer stop the tears streaming. All of her emotions swallowed regarding Alec's suicide; the death of her sister, this girl's namesake; her abandoned life; and everyone attempting to kill her; all came flooding out.

Woman—Ruby—managed the teeniest of smiles.

Through the tears, struggling to smile to be reassuring, Dia declared, "I'm going to call you Ruby, okay?"

"Okay." Ruby said. "What should I call you?"

"Ducky. Call me Ducky."

/ / / /

The standoff dragged on, neither gunman shifting his position from the instant the lights switched on. The simplest action for Bride was firing multiple 9mm slugs into the software mogul's heart. But what then? Bride's mind deduced Axeworthy had placed the contract on Dia's life, but he frankly had no proof. Without reasonable proof, Bride would be prosecuted for first-degree murder. Liptmann would void his agreement, meaning Greene's court-martial, Dia's trial for treason, and the NSA files unlocked for the world—or leastwise Axeworthy's people—to examine and exploit. Shooting Axeworthy became Bride's final option.

But Bride's options were running out. Chip was on his way, and Bride assumed Chip was coming from the apartment above the complex's external garage, which meant a minute perhaps. He hoped Dia carried on without him, finding the node, and disconnecting or destroying it. She might have escaped already. Hopefully, Dia assumed, as he did, they would meet at the Renegade, and if he didn't arrive soon she should leave without him. Dia had the second set of Jeep keys. He hoped she put this all together. But that was a lot of hoping.

He held one further hope. This one relied on something he observed added to the fact he'd locked the deadbolt upon entering the room. And a lot of hope.

/ / / /

"Sorry Ruby, we can't leave yet," Dia told her. "There's an electronic gadget I have to locate. I believe it might be somewhere on the ground floor. Can you show me? I spotted an iron door near the back gate—"

"That's my room," Ruby said. "There's nothing inside."

"Can I look?"

"No!" Ruby became belligerent. "You told me we were leaving, Ducky. I won't go back inside. Once you go inside the door locks behind you and you don't get out until the Mister calls for you."

Dia tried to calm her. "It's okay, Ruby sweetheart. I probably only need to peek inside. I won't go inside unless I absolutely must."

"It's okay?"

"Yeah, Ruby, It's okay. Everything's going to be okay."

Ruby took Dia's hand lightly in hers, gave her a teeny smile, and led her to the metal door near the back gate.

"Don't go in," Ruby begged.

"I won't." Dia turned the knob and slowly pushed the heavy door open. Inside the chamber was pure black, so Dia reached inside and found the light switch. When she toggled the simple switch, a single light recessed in the ceiling's center lit the ten-foot by eight-foot hold's bare cinder block walls. Ruby was right, the chamber held near nothing. A steel toilet hung from the wall in the far corner, a simple mattress lay opposite. A shower head above a drain occupied the near corner with a single valve on the wall between them. It was a slave den, only offering enough amenities to keep the girl alive and clean enough that Axeworthy wouldn't be repulsed during sex.

"Oh..." Dia became so sickened by the scene she forgot why she was looking.

"See. Nothing in there." Ruby tried to pull the door shut, but Dia stood shocked, hindering Ruby's effort.

Dia shook herself from her momentary stupor and said, "Yes Ruby, you are right. What I'm searching for is not inside here."

/ / / /

Bride estimated a half second. There would exist perhaps a half-second window between being square in the sights of Axeworthy's rifle and the moment Axeworthy's reinforcements burst into the bedchamber. After that all would be lost. At least a thousand half-seconds would slip away before the one Bride waited for would ultimately arrive. Through all the half-seconds Bride awkwardly held the 2-pound-plus XD Mod.2 with his right arm straight, awkwardly across his torso. He dare not move it one inch for fear of giving Axeworthy his own half-second. The pistol grew heavier and heavier as he held it trained on Axeworthy's heart. Bride's muscles in his arm and shoulder burned from the prolonged strain and nearly won out with their contention that lowering the weapon meant the accelerating pain would go away. But the harbinger of Bride's prize half-second came before the arm lowered the pistol. It came with a knock on the door. *Knock, knock, knock*

"Mister Axe, it's locked." The male voice penetrated the door.

Here it comes.

Bride watched anxiously as Axeworthy flicked his cyber-enhanced wrist to issue his voice command to unlock the door. As Axeworthy's wrist flipped, his finger slipped off of the rifle's trigger.

Go!

The instant the finger left the trigger, Bride rolled backward, spun, rose to his feet, and sprinted toward the rear wall of glass. The gun raised in his hand before he thought it, his muscles having forgotten their strain, and he fired again and again into the glass. He was glad to hear Axeworthy's voice frantically yell, "Unlock the bedroom door!" for he knew it would be that or the rifle firing. The twenty-foot tall pane of glass spider-webbed in front of him, fracturing the incoming moonlight into tiny dim sparkles throughout the wide bedroom. He lowered his lead shoulder and drove it at his full speed into the fractured pane.

The splintered glass panel flexed, but it did not give.

Bride bounced off, dropped his pistol in the process, and they both fell separately to the floor. Before Bride regained his bearings, Chip—who Bride thought of as Ponytail—stood over him with a rather large pistol of his own.

Bride had had no luck with glass panes this week.

34> **Caught**

"RUBY, I NEED TO FIND MY DEVICE. Is there another entry to the ground floor?" Dia asked.

"I don't know," Ruby responded. "Maybe in the front. I don't know. I'm not allowed to leave my area."

"It's okay." Dia understood Ruby was fundamentally still an emotionally fragile little girl. She would prefer to help her escape her prolonged hell right now, and if she had an easy answer, she indeed would. But Dia didn't believe Ruby capable of scaling the wall alone or surviving outside. "Can you follow me?"

"Yes." Ruby said.

They rounded the house's front corner nearest the highway and reached another wrought-iron gate set between the house and wall. Through the gate sat a second doorway that led into the ground floor level. Beyond that stood a spacious walled courtyard containing cars parked about the exterior, bushes in the corners, and an abstract marble fountain in its center. Beyond the cars, near the front gate, lay a multi-door garage with what appeared to be a second story apartment. She and Bride had noted this outbuilding while scouting the complex, but deemed it unimportant, deciding the node likely was kept inside the main house. At the base of the external stairway leading from the outbuilding's apartment stood the largest human being Dia had ever seen.

Dia quietly swore.

The behemoth plodded the courtyard on patrol, presumably watching for her and Bride. But with giant shoulders slumped and more watching his feet than the yard, the brute exhibited zero enthusiasm for his given task. He had been riled from sleep, Dia guessed. She determined they needed to continue, nevertheless. Dia glanced back to Ruby and whispered, "Keep quiet, keep low, and stay with me."

For several seconds Ruby did not respond before she uttered, "I don't want to go out there."

"The door is right there. Ten feet perhaps. If we stay low, he won't see us."

Ruby still hesitated.

Dia weighed not proceeding or leaving the girl behind because she could sense Ruby's mind was delicate. Instead Dia ordered the millionaire's sex slave with a quiet force, "You *are* coming with me."

Dia hated herself for using Ruby's mental state against her, but the concubine answered, "Okay."

Her signal booster out, Dia switched it on, and the gate magically clicked unlocked. With a light push the passageway opened enough for them to slip through. "Stay low and don't move until I do."

A quick peek over revealed the enormous man clearly showed no interest. His eyes drooped and his great body sagged against a Lexus. Apparently in his wearied judgment he decided it okay to try sleeping while standing on the job. They tiptoed through the gate toward the forward doorway, this one a simpler, hardwood door. Again the signal booster activated, popping this deadbolt open, and Dia and Ruby slipped into the dark windowless chamber. Dia wedged a screwdriver from her bag between the door and its frame in case this deadbolt automatically locked from the inside like the one leading to Ruby's cell.

Upon entering, the automated overhead light illuminated. *Thanks again, signal booster.* They stood inside a cluttered storeroom filled with various computer equipment and boxes. Dia understood this was the place she sought after noticing along the far, still-dark wall the telltale chaotic flashing line of LED lights of network routers. *Bingo.*

Dia smiled at Ruby and said, "My device should be inside here somewhere."

The ceiling lights followed the booster pack path as Dia and Ruby tracked back to the rack housing routers and Axeworthy's office CPU. From that point, Dia traced a loosely hung CAT6 cabling up the wall and down to a simple workbench. There, sitting in the center, stripped of its housing but still mostly encased in its protective resin, was the Las Vegas node.

A trick she learned reading about a roadie from the Grateful Dead, the black resin was a precaution to prevent her modifications from being copied or tampered with without destroying the device. Someone had carefully shaved away the Raspberry Pi's resin along one edge, but only enough to attach the ethernet cable. It appeared they had quit before they reached the major electronics. Disconnect this node, Dia surmised, and her self-made ordeal would be over. She searched the wall of tools above the bench until her hand settled on a ball-peen hammer. She grasped the wood-handled hammer with both hands, held it high over her head, and swung it down with her full might on top the Raspberry Pi. The miniature device sparked and shattered into several dozen pieces of resin, glass fiber, silicone, and copper.

And then she hit it again. And again. She continued the hammer strikes until the chunks pulverized to dust.

Satisfied, Dia stopped and panted, examining her handiwork. It was done. She was safe.

Or so she believed until she heard, "Who's in there?"

Dia cursed herself. There were surely quieter ways for her to destroy the device. She deactivated the signal booster instantly extinguishing the overhead light.

She turned to Ruby who cowered in the corner, dimly lit by the computer rack's blinking LEDs. Had it been the voice that frightened her or Dia's violent outburst? Dia searched the dark and found a pile of boxes. In a loud whisper, she called, "Ruby, see these boxes? I need you to hide behind them. Okay sweetheart?"

Ruby nodded agreement but remained motionless.

"Come along, Ruby, quickly. Over here, honey."

Ruby arose and stepped slowly toward the boxes apparently not sensing Dia's urgency.

Dia helped her new companion slip behind the box pile then stacked more boxes on top.

"Don't move from here, okay?" Dia whispered. "If I have to leave, I'll come back and get you, but don't move."

"Okay," Ruby said submissively.

Dia stacked one last box, blocking the final hole in the stack, but heard, "No, Ducky. I can't breathe."

Of course she would be claustrophobic. Rightly so. Dia shifted the box leaving a six-inch crack.

"Better?"

"Better."

Ruby was taken care of, now to—Too late. The man-brute's silhouette had breached the doorway. Dia grasped the ball-peen in her left hand and pulled the North American Arms .22 Magnum Wasp Revolver from her waist with her right. She prepared to defend herself against the giant who barely fit through the door. The man was more massive than he had appeared standing in the yard, and he carried a baseball bat choked up in his enormous fist. The other massive hand switched on the lights, exposing Dia and the brute who stood twenty feet away from her. He grinned.

"Oh hells," she moaned raising the little gun toward the brute. "Back off, Hulk!"

The colossus laughed. "You think that pee shooter will stop me?"

She aimed the pistol lower. "It'll stop you from reproducing. That'd certainly be a positive for mankind."

"You won't do it," the brute challenged.

The little gun fired.

A fresh rough circle of blood and flesh bloomed in the giant's crotch. The man-mountain dropped to his knees, stunned and howled a terrible, guttural scream. Like a tumbling boulder, he tipped over into a wall of shelves, knocking the shelves, books, and spare computer equipment over atop him. The scream melded into cursing—loud, harsh cursing.

Dia was debating whether to fetch Ruby from beneath the boxes when a second goon came through the door. She recognized him. It was the man from Myrtle Beach. The one Bride had called Roll. *That makes the cursing lump on the floor Rock*, she supposed. Before the new arrival could assess the situation, Dia leveled her tiny pistol at his chest.

"I warned you I'd shoot," she said.

"I believed you. I believed you," Roll said, putting his hands up by his side.

"She shot my 'nad, man!" Rock yelled to Roll. "It fucking hurts like a bitch's bastard! Kill her!"

Roll stepped backward to prove he was no threat. "No, no, girl. I'm cool. We're cool," he said to Dia.

Taking Roll's lead, Dia said, "That's right. Just back out of here."

"What are you doing?" Rock screamed, holding both hands to his groin. "Kill her, man!"

"Don't make me shoot you again." Dia shouted to the big man, though she kept her eyes and aim on Roll. She stepped wide around Rock as Roll continued backing out the doorway.

"Don't leave me here!" Rock pleaded. "At least call an ambulance."

From outside the door Rock called back in to his compatriot, "You know the boss won't allow that. Sorry, Rock."

The ailing brute continued screaming and pleading, though each successive gripe seemed to steal more of Rock's energy. As Dia reached the door, Roll had backed himself up to the iron gate.

Dia stepped through the threshold just as she realized Roll's behavior was odd. Why back up to the gate?

The answer came when an arm swept from beside her and knocked her arms and pistol downward. In the confusion, Dia's finger hooked the trigger and fired a shot striking the gate's iron rail directly between Roll's thighs. The unknown assailant's second arm snaked around her waist and pulled her from the doorway. Before she grasped what happened she was wrapped up by the arms of this third man, and the miniature pistol was stripped from her hands, knocking it to the ground.

Roll smiled, lowered his arms, and bent to look between his legs at the dent in the wrought-iron. "You really hate men, don't you?"

35> The Protocol

BRIDE WAS RELEGATED to being an audience as two ruffians pushed Dia harshly through the twin front doors into the great room. He had encountered the lead man before. It was Roll from South Carolina, who seemed to take tremendous pleasure keeping Dia's purloined gun leveled at her head.

Despite day breaking outside the glass wall, all the lights of the great room simultaneously lit bright as Axeworthy entered. With the lights providing a fuller inspection of the room, Bride thought it decorated with an Ikea credit card and the direction "Keep it clean." Axeworthy held court in the room's center as the goons escorted Dia to the party. Bride sat on a white leather couch, his hands laced behind his head. Ponytail stood behind him with the business end of a Remington rifle pressed hard into the crook of Bride's neck. When Axeworthy saw the young hacker enter, he devoted his focus to her. He smiled, and said, "The NSA turncoat I've heard so much about. Welcome to my seaside home."

Dia stood defiant, her arms poised at her sides. After their recent experiences, Bride was proud of her. Her attitude conveyed if they were going to shoot her then, damn it, shoot her. These underlings didn't treat her as a threat. They had taken her bag and had probably searched her thoroughly. They would know she held no other weapons. So she pushed her advantage. Bride guessed as long as she made no rash movements, they wouldn't shoot her without prior word from the boss. She looked to Bride with concern.

"Are you all right?" she asked Bride.

"He's fine," Axeworthy answered for Bride. "For now."

"Well then, you might as well release us," she said. "I've destroyed the one remaining node. Killing me no longer releases the password. The NSA files are locked forever."

This brought a smile to Bride's face. Axeworthy, on the other hand, was flustered. He inhaled through his nose and breathed out through his mouth, trying to hold it together.

But contrary to his boss's Zen moment, Roll spoke up, "She shot Rock, Mister Axe. You can't let her go."

Bride laughed. "Wow. Nice going, girl."

That earned Bride a rifle butt to the head.

While playing off the pain, Bride said, "Sorry, I didn't like that guy."

Roll added, "She shot him in the testicle."

That brought a stifled snicker from Bride. He felt the rifle barrel leave his collar again and prepared for another smack, but Axeworthy raised his hand halting the retribution.

"This disappoints me." Axeworthy said.

Bride couldn't resist adding, "Not as much as it does Rock."

Dia even laughed at that one, but it earned him another blow to the cranium.

"I'm not talking about that!" Axeworthy screamed at Bride. *"I'm talking—"* He stopped and calmed himself again. "I'm talking about your friend's program. We had important plans for that."

"Que sera, sera." Bride said.

"Oh, but our plans would benefit mankind and protect us all from Miss Reynolds' agency. Or should I say 'former agency'?" Axeworthy pointed at Dia. "Ironically, it's their program that will help make our plans feasible."

"Are you talking about that new protocol you had the node using?" Bride asked. "She told me about that. That's your glorious new internet?"

"Yes, that's what I'm speaking of, an internet free of government snooping. An internet no longer relying on giant cable and phone networks for its backbone. An internet communicating router to router, device to device, person to person, bypassing the mammoth central hubs. Fully encrypted, end to end. A better internet. A people's internet, not a corporation's, not a government's. Unblockable."

Bride was incredulous. "And we killed that? Shame. I suppose we're stuck with phone and cable companies instead of your company."

"Oh, it's not my corporation that's creating the new internet. We'll just facilitate it. In fact, the beginnings of this new infrastructure is already fully functional. Ninety-three percent of home and business networks running Axeworthy Software and nearly three percent of the current internet as a whole have the protocol available today. But obviously we'll need a vaster network if our superior protocol is to displace the current internet framework. Our patrons have tasked us with expanding the scope of their new protocol. Which is where Miss Reynolds comes in. She will help install the new protocol on a majority of the world's network routers."

"You want the NSA software?" Bride asked. "That software will grant you access to those routers?"

"Precisely, Mister ... er..." Axeworthy stopped his train of thought. "Sorry, I don't know your name, Mister..."

"I prefer to remain anonymous," Bride said.

"Whatever. It does not matter." Axeworthy appeared unfazed, still holding every eye in the room. "Anyway, I was saying, the NSA software will provide us with the hooks to install the new protocol on at least sixty-five percent of the routers worldwide. Then these routers will form a global mesh network capable of replacing the current antiquated system. Each router will pass through untraceable, fully encrypted transmissions to their neighbor's router. And with no clog points the network traffic will flow continually and consistently."

"Yeah, yeah, yeah. I've heard it before." Bride tired of the pitch. He unlaced his fingers to make air quotes. "'Free internet for all.' 'Ditch AOL.' 'Join the faster, better network.' 'All that's required is murdering an innocent young lady.' 'Sign up now.'

Brilliant. Except that Miss Reynolds has destroyed that last node and the password you require is gone forever. Ah well, I guess we'll stick with the internet we've got. Thanks though."

Axeworthy's patience stretched thin. "There is no need for murder." He spoke directly to Dia now. "Who said anything about murder? Miss Reynolds, is that correct? The password to the software is lost?"

Dia nodded affirmative.

"That's okay." Axeworthy's voice had smoothed. "We don't need the NSA software because we have you, Miss Reynolds. You can help us access the world's routers. You want a better, safer, more public internet don't you? Please understand, if someone tried to harm you it was not one of my people. We wouldn't want that."

"Really?" Bride interrupted again. "That bastard there," he pointed to Roll with his elbow, "and his gigantic friend broke into our condo in South Carolina and personally tried to inflict harm—"

The rifle's butt end stopped Bride mid-sentence. Dazed, Bride fought hard against an oncoming unconsciousness. He believed he had not succumbed, but he lost track of the events happening around him. When he snapped to, he felt blood trickling from the side of his head and through his still-laced fingers. And Axeworthy was speaking again.

"So you can see the virtues, Miss Reynolds? Our clients, who created the new protocol, are an organization named IPvØ. They've dedicated themselves to building a modern global internet outside the control of corporations and governments. Theirs is a noble cause. I realize you were part of the government, but you must understand how a better internet would benefit mankind as a whole."

"Except that's not how this so-called protocol operates," Dia spoke up.

"What?" Axeworthy's nostrils flared. He stared down the belligerent woman, his eyes savaging this female who dared to doubt his protocol's function.

"First your protocol sucks. I dug into the machine code. It has basic routing system calls," she explained, "but it's flawed, and that's not the program's core."

"Tell me then, woman, what does my program do?" Axeworthy asked scoffed.

"It a cyberweapon. Like the China's so-called Great Cannon. This program turns its infected routers into a single, massive denial-of-service attack weapon. Feed it an address, and it shares it with all your infected routers and each will launch an escalation attack on that URL's server. You infect a tenth of the routers as you claim and you'd wield the power to shut down the internet of First World countries. And keep it offline for as long as you wished."

"No!" Axeworthy yelled at her. "This program can already replace TOR with a simple, completely anonymize, lightning-fast, worldwide network. I've used it. It works."

Dia stayed perfectly calm, "Try it."

"I have. As I just told you, I've used it."

"No. Try the weapon. Pick a website. Go to the master router controller and key in the command Z-I-Z-O—as in zero in, zero out—and then type the address of the website. Then watch what it does."

"Is this a trick?" Axeworthy was fuming.

"No. I'm serious." Dia calmly continued to lay it on thick. "You've been duped. Whoever wrote this router controller for your protocol duped you. Perhaps your pet secret network project might work someday, but right now it's cake to pwn. How do you think we found you? I discovered your new protocol, worked out its flaws, and we followed the trail straight to your front door. Pwned."

Bride could tell Dia really had Axeworthy stirred up. But she stood on dangerous ground. It was like telling Hitler that his new radar system was actually an atomic bomb. Bride wasn't sure at all what Dia hoped to accomplish, but she had altogether removed attention from Bride, allowing him to devise a means of escape.

"All right, missy. I'll try your so-called weapon command. Let's say I want to attack eBay. What do I do?"

"Simple. Z-I-Z-O space ebay.com. Return."

"Kenneth, fetch my laptop from the bedroom."

Roll, apparently properly named Kenneth, scrambled up the stairs into the bedroom, returning thirty seconds later with a streamlined, ultra-lightweight laptop. He handed it to Axeworthy, who took it to the kitchen counter. Everyone except Bride and Ponytail, including Dia, followed Axeworthy across the room and watched as he opened the computer. From his position on the couch Bride couldn't see what was happening on the computer screen. He also had difficulties hearing them or even concentrating over his pounding head. His own blood now stained the shoulder of his shirt.

After perhaps fifteen minutes—hard to tell, though full daylight shone outside—the group returned to the living room area where Bride sat dazed, hands still on his head.

Axeworthy was speaking. "I'm afraid this doesn't change anything, Miss Reynolds. This improves the system's abilities. You've demonstrated, once installed globally, the new protocol will have the power to squash the old system from existence. And I'm afraid I don't believe you about the protocols flaws. So I still insist you help me ... us ... access the router firmware. I know it's within your skill set."

Dia remained defiant. "Not happening. Even if this were the world's greatest idea, I wouldn't trust it with a depraved psychoneurotic like yourself."

"Very well. I'll have to make you cooperate. Chip, Kenneth, strip them, search them, and lock them in the cell with the woman downstairs." He turned back to Dia. "We may not carry out our original schedule, but you will help. If not, we'll find other avenues, and I will have no purpose for you. No woman will ever thwart me. Remember: if the world already believes you dead, no one ever looks for you."

36> The Woman's Room

"WHY DOES HE HAVE A CELL?" Bride asked rhetorically. Dia had found the light switch and illuminated the overhead fixture exposing the cramped concrete enclosed chamber. The features were minimal: a metal toilet, a showerhead and drain, a neatly stacked pile of clothing, a cheap mattress.

"Axeworthy keeps his sex slave here." Dia said, grabbing a plain dingy-white shirt from the pile and slipping it over her near-naked body.

"Oh, I think I saw her." Bride carefully lowered himself to the mattress, sat, and leaned his bare back against the cold concrete wall. Still dazed from the multiple head knocks, Bride needed to rest. He tried to put his mind on the present situation but could barely process their recent humiliation. Under gunpoint, with hands zip-tied behind their backs, they were led to the courtyard's center by Ponytail and Roll, who used knives to strip them down to their undergarments; Bride in deep blue boxer-briefs, Dia in plain white cotton panties. While Ponytail held the rifle, Roll yelled, punched, kicked, and groped. All was an effort to make Dia admit she still held the password or was prepared to divulge the router exploits they desired. IPVØ seemed to need nothing from Bride, but he was nevertheless subjected to their brutality. Bride was kicked in the kneecaps, punched in the face and abdomen, and had his testicles squeezed and stomped. Bride resolved not to witness what the bastards did to Dia, diverting his eyes to not add to her humiliation, though, thankfully, Dia seemed to have suffered less physical harm than him. Eventually their tormentors led them to the heavy steel door Bride and Dia had found upon first topping the wall. Ponytail opened the hatch and Roll threw them into the tiny, dark room.

After she had explored the chamber, Dia knelt at Bride's side.

"Oh jeez, your head is bleeding," she said before picking up another shirt and using it to apply pressure. The pressure added to Bride's pain, but he allowed her to continue because he knew she needed to halt the flow of blood. Bride guessed he had received a concussion because it had grown difficult to concentrate. But he enjoyed her sitting with him. It brought a simple clarity with its calmness.

Dia apparently liked it too as she snuggled close, leaving only the thin, appropriated cotton tee shirt between them. The feminine warmth pervaded his skin, and the two captives sat still for minutes until finally she checked his head again and quietly declared his bleeding had stopped.

Bride expected Dia would move away, but instead she remained with his arm wrapped around her back and her arms around his bare torso.

Dia spoke again. "Eventually they're going to kill us."

"I know," Bride said.

"Without that password they have no reason to keep me alive. And you understand I can't give them the password."

"Yeah," he said. "They're likely only keeping me alive while they figure out who I am."

The pair sat quietly for several more moments, and Bride's head cleared a bit.

He asked, "You said Axeworthy kept his sex slave in here. I assume that was the woman I briefly met in his bedroom. What happened to her? Axeworthy said to 'put them in with the woman.' But she's not here."

Dia smiled a mischievous smile. "I've hidden her. But we need to help her or eventually they'll find her."

"We're not in position to help anyone, Dia."

"I know." She pressed her cheek against Bride's bare chest. "But sit with me now, please. I need to not feel alone, and you are the only one who has stopped me feeling alone."

"That's fine, Dia," he said, "but do me a favor."

"Sure."

"Turn off the light. It's bothering my eyes."

Dia raised her head from his chest and flashed the sweetest smile. "Sure, I can do that."

After standing, Dia stepped to the light switch and flicked it downward, returning the tiny cell to total darkness save two pinpoints of daylight at the door's foot.

When Dia returned, she did not go back to his side. Instead she straddled Bride's legs and laid her body across his stomach and chest. Except now there was no cotton shirt between them. Body to body, skin to skin, Henry Bride reveled in the young woman's warmth, aware of every inch where this beauty's skin met his. Her bittersweet aroma saturated each breath as he allowed her to continue.

The silky lips found his taut chest and kissed just below the edge of his neck. The soft, damp lips and tongue traced a passage up the side of the neck, over the thin soft beard, across the cheek. Just after Dia's lips brushed the corner of his, she wrapped her arms around his neck and drew in for a full-on passion-filled kiss.

Dia's arms traveled his body, both hands exploring his muscular figure thoroughly. The subtle pain of fingers pressing fresh bruises only enhanced his senses. Lazily he moved his hands to her torso, gently sampling the pleasures of her luxurious skin. How could he have resisted this back in South Carolina? But now it didn't matter. His career didn't matter. Her innocence didn't matter. Their situation didn't matter. This was lovemaking with no real world consequences. This was all that mattered.

For the first time entering the cell, Bride seized the initiative. His palms descended the hollow of her back sliding under the elastic waistline to the delicate but powerful mounds of flesh below the cotton panties. As he massaged the deep muscles of her behind, she moaned and rose to her knees allowing him to lower her sole garment to mid thigh. While one hand returned to her buttock, the other found the hairless skin around the front and discovered its folds and the petite item of jewelry dangling from them. Dia moaned louder and pleaded for him to continue. Her hands held his shoulders tightly to maintain balance as her body spasmed at his fingers' touch. Finally she screamed with pleasure again and again until ultimately grabbing his hand to stop its motion while she caught her breath.

When she was ready to continue her hands found his waistband and pulled out and down below the still tender groin. He was ready. She moved her hips above his and they connected.

Later, as she lay sleeping against him, Bride found himself able to contemplate their next move. The beginnings of an idea formed in his mind. He stood and found the light switch, shielding his eyes before flipping it on. When his eyes adjusted to the stark light, he slipped back on his shorts.

First, he observed Dia, still sleeping half on the terrible little mattress. He found her incredibly attractive, but only now noticed her bruises and welts from the punishment Roll had inflicted. *Concentrate, Bride.* He had developed the kernel of an escape plan, but he needed something to use for a tool. He searched the tiny cell top to bottom but uncovered nothing useful. Everything was either soft or firmly attached to the wall. With resolve, Bride undertook his plan without a tool.

After stepping to the light switch, he examined the plain American-style switch framed with a metal plate held in place by two standard screws. The switch plate was dented and worn but solid. He tried his thumbnail to loosen the screw but only ended with a broken nail. One by one he tried each fingernail, but as Dia would say, "No love." All he accomplished was destroying his fingernails. In frustration, he hit the plate with the side of his fist and swore.

"What are you doing?" a still groggy Dia said.

Bride turned to see her sitting up on the mattress, her knees to her chest and her arms resting upon her knees.

"I had a plan, but I don't have—" He stopped himself mid-sentence. There Bride saw what he needed. "Dia?"

"Yes?"

"You'll find this strange, but I need your jewelry."

"What?" She drew her legs in closer to herself, her feet crossing, attempting to better cover her exposed groin.

"The piercing, I need it." His voice insistent, he held out his hand for her to place the item.

"Okay," she said. "Don't look."

Dia spun toward the wall, back toward him. She opened her legs and proceeded to remove the piercing. When she had it loose, she reached back and handed the trinket to Bride. He examined the jewelry. Titanium, it appeared, shaped as a feather hanging from a tiny loop. *It should do.*

Dia dressed while Bride attempted to loosen the light switch's screws. She slid on the cotton panties, the shirt she wore before, and a pair of jean shorts that were too small to zip.

Using the little metal feather's edge the first screw finally rotated a quarter turn. Before loosening it anymore, Bride focused on the second screw, which came loose even easier.

As Bride removed the screws, Dia leaned next to him to see what he was doing.

Bride said, "I hope you don't mind being in the dark until they come to get us."

Dia smiled and said, "Not at all. I've had an awful lot of fun in the dark."

////

"I know who that guy is, boss. Well, sort of." Chip Ybarra's voice interrupted the silence.

Clarence Axeworthy was already fuming. After checking what the NSA girl and her companion had gained access to inside his office, he discovered somehow his computer had been compromised. This frustrated him greatly since the system used a 32-character password meant to keep anyone without his unique implanted chip from entering the system. He used a unique build of the TrustedBSD operating system optimized for stronger security.

"What?" Axeworthy said, belatedly acknowledging his underling with that silly ponytail.

"The man we captured, I know who he is."

"Well, spill it, Ybarra. Who is he?" Axeworthy barely gave Ybarra a glance from his screen. Axeworthy's mind focused on his system's security, connecting dots on how someone might gain access. He developed a chain of logic on what possibly happened. It went like this: The NSA was an original sponsor of TrustedBSD. So the NSA may have planted a mathematical backdoor into the operating system. Dia Reynolds knew this backdoor from her time at the NSA. The question became how to close a theoretical backdoor.

"That's the Homeland Security guy from St. Louis. The one who chased me."

"What?" Axeworthy finally gave Ybarra his attention.

"In St. Louis, with the Blind worm attack, the guy from the DHS who spotted me and chased me through the tunnels, that was this guy."

"He's with the Department of Homeland Security? Why is he with an NSA defector?"

"Maybe he's a defector, too," Ybarra suggested.

"No," Axeworthy's mind churned. "The girl, she's a trap, and they've sucked me in. The question is what division of Homeland Security, cyber security or human trafficking."

"Wait, what? Human trafficking? Are we involved in human trafficking?"

"Never mind that," Axeworthy said, sensing the walls closing. His system had been compromised. A mad gunman attacked his company headquarters. The Department of Homeland Security came to his door for any of a possible handful of reasons. And his project for IPVØ remained in danger of falling apart. His ultimate hope lay with the NSA girl. Trap or not, his focus must be Dia Reynolds. He must make her surrender the NSA router vulnerabilities and backdoors, but he refused to believe his future lay in female hands. Merely the idea repulsed him. His entire world was collapsing. What else could go wrong? Just then two notifications appeared on his screen.

```
Incoming Call: @π¡1å
Upload Complete. 121Gb uploaded.
```

Axeworthy screamed his frustration and slammed his fists down on his glass desktop, cracking the glass diagonally across its surface and cutting Axeworthy's hand.

"Find Kenneth," Axeworthy said, "and have him bring the NSA wench after I'm done with this call."

He closed his eyes for a moment and calmed himself. When he opened them, Chip was gone. He pressed a key on his keyboard and the silhouette appeared on center screen.

"Hello again, Attila. I have an update for you."

/ / / /

Henry Bride rejoined Dia on the hard, thin mattress and rested his back against the cinder block wall. It was pitch black again, but the mood had swung seriously.

"You sure this will work?" she asked.

"No."

For a brief stretch they relaxed in silence. Bride was convinced he heard her sulking. His mind attempted to occupy the time devising the next move if this succeeds. Instead, he fell asleep sitting in the dark quiet. Whether Dia sensed this or had only now gathered her thoughts together, she finally broke the silence.

"Bride, may I ask you a question?"

"Sure." He pretended he had been awake.

"What's your opinion of Edward Snowden? Was he a hero or a traitor? I want your point of view as an individual, not a government employee."

"Off the record, I've considered this before," Bride said, "and in my mind he's both."

"What do you mean? Should he be punished for leaking all those secrets?"

"Yes, Snowden committed treason, but I'll admit it was for the best to continue our free society. But also he needs to be punished."

"Huh?"

Bride continued, "We cannot allow every government employee to leak every minute secret and declare it 'the country's best interest'. Our democratic system would crumble. Each person must face that hard decision. Is this secret worth sacrificing myself? My way of life? My *life?* With no sacrifice you have no tough decision. Snowden decided these secrets were worth risking everything over. It needed to be done. But there's a necessity that the choice is difficult. If Snowden is not tried or is pardoned, then the choice becomes too easy for future would-be Snowdens. That choice needs to be difficult."

Dia contemplated Bride's statement before ultimately asking, "When you spoke to Axeworthy, you called me an innocent girl. Do you believe that?"

"Well, not anymore." Bride chuckled at his own joke.

Dia showed her opinion of his humor with an elbow to the rib cage.

He complained then apologized.

"Seriously," she said, "do you think I'm innocent?"

"I expect you've made a mistake, but, yes, I believe you are a good person."

Dia fell silent again until she confessed, "I've done considerably worse than posting the NSA's software."

Bride said nothing. He'd let her decide whether to continue. She did.

"I helped the NSA plant spyware inside the White House to spy on the President and his staff."

Now Bride had no words. This made zero sense with what he understood about Dia Reynolds. She was a free spirit, but she was a patriot. This bordered on a Nixon-level scandal.

"My boss, Anthony Thorenus; another programmer, Alec Holloway; and I built a worm intended to infiltrate the White House computer systems and other locations' systems important to the President. With this worm the NSA can monitor every action and file on the President and his staff's network. It also will access their system's internal speakers to use as microphones. Alec couldn't bear the shame and isolation, and he committed suicide. I was caught in the same trap: betray the NSA or betray the President. That's why I left. I didn't want to spy on our own country's leader. It goes against every reason why I joined the NSA. I couldn't be involved anymore."

Bride had a thousand questions, but settled for one. "Why? Why did you do it?"

Dia's voice betrayed the fact she was crying. "I don't know anymore. It made sense when Thorenus recruited me to the task force—something about not trusting the next administration—but I can't explain it or even understand why myself. I guess I trusted him.

"Alec sent me a note the night he shot himself. The guilt ate at him. He saw no way out. And you know what? Neither did I." She sobbed. After she composed herself, she continued. "Except I held this stupid idea. After Snowden left, I plotted how I might escape like he did. I was convinced I was smarter than him, and I didn't want to be a whistleblower. I love this damned country. But I want no part of this. I wanted out. I didn't want to die. So I ran.

"But instead of escaping, I've only made this mess. And I've dragged you into it. And Gordon. And Sunshine. And..." She choked on her words as she sobbed again. "...Ruby. My wonderful sister, Ruby, is dead because of my foolish actions. Alec was a wonderful, honorable man. And he's dead. And soon, soon we'll be dead. First you. And then after they're convinced I'm useless, then me. But, damn it, that's worse. I would rather we die together."

Bride sensed Dia wanted to hold him, but she kept her distance.

"Oh my sweet Dia, listen to me. Neither of us will die. We've made it this far. This will—"

He heard sounds, footfalls on the metal stairs. Someone was coming.

"I know—"

"Shh!" He cut her off as he rose to his feet. "This is it. Get ready to run."

"Okay." She stood, too, placing her hand on his arm to track his position. "In case we don't make it, thank you for everything."

Bride laid his hand across hers, both as reassurance and to stop her from speaking. The footsteps had reached the bottom stair and continued along the concrete walk. Bride hoped whoever was approaching was alone—only one set of steps—but he didn't count on it. She shifted in so their bodies touched again, and he felt her tense. Keys jangled outside, and the lock turned.

"Stay back!" The shouted command, though muffled by the thick door, was clearly Roll's voice.

Good.

The door parted from its frame, a vertical crack of light appearing before them. The column of light widened as the metal door swung cautiously inward revealing Roll's silhouette gripping Bride's pistol. Bride sensed Dia squeezing behind him and Bride placed his dominant hand on his back between them.

"Let's go," Roll ordered. "Move it."

Bride remained motionless. *Come on, you bastard.*

"Don't make me come in there."

Bride stepped backward deeper into the dark cell's shadows, and Dia matched his action in unison.

Roll stepped forward into the doorway. "Have you got something? You better drop it."

Come on. Just come inside.

Another step brought Roll through the doorway. "Why are you smiling? Where's Axeworthy's woman?"

Do it!

Without removing his gaze from Bride's eyes, Roll reached his left hand over to turn on the light. When it found the wall, his hand swept upward.

Yes!

With a violent spark, Roll's hand struck the two bare wires protruding from the switch's junction box. Bride swore he witnessed electricity flowing through Roll's body as he screamed in a shaking, frozen agony. The man continued violently trembling in place for a full ten seconds as the overhead light flickered a weak, macabre pulse, until Roll and the light abruptly stopped. The body slumped straight to the ground.

For a moment, the cell stood still. A thick wedge of sunlight invading the dark through the open door framed the motionless body. Wisps of smoke that shimmered around the sun beam was the only motion. Bride stepped into the light, the smoke swirling around his legs. He kicked the pistol from the Roll's grasp *just in case* before he re-appropriated it. He stepped to the doorway peering out to check if Roll had company. There was nobody. Finally he checked the body for a pulse. On the neck, Bride felt a faint, unsteady heartbeat. Roll was alive, but not likely for long.

Bride hastily examined the XD Mod.2 and its magazine—two bullets remained. It was better than none. He tucked the pistol into the elastic band of his boxer-briefs. It did a terrible job holding the gun, but it would serve for now. He reached into the injured man's pants pocket and found a key set with a fob and foible attached.

He untied Roll's mismatched Converse All-Stars—this time one white, one black—removing them from the near corpse's feet. They would need shoes. Hell, Bride thought, might as well take his pants. After struggling to wrangle the black jeans from Roll's motionless legs, Bride slipped them over his own legs. It was almost as difficult putting them on him as it had been stripping them off Roll. The jeans' waist fell roughly two-inches short, the legs roughly four. The top button refused to close, so Bride cinched the wide leather belt to hold up the jeans. It provided better support for his gun after he tucked it in the small of his back. The high-tops, however, were useless for Bride. His feet were too big. But the mismatched shoes worked for Dia. They were cut a size too large, but after she bound them tight, they sufficed. Roll's shirt would take too much time and hassle, he decided.

Bride stepped from the room. After checking that the way was still clear, he called to Dia, "Come on." After sealing the cell door and, most likely, Roll's fate, Bride laced his fingers together to boost her over the wall.

Dia exited the cell, but declared, "We're not leaving yet. We have to go get Ruby."

"What?" Bride was confused. How did Dia's sister become involved?

"Ruby, that's the name of Axeworthy's slave. We're not leaving her here."

With spirit Dia strode up the concrete walkway to the front gate she had opened earlier.

Bride pulled the pistol from his waist and said, "I suppose you're the boss."

37> **Hunted**

To Dia, Henry Bride epitomized a buffoon running about bare chested in undersized skinny jeans carrying his gun in one hand and Roll's keys in the other. But he proceeded like it were business as usual. He met her at the iron gate and they peered through its bars, scouting the front courtyard. Straightaway she noticed, near the center granite fountain sculpture, the guy with the ponytail was stepping from their Jeep Renegade. Of course, they had their car keys, why wouldn't they move it?

He spoke loudly to an unseen associate near the beach house's street-side entrance, but Dia failed to catch the words. Once the ponytail guy moved from sight, Bride handed her the keys, but before she tried any, the gate clicked unlocked. The foible's work, perhaps? Bride held his arm to block her so he could lead the way, covering the yard with his pistol.

The door unlocked as she reached it, so she headed straight in, examining the wall switch before flicking on the lights. Bride stood guard by the door, but he clearly saw the enormous carcass of Rock lying in a puddle of his own blood. Dia sidestepped the corpse like it were any other obstacle and faintly called out, "Ruby?"

Her call was answered with silence. Dia was worried now. Dia's mind had been racing for days now. With Alec's Suicide, her failed attempt to flee the country, this guy Bride showing up, her sister's death—for gods' sakes, she had just killed that giant man—all running through her mind, this poor girl, Ruby, had become her primary focus. Even if thrown in prison and hanged for treason, Dia couldn't help but feel her life had been a breeze compared to Ruby's life as a sex slave. She would make damned sure, even at the sacrifice of her own freedom, that Ruby would not spend one more day in captivity. Deliberately, Dia tiptoed toward the box pile in the storage chamber's rear.

Out in the courtyard a car door closed, its sound echoing into the concrete store room.

"Come on, Dia," Bride called, "we've got to hurry."

Upon reaching the pile of boxes, Dia inspected them before picking the top box off the stack. She squinted into the gap and saw Ruby's face appear in the invading beam of light. As soon as Ruby recognized Dia, she smiled.

Dia smiled back. "Hello, Ruby. We're leaving now."

After shifting a couple more boxes, Dia helped Ruby from her hiding place. Ruby's smile dropped the instant she spotted Bride.

"Don't worry, Hon," Dia reassured. "He's a really good guy. His name is Henry. He's my friend." She added, "And he usually wears better pants."

Ruby looked to Dia to read her face, then noticed what she was wearing. She said, "That's my shirt."

"Yes," Dia said. "And these are your shorts. And I'll give your stuff back, but, right now, we have to leave."

In the doorway, Bride had become antsy. So Dia directed Ruby around the giant dead body. A glance to the workbench and Dia noted the node pieces were gone. They removed the node's remains, but not the man's? The body must have presented a tougher job. *Oh hells*, Dia thought, Ruby had endured one final horror inside this house. She had helplessly listened to Rock slowly die and then had to remain inside the room with the body.

Dia escorted Ruby from the room out into the sunlight.

When they were near the courtyard's edge, Bride said, "Give me the keys."

Dia handed him the keys. Holding them high above his head, he pressed a button on the key fob. In the distance a car chipped.

"Wait here. I'll get us a ride," he ordered.

/ / / /

The video call had been lengthy, over an hour. Attila was rightfully upset and Axeworthy had striven to persuade the secretive cyber-cult leader that the NSA girl would cooperate. In fact, he'd lied and assured him she had already agreed, and they only needed to negotiate terms. The lie didn't matter. If the girl didn't cooperate, Axeworthy couldn't deliver and IPVØ would make certain he was done, by one means or another. Even without their threat, he was keenly aware everything he had built relied on this headstrong female.

For fifteen minutes after disconnecting, Axeworthy sat quietly in his stark office gazing out over his decaying landscape, his constant reminder of the world's advanced entropy. Finally, after his mind cleared all reflections of his future troubles, he stood and strode from his office into the beach house's great room.

He expected to find Kenneth waiting with the girl. Instead, he found three of his men. Cobb and Pitts sat on his couch staring at a blank television screen pulled away from the wall while Chip fiddled with wires behind the unit.

"Hey boss," Pitts said. "Did you know your TV isn't working?"

"Yeah," Cobb said. "We were binging *Benders* on Netflix and the TV went black and suddenly everything shut down."

Axeworthy glared at the men and all his frustrations returned. His world was collapsing, and they worried about a television?

"Where's Kenneth with the NSA bitch?" Axeworthy asked.

"Oh yeah. He headed down to fetch her right before the TV cut out."

"How long ago was that?"

The two men stood, finally realizing they should be concerned. At that instant, a vehicle's engine rumbled to life in the yard.

Chip said, "That sounded like Kenneth's car."

/ / / /

No one else was in the yard, so Bride had found the car that matched the key fob with a simple push of a button. He fired up the V8 engine and shifted the Blue Mustang GT's transmission into reverse. At idle, he rolled the car slowly backward through the courtyard he had just finished creeping across. He strove to roll as quiet as possible, but within seconds a commotion arose from all around the yard.

Upon seeing the new arrivals, Bride floored the accelerator, pedal smoking the eighteen-inch rear tires' rubber on the concrete paving stones until the Mustang shot rearward.

Before he reversed to where Dia and Ruby waited, a shot ripped through the muscle car's metal roof and into the passenger-side dashboard. But Bride continued back. While approaching the courtyard's rear corner, he stretched across the cabin and unlatched the passenger door. Bride then spun the steering wheel counter-clockwise causing the door to fly open as he slid to a stop directly in front of Dia and Ruby.

"Get in," he barked.

Ruby first then Dia, they did as told, both squeezing into the front bucket seat. Another bullet sunk into the open door's inner lining just as Dia slid inside. *Time to move before a stronger marksman arrives.* Before Dia reached for the door, Bride wrenched the pony car into drive and it rocketed forward, slamming the door closed with momentum. A panicked man rushed into the courtyard attempting to stop the escapees' car with his body. Bride swerved to miss, but Mustang's fender clipped the pedestrian on its route toward the front gate, knocking him over into a rose bush. With hope over belief Bride reached across and pressed all three buttons of the garage door opener remote hanging from the passenger-side sun visor. It worked. The courtyard's front gates inch by inch began ratcheting open. But the gate wouldn't open fast enough for the speeding Mustang.

Bride spun the wheel again and circled the granite fountain. Another bullet sunk into the Mustang's bulging hood. Bride counted three, possibly four, gunmen taking positions around the exterior yard. He squeezed the Mustang through the narrow gap between the Renegade and a Lexus parked on the outer side of the circle around the fountain. The Mustang's rear tire rubbed the Lexus' front bumper leaving a series of black arcs across its length. He'd be damned if he would pay for damages to the Jeep. When he rounded the fountain, the iron gates stood opened enough but now were closing again. Bride straightened the wheel and floored the accelerator, aiming directly at the converging gates' center.

"Get in the back!" he yelled.

Both women followed his order, climbing between the black leather bucket seats. Ruby went first. But Dia's legs still scrambled to reach the back when the 3,500-pound automobile smashed into the solid metal gates with a thunderous jolt.

The driver side airbag fired, slamming into Bride's face and chest. But Bride's foot remained pressed hard against the accelerator pedal. The six-foot-two-inch-wide Mustang continued boring through the five-foot gap between the giant iron gate. Terrible screams of metal against metal echoed throughout the Imperial Valley. The gates' denser metal was winning out over Flat Rock, Michigan's finest sheet metal. But somehow the bulk of the American muscle car managed to press through the narrowing gap, though not in good shape.

Bride pushed aside the wilted airbag and took stock. The ravaged Mustang still limped forward, but the car groaned and squealed its complaints. Dia was sprawled on the floor of the front seat.

"Is everybody all right?" Bride asked.

"Yeah, I'm good," Dia answered.

No word came from Ruby. He asked again. Nothing.

Finally Bride twisted to check behind him and found Ruby sitting buckled in her seat. She offered an impish grin and nodded, indicating she was okay.

Dia climbed into the front passenger seat, looked to Bride, and said, "Your nose is bleeding."

He rubbed his nose with his wrist and the fresh crimson streak confirmed her diagnosis. But he had greater issues. The injured muscle car propelled forward at around thirty-five miles-per-hour, if the speedometer could still be believed, along a dirt road toward Highway 111. But this was the battered Ford's new maximum speed as smoke poured from the left rear tire and trickled from the front right. In the rear-view mirror Bride saw Axeworthy's people struggle to pull open the mangled gates—that's a bonus—but he also spotted another danger rise above the compound's wall.

Another drone.

Bride swore aloud.

He caught sight of the highway ahead but also spotted another car turning off the pavement toward them.

He swore again.

Reviewing his options, Bride found bare desert on all sides, though buildings were visible to the north. The new car, some kind of generic sedan, still barreled straight for them.

Bride decided if this newcomer hoped to play "chicken" he'd volunteer for the titular role. He pointed more than steered the Mustang's remains northward, off the smooth dirt road and on the rough desert land. Though he had no guess how far they would get, his bet was farther than if they continued forward.

It wouldn't be as far as he hoped though. Within a few hundred feet, the left rear tire caught fire, and he spotted a serious ravine lying directly ahead.

"Get ready to bail out!"

While they were still rolling, Dia tried to open her door.

"It won't budge," she said.

He tried the windows; they only groaned.

"Break out your window."

Dia hit the window with her elbow. Nothing.

Bride realized he had forgotten something. "Where's my gun?"

Dia looked around.

"It's down by your feet," she said.

"I need you to get it," Bride said.

Dia studied the problem for a second then lay herself across the Mustang's center column. She bounced about but managed to stretch enough to touch the gun. But then the left rear tire blew, tossing Dia, the gun, and everything else in the car all around the vehicle's interior.

"Dude! Hold steady!"

Bride was already doing everything possible to keep the wrecked car straight and steady, but he was fighting the misaligned wheels, the rough desert surface, and now a shredded rear tire.

Ruby's hand came from the back seat and grabbed the waistline of Dia's shorts.

"I got you, Ducky," she said.

"Ducky?" Bride said, glancing down to Dia, whose head rested awkwardly on his knee.

"Can we not do—" Dia interrupted her own sentence, "I got it!"

She popped back up into her seat and handed Bride the pistol, which he grabbed with his left hand.

With his hand on the handle but finger off the trigger, he swung the pistol's butt-end toward his window. When the gun's corner struck the glass, it shattered into thousands of tiny cubes, most of which fell outside the rolling car. *Finally, cooperative glass.*

But the cruel desert ground refused to cooperate any farther. Until now Bride had managed to steer around the lesser ravine's branches, but all that had accomplished was leading them to the ravine's widest section. He checked the speedometer. It peaked at forty-seven miles-per-hour, not bad for a car with three tires, none pointing in the exact same direction.

"Buckle in and brace," he shouted over the engine and rushing wind. Dia complied. In the rear-view mirror, he saw Ruby already buckled, and he saw the trailing car had gained ground. Eight car lengths behind and closing.

When his gaze returned forward, the ravine was mere feet ahead, and they were heading over its edge. A second later the Mustang's carcass leapt the ravine's lip and dropped straight down into the natural ditch. Bride held a modest hope they would hit the far side and the car could climb it. Instead the Ford's grille dug into the hardened sand, showering the front of the car with dirt, and stopping the smoldering hunk of metal cold.

Dia's airbag fired, and Bride was thrown into the steering wheel.

/ / / /

"Go!" Ruby shouted from the backseat. Stunned, Bride was unaware of how much time passed since crashing the Mustang, but he recognized his surroundings again. Dia appeared slightly dazed. Bride snapped into full alert, unbuckled his seat belt, and checked if he still had his gun. He twisted to look behind him. The trailing Chevy Malibu had stopped short of the ravine's edge, but no one had exited. As quickly and carefully as he could, he slipped out of the missing window, still scratching his chest on the remaining glass. He then helped Ruby who climbed from the back seat. Dia had just moved toward the missing window when the Malibu's door opened.

"Hurry," Bride urged, giving Dia his free hand through the open window and training the gun toward the newcomer's car with the other. Dia took his hand and he practically yanked her from the car. The Chevy's driver stood over them and Bride could just make out the shape of the man and his skyward painting Mossberg 590A1 Tactical Pump-Action Shotgun.

"Stop! Don't move!" Bride commanded reinforcing his order with his pistol's aim.

"Whoa, whoa, whoa. Hold your fire Agent Bride. It's Watts, Charles Watts. I was with Liptmann. Remember? From Vegas?"

At last Bride recognized the man. "Burgundy!" Bride exclaimed. "So glad to see you again. I wish I knew that was you earlier."

"Hurry and climb out of that ditch," Watts said. "You have company coming. I'll take you out in my car."

Bride was helping Ruby up the side when an ethereal whistling filled the air. Bride thought he recognized the sound straight off and had his suspicion confirmed when the tiny rocket hit the Malibu and spread liquid fire across its roof, windshield, and hood.

It was the drone.

"Everyone down!"

Bride pulled Ruby back down on top of him, and Dia dropped to her stomach inside the ravine.

Watts leapt down to the ravine's edge, then rolled down its side holding the shotgun overhead to not have it get in his way. Bride recognized the roll had two purposes as fire spread along Watts' coat sleeve, but the roll failed to extinguish the chemical flame. Bride hopped up and pulled on Watts' collar and with a bit of shaking from the two men, Bride yanked the jacket away. He tossed it aside down the ravine.

From somewhere near the lingering sun, Bride heard a second rocket fire.

He yelled again, "Incoming!"

Everyone but Bride already lay on their bellies. But Dia scrambled away from the Mustang's wreckage an instant before the rocket's liquid fire engulfed the entire front end of the demolished car.

The rocket had made a direct hit to the Mustang's hood, a damned fine shot if your goal was to destroy something that's already been destroyed.

As he viewed the metal hunk burning, Bride had an epiphany.

"Get ready to run," he said. "We're climbing out the far side of the ravine. I saw buildings ahead a bit."

"No way," Dia balked. "They'll get us,"

"No, they won't. They still want you alive. That last rocket could have hit right in the center of us, but instead they shot the useless car. We'll run and they'll shoot their rockets toward us, but as long as we stick close together they won't hit anyone."

"I'm in," Watts declared.

"What if they just missed?" Dia asked.

"Then they won't hit us because they're a bad shot," Bride said. "So when I say 'go', we climb over this ridge and run together toward those buildings."

"Are you going to be okay running on this surface?" Watts asked, pointing to Bride and Ruby's bare feet.

"We'll have to be," Bride answered, searching the sky and finally locating the drone circling wide around to the south.

"All right, Go!" he called, and the four fugitives climbed the ravine's edge and ran across the cruel desert floor.

At first Ruby dashed ahead until Dia called for her to slow down and stick with her. Nice to know the frail girl could sprint fast when motivated. Together, running in a cluster, they rapidly progressed over the desert sand. The rough surface seemed to slice in to Bride's feet with each step. Once he was truly cut, he began suffering the sting of the arid basin's salt creeping into his fresh wounds. But Bride persisted. It appeared they might reach the unknown sanctuary ahead.

Then came the drone, its latest rocket striking ground ahead to their right. If Bride's theory held true—which he was more unsure of than he'd admit—the rockets weren't intended to hit them but rather to steer them. If wrong, its incendiary chemicals would consume the skin of their near naked bodies in fire with no recourse but to suffer.

The group easily skirted wide of the rocket's circle of fire. Watts twirled and ran backward while firing a load from the shotgun at the drone. It had no visible effect, but hopefully the shot served to warn the drone to keep its distance.

Another rocket shot struck the barren ground, again ahead to their right, obviously intended to encourage the runners to reverse course. But the four runners kept pushing toward the buildings ahead. As they neared, Bride observed a cluster of lesser wooden structures and a tower holding up an object. Also there appeared to be someone—or something—standing guard nearby.

Dia asked first, "What the hells is that?"

As they drew closer, the confusion heightened. Atop the tower rested what appeared to be a metal spaceship. Whoever or whatever stood near the fence rose roughly twelve feet toward the sky and was thin as a rail. The entire compound appeared to be surrounded by a barbed wire fence.

The hovering drone fired another rocket, then another, creating a wall of fire between them and the strange encampment.

Everybody stopped. "Keep running," Bride commanded, scrambling the far way around the fire. "This way. We must keep moving. We can't let them box us in."

Watts shot twice more as the drone skirted by overhead, but the flying mechanical beast stayed far above the Mossberg's effective range.

After rounding the fire, they arrived at the odd collection of buildings. Just outside the fence, a strange ad hoc sculpture of an alien, the compound's tall thin guardian, held a sign that read, "Believe."

"What is this place?" Dia asked.

"No clue. Perhaps a decrepit tourist trap," Bride suggested. "Or an art project?"

It didn't matter what its former life had been; now it served as shelter. They ran past the immobile alien greeter, with only Ruby slowing to marvel at the creature. Dia promptly pulled along her new friend. They entered through the wire fence into the nearest one-story crumbling building. The doors and windows were missing, the floors littered with trash, the walls littered with graffiti. Bride wondered when his last tetanus shot had been. His next thought was that the openings kept them in the drone's sight. Bride quickly checked the building while Watts fired another round out the doorway. Bride discovered only two rooms, the second room having another open doorway and two window openings. Plenty of exits should they be needed, but also plenty of ways to see or shoot into the building.

Bride searched the shack's clutter for objects to block its gaping doors and windows. A rocket flying into this building would mean disaster. The place was practically built of kindling. If a fire started on the crumbling shed's exterior, they stood a chance. If it started inside, all options could be blocked before they understood what happened. The first barricade was obvious. For whatever reason, a twin-sized mattress, complete with blue UFO sheets, sat in the rear compartment. It took minimal effort to prop the mattress against the rear door's frame. Bride removed the fitted sheet and hung it over one window. A loose chunk of plywood adequately blocked the other window. While Watts was guarding the front door with his shotgun, Bride doubted he could stop a rocket. So he searched, but Bride found nothing large enough to barricade the opening.

Then Bride noticed the liberated girl, Ruby, staring attentively at an object hanging on the wall. She was fascinated. In the front room's dark corner someone had hung a sheet of craft paper with a strange painted portrait featuring a nude woman sitting on a stool. Ruby reached slowly out to touch it.

"Ruby, I'm afraid I'll need to take that," he said. "But tell you what. I'll hang it over here instead." The craft-paper painting wasn't tall enough to cover the doorway, so Bride hung it to cover the window. He carefully slid the plywood board from behind the newly hung portrait and leaned the board against the front door frame. The quarter-inch plywood only covered the opening's bottom four feet, but it would have to serve. It decreased the drone's target while leaving Watts his sky view.

"Where's our drone?" Bride asked Watts as he watched Dia and Ruby clear an area to sit on the dirt covered floor.

"It's hovering," Watts said. "It hasn't moved much since I last fired at it."

The drone's distant whir helped Bride zero in on its location. "I think they're satisfied keeping us trapped inside here. If this drone uses the same design as the last one I encountered then it only started with eight rockets. That'll leave it with two now."

"Two's enough. Hell, with a butane lighter I could turn this place into a full-blown inferno in roughly ten seconds. You're right. They want us alive."

"They want her alive." Bride pointed to Dia with his thumb. "The rest of us they'd kill in an instant."

"They're bringing reinforcements." Watts said.

"That's what I was thinking. If we stay here, we're sitting ducks, but I see no options."

Watts was quiet. On the floor Dia entertained Ruby. The pair whispered and giggled about the painting. It was a good arrangement, Dia distracting Ruby who was distracting Dia.

"How's your partner?" Bride asked. "The one wearing the green jacket in Vegas?"

"Sutter?" Watts laughed. "Your maneuver pulled his shoulder out of its socket. He needs surgery."

"Ouch, I'm sorry. I didn't know you guys were G-men. A lot of people have tried to kill that girl in the past week. I thought you two were next in line."

"Don't apologize. I think Sutter's kind of an ass. I'm happy I'll be getting another partner."

"Speaking of which," Bride said, "you don't have any reinforcements of your own coming, do you?"

"No telling. I called in that I found you and Miss Reynolds, but I didn't ask for backup. I'm hoping since I haven't called back that they'll send someone. Unfortunately, my phone was in the car."

"That's too—" Bride stopped. He heard distant engines. Someone was coming.

"I hear them too. Sounds like company's coming from the highway. What have you got?" Watts nodded to Bride's pistol.

"Two. You?"

"Three."

The engines drew closer.

"Let's hope they don't bring more than five people."

Bride sought to gain a tactical advantage, but with the drone hovering overhead there'd be no secret moves outside the building.

Meanwhile, the engines' roars crescendoed then stopped and car doors opened. Bride discerned at least two engines and three car doors.

After a half-minute a familiar voice shouted across the desert land toward them.

"Dia Reynolds." It was Axeworthy's voice. "I will give you a choice. You can come out and help us with our router problem, and I will personally pay you a quarter-million dollars. Or you can stay inside and die with your friends and the woman. Consider my offer, Miss Reynolds, life and perhaps the single largest payday of that life, or die in *that* place. I shall give you five minutes to decide."

Staying squat, Dia stepped up next to Bride. "What do I do?"

"I won't blame you if—"

She cut off Bride. "The hells with that. Perhaps I'd consider leaving you two capable gentlemen to fend for yourselves, but Ruby, she has the mind of a little girl. I won't leave her. What do you want me to do?"

Bride drew a deep breath, delaying to gather his thoughts. "Okay, wait the five minutes and then negotiate. We need to buy time."

"Can do."

"Burg ... uh, Watts, tell me your full operation here. Where's Liptmann and your other people?"

"There's not really many others. Mostly we were letting you and Miss Reynolds do your thing. Liptmann gave you twenty-four hours. He believed he knew your plans and figured it was better to remain off-the-books. So, except for me, we gave you space. Sutter and Liptmann are holed up at the fire station north on 111. Garrett is south in Niland. Each is perhaps twenty miles away. Upshall is watching the sea from the other side in case you tried slipping out by boat. And Liptmann recruited the local police to watch the obscure back roads leading from the valley. That's all we have, Bride. This isn't the big operation. Liptmann's not exactly off-the-books, but he's kept us clear of the larger manhunt for your girlfriend there."

Bride ignored the "girlfriend" comment and gazed out the doorway opening. Axeworthy and his goon squad remained out of sight, but Bride contemplated the twin columns of smoke rising from the two burning cars.

"How long since the cars caught fire?" Bride asked.

"I don't know. Five maybe ten minutes," Watts said.

"Thirteen and a half." Everyone spun to find Ruby still sitting on the dirt floor in the corner.

"Why do you say that, Ruby?" Dia asked her.

"I know time," the delicate girl said. "I count minutes in my room."

"I'll take her word for it," Bride said. "So if it took five minutes for someone to call in the fires, the fire department will arrive in roughly seven minutes, assuming they're not at another call."

"And I'd bet Liptmann and Sutter will be trailing right behind them," Watts added.

"So after the five minutes Axeworthy gave Dia, we'll need to hold out another four minutes." Bride thought about their prospects. "If the drone's rockets hit us after his five minutes, we'll get trapped or flushed out before the fire department comes."

Bride went over to Ruby and knelt next to her. "Ruby, can you tell Dia ... er ... Ducky when she has one minute left in the five minutes."

Ruby acknowledged with a head nod.

"Good." Bride turned to Dia. "When Ruby tells you, negotiate even if Axeworthy says nothing. Continue the conversation as long as possible." Then to Watts, "I'll check how many guns they have. Watch the drone."

"Okay, but I rarely take orders from men in skinny jeans," Watts jested.

Bride entered the back room and examined its eastern wall. He waved his hand back and forth near the wall, searching for light sneaking through the decrepit outer wall. It didn't take him long. He found a loose board nailed to the wall where a sliver of light peeked through it. He set down his pistol on a five-gallon bucket lid and used both hands to grasp the loose board. With a good tug the rotted wood broke free, giving Bride what he required, a view of Axeworthy's crew. He leaned face first against the wall and peered out. In front of the Lexus with the marred bumper and an old Chevy Blazer, he counted five men standing in a cluster; Axeworthy, Ponytail, another man from the beach house, and two gun-toting thugs he didn't recognize.

Axeworthy stood in the center, in suit pants and a white shirt with that ridiculous collar holding a black handkerchief over his mouth.

Ponytail stood in the front, dressed ready for a Jimmy Buffett concert. The drone's bulky remote hung from a strap around his neck. The other three goons dressed in Goodwill chic, most likely hired local muscle. One carried a rather large Smith & Wesson, the other two brandished assault rifles— AR-15s, possibly automatic.

Bride stepped back and picked up his gun, then leaned into watch them again. If more men flanked them, he'd have no way of learning, but he suspected not. Only ponytail paid attention to anywhere but to this building, and he was watching the drone.

Dia yelled out to Axeworthy, apparently the five minutes were nearly up. "How do I know you'll give me the quarter-mill', Axeworthy?"

Axeworthy bit. "Miss Reynolds, you must trust me for now, but I'll deposit your money into your bank account before you do the work."

Good girl, Dia. Dig into the minutia.

"How would that work?" she yelled. "I'm an unemployed government worker who just emptied her checking account at the Penfed Credit Union. I can't see adding a fresh quarter-million bucks without raising eyebrows."

Bride ducked back to the front and said, "Get ready to run. When I say go, run. Run as fast as you can toward the sea. If they start shooting get down, but the three of you stick together."

"What about you?" Dia asked.

"I'll be right behind you."

Axeworthy yelled back, sounding frustrated, "We can set you up an off-shore account. You enter the password. We'll work it out."

Bride returned to his hole in the wall, but stood back and half squatted until the gap framed only Ponytail.

Dia shouted back, "I want Ruby to come out with me. It's no deal unless she lives and is set free with me."

Bride lined the Mod.2's sites through the hole, aiming squarely on Ponytail. At present the pistol held two bullets, but Bride only had one shot at this.

"Done," Axeworthy yelled. "But she says nothing about me to anyone. Her freedom for her silence."

Ponytail's eyes moved between the remote's monitor and the drone in the sky.

"I think we can arrange that," Dia replied. "Ruby's not very talkative, anyway."

"So we have a deal?" Axeworthy asked.

"Just one more thing," Dia said.

Bride pulled the trigger and the bullet fired.

Bride yelled, "Go!" before Ponytail's body slumped to the ground. He turned from his peephole and ran. He had barely cleared the interior doorway when a burst of shots tore through the building's side exactly where he had been standing.

"Stop! Stop! Stop! Don't hit the girl!" Axeworthy ordered over the guns' roar. The shooting trickled away.

With the plywood now on the ground and the women gone from the room, Watts fired at Axeworthy's gang as he exited the doorway. Bride followed Watts as the last to exit the shed. Like earlier, Ruby ran ahead and Dia pleaded with her to slow down as they dashed through a gap in the wire fence. Neither seemed to notice the drone heading directly toward them. Was someone else controlling the drone now? It seemed to be dive bombing.

"Watch out!" Bride shouted as the drone buzzed toward Dia's head. Dia was oblivious to the oncoming octocopter, but stopped and ducked her head when she heard Bride's plea. The drone zipped through Dia's former path and promptly crashed into the ground spreading a tumbling liquid fireball over the desert surface behind her.

Shotgun in hand, Watts leapt the wall of flames before it had a chance to grow. But the growing flames quickly cut off Bride's path. He was left with nowhere to go with Axeworthy and his armed thugs steps behind him. Knowing these miscreants held no qualms in killing him, Bride chose the only option he thought left. He stopped short of the desert inferno, dropped his gun, raised hands above his head, and prayed these men would have mercy on him. But before he turned, another volley of gunfire erupted.

"Drop your gun," the voice ordered, confusing Bride as he'd already done that.

"A'ight, don't shoot." another voice shouted.

When Bride finally spun, he gazed upon the two gunmen with the assault rifles lying dead and the Smith & Wesson thug on his knees hands behind his head. The last thug was being stood over by three local police officers with rifles, another plain clothes man with a Mossberg, Sutter with a Glock, and Liptmann, who was unarmed.

Beyond the fenced yard another uniformed officer held Axeworthy. The millionaire was unsuccessful asking the cop if he knew who he was.

"Sorry that I took so long, Agent Bride." Liptmann said. "We weren't able to triangulate Mister Watts' signal after his phone went offline."

38> Facing Justice

ALONG THE SHORE of the dying sea, Henry Bride's eyes traced along the desert floor. The dry sand glittered in the setting sun's golden rays and striped by sweeping shadows of the gathered crowd. His gaze followed these shadows across to Dia Reynolds and her new friend, Ruby. The pair stood near Liptmann's company car, a Malibu identical to the one the drone's rocket roasted. They were discussing Ruby's future. Colonel Liptmann himself stood patiently by the wire fence, a respectable distance away, allowing Dia time with Ruby before she surrendered. The investigator's eyes, too, seemed to appreciate the sea's splendor through rose-tinted lenses. By the Malibu, Ruby wept and pleaded with Dia not to leave her alone.

"I have to, Ruby," Dia explained, "I must answer for the things I did wrong. Just as Axeworthy must answer for everything he did. That means you need to testify against him. Will you do that for me?"

"But Ducky, I don't want to be alone."

"You won't be alone. My friend, Henry, will guarantee that."

"But you will come back, right?"

Dia failed checking her emotions as tears rained down her cheeks. "I don't know, Ruby. I hope so."

Bride stepped into the conversation. "Ruby, can you wait inside this car? I need to talk to Dia."

Ruby agreed, and Bride helped her into the Malibu's rear seat. Watts already sat waiting in the driver's seat, idling the engine to run the air conditioning. Automatically buckling her seat belt like a child pleasing its parent, Ruby's eyes met Bride's, and she offered a reluctant smile. Bride returned a wide, reassuring smile and carefully sealed the door.

Bride surveyed the other police vehicles. Axeworthy and his remaining man were handcuffed in the backs of the cruisers. Ponytail had been loaded into an ambulance. And black sheets covered the other bodies. How solid was the case against Axeworthy on charges of attempted murder for hire, cyber-terrorism, or the many other crimes? Bride couldn't guess, but was positive they had him dead to rights on sex trafficking, kidnapping, and any other crimes related to his enslavement of young Ruby. That should destroy Axeworthy and his company. The chips would fall where they may for Axeworthy Internet Security's other employees. No one knew who was involved with the hacking or the blind worm, but Bride was sure a thorough investigation would follow.

He returned to Dia, who wiped her tears with her shirt. "You okay?" Bride asked.

"Yeah, I think so," she said. "Is it stupid I'm more worried about that girl than myself right now? I guess I always understood I couldn't disappear with my freedom."

"Yeah, I suppose I thought that too," Bride said. "You'll survive intact, but it'll be a rough year. I've talked to Liptmann and I expect he'll make a deal. You're not the fish he was trying to catch."

"But I may get fried, anyway."

Bride noticed the sun's orb touch the mountaintops across the Salton. In this moment he saw this hell's paradise. He filled his lungs with the putrid air and said to this glorious young woman he had grown to care for, "Don't forget your bargaining power. Someone needs to remove that new protocol from the internet, plus someone needs to explain the depths of Wonderbread. Clever of you to host that file on whitehouse.gov. That, no doubt, has already forced the White House to audit its systems.

"The way I see it, Dia, you've committed two treasons," Bride continued. "Your first was committed under orders and for what you originally expected were noble reasons. When you realized it wasn't, you did something about it. Perhaps not the exact proper response, but importantly, you stopped. Your second treason ... without the world's cruelest password no one knows what's inside that file archive. Who's to say you weren't bluffing?"

"You know."

"Who me?" He turned and gazed into her sparkling eyes. "Oh, all along I believed you were bluffing."

As Bride walked away, he signaled Liptmann and Sutter that they could take Dia away.

While Sutter read Dia her Miranda rights, Liptmann, the investigator in charge, called Bride over to answer a few more mundane questions. The interrogation was brief, but Bride understood his future held more questions and more desk duty. For now, Bride was content. He climbed into the Malibu, opposite Ruby, who sat quietly with less fear showing on her face. A few moments later, Sutter and a local police officer escorted Dia Reynolds past in handcuffs. She smiled at Bride as she passed. Henry Bride understood what the smile meant and smiled back.

postscript

The Auction

IT WAS AN UNSEASONABLY COOL, rainy August morning in East St. Louis and Henry Bride worked his first Sunday since his transfer to the DHS Midwest office became permanent. After completing his required leave, he was pleased to return to active duty even if on a peaceful Sunday in the office. He sat at his desk in the office center, dubbed the bullpen. Bride used the day to catch up on the station's past alerts. He read the active reports twice to be prepared if called upon to join the case. So far he hadn't been assigned a case since the transfer, but he assured himself the time would arise after his new coworkers became more comfortable with him.

He studied a 2003 file involving a Grand Aire cargo plane landing in the Mississippi River, narrowly avoiding an important St. Louis bridge connecting Missouri and Illinois. Its pilots, identified as Saleem Iqbal and Mohammed Saleh, were rescued from the airplane, and after the incident both were taken to the hospital. The report had no further details.

Bride had never heard of this incident and was attempting to find further material regarding the incident when his desk phone rang.

"Agent Bride?" He recognized the voice of Neil Burton, the guard on duty. "Someone is here to see you."

"I'll be right there," Bride said and hung up the phone.

When he approached the guard desk, he recognized the short, bald man standing nearby in a light raincoat. It was Robert Liptmann.

Bride greeted the investigator. "Colonel Liptmann, what brings you to the fly-overs?"

Liptmann shook Bride's hand and said, "Have you read about the Shadow Broker's auction, Agent Bride?"

"I'm afraid I don't know what you are talking about," Bride said. "Why don't you come in and catch me up?"

Liptmann took the initiative and walked into the offices. Scanning the open bullpen, he said, "Can we use a private room?"

Bride obliged and led Liptmann into one of the conference rooms. Liptmann set down his case, opened the lid, and pulled a short stack of papers.

"Read this," Liptmann said, handing the papers to Bride.

Bride scanned the papers and read the following posting.

```
EQGRP AUCTION
Public Key
```

Bride flipped pages until he passed the extremely long public key.

```
Equation Group Cyber Weapons Auction -
Invitation
--BEGIN PGP SIGNED MESSAGE--
Hash: SHA256
From:
•>bitmessage = BM-NBvAHfp5Y6wBykgbirVLndZt
EFCYGht8<
i2p-bote = o1uHOkOcMoFEa7O7dbEilzfMvWzo7bDu
\~td3x9gYz4b4t5OriJ7U6GUWr5GZoWxQ9f2TrIY5Rzhp
IMVP6hTLXZ
Equation Group Cyber Weapons Auction -
Invitation
----------
!!! Attention government sponsors of cyber
warfare and those who profit from it !!!!
How much you pay for enemies cyber weapons?
```

Not malware you find in networks. Both sides, RAT + LP, full state sponsor tool set? We find cyber weapons made by creators of stuxnet, duqu, flame. Kaspersky calls Equation Group. We follow Equation Group traffic. We find Equation Group source range. We hack Equation Group. We find many many Equation Group cyber weapons. You see pictures. We give you some Equation Group files free, you see. This is good proof no? You enjoy!!! You break many things. You find many intrusions. You write many words. But not all, we are auction the best files.

Picture Urls

Bride skimmed over more cyber-gibberish.

Auction Instructions

We auction best files to highest bidder. Auction files better than stuxnet. Auction files better than free files we already give you. The party which sends most bitcoins to address: 19BY2XCgbDe6WtTVbTyzM9eR3LYr6VitWK before bidding stops is winner, we tell how to decrypt. Very important!!! When you send bitcoin you add additional output to transaction. You add OP*Return output. In Op*Return output you put your (bidder) contact info. We suggest use bitmessage or I2P-bote email address. No other information will be disclosed by us publicly. Do not believe unsigned messages. We will contact winner with decryption instructions. Winner can do with files as they please, we not release files to public.

```
FAQ
---
Q: Why I want auction files, why send bitcoin?
```

Bride flipped through the FAQ until he came to the big finish.

```
Closing Remarks
---------------
!!! Attention Wealthy Elites !!!
We have final message for "Wealthy Elites".
We know what is wealthy but what is Elites?
Elites is making laws protect self and
friends, lie and fuck other peoples. Elites
is breaking laws, regular peoples go to
jail, life ruin, family ruin, but not Elites.
Elites is breaking laws, many peoples know
Elites guilty...
```

The rant continued until finally...

```
END MESSAGE
```

Bride's heart sank. "Is this what it appears to be? Are these Dia's files?"

"That's the mystery, Mister Bride." Liptmann said. "Did someone crack Miss Reynolds' password?"

Bride scanned the directory of programs included in the online sale. "It doesn't appear to be the same programs. There's no StasisZero."

"No, the lists don't match. There's overlap, but each list contains files not present on the other. In fact, the information from this auction appears to predate 2013. Many of Miss Reynolds' files are post-2013."

"So the NSA has sprung another leak? Or are the auction files from Snowden?" Bride asked.

"We believe Mister Snowden didn't have access to various items from the auction."

"That's never stopped him before," Bride said.

"So I've been told."

"You tell me, Colonel Liptmann. Where do you suppose the auction items originated?"

Liptmann paused a moment perhaps to consider whether he should share his suspicions with Bride. "I've theorized these files were leaked by Anthony Thorenus, Miss Reynolds' boss."

"I don't understand. Didn't you arrest him for treason?"

"We did." Liptmann almost smiled. He was evidently proud of Thorenus' arrest. "And Miss Reynolds has been offered leniency to testify against him. I suspect Thorenus leaked this information to cast further doubt on Dia Reynolds' story. She maintains no password can decrypt the files she posted. If those files suddenly appeared..."

"I see," Bride said. "Have you seen her, by the way? How is she doing?"

"Yes, I've visited her. With her charges reduced, she's out on bond. And I believe she'll beat the charges. She's hired the best lawyers money can buy."

"How can she afford that?" Bride asked.

"Bug bounties. Companies like Google, Apple, and Microsoft offer bounties to white-hat hackers who find and report exploits in their operating systems. In the past three months, Miss Reynolds has earned over a quarter million dollars in bounties for bugs and exploits."

"Good for her." Bride said. "Were those NSA exploits or new bugs she found?"

"I can't say. If they were NSA exploits, the agency won't ever admit to it. Miss Reynolds sold those exploits to American software companies the NSA is supposed to protect. If she had sold to exploit resellers, she may have gained millions, but her old agency would scrutinize such a deal. And perhaps bring charges."

Liptmann pondered a moment. "Also in her favor," he continued, "Miss Reynolds donated a large portion of her earnings to the shelter that's helping transition Miss Doe."

Bride understood Liptmann was referring to Ruby. Bride sought help from Crisis Aid International's shelter here in St. Louis to assist the former sex slave. They had given her the surname Doe until her real name could be found. Originally Bride visited her six times a week. Then Ruby's counselor said she worried about Ruby only imprinting on a male companion. After that Bride backed off to about twice a week, but still checked on her daily.

"So," Bride said, "this doesn't explain why you flew to St. Louis to tell me this."

"I felt you should know," Liptmann said. "Also that all charges have been expunged for your friend Greene. I'm visiting him to tell him personally next. And..." Liptmann paused.

"Yes?" Bride urged him to continue.

"Did you read about the new troubles for our friend, Mr. Axeworthy. A body has surfaced in near the Salton Sea. The local police believe it may be that of his secretary, Irma Vaughn, who went missing around the same time as your visit."

"Hmm... Doesn't surprise me. From the little I saw of him and from what I've read, that man lived evil as if evil was normal."

There was an awkward silence as Liptmann hesitated. Bride looked over the man. He wasn't saying something. Bride stood to show him out, thinking it might prod him to spit it out.

"Oh," Liptmann said, "Before I go I want to say thank you. I wanted you to know, even though the whole matter will stay secret, I appreciate and my boss appreciates everything you've done for the country in this matter."

"That's nice. It'd be helpful to earn favor from the head of the NSA."

"Oh, my boss doesn't work for the NSA. I report directly to the President of the United States."

acknowledgements

THE AUTHOR WOULD LIKE TO THANK the following wonderful people whose invaluable assistance made this book possible:

Charles Axworthy, Ticia Rani, Patrick Dorsey, Kay Cochran, Jim Stoeppler, Gordon Green, Randy Willnow, Bill Franco, David Winter, Ronald Willnow, Elizabeth Willnow, Zoe Willnow, Brennon Fort, Anne Watts, Sela Carsen, everyone at the Plethora of Pens Writers' Group, and the memory of Dudley Batchelor.

/ / / /

The author would also like it known that the auction, which portions of appear in the postscript, is an actual email of unknown authorship and not a creation of the author. As of publication, the manifesto can be read in its entirety at:

wired.com/beyond-the-beyond/2016/08/
shadow-brokers-manifesto/

preview

And now, a pulse-pounding peek at
the next Henry Bride Thriller,

OVER TIME

EVAN WILLNOW

1> Bloody Island

THERE CAN BE TERRIBLE days in the life of a Department of Homeland Security agent. The previous twenty-four hours fit that category for Henry Bride. The day just plain sucked. The week sucked. Hell, the month sucked.

For the past month, Agent Bride had been on loan to ICE, US Immigrations and Customs Enforcement, a branch of the DHS overwhelmed by the latest presidential mandates. Those mandates temporarily moved many local ICE officials south, and Bride and his comrades were assigned to fill their local duties. Had the word "temporary" not been liberally spoken regarding the assignment, Bride would have already put in his two weeks. Splitting up families trying to get by was not why Bride signed up.

At least, it seemed, it was over. The temporary post was to end today. But as he prepared to leave the office, he and his fellow agents were warned the "temporary" duty would continue another week. Bride huffed as he left the office and walked to the rusted red and primer Buick Reatta he not-so-affectionately dubbed "The Beater" parked inside the fenced lot. After slipping into the driver's seat and putting his gun up, Bride coaxed the old engine to life. A few seconds later, Bettye LaVette's "Things Have Changed" continued mid-song through the car's stereo. He realized the song had taken up from when he shut off the car, but it felt like some sort of cosmic message. He backed from his parking spot and headed for the lot's gate.

Common knowledge says East St. Louis, Illinois is a dangerous place. Despite this, the Department of Homeland Security placed its local office smack in the city's center. Thus far, it had never been an issue since he transferred to the midwestern branch. In fact, Bride found it rare to see an actual person outside in the decaying city's downtown.

He exited from the office's gated lot on a Thursday afternoon that still felt to him like an extension of Wednesday. He told himself again it was over.

As if out of spite, though, the terrible day struck again. Just as Bride pulled the Beater onto Fifth Street, he nearly collided with a teenager on a motocross motorcycle performing a wheelie down the street. Bride slammed the brake pedal to the floor. The old ceramic pads screamed in mechanical agony. The rider dropped back to two wheels and barely swerved around the Beater's front fender. This child, a blond teen entirely out of place in the predominately African-American community, offered Bride the single-finger salute as he sped off on his undersized white motorcycle.

Bride took a sharp breath and uttered a string of swears—not at the kid, but at himself for not paying close enough attention. *Fuck this day.*

Bride had much on his mind. He and his partner, Harrison "Spiro" Agnew, had just arrested a 57-year-old grandmother, separating her from the four live-in grandchildren. The grandchildren were all natural US citizens, but the grandmother was not. Now the kids would be entered into the foster care system, and the grandmother would likely be deported. Had it been up to him or Spiro, the whole affair would have been ignored, but their temporary boss from ICE would have none of that. Bride daydreamed of punching that guy in the face. Instead Bride finished the day with a pile of crap paperwork that the ICE bastard should have done on his own.

Right now, his saving grace was that both he and Spiro had been granted four comp days, giving them a six-day break, when added to the weekend, from ICE duty. The rest of the day and well into tomorrow would be used for sleep. Then, perhaps, with his remaining time, he'd do some investigation on his pet project.

Thirty seconds or so had passed with Bride blocking the lot's exit before he realized the Beater's engine had died with the sudden stop. He turned the key to off and cranked the engine back to life. He took a deep breath, looked both ways, then proceeded toward his normal commute home. The two-seater Reatta, in hindsight at least, was not the century-old car company's finest moment. If the car ever had any pizzazz it was lost with erosion and '90s sensibilities. Today the only thing special about the car was that it lacked a back seat. Bride had only spent four-hundred dollars on the Beater, and another three- to make it reliable enough to drive. That was until his true automotive passion, his 1963 Apollo GT was restored back to working order.

Now on a straight shot to the highway, Bride noticed ahead that the motorcycle kid was in the opposite lane heading toward him. No, this was another kid, this dirt bike was red. Not knowing what to make of it, other than recalling a recent news story about "stunt riders" in downtown St. Louis, Bride prepared to merge onto the highway entrance ramp. As the new bike approached, he noticed the kid had the same tee-shirt as the first, a black shirt with red type proclaiming, "I ♥ Crack Whores".

At the last second, as the two red vehicles crossed paths, the kid—this one maybe a year younger—tossed something at Bride's windshield. Bride didn't get a look at the tossed item, but it thudded against the windscreen and spider-webbed the glass before pounding across the Beater's roof.

"What the hell?" Bride spat. He turned his head to see the red bike join the white bike before they sped back into East St. Louis. Not sure what he planned to do, Bride violently whirled the Beater around and raced after the two juveniles. On the stereo, Bettye LaVette had at some point shuffled to her cover of Dylan's "Do Right to Me Baby". *Damn, Bettye was on point today.* But he couldn't decide whether the soul singer's croon of "do unto others" was encouraging or dissuading this current bout of road rage.

Maybe he'd just scare them, Bride thought. At least these little punks would know that some people give chase.

Ahead, the two motorbikes tore through the empty streets, the Beater no match for their speed, but Bride managed a longer look at the pair through the cracked windshield. He'd guess the pair were brothers, and despite the two appearing too young to ride legally, both bikes were too small for their riders. Bride guessed the teens received the bikes years back and since outgrew the vehicles.

Bride lost sight of the bikes when they turned into an old, well-graffitied industrial zone, but he surmised that they were headed toward the river.

He slowed and turned where the pair had, but he probably should abandon the chase. What was he thinking, going after them in the first place? Still, he'd take a cursory scout around before turning back toward the highway near the casino.

He followed the flood wall toward the Casino Queen. Directly across from downtown St. Louis, Missouri, the casino was the safest area in East St. Louis. When the casino came to the small city, its taxes funding the city quadrupling the size of its police force—half of that extra force continually patrolled the casino's grounds and the surrounding area.

Bride passed the casino's hotel. Nothing. *Okay, time to head home,* he thought, but then he noticed a third motorcycle in his rearview mirror—another teenager on an undersized dirt bike. This one was smart enough to wear a helmet and lacked the other two's affinity for crack whores.

Defensively, Bride assumed the newcomer on the black motorcycle was related to the other two, but, offensively, he could make no action toward a potentially innocent bystander who also owned a runt-sized dirt bike.

Bride slowed, deciding to continue straight. Perhaps the newcomer would lead him to the Crack Whore Brothers. For safety, though, Bride reached over, removed his service pistol from the glove box, and set it on the tattered passenger seat.

The black motorcycle swiftly caught up. For a moment, the new kid paced a mere yard behind the Beater before pulling into the far lane and passing Bride on the left. When he was even, the mirrored sunglasses under the helmet turned and looked in at Bride, either examining or taunting him. The kid then sped ahead spitting loose gravel and dirt from his rear tire as he merged back in front.

Only then did Bride notice the fourth motorcycle just outside his right window. This rider, the youngest yet, almost fit his junior-sized Kawasaki-green dirt bike. The kid banged the ball of his fist against the Beater's window before popping a wheelie and speeding north. The kid on the Kawasaki also sported the "I ♥ Crack Whores" tee-shirt. One wearing that shirt was kind of funny, Bride admitted. Three was sad.

Bride floored the gas pedal and surprisingly the Beater spat its own dose of gravel before the rear tires gripped. The old Buick shot forward in pursuit under first the Eads and then the Martin Luther King bridges northward along the wide Mississippi River. The road followed the flood wall north toward the area of East St. Louis known as the Island. If the casino area was safe, the Island was infamous for being the opposite.

In the days of the early Nineteenth Century, Bloody Island was the lawless land in the middle of the Mississippi River that men would go to duel because it legendarily didn't fall under the laws of Illinois or the then territory of Missouri. It lost that status after young Lt. Robert E. Lee and the U.S. Army Corps of Engineers blocked the river on the Illinois side allowing silt to fill in and permanently attach the Island to the Illinois side of the river, ensuring the Mississippi eternally flowed along the banks of St. Louis on the river's far side. Though no longer an actual island, the Island's reputation still survived nearing on two centuries through the Island's years as a railroad depot and even more now as nature had reasserted herself and the Island became a good place for body dumps.

As if to underscore the Island's reputation, the two original dirt bikes waited for their friends near some overgrown rail tracks. Bride slowed. It was now obvious how bad his situation was. He had foolishly fallen into the trap. For what purpose, he didn't know. Did they know the parking lot he was exiting was the DHS office? Was this all some scam, or was it over-zealous revenge for almost wrecking the white motorcycle as he performed his dangerous stunts on public streets? With the concrete flood wall on his left and the overgrown railroad tracks to his right, whatever the bikers' reason, Bride knew his best course was to retreat.

But before Bride could turn around, White and Red moved again, traveling behind the Beater and soon all four dirt bikes circled the old car on the crumbling asphalt.

Bride put the Beater in reverse, hoping the reverse lights would warn them he was planning on running them down if they were behind him—assuming the reverse lights worked.

The dirt bikes continued to circle, spraying up a cloud of dust as their tires ground the remnants of the old road.

With one foot on the brake and one on the gas, Bride eased up off the brake pedal and gave the accelerator a punch of gas. The Beater lurched back a foot, nearly hitting Kawasaki, before Bride's left foot stuck the brake pedal again.

Still, the bikes circled.

He repeated the action, this time nearly clipping Black. But the dirt bikes were undaunted.

Hell, even if he had to do it a foot at a time, he was getting out of the Island. But instead, he lurched forward, clipping Red's rear wheel. The bike leaned to and fro under its rider as it sped toward a large clump of scrub brush growing through a pothole near the street's edge. But Red righted the bike to rejoin the other teen terrors circling the Beater.

Bride had had enough. He considered the juvenile pack suitably warned. If he runs one over on the way out, that's on them.

But then he noticed Black had stopped at his driver's side window. The helmeted teen was pointing something plastic and white at him. It took Bride a second to recognize the 3D printed gun. He tossed his arm behind him to the passenger seat and grasped for his pistol. But he didn't find it.

"Get out," Black ordered. This kid barely could grow facial hair, and he was barking orders with a gun.

Bride looked over; his gun had fallen onto the floor, out of reach. *Shit.*

Resigned, he looked at his steering wheel just for a chance to think of something. He got nothing. *Don't try something stupid, Bride,* he thought.

Or do try...

about the author

A BORING WEEK of jury duty and a stack of Ian Fleming novels jumpstarted Evan Willnow's interest in thriller fiction. He never did get picked for a jury, but he finished every James Bond literary adventure from *Casino Royale* to *The Man With the Golden Gun*. An award-winning digital artist, his career has ranged far to include bicycle mechanic, computer programmer, roadie, and cartoonist. He introduced digital age action hero DHS Agent Henry Bride to the world in his first thriller, *Mightier than the Sword*. Bride now faces his newest dangers pursuing his latest threat in *Zero In, Zero Out*, published by Legendary Planet.

evanwillnow.com ✈ @EvanWillnow

also from Legendary Planet

Made in the USA
Coppell, TX
10 November 2019

11172277R00201